HEADS YOU WIN

Ferdinand Mount, editor of *The Times Literary Supplement* from 1991 to 2002, was awarded the Hawthornden Prize for *Of Love and Asthma*. Of his most recent novel featuring Gus Cotton, *Fairness*, the *Evening Standard* critic wrote: 'Were more novels like this, more people would read novels.' He lives in London.

ALSO BY FERDINAND MOUNT

Tales of History and Imagination

Umbrella
Jem (and Sam)

A Chronicle of Modern Twilight

The Man Who Rode Ampersand
The Selkirk Strip
Of Love and Asthma
The Liquidator
Fairness

Very Like a Whale
The Clique

Non-fiction

The Theatre of Politics
The Subversive Family
The British Constitution Now
Communism (ed.)

Ferdinand Mount

HEADS YOU WIN

A Chronicle of Modern Twilight

VINTAGE

Published by Vintage 2005

2 4 6 8 10 9 7 5 3 1

Copyright © Ferdinand Mount 2004

Ferdinand Mount has asserted his right under the Copyright, Designs and Patents Act, 1988 to be identified as the author of this work

First published in Great Britain in 2004 by
Chatto & Windus

Vintage
Random House, 20 Vauxhall Bridge Road,
London SW1V 2SA

Random House Australia (Pty) Limited
20 Alfred Street, Milsons Point, Sydney
New South Wales 2061, Australia

Random House New Zealand Limited
18 Poland Road, Glenfield,
Auckland 10, New Zealand

Random House (Pty) Limited
Isle of Houghton, Corner Boundary Road & Carse O'Gowrie,
Houghton, 2198, South Africa

The Random House Group Limited Reg. No. 954009
www.randomhouse.co.uk/vintage

A CIP catalogue record for this book
is available from the British Library

ISBN 0 09 947226 0

Papers used by Random House are natural, recyclable products made from wood grown in sustainable forests. The manufacturing processes conform to the environmental regulations of the country of origin

Printed and bound in Great Britain by
Bookmarque Ltd, Croydon, Surrey

Contents

In heaven it is always autumn, his mercies are ever in their maturity.

John Donne, *Eight Sermons*

It was choppier now. The launch was rocking in the shadow of the wharf, its blue plastic fenders squeaking against the wet posts. This far downriver I could smell the sea, or the sewage. The river policeman saluted when we came aboard, keeping his other hand on the wheel. I stumbled coming down into the boat and the other policeman steadied me. Then I turned to help the stretcher-bearers, but they already had him laid out down the middle of the boat. The stretcher poles fitted into metal rowlocks fixed to the transom at the back and to a crossbeam halfway up. They must be used to this sort of cargo. Most were probably dead already, hoicked out of the river dripping with mud and seaweed, things that had to be touched with a bargepole. There was only just room to squeeze in alongside him. Three of us either side: the photographer and the girl and me, and then opposite us the Superintendent and a couple of uniforms, and the St John men at the back.

Like the figures alongside the tomb of a recumbent knight, I thought, or King Arthur's companions in the barge. Perhaps our friend too would raise his arm before we reached the other side and grasp, not a sword obviously, but an oar or something. Then I remembered that it wasn't Arthur who grasped the sword but another unidentified arm, the one clothed in white samite, mystic, wonderful, that had risen dripping from the lake and waved the sword about a bit before taking it down below. So not a replay at all, nothing like it. On the whole life didn't go in for replays. That was the mistake we had made, most of us anyway.

Better if we had been on a barge and had to row across. At least the exercise would have kept us warm and taken our minds off him. As it was, there he lay between our legs and there was nothing to do but sit there numb and sad, feeling underneath us the thrum of the engine reversing out into the river. We stopped engines for an instant to allow the current to carry us round and I could hear his urgent, uneven breathing like a lorry grinding up a steep hill. Not long now, the Super said, as we went into forward gear and cut across the tide, but I wasn't sure whether he was talking about the time it would take us to get to the hospital or about how long the man on the stretcher would last.

A glint of silver caught my eye and I saw that the snapper was taking pictures with his digi-camera, not surreptitiously exactly but pressing his forearm against his ribs to keep the camera steady. Who the hell did he hope to sell them to? He had charm, bags of charm, even so it was hard to imagine him strolling into the offices of *OK* or *Hello!* and persuading them to pay thousands for pictures of a man dying on a police launch.

We were in the middle of the river now. I could see the pier and the white ambulance waiting. Only five minutes to the hospital from there, the Super said, they were holding the traffic on the East India Dock Road. I thought he had gone already because I couldn't hear his breathing but when the helmsman cut the engine again there it was, in-out, in-out, he needed a cox to call the strokes. Except that he had had a stroke of his own, several of them in fact – stroke, what a strange feline word, covered everything from a caress to a *coup de grâce* and now he had experienced the whole range.

How long to high tide, the Super asked, and the river policeman said ten or fifteen minutes, making a swivelling gesture with his free hand to show that he couldn't be sure exactly. Somebody died at the turning of the tide, but I couldn't remember who. Anyway, it wasn't the sort of thing people noticed these days. Died on his mother's birthday, they used to say, or on Easter Sunday, but now they just said 'peacefully', as though they could possibly know. 'Noisily' would be more accurate in this case.

'Don't be sad, Gus, he'll be all right,' the girl said, 'and anyway he's had a wonderful life.' Yes and no, I thought, but I was grateful all the same, when she put her hand on my knee, and I put my hand over hers.

'Life goes on,' the photographer said. Well, yes and no again and up to a point. The photographer had finished snapping now and he had put a consoling hand on the girl's knee so we must have looked as though we were playing one of those stupid party games which is supposed to break the ice. Not a precaution ever needed when our friend was around. He always plunged in, utterly insensitive to froideur or to anything else much. In social terms he was one of those swimmers who is first into the water on New Year's Day. And we were grateful for the splash, most of us most of the time.

'You'll have to charge him I suppose, if he recovers?'

'Oh, not till he's in a fit state. But then yes, we will, he could have done a lot of damage. Funny to see him there sleeping like a baby when an hour ago . . .'

The Superintendent left the sentence unfinished, as though he needed the space for musing. He would have done better to keep his thoughts to himself. There really wasn't much of a funny side and no baby ever slept with such a desperate, rattling, sighing breath.

The stairs were steep on the other side, and the St John Ambulance men had to back up carefully, watching each step. For a moment, he was almost vertical on the stretcher and without the red straps he would have tumbled off down into the black water. Even so his head lolled away from the blankets covering him and his face glared out at us, purple, throbbing-veined, his sandy-grey hair all over the place, a gorgon rearing out from the sodden mossy pier. Just then he gave a huge groan, a sonorous stagey noise like someone trying to draw attention to their despair, and I thought that was it. 'On 7 November, between land and water, unpeacefully . . .'

But it wasn't. The groan faded to a whimper, a jerky little whimper, and they managed to haul him up on to the quay.

I

The Fairy Glen

It started with the Finchers or rather at the Finchers', at their place in
Ireland, the place Francie Fincher thought of as home, though he had
spent the past forty years slogging away at the English bar. I needn't
have gone, but it was hard to resist Francie. He was so warm and
compelling when he asked you things, you felt mean if you turned him
down. He hadn't an ungenerous bone in his body and it didn't take you
five minutes to see how the same was true of his wife, Jonquil, Jon for
short, and how she shared his fine impetuousness. He liked to rush his
fences in life, and on horseback too. As he drove me from Sligo station
through the boggy meadows of his native country, there seemed to be
scarcely a tumbledown stone wall he hadn't broken his collarbone at.
And when his children tumbled out of the grey creeper-clad manse to
greet him, they too seemed to be the fruit of a reckless spawning.

'This is Brigid and that's Fionnuola, and that one skulking in the
laurels is Conor, Aisling's away at Trinity but she'll be back this
weekend, and Eileen has the colic. It's a bit like sardines here at the
best of times. When Mr Moore had the house he had just the two
children, a nice Protestant family as the nuns used to say.'

He rattled on, which was nothing new to me – that was why I had
taken to him in the first place – but there was a new freedom about the
way he talked, a quality that hadn't been there back in London. It
wasn't that his voice sounded more Irish (perhaps it did a little), more
that he sounded unconstrained, as though he was no longer being
watched.

'I'm so sorry your wife couldn't come,' said Jon, looking up at me anxiously. She was short and round and jolly, and the anxious look was out of place on her.

'She was desperate to miss it,' I said. 'She had to go to this conference, on diaries.'

'Diaries, that's a funny thing to have a conference on.'

'Well, it's her subject. She edits seventeenth-century diaries.'

'Does she now? It must be a lot of work finding out who everyone is. Think if she had to put my old diary in order. How would she know which Mrs O'Brien I meant or who the Alligator was?'

She was as zesty as her husband, a warm, bustling person who herded her children to the dining table with cuffs and kisses which they scarcely seemed to notice.

'Who is the Alligator?'

'Oh, the man from the drainage board, he has these teeth. He's always round here, fancies himself. I thought he fancied me but my dear kind husband said it must be Georgina Rowan up the road, because I was giving away ten years and a couple of stone. Such flatterers, aren't they, husbands? Take your elbows off the table, Conor, you're not an uncle yet, unless there's something I don't know.'

She turned away from the children and back to me.

'Tell me about your wife and family, Gus.'

The most natural question in the world, but it had me groping. Would Jonquil want a physical description? Nellie, Nell, Eleanor – she answers to all three in different moods – is tall with a long back and a warm, blushing smile which exposes the missing pre-molar and paradoxically makes her look toothy. Her long hair goes frizzy in the rain like a spaniel. Most of her cousins are Catholics but for some complicated reason she isn't. She is unworldly, no, disdainful of worldly things and never swears, but sometimes she will surprise you by using words like vagina in contexts when much ruder people would not. By trade, if you call it a trade, she is a population historian but since we married what she mostly does is edit diaries. Her edition of the diaries of Thomas Crupper, a fifteenth-century asset-stripper, was well received, but for what seems like an eternity she has been editing the diaries of a collateral forebear of hers, Scrope Dudgeon, sometimes dubbed, unfairly she claims, the Butcher of Baldock on account of his high kill rate in the Civil War. She pursues this strange quest across most of the East Midlands in an old Peugeot 205 mostly driven by her helper, Chris Alison, known as the Chrysalis or the Bug for short, who is assistant librarian at Mablethorpe and picks her up from the station or occasionally comes down to London. The Bug is small, dark and squinny-faced. He doesn't like to come into the house, prefers to sit hunched in the car which is piled high with cardboard boxes, containing Dudgeon stuff according to Nellie, cling-wrapped body parts according to me.

Not much, if any, of this seemed suitable material for Jon, so I simply said we had two children, Thomas and Elspeth, who had fled the nest, which gave Eleanor more time for her research, and I said again how sorry she was not to be able to come.

'Ah well, next time she won't get out of it so easy. Now then, let's have a bit of hush.'

Francie mumbled a quick grace. It was a long, gloomy room with fir trees blocking the view through the tall window. There were a couple of hunting prints on the wall, but otherwise it probably hadn't changed much since the time when it was the rector's dining room (even the hunting prints might have been inherited – the Finchers seemed too busy to bother about decor). Still, it was odd to think of grace still being said at the same table, even if the denomination was different now.

It can't have been more than a couple of minutes later that he turned from spooning out the stew and said to me the words that I dreaded, 'Do you know, the most extraordinary thing, we have these English friends a few miles over the hill there, and when I told them you were coming to us it turns out they're your oldest friends in the world, Joe and Gillian Follows. Did you know they were lurking here in the bog now?'

Yes, I said, I did know but I hadn't known they were quite so close, which was a lie. As soon as Francie had asked me to Ballyturbet, I looked up Drishill on the map and saw where it was.

'Well, I thought to myself,' Francie said, 'it'll work out a treat, because Saturday is Brigid's birthday party and the place'll be full to the gunwales with screaming kids doing God knows what into the small hours, so why don't we park you with Joe and Gillian for a couple of nights. So anyway, it's all decided and she's longing to see you. Did you know she's got what she calls just a little touch of cancer, rather more than that if you ask me? I love her, don't you?'

I did know and had loved her too, long ago, years before she had married Joe and had the first cancer scare and the operation which meant she couldn't have children. Later it turned out she probably hadn't had cancer at all then, though she certainly had it now, but then it was hard to be sure about all that, because Joe had told me that she had had the whole lot out but she still talked about having the curse. Anyway, I loved her still.

Joe and I first saw her just after we had left the asthma clinic where we met. She must have been about eighteen, and she wore this thick pink wool suit and she had this unstinted enthusiastic way of talking. She was so unlike Peggy, her slender, elegant mother. Peggy's every word had a drawling charm and she didn't even have to whistle to make men come running, among them Joe, who had lived with her for a year or two. So at first when Joe took up with Peggy's daughter, relegating me to the sidelines, it seemed as though he was simply completing his programme of scoring every woman within striking distance, a sort of gender cleansing.

Strange, really, that I should have gone on thinking of Joe as a friend. Even his making Gillian unhappy at regular intervals had not driven us apart, although I knew from her letters how much she minded and how seriously she took marriage. You wouldn't think it from her rude laugh and her lewd prattle but she took most serious things seriously.

It's easy to see why I never stopped being fond of her, but why did I not resent Joe more? We didn't share a single interest. In fact, he didn't seem to have interests except in the business sense. He cared only for the next big thing coming up and he cared for it with a ruthless, boyish innocence. Not my style at all. I'm much more like my long-time colleague and equally old friend Ian Riley-Jones. We see the world through a flimsy filter of irony. We have taken the guarded manner and oblique discourse of our profession (we are both senior civil servants) and turned it into something of an art form. But Joe takes things straight, gulps experience down as it comes, scarcely giving it time to touch the sides of the glass. He was my native guide to the real world, he spoke that odd dialect which comes naturally to people who take it all at face value. Perhaps that was why, despite myself, I wanted to stay friends with him.

'When we bought the Lodge, oh six, seven years ago,' Jonquil said, 'we didn't realise they were neighbours. And you know, nobody told us, that's the funny thing. Not a soul. You would think, wouldn't you, that the first thing they'd be bursting to tell you is just over the hill there's the couple that were kidnapped. Oh, but they're peculiar, people in this part of the world. They'll talk the hind leg off a donkey about some nonsense or other, but when there's a bit of really interesting news they clam up. So it wasn't till I was standing behind Gillian in O'Brien's the chemist and I said don't I know you from somewhere and she says, oh dear I've got such a fucking awful memory for faces, you know the way she talks, that I remembered seeing her picture in the papers at the time and we became friends on the spot. But they've had a hard time of it, very hard. I don't just mean their health, though that's been miserable enough, but half the people round here won't speak to them because they think they were in cahoots with the IRA and the other half think the IRA should have finished them off instead of dumping them in that cowshed in Dundalk.'

'It wasn't a cowshed, Jonquil, it was a council house,' her husband said.

'With those pigs, who'd know the difference? You try living bound and gagged in your own filth for a couple of months with only murdering eejits for company and see how you like it, I tell them.'

'She does tell them, too.'

'But they just purse up their evil little lips and say, I'm sorry, Mrs Fincher, but there's something fishy about that business. Oh, is there now, and how would you know, Eileen Lavery, have the police taken you into their confidence? You wouldn't credit it, Gus.'

But I did. From the moment the news had broken, the whisper had run on both sides of the water – almost simultaneously – that it was a put-up job. Even the man from the Fraud Squad, Jervoise, a dark, creepy fellow who spelled out his surname every time he called me, mentioned the possibility right at the outset. The fact that he was from the Fraud Squad showed what the authorities thought about the case, and although the police gradually settled into a conviction that the ransom note (demanding 2 million) was genuine, and that Joe and

Gillian really had been snatched and were being held against their will, they never stopped thinking that the whole affair had hidden depths which were not to the credit of its victims.

Anyway, by some ingenious means which I never quite got the hang of, Jervoise and his associates persuaded the kidnappers that they would create more trouble by releasing the couple than by killing them – because Joe was such a hot potato to the authorities in both countries. So they let them go.

The irony was that a week after they had been found, shivering, soaked and lousy in this place just outside Dundalk, Joe and Gillian became the coldest of cold potatoes. Nobody wanted to interview them, nobody talked about them, none of their friends went to see them. I had been over there once before it all happened but I didn't think of going again, although Gillian wrote to me and I wrote back. Every now and then, when some other unfortunates were snatched and held in captivity in equally appalling conditions, I wondered why their sufferings were so eagerly rehearsed for months afterwards, why these other names stuck in people's minds in a way that Joseph and Gillian Follows did not, but because I was myself part of this involuntary conspiracy to forget about them I didn't wonder very hard.

After the early dinner – more of a high tea – we played Oh Hell with the older children and a storytelling game in which you had to carry on from the last sentence of the previous speaker and finish with the last sentence of the one before, or was it the other way round? We had bottles and bottles of wonderful wine – Francie belonged to some lawyers' wine club – and with the wind howling and Brigid's sweet rosy face opposite me, I should have been happy, but a brooding unease settled on me until, for all the wine I had drunk, I could feel my heart battering against my ribs.

There was no sleep to be had either in the pleasant shabby old attic bedroom with its blotchy mirror and bluebell-clustered wallpaper. The branches outside knocked against the gutter to make a tinny scraping noise, but it wasn't an eerie sensation of the ghost-story sort that disquieted me, rather the opposite. What unnerved me was the Finchers' down-to-earth contentment, their confidence (which you couldn't miss) that whatever might happen, terrible things perhaps, would happen and would pass and all was as it should be. They were substantial people, that was what had me turning in my bed (which was sopping damp somewhere in the nadir of the mattress). And if there was any ghost story being told, it was I who was the ghost in it.

The next day we had a picnic at the head of the glen beyond the house. There was a squall just as we arrived and then it washed away to leave a clear blue sky and a gauzy view of a string of lakes and mountains beyond, but none of it made me feel much better.

They loaded me down with kindnesses – devilled kidneys at breakfast which I then saw none of them ate (when I had said I liked kidneys I was thinking of them as a main course at dinner, not glistening dark and fatty at 8.45 a.m.), and a book by Surtees by my bed the next night because I said I hadn't read any, which was another lie because I had got stuck in one years before, the same one probably, and then Francie drove me miles up in the hills again to a place where you could see over into the next glen, the famous Fairy Glen where the River Turbet sprang out of the ground, foaming at the touch of the fairy's wand, although some said it was the staff of St Brendan, the one who circumnavigated the world and discovered America, who although not strictly speaking a Ballyturbet man had passed through the country just before he stepped into his little leather boat. The men of the Glen were remarkable for their fighting spirit, Francie said, not that there were many of them left now.

'The Famine?' I queried brightly, peering through the car window at the luminous watery-green valley opening out far below me, with the curl of the river lost in the hazy fuzz of the trees.

'No, no, the place still had a population of several thousand in 1914.'

'Emigration then?'

'A fair bit of that, yes, but it was the wars that did for them. A couple of hundred were killed on the Somme, quite a few in the second war too, they volunteered like lemmings.'

'And now?'

'Oh, half the lads were in the Maze. A peculiar place, that. You ever do any prison visiting, Gus?'

'No,' I said. Another question which left me uncomfortable. The idea of doing such a thing had never crossed my mind, which I then admitted.

'You should,' Francie said, but gently. 'It's a kind of education.'

'I'm sure it is,' I said.

'I think you'd find it rewarding.'

'Mm.'

'I could fix it up for you if you liked.'

'I'm not sure I'd be up to it.'

'Oh, it's not like that at all. Everyone's so pleased to see you. Nothing's expected. Your being there is the thing. And then, surprisingly soon, you get fascinated by it and you look forward to your next time. I can see you're doubtful. Well, I'll leave you in peace, but think about it and when we're back in England – ah, there's Jon now with the lunch.'

It doesn't often happen that you spend four whole days, or even half that time, with thoroughly good people. And by the time I came to say goodbye to Jonquil and Brigid and Conor and Fionnuola and Aisling (who was back from TCD and was just as lively and rosy as the rest of them), and Francie drove me over the hills to Drishill Abbey, I was eaten up with self-loathing and impatience to escape. Even when we were bumping along in the old Volvo with great silver-marked veins of moor and mountain unfolding at each bend I was counting the minutes till I could say goodbye to him.

Why is it so difficult for us to contemplate goodness? We like to pretend instead that goodness always has a phoney streak running through it, that it is stained with unacknowledged motives – ambition, spiritual pride and so on – but deep down what we find intolerable is not that the goodness is phoney but that it isn't. It sits there before you, shining, and won't go away or go out of your head afterwards.

The only reason I bring in Francie and the other Finchers at all is to explain my peculiar intense relief at falling into Gillian's arms on the doorstep and, even more bizarre, giving Joe a huge hug. The dread I had felt at the prospect of seeing them had instantly turned into delight. True, in sloppier moments I had always thought of my old comrade in asthma with some affection, even regarded his crass word-fluffing, sex-frenzied persona, the very obverse of my own, as somehow my other half. But the relief I experienced on seeing Joe was mostly due to the thought that after he had poured a couple of drams down Francie's throat, that would be the last I would see of the Finchers for a bit. This is an uncomfortable admission and one which would be met with complete incomprehension by the entire population of Ballyturbet, not to mention the membership of the Garrick Club in London and most of Francie's fellow high court justices. But there it is, and it is necessary to spell it out to help account for a couple of things which happened over the next twenty-four hours and which were to have such an assortment of consequences and ramifications.

It isn't worth listing all the companies Joe once controlled, though I sometimes used to count them as a way of getting to sleep. But here's a sample: the Genuine Knitwear Company, Merrythought Property Developments, Jenny Wren Estates, Dudgeonvest, the Broderia Mill Company, Potter Forest Heritage, Follows On Inc. (USA).

The sad thing about capitalism (the consoling thing for those who hate it) is that it lacks any collective memory. The heroic takeovers of yesterday melt like snow in spring. Nobody can remember who took over what. In any case by now the company will probably be as dead as its creator. Joe will be remembered longer for the women he screwed than for the companies he did the same to. After the stroke he wasn't capable of much in either department. What he had achieved, though, over the ten years since I had last seen him, was to defy the doctors' glum prediction that his speech would never recover to more than 10 per cent of its old capacity – not that his old capacity was much to write home about. The way he talked had always been slightly chaotic even when he wasn't tossing in one of his wrong words. These were not spoonerisms or even malapropisms exactly but words that sounded quite like the right ones and might have a meaning that was more or less adjacent. Yet here he was, talking away at something like his old speed, with only the occasional aphasic blip. And walking, too, with only a slight drag of the leg, again in defiance of the doctors' prediction that even if he did learn to walk a little he would never manage without having a crutch handy.

All the same, I could hear how uneven his footfalls were on the worn stone of the passage from the cavernous hall to the damp dining room with the family portraits of the previous owners and the mildew on the sage-green damask. And when they took me out into the moorland beyond the paddock, his foot kept on slipping on the boulders and Gillian had to hold on to him.

'Like a macaroon,' he gasped pointing at the low, round-topped mountain beyond the tumbled landscape of gorse and grey rock.

'Or a McDonald's bap.'

'No, no, spare us.'

'Or a giant mushroom?'

'Or the beginning of a nuclear explosion.'

'That's the same as a mushroom.'

'It's called a turlough,' Joe said.

'No it isn't, that's the lake.'

'There isn't a lake.'

'There is in winter.'

'It's strange,' I said, 'that you can remember a word like turlough and you can't remember words like butter.'

'Anything that gives him a chance to show off. Anyway, he was always inclined to mangle his words, you must remember.'

'Please,' Joe said, 'I'm not quite dead yet.'

'You will be if you go on drinking like you did last night,' Gillian said.

We went on staring at the grey mountain with its strange rounded top and the limestone wilderness stretching away up to it. Very quiet, only the skittering of grey wagtails in among the scant bushes and boggy patches. The limestone was cracked into huge slabs, a tray of giant's toffee. They called it a pavement – Cockburn's Pavement, according to Joe in his unlikely new role as tour guide – but the word was wrong for such a wild, cracked place.

'Look there, the first cranesbill.'

'Bloody cranesbill.'

I thought Joe was still calling everything bloody as he did just after the stroke when he couldn't remember an adjective let alone a noun to save his life, which is what he needed to do to save it. But then I looked down into the crack between the two man-sized slabs and there were the petals poking out bright scarlet.

'It seems to be growing out of the rock. I can't see any earth at all.'

'Oh, we're hardy plants out here, left over from the Ice Age.'

But Gillian did not look hardy, not as she had when I first knew her. Even when I had come out to visit them just before the kidnap, she had a colleen's bloom on her (had I actually said something embarrassing along those lines?). She must have been in her forties then, but didn't look it at all. Now she looked what she was – ill.

'You won't see wild flowers like it anywhere else in Ireland.'

'Except the Burren,' Gillian footnoted.

'That's just a tourist trap.'

'You can walk for miles on the Burren and not see a soul,' she continued sweetly.

'Well, so you can here.'

'Except for the border post on the hill to the right, and the peat-packing factory over towards Cockburnstown which is being turned into some computer thing and that place next to it just there, you see? They make the fencing for the Maze, except they've closed it down since the Agreement. But then I think I showed you the sights the last time you came over. Oh, you are a goodster. Nobody else ever comes twice to Drishill. Now we'll show you the Fairy Glen.'

'Francie pointed it out to me from the other side of the hill.'

'Oh, you have to see it close up. You can't go back to England without.'

'Do you ever think of going back?' I asked as she drove us out of the moorland towards the mountains.

'Are you including me in that question?' Joe put in gruffly.

'You mean, you're not on the run any more?'

'They'd have caught me by now if they were really trying, wouldn't they?'

'I'm afraid we're too stuck in the bog to budge,' Gillian said firmly, rather as if her husband had not spoken. His hand began to tremble and he held on to the armrest in the Frontera, although it might have been because Gillian was taking us up a twisty single-track lane and at a fair clip.

'They can't even run a fucking insurance market,' he said.

'What?'

'That's what's wrong with England.'

'Oh –'

'Poor darling took an absolute wallow at Lloyds. Well, I did really because it had to be in my name because he thought if he tried to be a Name – such a silly word, isn't it – they'd grab his absolutely enormous profits, you know, the creditors, only there weren't any profits to grab.'

'But we've still got the Glen,' he said.

'You mean you own it?'

'Well, we bought the caves years ago, with some money the Colonel left Gillian. Didn't do a thing with them for a bit. But then I thought there's the new road to the airport and this part of the country crying out for tourist attractions. So I got this chap Tooley in to manage it, his family used to work for us though we had to let them go. He's an obvious rogue but he's got a bit of poke about him and if you just keep your eye on him –'

'I am sure you would like to hear the Legend of the Glen.'

'I'm not sure I would.'

'This is the Legend of the Glen,' Gillian began, undeterred. 'When Aengus of the Red Hair had grown as tall as his wolfhound Fern, he went riding down the glen on his brindled horse Ennel and there came a storm and he went into a cave to shelter –'

'And that was the last anyone saw of him?'

'Don't interrupt. The storm came to an end and there was the greatest rainbow the world has ever seen and his horse followed the rainbow across the country which today they call Cockburn's Country, but its old Irish name is the Country of Aengus. And Aengus became afraid because they were many leagues from home and he tugged on the horse's mane this way and that but the horse paid him no heed and went on chasing the rainbow until they came to a great lake and they went into the lake and the wolfhound was drowned but the Little People carried Aengus and Ennel across the lake and they came to the other side dry as a bone without a drop of water on them.'

'Must have been a turlough,' Joe grunted.

'It was not,' Gillian said. 'The lake was thirty fathoms deep. In fact it was the deepest lake in all Ireland.'

'So it's a happy ending,' I said. 'I thought the Little People were usually rather malevolent.'

'That is not the ending of the story. Because Aengus went out riding again to find the magic lake and as he passed the cave he met a dwarf. And the dwarf said, are you Aengus of the Red Hair and Aengus could not deny that he was. The very same that galloped across the lake and came out dry as a bone? The same, said Aengus, pleased that his great deed was so well known in the country. Ah, said the dwarf, and what are you doing here? I have come to find the lake again, said Aengus. You would have been wise not to come back, the dwarf said. Why not? said Aengus. Because now you must pay the price. What price? said Aengus. It was my people who carried you across the lake or you would have drowned else, the dwarf said. I owe no man so much as a farthing, Aengus said, for he was a proud youth. You must marry my sister, the dwarf said, that is the price. And who is your sister Aengus enquired. She is Deirdre the Hag of the Bogs, and after you are married to her for a month, you will wish you had gone to the bottom of the lake. I will not marry your sister, Aengus said, for it was my own brindled horse Ennel that galloped after the rainbow and carried me across the lake so that we came out dryshod without a drop on us. The dwarf laughed and said, it is a poor horseman who lets his horse lead him where he does not wish to go, you will be married to my sister in seven days' time.'

'What the fuck is that?' Joe growled, swerving.

Beside the road there was a sign in brilliant shamrock green saying 'Only 2 miles to Tooley's Fairy Glen – it's another world'.

'That was not part of the agreement. I said he could put "Thomas Tooley, director" at the bottom of the sign if he insisted, but *this, Christ.*'

He beat his fist on the passenger's airbag with a glum despair which was accompanied a couple of minutes later by a groan as we passed another sign saying 'Only 1 mile to Tooley's Fairy Glen – where the Little People will make you feel at home'.

We were approaching the head of the pass and a golden light was moving across the dark rocks. Across the immense sky beyond the valley the mist cleared and a full-arched rainbow came into view, presenting a scene so huge and lovely that it would have been hard to think of anything to say if there hadn't been another sign saying 'Only $\frac{1}{2}$ mile to Tooley's Fairy Glen – where the rainbow really ends'.

'Fuck, fuck, fuck.'

'What's this?' Gillian exclaimed, as we came round the bend and she had to brake sharply not to run into a police roadblock. Three policemen were standing behind a tape strung across the road. They appeared to be armed with automatic weapons.

Joe clambered out of the Frontera with furious haste, his bad leg giving under him as he stood on the gravel.

'What the hell's going on?'

The garda told him we couldn't go any further. He sounded nervous.

'What do you mean? This is my property from here down this whole glen.'

'Sorry, Mr Tooley, sir, but it's a security operation.'

'I am *not* Mr Tooley.'

'Sorry, sir, whoever you are, I can't help it. It's security.'

'Look, I'm not going to be ordered about by a – Gillian, drive on. It's only tape.'

'Don't be silly, darling. It's not his fault. And anyway you don't own the whole valley. He only owns to down to the dear little stone wall before the bridge.'

Whether or not Gillian had intended it, her remark provoked Joe to get back in the car and start shouting at her to the effect that he had never wanted to buy the useless slagheap in the first place and every single piece of advice she had given him since the day they were married was ballsachingly cretinous and if she hadn't been so stupid, he 'would never have had even the teeniest-weeniest little stroke. I drove him to it, you know,' Gillian intervened sweetly, reversing across the narrow road to begin what must have been a ten-point turn. 'And now he's going to have another one, all because of me.'

As we finally straightened and started back down the road again, I twisted my neck for a last look at the Fairy Glen. The sun had slipped behind the clouds and the light had gone off the rocks. The three policemen stood remarkably still, not joking among themselves at all.

Then it came to me that I had actually met the Tooleys on my last visit. It was little Seamus Tooley who had thrown gravel at the taxi bringing me to Drishill and later there had been strange incidents – Gillian's beloved hens let out, a window broken, soot flung all over Joe's computers. Joe had sacked Mr – or was it Mrs? – Tooley or both for some reason and it seemed they had taken it hard.

'The Tooleys? Oh, we made it up with them ages ago. He went off to Galway City and did rather well apparently, then he came back here and went into leisure management, so we thought he would be just the ticket and little Seamus is rather sweet now; he's designing websites in

Hammersmith so we don't see much of him but Tom and Doreen are our absolute bosoms. They looked after Father O'Kelly Mahon when he was on his last legs, because his housekeeper had Parkinson's. You remember OK, don't you, with his basilisk stare? His nephew's my doctor, they call him OK too, perhaps because he has just the same look in his eye when he gives you the ghastly news. Oh shit, I've forgotten to get the cream for my tits. It smells absolutely foul because it's made of cabbage leaves, marvellous for nursing mothers apparently, so now they give it to women who've only got a baby C to nur—'

'Tom?' Joe bawled down his mobile. 'What the fuck is going on? The Glen is swarming with gardai ... No, I do not believe it ... Who put the fucking stuff there? ... All right, I take your word for it, but nobody dumps a dozen crates of explosive and automatic weapons without somebody knowing about it. And anyway you said the lower caves were securely blocked off. Jesus.'

He had the mobile jammed so fiercely against his ear that it looked as though it was some device for extracting the wax. His cheeks were flushed an unnerving purple. His free hand was beating against the passenger airbag again.

'Well, you see,' Francie explained over the phone when Joe got hold of him, 'they can't use the slurry pits or the potato clamps any more because the gardai are on to them now. Deep inside the mountain is your man's only hope but I wouldn't fancy being the officer who wriggled the last hundred metres or for that matter the guy who put it there. Some of that stuff's as unstable as old jelly, breathe on it and it'll blow your bollocks off.'

But Joe seemed less interested in the threat to life and limb than the insult to his property and the ingratitude shown to his efforts to regenerate the Cockburn Country. 'You knock yourself out to give the micks a leg-up and they spit in your face. You would have thought the Glen was the one place they wouldn't dream of putting their kit. Apart from the impact on tourism, the place is supposed to be fucking sacred.'

We were sitting by the long windows that had the view over the lake and the hill. Another shower had just shimmied across the panorama and left a patch of golden-green on the shoulder of the hill. Gillian had absent-mindedly brought one of her hens with her and was stroking its feathers as it nestled in her lap with a perky look in its eye.

Joe was stabbing his mobile with a furious finger, trying to find a police officer he could get some sense out of.

'Now look here, Inspector,' Joe said, 'you barge into my property without a warrant, you put up roadblocks all over the place and you don't have the courtesy to tell me a blind thing. One telephone call, that's all I ask, one fucking telephone call.'

Joe didn't give the Inspector time to reply, or perhaps the Inspector had nothing much to say before he began jabbing his mobile again. A sallower tinge had come into his face. That merry freckled melon face that had once looked ready for anything had a battered glare on it. When he raged and swore, there was at the same time a kind of flinching in the expression, as though he was possessed by an outside force which he would prefer to be rid of. Sitting in the high-backed chair hunched in his green puffer waistcoat, he was unmistakably beleaguered, at bay.

'Why do you bring that bloody hen in here? Nobody else brings hens into their sitting room.'

'Irma is my therapist. She clucks and I am calm.'

Oddly enough, I too was calm. Surrounded by debt and illness, in this tall, draughty room with the rain coming on again and beating against the windows, and the faint smell of hen in the damp air, I felt among my own fallen purposeless kind. No credit to be gained from this thought; the reverse, in fact. To have felt so out of place with the Finchers was nothing to boast of. Still, there we were with death just around the corner even if you sat indoors and didn't go crawling down fairy caves.

'You ever read that book?' Joe said suddenly.

'What book?'

'Joe's never read a book in his life, doesn't know what those things between hard covers are.'

'You've probably all read it years ago,' Joe went on unmoved. 'I found it on the shelves with the other ones they left behind.'

'Give us a clue.'

'First letter of author's surname?'

'It's about an old man – well, actually, he's probably about my age, fifty-eight – who's feeling a bit seedy and goes to his doctor and the doctor tells him he only has six months to live. So he resolves to break out of his old life which he's totally fed to the teeth with and embark on one last adventure, and he remembers that there's this amazing green valley thousands of miles away in the Canadian wilderness and he went there once as a young man and he wants to find it again and by an extraordinary coincidence there's this man who's disappeared and the man promises his wife he'll find him and the man, the one who's disappeared, turns out to have been heading for this amazing green valley and –'

'Sounds like total crap,' Gillian said.

'It's called *Sick Heart River*,' I said. 'It's by John Buchan.'

'Smartass,' Gillian said.

'It's his last book. He wrote it when he was dying.'

'Double smartass.'

'In fact, it wasn't published till after his death. It's one of my favourites.'

'Is it really?' Joe seemed pleased, indeed grateful, as you are when somebody turns out to like a book you like. 'You think it's good, then?'

'Well, I suppose it's a bit sentimental, but I don't mind that.'

'Exactly, crap,' Gillian said.

'You know,' Joe said, 'I thought I might do something like that.'

'What do you mean?'

'Go on one last adventure before I snuff it.'

'Don't be morbid,' Gillian said. 'Anyway you already live in a green valley at the back of beyond, so you only have to go for a short walk.'

'No, no, you don't understand. You have to do it the other way round.'

He leant forward in his chair with his hands clenching the arms, looking earnest and pugnacious, a bit like Churchill in the portrait Churchill's wife burnt.

'You have to find the wilderness.'

'Yes, so –'

'There's only one wilderness left. All the rest of it is fenced in and tidied up, even the Fairy Glen.'

'You wouldn't believe the rubbish we had to get rid of when we were cleaning it up, three skiploads.'

'That's probably what gave the lads the idea,' I said. 'There must be plenty of room in those caves now, they thought.'

Joe paused and glared. He had thought this speech out carefully and he was having no interruptions.

'There's only one wilderness left,' he repeated. 'And it's the City of London. That's the last hideout for the bandits.'

'So what do you mean?'

'I'm going back. To take one last hand in the game.'

'But you can't possibly, my poor old hemiplegic. You can't do a full-time job, not in a million years.'

'I haven't got a million years,' Joe said, 'all I've got is a window. I know I have, just a few months, perhaps a year, when I'm ninety per cent fit and still with a bit of juice left in the tank.'

'And what am I to do? Just sit here by your precious window and languish, murmuring he cometh not, he cometh not?'

'You are to stay here and get your strength back, and when I've made enough money we'll go to Texas and see Dr Lenz.'

'That's mad, Gus, tell him it's mad.'

'It's the only way,' Joe said. 'Got to have one more throw of the dice.'

He sat back in the chair and unclenched his hands. There was a little smile on his face, the smile of a lawyer who has just scored a point the other side wasn't expecting.

'You've been plotting this thing, whatever it is, for weeks. I think that's monstrous,' Gillian exploded. For a moment the colour was back in her cheeks.

'Why is it monstrous?'

'You didn't say anything about it because you wanted to stop me nipping it in the bud.'

Joe grinned, one of his old truculent grins. He seemed pleased that Gillian was so agitated.

'Anyway,' Gillian said, 'I don't think I want to go to Texas. Dr Lenz is a total phoney.'

'OK says there's nowhere else in the world they do the treatment.'

'That doesn't mean it works.'

'Dr O'Kelly Mahon thinks very highly of it. It's a new form of chemotherapy, a different combination of the standard –'

'Gus doesn't want to hear about it, do you, Gus? I hate illness, I mean talking about it, it's so humiliating.'

'How do you mean humiliating?' Joe looked slightly aggrieved.

'Oh, if you can't see –' Gillian jumped and ran from the room to stop us seeing that she was crying. The hen, startled by the sudden movement, broke into a frenzied clucking which continued as Gillian ran down the stone passage outside, so that you could hear the flapping of her slippers and Irma's clucking all the way till they reached the back door.

'Silly to rush out in the rain like that,' Joe said contentedly. 'Would you like to borrow the book?'

He handed me the grubby little scarlet book which said 'Maj. G. H. Cockburn, Haifa' in slanting blue ink inside the cover. I took it up to my room and lay on the rattly old bed, which had a dip in the middle like my bed at the Finchers', and surrendered to its enchantments. Reread after thirty years – no, more – it was a surprising book, not better than I had thought it the first time round, not so good in fact, but more surprising. Not that my memory of it was at all accurate. For one thing, I thought it was all written in the first person, by the old dying lawyer Sir Edward Leithen; that was what I had remembered as being so touching, this old man describing himself going to the doctor and being given the death sentence (lung trouble left over from the war) and then going to his chambers and his bankers and his solicitors and so on, to tie up the loose ends. But in reality the book was told in the third person throughout and, Joe was quite right for once, Leithen couldn't have been as old as all that because he had been in the first war and the second war hadn't yet started, although the Chief Whip tells him 'things are pretty insecure in the world just now, there may be a crisis any day'. That's the kind of thing important people are always telling Leithen. As he keeps on saying himself, he's a dry old stick, though he occasionally goes into raptures about some fine young man who is straight and clean-run. But as I shifted about in the bed, it wasn't Leithen's homoerotic tendencies that struck me so much, or the fact that Joe was right about his being only the same age as we were – it was more that the book started being about a man dying and ended with him being dead. In fact, as I discovered when finishing it on the plane back to England, it ended after he was dead. And I tried to think of other books that were specifically about a man dying. Books in the normal way of things were littered with corpses, but they did not normally start off with the character being an apprentice corpse, even if he or she was already old. But in *Sick Heart River* the dying is the thing. The adventure in the wilderness is merely a diversion to keep the reader amused until the dying bit. That made the book interesting, creepy but interesting, or to be more precise, interesting because creepy.

No more had been said that night about Joe's last adventure, at least not in my hearing. Perhaps they had had words about it between the two of them upstairs and agreed to keep off the subject for the time being. They both seemed sobered, either by the business at the Glen or by the thought of Joe leaving Ireland, or the combination of the two. At dinner we sat under the portraits of the dead-and-gone Cockburns, canvases where the paint was as thin as the old turkey rugs were threadbare. The last time I had dined here, Gillian was teaching Joe to speak again after his stroke and making him repeat the names and titles of the Cockburns in the pictures. The atmosphere had been sad then, but animated. Now it was just sad.

At about half past three in the morning I woke in a sweat with a full bladder. I clambered out of the dip in the bed and flexed my toes on the stringy bedside rug, then creaked across the floorboards in what I thought was the general direction of the door. A wedge of grey shadow in the blackness showed me that the door was half open, though I thought I had shut it. Out in the long passage I again tried to remember where the bathroom was, beyond the bend in the passage where it turned towards the long window with the view of the lake, was it? There was just enough light to grope my way through the chilly gloom. Then to my amazement –

'Oh, there you are,' she said. 'Can't you sleep either? Joe makes such a racket snoring I have to go walking at this hour like Lady Macbeth. You do look sweet in those jarmies.'

She came close to me and it seemed – natural isn't quite the word, but near enough – to take her in my arms and kiss her on the mouth, which was where she always kissed people, even people she didn't know well. That was all right but the way my body reacted was not.

'Down Fido,' she murmured, and accompanied it with a stroking gesture that was both friendly and dismissive. 'It's a bit too late, don't you think?'

'G, I really didn't mean –'

'Didn't you? I wouldn't have minded.'

'No, no, I was just –'

'Oh, yes, of course. It's second on the right. The switch is just behind the door. Pity my mother isn't alive, she'd have enjoyed it: "Gillian always thinks the men are after her when they're just looking for the loo." '

Her imitation of her mother's confident drawl added a sneer which wasn't in the original. She kissed me again, this time on the cheek lightly, then moved past me the way I had come, a pale spectre on the creaking boards until the dark consumed her. And after she had gone – perhaps before – a faint cabbagy smell, green and pleasant not rotting, so she must have found the cream after all.

The next morning Joe was full of zest and bustle. While Gillian had gone to fetch the car to drive me to the station, he took me to one side of the hall so that I was almost backed into a wooden stand full of walking sticks and fishing nets. There was nobody else in the hall or probably in the house (they didn't have a cleaner any more), but he seemed to need a corner to conspire in.

'What you reckon?'

'Reckon about what?'

'My little caper, the last throw.'

'Oh,' I said, 'well, it's up to you and I'm not a doctor, but I don't think you're well enough.'

'That's why I'm doing it, because it doesn't matter, because if I don't do it now there won't be another window. Now or never – doesn't that say anything to you?'

'What about G? It matters to her.'

'I'm not talking about Gillian. I'm talking about you and me.'

'Me?'

'Of course. That's why I mentioned it – well, I suppose partly because I was so pissed off about the Glen. But I wanted to sound you out.'

'Well, now you know what I think.'

'No, but are you on?'

'On? On what?'

'Are you up for it?'

'Don't keep talking in prepositions. What do you mean?'

'Can't you understand plain English? Will you come in with me?'

'You mean you want me to become a partner or something in this loony enterprise whatever that is?'

'I always said you had a first-class brain.'

'Are you serious? You can't possibly expect a civil servant to moonlight for a private company, especially one as dodgy as anything you dream up is obviously going to be.'

'You could always stop being a civil servant. Change of direction, new challenge. Come on in, the water's lovely. Just think about it, that's all I ask. I'll fax you the details in a week or two. I'm not going to tell you now because you're all agitated. For the moment, I just want you to think about the possibility, the outside possibility I put it no higher, of taking early retirement. You'd have your pension of – what? – 35k, not a lot of difference from what you'd get if you slogged it out to retirement, and you could do something exciting with those last few years of active life, venture closer to the edge. Doesn't even your flabby old heart beat a little faster at the thought of it?'

He was right up close to me now so that I could feel some walking stick or umbrella jutting into my hip. His breath was sweet-smelling, violets I think, and he had his arm round my neck which I didn't mind, but his mottled face still had that sad expressionless look which he had had ever since the stroke, so that his excited words sounded more like someone tonelessly reading a communiqué. Was he just trying all this on as a tease, to remind me of how dim and unadventurous I was, how perfectly my work suited me, regular, secure, virtually risk-free? Yet he had taken the trouble to find out roughly what I could expect in the way of a pension – I wouldn't have dreamt of giving him the details myself.

'Oh, all right then,' I said, to get rid of him really, 'I'll think about it.'

'I always knew you were a couple of poofs, but must you do it in the hall in front of the servants, if we had any servants?'

Gillian came in jangling her car keys.

'Just saying goodbye,' Joe said. 'Totally innocent.'

He stood back from me, spreading his hands to show we had not been up to no good. For the first time I registered what I had remembered about him when we met in our teens, that his arms were not long enough for the breadth of his shoulders and his fingers were so stubby that they might have been short of a joint. Jackets hung uneasy on him, as though he was hunching his shoulders against the cold. He wasn't all that short, but he somehow made you think of dwarfishness, or perhaps of being physically unfinished, so that after all these years it seemed surprising that he hadn't made up these deficiencies.

'We'll meet again, in London,' he said. 'And you'll probably see G on her way through to Dallas.'

'I'm not going to Dallas, my darling,' Gillian said. 'I'm going to stay here with my hens, and OK can cure me.'

'Anyway I'll fax you,' Joe said, paying no attention.

He clasped my hand in his unfinished freckled fists and I concentrated on saying goodbye.

I got into the car and turned to wave while Gillian switched on. He was standing in the doorway and holding his walking stick high above his head with both hands as the hurley players did at moments of triumph and that reminded me too of the way he used to display his body at the asthma clinic, standing naked in the middle of the room or clambering up on the cornice of the dormitory to see if he could walk round the room without touching the floor. He seemed impervious to the cold or to the eczema we shared, which left minute fragments of skin in our socks each night. I suppose that was what women liked about him, the innocent way he attacked the world. I liked it too – no, liked is not the word, envied would be nearer the mark. But I would have preferred to watch him from a distance. If this scheme, whatever it was, was going to be his last throw, I could see no reason why it had to be mine too. All the same, there it was, I had said I would think about it, which he clearly took as a yes and, partly, I meant it to be a yes, out of pity I suppose, with a spoonful of guilt for my mistakenly embracing Gillian, which cannot have been pleasant for her and which, if I was to be absolutely honest, was not as mistaken as all that from my side.

II

Thursby

How long was it, a day or two, not more, before a deceiving mist had engulfed those unsettling days across the water? I found myself dreaming, no, daydreaming, of Drishill and its Gothic crenellations, and the little summerhouse with the pointed roof where Gillian kept her hens and the view across the lake to the moorland where we sat and watched the sun go down. I forgot about the mildew on the damask in the dining room and the slimy cement the whole Abbey had been encased in back in 1950 in a futile effort to keep out the damp. I no longer felt the chill in the passages or noticed the brown marks on the walls where some of the Cockburn portraits had been before they were sold off to a shyster from Dublin who knocked on the door and offered five hundred quid for the lot. Without any conscious effort, I began to experience in recollection a kind of relaxation, even charm, which had not actually been present at the time. Their shortage of cash came to seem almost like a blessing. Joe's absurd plans for one last breakout dropped out of sight. No doubt he would fax me some nonsense or other, but it would be no more menacing than a travel brochure and just as easy to chuck in the bin. Obviously he could not think of leaving Gillian in her present state. They would probably find a first-rate man in Dublin or Belfast who could help her.

As for the Finchers, I was sorry I had allowed myself to be irritated by their contentment and only hoped they hadn't noticed. They deserved whatever luck was going. The general opinion was quite right: Francie was one of the best. And I thought with affection of him leaning on the bar at Gilligan's with his cap on the back of his head swapping the latest on Munster's new stand-off with young Gerry Gilligan, in his element, while further down the counter Jonquil was stocking up on groceries and gossip with Máire G. This was the way to live. You would be mad to abandon it just because of a drop of rain or the odd terrorist incident.

So it was not surprising that I should have been such putty in Francie's hands when he rang me a month or two later to fix me up, as he had threatened, with a little light prison visiting. Just to hear that gentle, quick voice down the line — a touch more Irish than I remembered but then that's often the way with the phone, it makes you hear where people come from. Though I had expressed zero enthusiasm for the idea, I couldn't let Francie down. He didn't need to appeal for your help. He simply expected that you would do the right thing, expected it in the gentlest possible way so that not doing it was like wrenching a delicate piece of machinery out of shape, cost a bomb to mend and you regretted it ever after. Even the roughest witnesses who came before him had felt that expectation of his and glowed because this was probably the first time in their lives anyone had expected anything of them.

'You would not believe how difficult some of them find the transition to ordinary life.'

On the contrary, this seemed all too easy to imagine, seeing how difficult ordinary life could be even if you were in practice for it. But all I said was ah yes.

'So I've fixed you up at Thursby Grange. They're a bit short of visitors up there. The Governor's an old mate, Ninny de Burch. Just give him a bell. The thing is to stay the night, it's miles from anywhere and that way you can really get the feel of the place. There are excellent trains from King's Cross.'

It was hard to say which dominated, the gloom or the resentment, as I sat staring out at the fields of blackened stubble and the dismal dykes. The excellent train ground to a halt for a couple of hours somewhere north of Grantham, so night was falling across the wolds as the station taxi rattled over the brow of the last hill and down through the gates of a large beige-brick mansion – Edwardian, probably, it was hard to be sure in the gathering murk – standing in its own flat grounds with here and there a few tall firs snapped off halfway up. A bleak scene, as bleak as I had expected, but then in the grey half-light, the grounds took on a startling silver shimmer, as of some huge dew. Pulling down the grimy window of the taxi, I discovered that fields of young kale stretched right up to the house, and as I got out the fierce smell of cabbage made breathing difficult for a moment or two, and reminded me of Gillian and our awkward meeting in the small hours.

From his name at least, the Governor sounded like a sensitive person, whose liberal views might be a bit laughable but sympathetic. These expectations shrivelled when the elderly man who answered the door said, 'The Colonel's just finishing his supper, but he'll be down in a minute.'

Place must have been a school, I thought, as I mooched around the umbrous hall. Behind the classical wooden pillars, there were honours boards, the gilt lettering still fresh enough to gleam in the gloomy recesses. I stared idly at the boards:

Table tennis

De Burch Salver
1995   J. Pugg
1996   A. Adebayo
1997   R. Smith

All surprisingly recent. Ditto **Gymnastics**: Victor Ludorum (*MacInnes Cup*) G. Beck. And how about the de Burch element? Had he been headmaster of the school before it became a prison?

'Ah, I see you've noticed my little honours system. It gives the lads something to aim for.' A voice at my elbow, crisp and boomy at the same time. I turned to find a huge man with crinkly pomaded hair and mini-Kitchener moustaches stamping to attention in front of me. He was wearing a jacket of garish heathery tweed and an even more brightly coloured kilt over his paunch. His appearance wasn't so much military as theatrical – a ringmaster or an MC at a palace of varieties.

'My grandmother was a MacInnes,' he said, picking up my stare. 'You must be our esteemed visitor.'

'I'm sorry I'm so late,' I mumbled, 'train got stuck.'

'Don't worry. Mrs Boothby's put by some of her bread-and-butter pudding for you. You're very welcome. Any friend of Francie's . . .'

'Did he tell you it was my first time?'

'I wouldn't give it a thought. You'll find you just slip into it, much easier than losing your virginity I always say.'

'Oh, good.'

'Anyway you'll find plenty of your sort in this place. And of course the great thing is they're all raring to get the hell out of here.'

'Yes.'

'If you wouldn't mind doing a bit of beating tomorrow. It's the best way to get to know the chaps. Companionship in misery.'

Through my tired brain tripped images of men stripped naked and bent over vaulting horses while the Colonel, kilt swirling, swung some murderous tawse or cat-o'-nine-tails, before, panting with exertion, he passed the hideous instrument to me.

'You needn't if you don't fancy it. The forecast says it's going to piss.'

'Oh, I –'

'The local syndicate takes a couple of days on our land. We don't tell the Home Office, of course, the cash comes in handy for life's little extras. I hope I can rely on you to stay shtum.'

'Of course.'

'Kick-off's nine thirty sharp. We can lend you some wellies. You haven't got a drink. What do you fancy? I've got a single malt that smoothes out the wrinkles.'

He put a heavy cut-glass tumbler in my hand and trickled a generous measure of peaty fluid into it.

'Would you like to have a look around? It's after lock-up but the comrades will still be up and about.'

He unlocked a door at the far end of the hall with a flourish of a key from a large ring which appeared to be somehow connected to his sporran.

'Not strictly necessary, but the sleepwalkers seem to prefer it.'

We were in a long passage painted a sickly cream, recently added on to the old building by the look of it. The rich aroma of Mansion House polish and de Burch's cigars in de Burch's quarters faded the moment the door clunked behind us. Instead, the passage smelled of lavender haze disinfectant and stale fags. The air seemed different too, raw and dank, though not exactly cold. I recognised it all instantly. It was like when you went from Dr Maintenon-Smith's quarters – the private side – through to the dormitory corridor in the asthma clinic where Joe and I had been banged up all those years ago. Two or three men in green overalls were loafing about, leaning on the doors to their rooms and ashing out in the ashtrays they were holding in their hands. Halfway down the passage it broadened out into an open space where half a dozen more men were watching a game show on a large TV.

'This is all crap, you know that, sir? Can't you get us some vids?'

'The place is too much like a holiday camp as it is. I must warn you, this gentleman is from the Home Office.'

'I'm not,' I said weakly.

'Well, he can get us a fucking video then. Aren't we supposed to be improving our minds in here?'

'On the contrary, George,' the Colonel said, 'you are preparing for life in the outside world where you will be watching a good deal of this sort of thing.'

'Oh, Governor, pul-lease.'

'Nine a.m. in the yard sharp tomorrow for those who are coming out with the guns. You up for it, Terry?'

'You know I'm anti-blood sports, Governor.'

'Only where animals are concerned, it seems.'

'That's not fair. He was an animal himself, even the judge said so. Anyway, we're trying to put our past lives behind us, isn't that right, sir?'

'Oh, God, they know all the answers, don't they?'

The Governor was gratified by this badinage, taking it as a tribute to the success of his regime.

The next morning, out in the yard with the wet still on the cobbles, I recognised a couple of faces from the night before, but looking brisker and cocking an eye to the weather like born countrymen, which for all I knew they were.

The Colonel, now clad in a complicated waterproof with flaps, was already greeting the local farmers who had come to shoot. He had barely time to give me a friendly wave.

'Sleep all right? You go with George, he'll look after you. Cocks only, remember. Don't start yelling when you put up a bloody hen.'

George turned out to be the neat little man with a bald head who had asked the Colonel for a video the night before.

'What are you in for, then?' I said as we trudged down the main drive past the long fields of kale which seemed to stretch a glistening silver-green all the way to the horizon.

'Glassed a geezer who was going on about my wife. It was in the pub. Bled to death, he did. Manslaughter, verdict was unanimous.'

'That was the only charge, was it?' An unholy jubilation took hold of me, the thrill of the first kiss, the duck broken.

'Course it was. An unmistakable case of provocation, the judge said. I was rat-arsed at the time, so was he, come to that.'

Our boots crunched through the thin ice in the rut puddles. Cabbage-tanged breath steamed into the iron-blue sky. The endless vistas beyond the fir plantation made me think of Siberia. We could have been a detachment of prisoners from the Gulag off to dig a canal through the tundra, our guards marching along beside us with guns on their shoulders.

'Right, lads,' George said, 'line out along the end of these fucking cabbages and don't start till I blow the whistle.'

I clambered over the barbed wire and stumbled and slithered through the dripping kale to take my place in the line. Recovering my breath, I turned and nodded to the next man in the line. He was wearing a woolly hat with 'Armani' emblazoned across the front and some other writing below it, and war criminal's spectacles. He returned my greeting in the most extraordinary way, running towards me through the kale and seizing me in one of those masculine embraces which involved a good deal of shoulder-patting followed by arm's-length gripping and a frank manly exchange of stares, at the end of all which he said, just as George's whistle blew, 'You didn't recognise me.'

And I said of course I had as soon as I got a proper look at him, but the truth was that the recognition was slow-dawning because he was so much thinner and he had that face which after less than a day in the place I was already beginning to recognise: a depleted look, dead-eyed, flat, a look which even being fit and having your muscles nicely toned didn't quite conceal.

'Trull,' I said.

'Keith,' he corrected. 'It's all first names in here, Gus.'

'Hey, break it up, you nonces, keep the line straight.'

'Cock over!'

We cheered at the first whirring of wings and then a little later the crack-crack of the guns as the birds passed over the end of the field where the farmers were lined out. The guns sounded quieter than I expected, dulled by the distance and the wintry air.

'What on earth –'

As he filled in 'brings me here?' with a quizzical twitch of his rude cherub's lips, I read the other lettering under the Armani on his bobble hat. It said HM PRISON THURSBY. The writing had to be quite small to fit it all on.

'Well,' he went on. 'It is quite an *histoire*. You remember the butterfly farm I had with Peggy, actually not really with Peggy, she had a thing against butterflies, but then she had quite a lot of *things*, God rest her soul.'

'Gillian told me she was –'

'Oh, yes, didn't live to see me go through all this, which has really turned out to be rather a blessing.'

I wasn't sure from this whether it was Peggy dying first that was the blessing or his incarceration itself, which sounded improbable, but then Trull had often been improbable and in any case I wanted him to get on with the story, as we were halfway down the field with the wet cabbages slapping against our calves and the yells and cluckings of our fellow beaters making it hard to hear what he was saying.

'The butterfly farm, yes, it was a pretty spot – you came there once I think – but doomed I'm afraid, utterly doomed.'

'How do you mean?'

'We were prosecuted, you know. A frightful man reported us for illegal importation of endangered species. Guilty as hell, of course, the endangered species were the only ones the punters wanted.'

'But you weren't sent here for that surely? I know the British are crazy about animals, but that seems –'

'A little excessive, yes.'

'Hold the line, hold it.'

We had reached the last twenty yards of field, and pheasants were rocketing out of the kale and falling in tufty bundles almost on the farmers' heads. The prisoner-beaters whooped and rattled their sticks.

Trull took off his bobble hat and waved it languidly as though fanning his face.

Sitting beside me, on a straw bale at the back of the open lorry on the way to the next drive, he continued, 'No, that wasn't the whole story. Other matters came to the attention of the police in the course of their enquiries.'

'Other matters?'

'Quite illegally, I believe, or so my unlearned friend attempted to argue on my behalf at the trial, the pigs began to intercept our consignments. And what did they find when their little piggy trotters had unwrapped the parcels that had been so carefully wrapped back in Bogota? Not just the most beautiful Peruvian Blues and Parrot Fritillaries, all, I may say, in wonderful condition — Hernando is an absolute genius as a butterfly exporter. Alas, in other departments he is something of a klutz and it was not long before little piggy eyes noticed that there were envelopes taped to the bottom of the carrying cases, somewhat crudely taped, I have to say.'

'Envelopes?'

'How sweetly you say the word, like Lady Bracknell. Yes, envelopes, containing certain substances which our nanny government does not wish us to enjoy.'

'Oh, I see.'

'These modest extras, mere *bonnes bouches* you might say, added roughly 10k to the value of each consignment and thus enabled our little operation to tremble on the edge of profitability — no, I am too modest, it enabled us to take our rightful place in the vanguard of the enterprise culture.'

'Right, lads, out you get. And don't make too much noise. We're doing this lot on the way back.'

'And?' I enquired as we began to hack our way through the next brambly thicket.

'Five years. Rather steep, I thought. The judge said that a particularly distasteful feature of the case was the abuse of wildlife for the furtherance of this vile trade. But as I say, the whole business has been something of a blessing.'

'How so?'

But before he could answer, a rough voice said, 'Oy, you two, out of there. I want one of you to walk outside with the Major and the other one to go back along the ditch.'

I was the one detailed to walk along the fence, rattling the barbed wire to keep the birds in and make them run forward.

The Major was a tall, lugubrious man in dung-coloured plus-twos. 'Beautiful morning,' he said.

'It is.'

'You must be glad to get out, see a bit of the country.'

'Absolutely.'

'I mean, I know it's an open prison and so on but all the same –'

'Yes.'

'I hope you won't mind my asking, but what exactly are you in for?'

'I'm not –'

'If you'd rather not say, I'd quite understand. I expect it's the first question everyone asks.'

'No, actually, I'm just visiting.'

'Just visiting? Like in Monopoly?'

'What?'

'When you land on Go To Jail but you're all right if you get the Just Visiting card, at least I think it's a card.'

'Ah,' I said.

'I say, I'm most awfully sorry, I didn't mean to imply you looked the type who . . .'

'Is there a type?'

'No, probably not. Well, I must say in that case I think that's a first-class effort.'

'What is?'

'Going out with the chaps like this, you seemed to be getting on awfully well with that other fellow.'

'He turns out to be an old friend.'

'Really? What an amazing coincidence. Well, I suppose there but for the grace of God and so on.'

'Yes.'

Some vague glimmering of not having hit exactly the right note seemed to trickle through and he sank back into a reverie. For a while, the only sound was our boots squelching through the boggy ground along the edge of the wood. Then the birds began to rise ahead of us, lumbering up through the bare birches until fully airborne and then gliding between the silvered branches in a silence that seemed tremulous because so soon cut off by the anger of the guns (anger was the right word, the guns sounded aggrieved, alarmed even, as though it was the birds that were attacking them).

'You a friend of Ninian's?' the Major said as the wood went quiet again.

'No, they just sent me here.'

'Ah, is that how it works? Well, he's a great man, can't shoot for toffee, but a great man. We were in the army together, real muckers.'

'A Scottish regiment I suppose?'

'No, why should you think that?'

'Well, the kilt.'

'No, no, not Scottish at all. The Reemy actually, spanner wallahs.'

'Really?'

'And your friend, the one you were beating with, how did you come across him?'

'Oh, years ago, in London, I think. He's –' but then I couldn't think exactly how to describe Trull.

Writer? Traveller? Wit? No, wit isn't the word, his knowing, playful kind of talk was more insinuating, occasionally even charming, but not exactly witty. His high point, I suppose, had been as a rather popular novelist about twenty years earlier – somewhere between science fiction and magic realism: time travel, metamorphoses, with added sadism. He had done quite well to start with, with a creepy gothic type of novel, but then what he called his magifiction really took off (*Cybertyphoon* was supposed to have sold a million, or was it *One-Eyed Dwarf*?). Then he had taken up with Peggy, after Joe had chucked her and married her daughter, and they had gone into butterfly farming (or rather he had, Peggy couldn't tell a Painted Lady from a Red Admiral). They stayed friends, Joe and Trull (we always called him Trull; he never used to care for Keith then, and that was the kind of thing he could impose his will about, as about most things in fact). Perhaps that was not so surprising. After all, Joe and I had stayed friends after Gillian had gone from me to him. Their continued friendship might be less surprising, because both of them were so much younger than

Peggy was, Joe a full fifteen years, Trull probably about ten, although I never knew his exact age — it was one of those pieces of information that he had seen from the beginning it might be useful to keep darkish. So they might both feel that she had taken each of them merely to amuse herself. They were playthings, not quite full partners in the long drawling war against boredom that was her life. From their point of view she was a rite of passage they had shared, a unique encounter with style.

Not that Trull didn't have his own style, which he had pretty much worked out for himself before Peggy came along. Through all his ups and downs he had never lost his air of knowing something you didn't know, something which was very soon going to pop up and smack you but not him in the face. Despite his present situation he still had that superior nonchalance. It was hard to put all this into words so I just mumbled something about him being a bit of a character.

'Looked like a lively sort. Tell me, what's he in for, or is he just visiting too?'

'No, he's doing five years for drug smuggling and illegally importing butterflies.'

'Strange combination,' the Major said.

'Mm,' I said.

I didn't see Trull again until after the last drive of the morning. We were sitting in the ruins of a keeper's cottage in the middle of a fir wood, eating our sandwiches with a crate of beer cans dumped in front of us.

'I know why you're here, of course,' he said, shifting his buttocks on the block of masonry we were using as a bench.

'Do you? I wish I did.'

'There's no point in being so evasive, Gus. You might just as well tell me straight out, nobody's listening.'

'Tell you what?'

'Joe sent you, didn't he? He told me there would be a messenger. It's great that it should be you.'

'A messenger?'

'To summon the Four Horsemen, for the Last Day. I happened to be studying the Book of Revelation when I got his letter so the whole thing fell into place nicely.'

'What are you talking about?'

'Well, we don't need to go into details now. The messenger was merely to bring a summons, nothing more. I'll be out in a couple of months, which should give me just enough time to finish the course.'

'Course? What course?'

'BA Theology. Open University. I'm afraid the teaching is rather bog standard, but the texts are what matters.'

'Theology? You?'

'Ever hear about the lost sheep, Gus?' He blew me a rude kiss with his cherub's lips and suddenly looked about eighteen again.

'Is it a way of earning early release or something?'

'Oh dear, you have become awfully cynical in my absence, and you used to be so sweet and trusting. Well, there's hope for all us sinners and I wouldn't dream of giving up on you, Gus, least of all you. We must have a proper little talk while you're here, and then, when I'm out and about –'

'Right, lads, on your feet, no peace for the wicked.'

For the next drive we were separated again, either side of a muddy stream that fumbled its way through a swamp of willows and alders. As we heaved ourselves over the barbed wire, wild duck got up all over the place and whirred off into the clearing sky. Swearing at the ducks and following their flight, we had to shade our eyes from the sun, which came out high and bright as though it were still summer. I slithered down the bank through the reeds and found a squelchy tuft to stand on while I waited for the other beaters to come into line. It was a quiet place. The sun streamed down upon the little boggy pool at my feet and a peaceful feeling, quite unexpected but intense, came over me. The reeds looked fragile, almost papery with sun shining through them and through the white foam of the old man's beard on the thorn bushes. This miniature patch of swamp seemed at once precious and entirely familiar to me, and my heart began to thump as though I had been away from it for years and this was a homecoming. Or that was how it seemed at first, one of those moments that catch you when your mind is somehow receptive to such things and then stick with you for years, to be triggered off again by some sudden analogous experience, like the sun winking on a puddle in an empty street. But there was another element here, less pleasant, colder to the touch. I knew it at once for what it was, though not able to recall having had a feeling quite like it before. Not so much you have been here before as you won't come here again, and quite soon this here might as well be anywhere as far as you're concerned. A harsh voice somewhere was telling me to start saying my goodbyes, or rather to save my breath because nobody was listening and nobody cared. It was dealing out this memento mori in the harsh slangy voice of a hit-man in a basement, but it was my own voice. It was a moment of dread, utter wretchedness, all the worse because so unexpected.

The boggy tuft was sucking at my borrowed boots and my feet were cold as the tomb. The heart-thumping slowed and I felt the comforting waves of self-pity washing over me. Then George blew his whistle and we began tramping through the swamp, our cluckings echoing off the sides of the valley and jinking across the water with a mournful syncopation. I stopped again, this time to take a leak. The golden arc dibbling the murky pool seemed to act as an antidote and I holloaed with the rest of them as a bird, perhaps two of them, crashed through the willow branches ahead of us.

But it wasn't a bird at all. What came belting out of the brambles, its head held high as it searched for a way up to the high ground beyond us, was a big red fox. It ran up out of the bog and you could see that its underside was smeared with the mud, and the brush too, but the head and shoulders were still a gleaming chestnut-red. As it ran across the line of beaters, the holloaing changed to another noise I couldn't quite get the hang of, more song-like, a football chant perhaps, I thought, but one I didn't know. And they stopped beating and made no effort to thrash the scrub and turn the fox towards the guns. In a couple of seconds he was scrabbling up the bank and off into the fir trees. Then he was gone and the beaters gave a long warbling sort of cheer, and even I could hear that the cheer was full of fellow-feeling.

'That was a poor show,' the Major said as we came out of the wood. He recognised in that cheer a little upsurge of rebel spirit and he didn't care for it. He looked at me with some suspicion as though to check whose side I was on.

But the sudden appearance of the fox – and the welcome the beaters had given it – had transported me a long way back, to the time when my father was trying to teach me to shoot and we were splashing through a marsh belonging to a friendly farmer (he even lent us the gun) and I was loosing off at everything that moved because I hadn't fluffed a feather all afternoon and I wanted to show my father I wasn't a total dud. It was near dusk and we were coming to the end of the marsh. There was a fir plantation on the higher ground beyond, between us and the setting sun, which made the light worse still. When the bird got up out of the rushy tufts, its slow flapping flight should have told me it wasn't a snipe. But in my trigger-happy frustration I put up my gun and more by luck than aiming (I don't think I even had the gun up to my shoulder properly) winged it. Even as I sploshed across to the tussock where it had fallen, I somehow knew it was all a mistake and didn't need my father calling from the other side of the stream where he was trying to flush the birds for me, 'I'm afraid it's protected.'

'What?'

'Pro-otected.' As the syllables rolled through the damp twilight, I was cradling the lapwing, its soft white breast still warm and trembling but its eye already shut. I never troubled to find out whether lapwings are in fact protected by law, consoling myself with the thought that my father was usually unreliable on such matters, but it is true that I have never heard of anyone deliberately shooting a lapwing. And beyond the humiliation I remember experiencing a deep sadness and wondering whether I had ever felt so sad about a human being. But then it may just have been my first encounter with death. I never learnt how to shoot properly and gave up trying a few years later, not because I was still mourning the lapwing but because missing every time had become unbearable. Still, I wished I had joined in the cheering when the fox escaped.

We were just getting back into the trailer when the sun went in, abruptly as though it had lost patience, and within minutes the sky was bruised-black and a coarse squall came down, which turned into unkind unceasing heavy rain that made you shiver and caused de Burch to call it a day.

There was a Gideon Bible by my bed and I sat reading the Book of Revelation in the hot bath that de Burch had insisted on running for me himself. These horsemen in Chapter Six were not the sort of role models most people would choose.

'No,' agreed Trull when I called in on his clean, sparse cell, 'famine, war, death, and I can't remember what the other one symbolises. I think Joe must have got them mixed up with the Four Just Men. He's probably thinking of himself as a Clint Eastwood type, you know, the lean, hard-faced man riding into town to sort out the baddies.'

'You wouldn't say Joe was a goodie exactly.'

'No, but nor is the Clint Eastwood type. There's always some unpleasantness he had to ride out of town to forget, before he could ride back in again. We only do flawed heroes nowadays, so Joe qualifies easily. Sinners come to repentance are the hottest ticket in town.'

Trull gave his rude cherub's smile. He was wearing a T-shirt in the regulation Thursby green which gave him a priestly look. In fact, his whole cell had a chilling monastic feel. Perhaps the cells were all bound to be rather like that, but the couple of others I had peered into through half-open doors had been cheered up by a family photo on the shelf behind the bed, or footballers and Page Three girls cut out from magazines and Blu-tacked to the cream roughcast wall. Trull, though, had bare walls relieved only by three or four paperbacks piled on the shelf and a little bunch of flowers, old man's beard mostly, stuck in his toothmug. But then whom would he have pinned up? It did not sound as if he was still worshipping Peggy's memory. Anyway, it was not necessarily Trull's new religious enthusiasm that was responsible for the austerity look. It came naturally to him. Even after those creepy gothic novels took off, there was never much more in his flat than a tip-up chair and an army surplus table with a bean bag for relaxing on. His uniform then was a sweatshirt and baggy check chef's trousers. Later on, when he had switched to the magifiction, he dressed as if he was about to go into the operating theatre with green top and trousers and Green Flash tennis shoes (that was when they had the butterfly farm). So he didn't look very different now in the green T-shirt and tracksuit bottoms. He was, as always, stripped for action.

'What is this religion thing you are into?' I asked.

'Ever heard of Ortho?'

'No.'

'Neo-orthodox evangelical group, based on St Thomas Didymus

down in Docklands. The chaplain here, Malcolm Tedder-Brown, is Tommy D's outreach officer. He's lent me some of their better stuff.'

He spoke as though given access to some rare wine or hashish, difficult and expensive to get hold of.

'What,' I said, casting about, 'what exactly is it all about?'

'The general idea is to reboot the sacraments as the software for your spiritual life, to get you on-line for the epiphanies that religion used to deliver. I quote.'

'I haven't a clue what you're talking about.'

'Well then, think of the most intense moments you've experienced, grief, joy, terror, doesn't matter which. The telegram bringing you the news that your mother has died, the time you first got it in properly, seeing your father's body in the mortuary, the day you –'

'Yes, yes, I've got the idea.' (How had he remembered all this? Had I ever told him so much?)

'Now shouldn't religion bring you moments like that, if it's serious? Surely it ought to be more than a rubber underlay to one's life.'

'If you say so.'

'So it can't really count if it's just a matter of vaguely believing something in a more or less metaphorical sort of way.'

'I suppose not.'

'There has to be a passionate, direct experience and the only hope of anything like that is to belong wholeheartedly, to accept every single dogma, sign and symbol of the traditional faith. You have to make the most daring jump of all, which is the jump into orthodoxy.'

'Ye-es, I see,' which I did more or less. I sounded hesitant only because there was something familiar about the spiel which my mind was having trouble identifying.

'According to Malc, sometimes the best way in is to think of a really memorable fuck, with someone you hardly knew, say, or during a thunderstorm.'

'Oh.'

'But of course it doesn't have to be sex. A thunderstorm by itself might have the same trigger effect. You looked a bit shaken when we met up after going through that swamp.'

'Yes, well, as it happens I did have a bit of a turn. There was a little pool in front of me and the sunlight caught it when the sun came out and I suddenly had this intense sensation that I was going to die very soon and would never see any of this again.'

'There you are, an epiphany.'

'Of course, it's unlikely I would ever see that particular pond again in any case, but –'

'Utterly irrelevant. The pond was simply synecdoche, a part standing for the whole of creation, it's the characteristic method of religious experience. Pity you're not staying on here a bit. Malc could talk you through the rest of it in no time.'

'Chesterton,' I said, 'that's what it reminds me of, G. K. Chesterton.'

'Right,' said Trull with a lazy assent which gave no hint whether he could have passed a stiff exam on Chesterton's religious writings or barely knew his name.

Then Trull began again to talk, but much of what he said passed over my head or rather swirled around in the fumy haze from his Silk Cuts. Thrashing around in bog and bramble all day had frazzled me, and I lay back in the cell's mauve utility-style armchair and ambled off into something approaching sleep, until roused by a clap of thunder, which turned out to be only a hammering at the door, followed by a remarkably hairy man with big teeth putting his head round it.

'It may interest you to know, young Keith, that I have just had the shag of the decade. Ah, you must be the visit*or*' – he gave the final 'or' comic emphasis, as though prison visiting was a way of showing off like acting, which perhaps it was.

'Malc, this is Gus, an old friend from my days of innocence.'

'In that case you must go a very long way back. I apologise for my rude language, but once you two have set eyes on Carole in the dispensary, you will forgive me.'

He was wearing a short-sleeved shirt in Thursby green and, to my surprise, a dog collar from which black hairs sprouted vigorously but not too vigorously to cache an Adam's apple the size of a baby's foot.

'When you say "in the dispensary"?' Trull hazarded.

'I mean in. There's a little storeroom at the back, might have been made for it.'

'While you have been disgracing yourself with defenceless dispensers, I have been giving Gus a short course on neo-orthodoxy.'

'Splendid,' said Malc, 'I find the response in this place is first-rate. But then there's no place like a nick to preach the word.'

'Captive audience.'

'Right, and receptive too. In thy service is perfect freedom, not exactly the screw's motto, but being inside does give you a bit of time off in a very real sense, as we padres like to say.'

His voice was vibrant and eager, with just a hint of West Highland peatiness to it. At pauses in the conversation he gave a big-toothed grin not apparently connected to anything any of us had said.

'When Gus was out beating for Ninny, he had a terrible sensation of approaching death, a Grade-A memento mori.'

'Did he now? Excellent.'

'Yes, surely you must see, Gus. It's the only way to be sure you're alive. If you can't hear the hiss of the reaper's scythe, you might as well be dead already.'

Then Malcolm Tedder-Brown took over the controls. He moved effortlessly from his amorous adventure into a sort of homily, so that Carole in the dispensary became a figure in a parable, their grapplings brilliantly lit for an instant before the preacher pushed on to expound the lesson to be drawn from the incident. Now and then he mentioned names unknown to me – Burberry, Fieldspar, van Donck – presumably theologians or charismatic leaders of this new cult. Once or twice he gestured at Trull with his meaty hand asking for corroboration – 'isn't that what we found, Keith, when we were giving the Real Presence a going-over?' or 'I seem to remember you had some doubts about the gnostic approach in this context'. I could not tell whether these were mere courtesies to keep his audience with him or whether he genuinely respected Trull's input. He was not a large man, no more than average-sized in fact, but he somehow suggested burliness. He might have trained as an engineer before receiving the call. The way he injected a kind of muscularity into these elusive concepts was attractive, not that it made his drift much easier to catch.

A bell began to ring somewhere beyond the end of the passage, not like a fire alarm or an electric doorbell, but clanging, hand-held, the bell of a town crier. And outside Trull's cell came the sound of passing feet and cellmates' chatter.

'Roll-call,' Trull explained, 'they don't bang us up here but they do make us check in. Like being back at school.'

That limp-trot clanging and the sound of feet on the lino and the grumbling chat did bring it all back, the surly pace you walked at to the assembly point to show you were cool and the way you talked, idly, preferably about something as far away as possible, and the way you answered your name – all to show you were free when you so clearly weren't.

De Burch was standing a couple of steps up on the stairs leading to his flat where we had had the single malt the night before. He was wearing a strange upper garment, dark-blue or black, flowing to mid-thigh, halfway between a boxer jacket and a frock coat, but looking more like a schoolmaster's gown than anything else. He began abruptly without preliminary, as though to take the audience by surprise.

'The first eleven will play Pottersfield Tech on Thursday, kick-off two fifteen sharp. The toilets on the upper corridor are closed until further notice. Abbot?'

'Yes sir.'

'Adams.'

'Yeah.'

'Adebayo.'

'I'm here.'

'Allen.'

'Here, Boss.'

There was something hypnotic about the ceremony, something universal too: the naming and the responding, the necessity to go on until everyone present had been called and named, the little thrill when someone was slow to answer or didn't answer at all and then the half-felt disappointment when someone else piped up 'he's got the flu, sir', or 'he's gone to Huddersfield, for his appeal, sir' and again I remembered the same thrill, the same let-down forty years earlier, when we too were banged up and the one glorious moment when Courthope had run away and got as far as the amusement arcade at King's Cross before being spotted.

'In most nicks one of the screws calls the roll,' Trull said, 'but Ninny can't bear to be out of the limelight.'

'Ninny's a good bloke,' Malc said.

He had a curl at one end of his full red lips, leaving an aperture which nature had meant for a pipe but at present was affording only a balcony space for one of his heavy-duty canines.

'As I say, in a funny way there's lashings of freedom in this place,' he went on, 'and I don't just mean that you can bugger off down to the pub and get pissed if you please, though you can. There's a kind of spiritual space in here which you don't always find outside.'

'Would you agree with that, Gus?' Trull said with one of his dangerous rude-cherub smiles.

'Well, I've only been here twenty-four hours.'

Which was beginning to feel like a lifetime, and it was like another sort of bell going when one of the prison officers knocked on the door to say that the taxi had come to take me to the train. Yet it was true that in a way I didn't care to admit the appearance of the Reverend Malcolm Tedder-Brown had brought out, incapsulated even, what I was beginning to feel about the whole visit: that being banged up was a kind of backhanded liberation but only because it was so horrible. Walking down the long passage back to Ninny's quarters, I heard the now familiar grunts, snatches of ill-humoured talk, the odd fart – the puttering sort like an old Vespa engine – the cluck of a ping-pong ball being idly bounced on the floor. No, not again. Not ever again. Some people, softer or harder of heart, might find a vocation here, but not me. From the spiritual point of view life on the outside might be one big prison but it had its compensations.

III

Lower Marsh

Once you have gone down Monmouth Street and after you have slalomed round the new Seven Dials monument, you can begin to freewheel. If the lights just after Stringfellows are with you, you can keep going the whole way to Trafalgar Square unless you have to brake to avoid a couple of winos crawling out of the crypt of St Martin-in-the-Fields or a party of Japanese crossing the zebra to the National Portrait Gallery. You can let your feet rest on the pedals, with the morning stiffness only just worked out of them, sniff the coffee fumes already strolling out of the new Starbucks with the customers standing upright in a line inside as though waiting for some secret monorail service, the Jamaicans in the yellow waxed jackets shifting the first cars into the NCP and the commuters marching up from Charing Cross, the women all in black holding their briefcases with a certain pride, suggesting that they might be making a big entrance in the final scene with the crucial documents that can allow the prisoner in the dock to walk free, the men in their flappy Rainman coats more beaten-looking, and the cleaners at the Albery putting out the empties. Sometimes, not often, the lights at the NPG are with you too and you can get as far as the Cenotaph without pushing the pedals. That is the best moment of the day, not a thought in your head, your eyes washed clear of last night's Rioja and the pleasant diesel fumes of the white vans calming your tubes.

But that Monday morning had an added zing to it. Almost the moment I had got on the bike, I could not stop thinking how wonderful it was not to be inside HM Prison Thursby. A man in a Volvo Estate swore at me and I swore back, and liberty seemed infinitely sweet. Even the looming towers of the office the other side of Victoria Street beckoned me on. The Lower Marsh complex, not thirty years old but already marked for demolition, looked like a Hong Kong tenement, its window frames corroded, the coloured panels cracked or discoloured, the ridgy cement podium chipped and soiled at the corners as though a pack of gigantic dogs had lifted their legs against it. The air conditioning, noisier than ever because they were economising on maintenance now, still managed to keep its inmates freezing in winter, baking in summer. Each fresh batch of recruits clung to the consolation of the one promise the Civil Service did usually keep, that wherever they put you they would move you somewhere else quite soon.

'What makes you so cheerful?' Teresa, the PA I had shared with Ian Riley-Jones ever since he had come back from the trouble with his testicles, looked, not excited – excitement was not part of her repertoire – but attentive.

'Oh, nothing, it's a nice day.'

'Nice for some. Hilary wants a word at ten.'

'Does he now? In that case could you tell the doctor I may be a bit late?'

Hilary Puttock only had a few months to go before his sixtieth birthday, that bourne which for us is the one that really counts, the Styx being by contrast a mere muddy ditch in the middle distance. He had referred to the subject several times recently, perhaps to show that the thought of retirement might scare others but it wasn't going to leave a scratch on him.

'Not long to go now. I can see the grass the other side of the fence and it looks good.'

'You got something fixed up, then?'

'Emerging Markets at Paris-Bas but keep it under your hat, Gus. They're being awfully good to me.'

He was walking up and down a huge sheepskin rug in his even huger office, not walking fast but giving an impression of stoking up energies for some terrific physical feat that he was about to undertake, a triple jump perhaps, or a double lutz, finishing with a forward roll through the window. He had that burly build which, if you hadn't seen him for some time, made you think he might be putting on weight but on closer inspection you could see he wasn't.

'Don't know a great deal yet about what's entailed, but then that's one thing we're used to, isn't it?'

'Ignorance, you mean.'

'Yes,' he said, meaning no.

'Perhaps they'll send you to the Lords,' I ventured. What was making me so uppity this morning? Some weird reaction from my trip to Thursby, was it, or perhaps just the thought of never seeing Hilary again after, God, thirty years.

'What? No, no question of it, I can assure you. K's just about my natural place in the batting order and then, of course, I wouldn't want to cramp Helen's style.'

'No, of course not.' His wife Helen was my oldest of old friends in every sense, well, almost every sense, but since she had become Baroness Hardress of Minnow Island and married Hilary (the two events happening at much the same time) we had seen less of each other. In fact, we hadn't met at all since the day I had watched her tiny golden-haired figure processing up the aisle in scarlet and ermine to take her place among her peers. I did think of her, though, as you often think of people you have not seen recently when you get older, especially when the reason for not seeing them is that they are dead, but being a member of the House of Lords comes into much the same category.

'Anyway, before I shuffle off into the wings I thought it would be helpful to have a little talk. One of the many things I shall miss about the Service, Gus, is the immensely fruitful and congenial relationship you and I have enjoyed over the years.'

'Me too.'

'It was at UPARS we first came across each other, I think.' Like his senior colleagues, Hilary called it Yew-Parze. To us the Under-Secretaries' Policy and Analysis Review Staff, where some of our happiest days had been spent, had always been known as Up-Arse.

'Yes.'

'And then Technical Support. And of course Social Security and so to our present billet.'

'Yes.'

'I don't imagine you thought it was entirely a coincidence our paths crossing so often.'

'I hadn't thought about it much, to be honest.'

'Well, I have made no secret of my high regard for your capabilities and whenever I've had a chance to put in a word, I've asked if I could have you somewhere on the team.'

'I'm very grateful.'

'I'm conscious, in fact, that this preference of mine may not always have served your best interests. Though it was the last thing on earth I intended, I may perhaps even have held you back.'

'I don't believe it for a second,' I said, believing it instantly.

'No, no, there was a moment, a year or so ago, when Aidan asked for you – but that's water under the bridge now. The important thing is to look ahead.'

'Absolutely.'

'Now, as you may know, Andrew is going to take over from me here.'

'Ah' – a long ah, nowhere near as long as it would have been if I had been by myself, an ah of abjection, disappointment, resentment, gloom, indignation, bafflement, consternation. No, I had not known that Andrew was going to take over. Indeed, discreetly placed at the back of my mind as I had freewheeled so gaily down St Martin's Lane was the thought that this would probably be the week in which Hilary would call me in to tell me that I was to be his successor or at least his successor's Number Two and to boast that he had fixed it for me, in view of his limitless regard for my abilities. Not, however, so, it seemed.

'I think he'll do a splendid job. He has all the qualities for this particular post, we were all agreed on that.'

What qualities did 'we' have in mind, beyond the usual ones – staying sober (though exceptions were made on that front), turning up on time, greasing to ministers (no exceptions there) and double-greasing to the Cabinet Secretary (ditto), oh and looking optimistic at all times. Optimism came in two approved varieties: gravely cheerful to make it clear that your minister's inspired long-term strategy was making the progress it deserved, or manic-bonhomous to express your sheer delight in working for such a genius who should by rights be PM already. I could think of no special qualities beyond these which might be required for our relative backwater in Lower Marsh, so all I said was 'Absolutely'.

'Personally, I don't mind telling you in confidence, of course, that yours was the name I had pencilled in, but others felt' – he paused for a delicate instant, to find the exact phrase for how others felt: their lack of percipience in not seeing the matter his way; at the same time, their broader perspective on the demands of the Service, the weight of their combined experience, in short, the reasons why it was ultimately right to bow to their wisdom. No, there was no way of expressing it in mere words, it was too fine and subtle a perception, so all he said was 'they felt that Andrew was the man'.

Which was my cue to say 'Yes, of course, I quite see. He is first-rate.'

I managed that bit, but already my mind was far from Andrew Whittinghame who was in truth not a person to linger on: apart from the 'e' on the end of his surname, all that stuck was that he had had a trial at wing-three for Leicester and Riley-Jones had once told me he knew for a fact he was gay but could produce no evidence for this. My mind had wandered off, or taken flight rather, as it tends to in moments of stress (humiliation to be more precise), and I was concentrating on the sheepskin rug on Hilary's floor.

It was a strange thing to find in a Permanent Secretary's office, so wild and hairy and huge – too big to have lugged back from a holiday in the Greek Islands. Yet I couldn't imagine him choosing it at Harrods or Peter Jones. Was it perhaps a gift from some oil tycoon grateful for a long-awaited tax relief? But in that case it would have been declared and placed in the government store. Perhaps Helen had bought it for him as a wedding present. That thought was somehow depressing, although she must have given him something.

'Helen bought it for me,' he said, following my glassy stare, 'as a wedding present.' Him telling me was more depressing still.

'So then,' he said with the relieved briskness of a rider who has cleared one tricky fence and is eager to press on to the next one. 'We need to think very seriously about your own future.'

'Oh, I'm perfectly content as I am. I wasn't looking for a move.'

'Now, Gus, you know how we operate. You are certainly due for a move, overdue I would say if it weren't for your excellent performance.

We all want to hang on to our best men. But in view of your seniority it wouldn't be fair to you to have you reporting to Andrew and I don't think it would really be fair to him.'

Ah, so Whittinghame was not as innocuous as he seemed, had no doubt asked to have me removed, perhaps even made it a condition of taking the job.

'In any case,' Hilary went on, his stride visibly lengthening, 'Bill is just ripe to take over from you. Leave him another year or two and he'll go off the boil.'

These fruit-bottling or jam-making metaphors seemed inappropriate to describe our fraternity. On the contrary, what struck me in thinking back to our early days was how utterly unchanged we were, how we had arrived in the office fully formed, more like ingenious rubber toys which would give satisfaction for years until they had to be replaced because of long-term fraying or loss of elasticity. But this kind of speculation would not be calculated to appeal to Hilary, even in an hour of leisure which this certainly wasn't because with that art of being able to read upside-down (another desideratum to be added to the list), I could see he had another appointment at 10.15, with lucky old or not so old Bill, in fact.

'Which places us in a quandary. As you know, there is something of a logjam at the upper end just now. An unusually able generation is just coming to fruition. There must be disappointment, perhaps, I fear, even injustice.'

'Errm –'

'After a careful review, a very careful review of all the options, I'm afraid that all we were able to come up with – and I don't begin to pretend that it is remotely worthy of your exceptional talents – is . . .'

As he was talking, I thought very hard indeed about the rug, its whiteness, its hairiness, about the sheep, or were they goats, standing on a sun-silvered crag above a violet sea, and so when he said 'the Vehicle Licensing Department, Swansea of course, do you have any Welsh connections? – country can be rather agreeable, I believe?' I was able to maintain a totally stoical front and murmur my thanks.

'There is also, as I am sure I don't need to tell you, the alternative solution.'

'Yes?'

'The package. What you may not be aware of is that it has been redesigned by the CSD, rather cunningly I think for once, so that the full pension kicks in straight away and you can take the lump sum as and when you prefer, tax-free.'

'Early retirement?'

'Staged retirement is the way we prefer to think of it.'

'Or Swansea? Perhaps you should send Andrew, he'd like the rugger.'

The first spasm of disquiet, nothing so gross as ill temper or even impatience, passed across Hilary's smiling face. 'Naturally,' he said, 'you need time to reflect.'

'No,' I said, 'I don't think I do. I'll go for the package.'

'Good man,' Hilary said, 'I'm sure you'll find you've made a wise decision,' which he would have said, whichever I had chosen.

He clasped both my hands as I left and gave me a look of intense friendliness, managing somehow to remain his usual high-spirited self and yet to convey that he was deeply moved.

'If you were thinking of holding a leaving party,' he said, 'I would count it a privilege if you were minded to hold it here.'

'That's fantastically kind of you,' I said.

I wondered whether they would remove the white rug for the party and if not, whether I could manage to spill a bottle or two of red wine over it.

Teresa was still looking attentive but I had no intention of satisfying her curiosity and paused merely to snatch up my briefcase and tell her I would be gone for the day.

'I hope —' she began.

'We live in hope.'

'Would you —' but I was gone, surging down the corridor like an executive tornado, but unlike an executive tornado blinking back the tears.

The tears lasted through the lift journey to the bike store in the basement. The lift I luckily had to myself, but outside the lift doors at Level Minus One (as the CSD had recently sent round a memo instructing us to call it) before you got to the fire doors there was a small cubbyhole of roughly painted breeze-blocks where a few old plastic chairs were set out round a small green Formica table. This was the Clerical Smoking Area where a few derelict addicts were currently puffing away. It had formerly served as the Smoking Area for the whole of Block A, but then on the way to pick up his Rover from the underground car park one evening Hilary had found Ian Riley-Jones with his small panatella sitting there with a couple of clerks and electricians, and decided that decorum demanded that an Executive Smoking Area be designated on Level Five to serve both Blocks A and B, while the basement sanctum would in future serve the lower orders throughout the building.

'How you doing, Gus?'

'Not bad considering, Lionel. You lot look like death warmed over.'

'Well, it's the stress, isn't it? You ought to try it some time,' someone else said.

'Here, have one, got plenty left.'

The egg-domed, bogbrush-tashed Lionel, the messenger, who had a bad limp, thrust out a packet of Silk Cut and, to my surprise as much as his, I took one and plonked myself on the last remaining dusty chair, next to Smudger Smith, the laconic sharp-eyed sparks, who always won the hundred metres at the CSD sports day, despite being a forty-a-day man. Alone of the little circle he suffered from no visible physical handicap, electricians being presumably exempt for safety reasons from the service's equal-opportunities employment policy, which had been given an extra twist, I don't know whether deliberately, by assigning the employee to the work in which his or her defect would be most conspicuous, with Limping Lionel being one of the messengers dispatched to the furthest corner of Block C, partially sighted Anona scrutinising your pass in the front hall and Jock, the Scottish midget with a paralysed arm, in charge of humping the stationery. It was my first cigarette for twenty years or more and when I said so they gave an ironic cheer. As I lit up, the old swoony first-of-the-day lift kicked straight in and I felt as though I were planing through the endless vista of the intervening years, and a wave of self-pity the size of Niagara washed over me, but not the sort that bemoans the wasted years, the missed opportunities, the promise unfulfilled. Rather the opposite. My career suddenly seemed heroic, a saga of self-sacrifice, dedication, integrity. Its ending with a fizzle was only proper to a life spent without thought of personal advancement.

'You look a bit pale yourself.'

'Unused to this poison,' I said, wagging what was left of the cigarette.

'No, when you came out of the lift. As though you had had a bit of a shock.'

'No, only a liberation.'

'Oh, ah.'

This courteous lack of further probing was, I felt, a rule of the house, this breeze-block opium den being a refuge from the intrusive jostling to be found on Levels Zero to Five.

'Well, I must be pushing off. Got to see the doctor.'

'Expect he'll tell you to give up smoking.'

As the oafish cackles died away behind me and I pushed through the fire doors to the bike store, the nicotine high melted away and the abjection syndrome returned but with extra sag. For I had not admitted to myself till that moment that the hope of promotion had been buoying me all morning and keeping out of my head the doctor's appointment that would otherwise have filled me with dread, a dread which had politely remained in the background even after the hope had been shattered, as though to allow a decent interval before coughing gently to remind me of its presence. This was peculiar since I was only going to the doctor because I thought I needed to be checked over before taking on my onerous new duties. Pity I hadn't the brio to tell this to Smudger and Lionel. They would have liked the irony.

But then it wasn't entirely true that the only reason I was going to the doctor was because I had thought I was shortly going to be a Permanent Secretary on £96,000 per annum with an office big enough to accommodate the XXL size of sheepskin rug. That prospect was really a pretext for settling the worries I had had ever since the night I wandered through Drishill Abbey and had that awkward meeting with Gillian. The Health and Safety Council poster by the urinal in the Lower Marsh gents – 'Waterworks trouble? Don't ring the plumber' – also made it difficult for me to forget.

Ever since the asthma days I had had a clear run. A couple of teeth had cracked or crumbled over the years, so that I now had a plate filling in the gaps at upper right 3, 4, and 5 and upper left 2 – the mildest convenience, no more troublesome than having to buy the next notch up in reading specs when I lost the incumbent pair (x 2.5 suited me now). The left knee had given trouble for a year or two, the knee man said the meniscus was ragged and flicking against the other cartilage but it could easily be trimmed off by keyhole surgery. Otherwise, not much to complain of – so far.

It was only five minutes' pedalling through the swamplands of Pimlico to Dr Playfair's office, in a red-brick block wreathed in sickly laurels just behind the Tate Gallery. He had cheered up his consulting rooms with high-quality reproductions of Turner seascapes, so high-quality that while lying on his couch trying to distract myself it was easy to fancy that a little door might lead on from the Turner wing of the Gallery and inquisitive tourists, glimpsing yet another roomful of the Master's works, might swarm through, only to find Dr Playfair bending over my prostrate or prostate form. Not much of a fancy, perhaps, and a worse pun, but any form of distraction was to be grasped at and I had too often repeated my old drill of going through the alphabet with composers' surnames to be stumped by I (Ireland) or Q (Quilter). But still as the consultation wore on the old drill offered the only comfort. I don't know why I do it, not being at all musical and half of them only being names dimly heard on Classic FM, but it does help.

'Mm, yes, there does seem to be a little bit of swelling there.' Janáček, Kodály, Lully, Massenet, Nielsen, Orlando Gibbons – no, cheat, I'll come back to that one, Purcell, Quilter, Ravel.

He was silent as he gently palpated, I believe the word is, the obscure area in question, as though to prolong the exquisite contact. Stravinsky, Tallis, Forgotten, Vivaldi, Walton, and we don't do X, Y and Z.

'Yes, there it is. Nothing out of the ordinary, of course. At your time of life, some degree of swelling is almost inevitable. We'll get a better look with the ultrasound. And we'll do the usual tests, the PSA I'm sure you know about.'

'Yes, indeed.' Arne, Bach (J. C. this time), Chopin, Delius, Elgar (no, had him first round), Franck, Grieg, Handel, Ives, Joplin, Kodály (no, had him before too), Liszt, Mozart, don't know another N, Offenbach of course.

'But it could be . . .' I let my sentence trail away for him to finish, not sure whether I could complete it without letting the sob show.

Doctors must be trained not to complete their patients' sentences. To retain therapeutic mastery, I suppose it is important to continue discourse without directly responding to interruptions any more than one would respond to the buzzing of a wasp that happened to be trapped in the surgery, or rooms, as Dr Playfair calls what is in fact only one room and not a huge one at that, unless you count the waiting room which he shares with two dentists and a chiropodist. To be honest, though, his smooth only faintly chilly manner was reassuring. He was short and plump, his striped shirt hugging his shimmering grey braces. His face was one of those round non-merry ones with a somewhat affronted pout to the mouth.

'In the great majority of cases the swelling is merely as I say a natural side effect of middle age and there are a variety of treatments. Surgery is by no means the only option, there is benign though watchful neglect, there is radiotherapy. The Prostatic Specific Antigen test indicates the presence of swelling. Of course, we have some idea of the degree already from the digital examination' – I found the flow of his voice comforting and wanted it to go on – 'but the PSA acts as a pretty reliable negative indicator, a lowish PSA and the chances that any tumour' – ah, the word at last, but how inconspicuous, how nicely smuggled in – 'may be present are minimal. Even a higher PSA may mean no more than that the prostate is decidedly swollen. We might then also proceed to a biopsy to gain a more reliable picture.' I liked the lazy subjunctive of the 'might', suggesting a decision no more urgent than whether to order a side salad. 'If you could fix up an appointment for a blood test across the river, I'll give you the bumf. As I say, in the overwhelming majority of cases the symptoms are entirely benign. I wouldn't worry too much if I were you.'

This last statement was, of course, false. If he were me, he would worry every waking hour and there would be a great many more waking hours to worry in.

Still, as an activity to take your mind off a death sentence I do recommend cycling, especially uphill. Not only does the exertion fill up the mind, any upsurge of self-pity can be burnt off by shouting prat or prick when a white van cuts you up. The full melancholy only descended, thick and damp like a ground mist in November, when I wheeled the bike into our front hall.

The house was empty. My wife was with the Bug somewhere in Lincolnshire, perhaps not all that far from HMP Thursby, the children abroad (Tom working for a TV network in New York, Elspeth learning Spanish in Salamanca). The heating had been off all day and the house was dank and cold. By some confused train of thought, it seemed as though I was already drifting through it, looking at it as a ghost, as it would look after I had died and Nellie had sold it because it was now too big, though the new owners had not yet moved in and all the furniture was still there. I wandered from room to room, wondering if anyone would want the green armchair whose springs had gone and how they would share out the pictures, especially the Bartolozzi prints that my parents had collected for not much more than a fiver each and which really looked better hung together on a single wall. The ghost then got above itself, soaring off into thoughts of how probably none of the houses in this street would be standing in a hundred years' time and these comfortable cluttered little sites of late twentieth-century life would be unimaginably lost, as mysterious and impossible to reconstruct as the temples of Machu Picchu.

This would not do and in any case hunger put in a couple of pangs, familiar and welcome in the context. A selection of M&S complete meals, hot and cold, were neatly piled in the fridge and I was hesitating between the cannelloni with mushrooms and the spaghetti carbonara when the telephone rang.

The voice was a strange hollow booming but also rather breathless and it said without any other preamble, 'And when he had opened the fourth seal, I heard the voice of the fourth beast say, Come and see. And I looked, and behold a pale horse; and his name that sat on him was Death, and Hell followed with him. And power was given unto them over the fourth part of the earth, to kill with sword, and with hunger, and with death, and with the beasts of the earth.'

'Who the fuck is that?'

'And you are the fourth horseman,' the voice concluded in a portentous basso profundo.

'What are you talking about?'

'From the Book of Revelation,' the voice said, sounding more normal now and a fraction aggrieved. 'You must know it, Chapter Six, we had the hell of a time finding it, Gillian found it in the end.'

'You scared the hell out of me.'

'Excellent,' Joe said, 'that's our mission.'

'Have you gone completely mad?'

'Trust Uncle Joe. This will be a perfectly solid business proposition and we're on track for a spring launch. Trull says market conditions look great.'

'So Trull is in on this. You know he's got religion? He's as bonkers as you are.'

'That only shows how out of touch you are, Gus. Religion's absolutely huge in business circles right now, especially with the New Tech people. I've been to Tommy Ds myself a couple of times. It's a most impressive show.'

'You're in London?'

'Of course.'

'And Gillian?'

'She's at Drishill tying up a few loose ends.'

'Loose ends of what?'

'Didn't she tell you? We've sold it to the Tooleys – hotel, conference centre, nine-hole course. If anyone can make a go of it he will. The price wasn't brilliant, but at least we've washed our face. She's renting a nice little bungalow with a view of the Fairy Glen.'

'What about the treatment?'

'Oh, Texas you mean. That's still very much an option, but as of now we haven't got the readies.'

'But you just said you sold Drishill.'

'Well, we haven't actually got paid yet, but that money will of course have to go into Project Apocalypse.'

'But –'

'Look, I'll tell you more at the planning meeting: 9 Bagge's Head Wharf, the e-mail is . . .'

I took down the details in a trancelike state of bafflement and irritation. It was only after I had put the phone down that I realised that at some point in the conversation I had said yes, not just yes I've got all that down, or even yes I'll try to be there, but yes as in I'm on, up for it. And though it would be pushing it to classify this as a yes to life, there was no denying it was an affirmative.

The telephone rang again.

'Greppin. Establishment. Is that Aldous Cotton?'

Not much good ever came from anyone using my proper name, but there was a certain deliciousness in hearing someone actually proclaiming himself to be the Establishment, a deliciousness that hadn't struck me before.

'Yes, Gus Cotton here.'

'I had hoped to catch you at the office. I didn't realise you were on leave.'

'I'm not, I had to go to the doctor.'

'Ah,' an ah that exhaled disbelief and lack of interest in roughly equal proportions. 'HP suggested it might be useful to have a word. About the Package. You are probably familiar with the general shape of the arrangements, but you may wish to tie up a few little ends.'

The vision of an awkward-shaped parcel and Greppin's long white fingers, rendered supple by constant practice on the viola, deftly knotting the string round its knobbly corners diverted my mind and then drew me on to the vague intimation of some other connection, another context which wasn't the conditions of my early retirement and wasn't Gillian completing the sale of Drishill either.

'Computation of years of service . . . rank attained on actual date of retirement . . . may be uprated . . . the tax advantages of the lump sum option . . . capital gains tax exemption well worth bearing in mind.'

About halfway through the dispiriting litany it came to me and I wondered how I could have been so slow.

It was I who was Sir Edward Leithen, not Joe. I was tying up the loose ends of my life, or rather having them tied up for me by my professional advisers. The death sentence was not as emphatic as the one handed out by Leithen's doctor – what was he called? I looked it up in the battered scarlet copy of *Sick Heart River* on my own shelves and discovered that he was called Croke – had Buchan intended this fetching wordplay?

And now here I was, setting off for the badlands of the City of London with my half-wild native tracker in the shape of Joe. Half-wild and half-crippled, unlike Sir Edward's guide Johnny the half-caste. About all Joe and Johnny had in common was being five feet six tall and having bandy legs. And Leithen and me? Well, we shared a certain dryness of temperament, for one thing, and just now a general sensation of extreme fatigue. Leithen in his prime could walk down any Highland gillie. The best I could claim was to be able to cycle to Whitehall and back, but today even that trip had left me limp and short of puff. There wasn't much doubt about it. Dr Croke had booked me in for an appointment.

To come to this conclusion was curiously soothing. Perhaps to come to any conclusion has its soothing side, the way some people pat a pillar box after they have dropped in a letter which has given them trouble. Shakespeare is full of bits about worrying being the worst part, Woody Allen too. Can't be quite true, of course – the worst part ultimately must be the worst part – but it would do to be going on with. And I walked slowly round the garden, looking at the little soft-blue clusters of michaelmas daisies and the few pale-pink geraniums that were left, and thought how far we had been depleted since seeing the bloody cranesbills in the cracks of Cockburn's Pavement. Still, we might see another spring at least and even perhaps another century.

What season would it be best to die in? It had always seemed odd to me that people with fatal diseases always wanted to be told how long they had got. After all, it only took Sir Edward Leithen a day to put his affairs in order and it wouldn't take all that much longer to arrange something that you had always wanted to do before you died, like seeing the Taj Mahal or Ayers Rock. But now that I was in rehearsal for the real thing there did seem to be some obscure satisfaction in having a closing date nominated for you. Was it so you could strive to beat it and survive beyond D-Day, thus giving some meaning to the 'fight for life' which otherwise was bound to be an uphill, not to say ultimately one-sided, contest? Or was it the opposite, that on the contrary you could subside gently as the date approached, in the knowledge that you were not disgracing yourself?

I couldn't find Bagge's Head Wharf in the *A–Z*. Perhaps it was the name of the building, not the street. But the new Docklands Pevsner had it: 'Bagge's Head Wharf: plain-pediment warehouse (F & H Francis 1870) with oculus and forged-iron wall-crane, collars and loading doors much decayed, interior aisled with cruciform columns carrying king-rod timber trusses on a riveted iron-trussed valley beam. Orig. Prosperity Wharf, renamed after celebrated prostitute Nellie Bagge whose severed head was found dangling from the crane. Unrestored.'

There it was, no hesitation or perhapses: Sick Heart River.

IV

Bagge's Head Wharf

The black water slopped against the slimy weed and the weed slapped the dirty stone wall, making a skirt of fag packets, beer cans and general trash flounce out into the narrow mooring and then back to the wall as the wash of the police launch passed on downriver. Behind the brick arches of the wharf I could see the dull gleam of the Mercs and Beamers stabled there so that their owners could nip down in the lift from their river-view lofts and zoom off without having to set foot in the dingy streets.

No answer from the entryphone at No. 9, so I had time to watch an ancient Bangladeshi painfully making his way across the cracked and puddled roads to the Londis store on the corner. His stick slipped on the uneven cobbles and he looked like falling but he knew how to lean out with his wobbly knees and stay upright somehow. Even the immigrants were getting older, except, of course, for the ones with the 2.9 X-regs.

Across the road I saw a stubby man, not young, standing on the perron of a warehouse that was still unconverted with a buddleia sprouting out of one of the round windows along the top and ferns taking hold where the brickwork had crumbled. The stubby one was looking up and down the street, turning his neck rather stiffly as though constrained by some invisible harness but at the same time conveying even at this distance impatience, enthusiasm even, for whatever it was he was waiting for. It was only after processing these impressions that I realised that it was Joe. I felt chagrin for being so

slow on the uptake and double chagrin when I looked at the door I was
pressing the bell of and realised that its snazzy script said 2 and not 9.

'This is the place to be,' he said as we embraced, with a warmth on
my side which was partly for stupidly standing on the wrong doorstep
but mostly because as you get older the sight of an old friend still on
his feet is a cause for celebration.

'Bagge's Head is going to be a new-concept space, essentially
minimalist, state-of-the-art and all that.'

'What?' I said, already feeling weak.

'Come on in, you'll see.'

He led me down a narrow passage and after cracking my head on the
first beam I followed him at a loping crouch.

You could still detect traces of the stroke in his jerky strut, but only
traces. All the same, he wasn't too quick up the open wooden staircase
at the end of the narrow passage. Staircase was too grand a word for
the contraption (which took us up three floors). It was not much better
than a built-in ladder with creaky treads that looked as if the rats had
been at them.

'Original feature,' Joe gasped, pointing at the treads while he paused
for breath as the steps turned back on themselves for the third time.

At the top, he kicked open a door which had one corner sliced off it
by the angle of the roof, and we came out into a long, low attic which
he could just about stand up in but I couldn't. It was lit by a couple of
small square windows with grilles on them, suggesting a low-security
wing of the Bastille or the economy-class sector of a debtor's prison.
From the far end of this long room came the drone of an appliance
drilling or honing something. There were a couple of Ikea desks and
spindly gingerish office-surplus chairs. On the furthest desk there was
a grubby beige PC and a tangle of white flex, which was being sorted
out by a slender girl with long dark-brown hair. She had her back to us
and did not turn round. Squatting on a mat in the lotus position was
Trull. He was positioned disquietingly close to the door as though he
were some ancient, perhaps distantly related to the family, who was
licensed to collect alms from visitors on arrival.

'Great to see you out,' I said.

'Yes, isn't it? Though I was sorry to say goodbye to the lads. Not all
of them, mind you. Some of the hard nuts in G Wing could be the most

frightful nuisance. You've met Jade, our IT wizard? This is Gus who's going to make us all look respectable.'

The thin girl turned round, said 'Hi' and shook out her hair as though the shaking out was part of the greeting ceremony. You wouldn't have said she was unfriendly, or even showing off how busy she was. She just left you feeling that anything in the way of an introduction was old-fashioned and made too much of the difference between one person and another.

Or perhaps she was just busy. Oddly, though, I felt there was something familiar about her, but then my feeling might only go to show that if you weren't all stiff and introductory when approaching a new person you would both transmit and receive this sense of familiarity.

'When you've finished making eyes at Jade, who's *much* too young for you, I want you to come and meet an old friend.' Trull hadn't lost much time (how long could he have been out of Thursby? Not more than a few weeks) in regaining his old manner, the sinister edge-of-camp way of talking at you to show how many jumps ahead he was but making it clear at the same time that being jumps ahead was a kids' game really.

He de-lotused himself and led me over to the far corner of this wizened attic where a bald man in a white T-shirt was planing something. Light from the dusty little prisoner's window poured down upon his pate and shone on the wood shavings dancing in the air, giving him the look of a medieval saint who had, rather late in the day, received divine blessing for his gruelling labours.

'There,' he said, 'George,' rather as if christening the bald man with a name he might not otherwise have chosen for himself. 'You remember Gus, don't you, George.'

'Course I do, we was out shooting together.' He too seemed to have developed a touch of the sinister campiness from exposure to Trull. Perhaps we all did without knowing it. At any rate I didn't recall George talking in this gangster cockney with the words spilling out of the side of the mouth.

'Right,' Joe said. 'We're all assembled together at long last, so I think we should start with a toast.' He was carrying a bottle of champagne and a stack of plastic cups, which he set out on George's workbench.

'To the Four Musketeers,' he said.

'Musketeers?' I said. 'I remember you talking about the Four Horsemen.'

'I did point out to Joe that the Four Horsemen were war, famine, pestilence and death, and so not exactly the right image for a new venture entering the market place. The Four Musketeers just says Adventure, Fellowship and plenty of humour – ideal for any company operating in the Human Relations Field.'

'But there are only three of us,' I said.

Joe had his mouth open to answer this, but he was beaten to it by a cool woman's voice behind me. 'I suppose you think girls don't count.' Once again that sense of familiarity and yet beyond the familiarity a kind of strangeness. Perhaps this is too fanciful, perhaps her voice just sounded odd because it was coming from behind me.

Anyway, there was no way to answer her without revealing that she was right, I had thought she was only a technical assistant and far too young to be one of this decayed brotherhood which I once again had failed to point out I was still not a committed member of.

This last point had to be made clear straight away, or I would find myself shackled for ever to this grisly crew: a disgraced wheeler-dealer who might have only a couple of months to live, a convicted drug smuggler and butterfly torturer who was probably only out on parole and a sulky girl who, although we had scarcely spoken, was obviously peculiar, if only to have got mixed up with these no-hopers twice her age. As for me, while I could not pretend that my CV was electrifying, it contained no criminal conviction except for a six months' disqualification for a sequence of minor driving offences, the worst of which had been to make a forbidden right turn in Camden Town ten years ago. True, I had no other plans yet to fill my early retirement, but surely somewhere there must be some organisation to rebuild neglected churches or save the Wolds or some somnolent unit trust or building society that could make use of my rare administrative skills.

At present, I seemed to be entangled in one of those enterprises which did so well in the South Sea Bubble raising huge sums for a Purpose Yet To Be Disclosed.

'Look,' I said, 'please, before all this goes any further all I said was that I would come down here and say hello and see what you were up to. I'm not committed to anything.'

'You never are, Gus, are you?' Joe gave me one of his forlorn looks which made him look pitiful and pitying at the same time.

'You said, three of *us*,' the girl said.

'That was a joke.'

'Rather beyond a joke, my dear, I'm afraid,' Trull said. 'You obviously haven't seen our prelim letter to clients. Jade, darling, could you fish us out one for Gus? We meant to show you first, but time's rather pressing. Don't you think the masthead sketch is rather charming. Jade, of course, she's a girl of many talents, she really is.'

I stared at the sheet of paper with a little two-tone drawing of 9 Bagge's Head Wharf just above the address, every bit as charming as Trull claimed. I read it through with that glazed sort of fascination which the brain slips into for the reception of news that is overwhelmingly unwelcome and which you can do nothing to palliate. Perhaps it is better not to give the full text with all its ponderous come-hither verbiage but merely to set down the few phrases that stuck and which still run howling through my head on sleepless nights:

HEADS YOU WIN ... Executive Search for the Twenty-First Century ... Whether you're up-sizing your life or downshifting in search of fresh challenges, we can make every Job change a Life change. Our partners are your partners in adventure ... We have seen life from every angle ... Other firms try to put each square peg back into the same round hole ... We see you as a person looking for a life, not as someone who just wants his old job back.

There was much more along these lines. Quite often it was hard to know exactly what it all meant, but then that was nothing unusual in brochures which even I knew were intended more as mood music than as hard information. But it was the final section, the stuff about the management team, which was so terrible, not because it was vague or evasive, on the contrary because it was so unforgivably forthcoming. Again, I give only the most awful phrases that stick with me like plaque to the walls of a tired artery.

Joseph Dudgeon Follows (Chief Executive Officer) aged 59 ... (then a list of all the companies he had founded), voted Young Businessman of the Year 1969, caught up in the property crash of 1974, censured by Dept. of Trade inquiry, retired to Ireland, founded heritage and leisure business (Fairy Glen plc), Drishill Modern Poultry Company, etc.

Keith St John Trull, 60, sailed 14-ft yacht *Peewit* to Valparaiso single-handed, author of nine novels selling 2 million copies worldwide (Golden Asteroid Award 1975), founded Swallowtail Butterfly Farms Ltd 1983, sentenced to five years for drug trafficking (reduced to three on appeal), co-founded Ortho-theological study group HM Prison Thursby, since release churchwarden St Thomas Didymus, Docklands.

Dr Jade Treviso, 26, BA Oriental Languages (1st Cl. Hons) University College London, Ph.D. Information Technology, Imperial College. With ex-husband, Andrew Treviso, founded software company Blotting Paper, convicted of three offences under the Companies Act 1995, joined Alcoholics Anonymous 1997, now counsellor, East Ham alcohol abuse unit, former England hockey international.

And then me. Most of it isn't worth repeating, except: Took Early Retirement 1998.

Now taking early retirement isn't a crime and even during the squalls of self-pity that had drenched me in the course of the past few weeks there stayed on duty a sensible alter ego which persisted in saying: so what, this is all a million miles from being the worst thing in the world; think not only of starving children in Ethiopia and babies hacked to pieces in Rwanda but of men who lost their jobs when they were twenty years younger than you are and never found another one, of women who never had a lover or a child, men too, come to that, of people who have no inflation-proofed pension, of people who have no money at all. This sensible homunculus was still saying all these things, but for the moment his voice was drowned in the sickening rush of panic which was set off by the joyous clanking of all these chains by what now seemed to be my fellows in the chain gang, links which were firmly hammered in place by the sign-off under this deplorable staff list:

They picked themselves up, so can you.

'Christ,' I said. 'At least you didn't mention about murdering butterflies.'

'There are limits, Gus.'

'But you can't, I mean surely there are rules about, well, about people who've been inside being company directors and so forth, especially when they've only just come out.'

'Warned off the turf, you mean,' said Trull, turning his gaze to the ceiling, his war criminal's specs glinting like George's pate in the dusty sunbeams. 'The trouble is, Gus, you're still living, like so many people, in the bad old days of disgrace and retribution. Think rehab, think forgiveness, wiping the slate clean. I admit some old-style stuff does still linger on the statute books, but it doesn't apply to us headhunters. As befits a profession like ours, we are totally unregulated, free as air to follow our vocation, which is to help our clients follow theirs' – here I recognised him quoting from the letter – 'how could it be otherwise? If A wants to help B discover what he's going to do with the rest of his life it would be crazy to put stupid little obstacles in his way.'

'But what about the employers? Are they really going to want someone who comes recommended by a bunch of ex-cons?'

'You haven't got it at all, have you? This isn't just an employment exchange for no-hopers fresh out of the nick. We're going to be a one-stop universal exchange which will offer every kind of opportunity from a 200k MD's job in a multinational to a trainee zookeeper on the Isle of Man. Sometimes the client will come to us without a clue what sort of job he's going to be applying for. And the potential employer is going to be accessing a range of talent he wouldn't have got a sniff of before.'

'And who is going to put up the money for this totally crazy and confused venture?'

'We have seed money from three charitable trusts even you will have heard of and firm expressions of interest from a couple of VCTs, and as soon as the DTI heard you were going to be on board –'

'Well, I'm not on board. For one thing, there may be no rules for headhunters but there certainly are for civil servants. We aren't allowed to accept any position of profit for at least six months after leaving the Service if there's likely to be any contact with matters dealt with in post and I haven't even left yet.'

'Oh, you don't have to worry about that. You won't be paid for the first year at least.'

This caused unseemly mirth all round. Even Jade's pale face came alive with a seraphic smile, which brought back the unexpected sense of familiarity – or perhaps that was just the effect of a pretty smile on a solemn face.

We stood, the four of us, in the dismal attic (George had gone back to his bench in the corner and the zissy hum of his planing seemed to tremble in the sawdust sunbeams or made the sunbeams themselves tremble) and in response to no particular stimulus that I was aware of an odd feeling overcame me, not elation exactly, more like a weightless, reckless calm, possibly akin to those states attained by adepts of Eastern religion only after considerable mental and physical exertion. Not giving a damn might be a useful shorthand way of putting it, but it went further: for that moment not giving a damn seemed like the most important thing there was and any falling away from this exalted state of mind would have been a deplorable comedown.

'Oh, well,' I said, 'I suppose I might string along for a bit.'

'We intend to operate as an informal partnership for the time being,' Trull continued in a matter-of-fact way, disdaining anything so banal as gratitude or welcome, let alone relief. 'As you so unkindly surmised, anything in the nature of a plc will remain off limits for legal reasons in the short term.'

The exhilaration refused to die down even when I was sitting in the Tube on the way back to Whitehall reflecting on the absurdity of the project and the total unsuitability of the personnel. Perhaps I was just demob happy, but I continued allegro, even vivace, even when addressing the dismal task of drawing up a guest list for my farewell party.

'So difficult to know who to leave out,' said Teresa, determined to squeeze a drop of enjoyment out of each stage in the dreary business –

the list, the venue, tasting the wine, whether to bring in someone from outside for the nibbles.

'No, it isn't. What's difficult is to fill the room,' I retorted.

Hilary and his wife, the once beloved Helen, obviously came high on the list. There was my battered companion in arms, Ian Riley-Jones, and the rest of our present office. Then it was a matter of going through back numbers of *Vacher's Parliamentary Companion* to remind myself of former colleagues, now scattered to other departments or retired, plus a few ex-ministers who might remember me, not too many of those, then the more amiable secretaries, messengers and other denizens of the basement smoking area. You couldn't expect these elements to mix particularly well. All the same, the mixing was the point of it. After a couple of drinks the barriers didn't exactly come down but people tended to look passably merry. At least that was my experience of other leaving parties.

But somehow mine was going to be different, for me, anyway. I knew it as soon as I stepped into Hilary's huge office to see that everything was ready. He had had the big white rug removed and with the chairs pushed to the side of the room it was a cheerless place, not least because Hilary had been on holiday in Norway and the heating had been switched off.

'Expecting a big crowd?' enquired Limping Lionel, staggering across to put half a dozen cartons of orange juice on the thick white paper tablecloth that now shrouded Hilary's desk.

'No.'

'It's a big room.'

'I can see that,' I said.

The Level Minus One crowd were first in. In fact, most of them were already there, since Limping Lionel was roving with the drinks, while partially sighted Anona with her wiry hair and sprawling bosom, though not the fag drooping from the corner of her mouth this being a no-smoking zone, was in position behind Hilary's desk wearing an unexpectedly frilly apron. Others of the doomed crew now trooped in by the door leading to the medieval flagged passage, led by my oldest work friend, Ian Riley-Jones, who, although he had not had the Package dumped on him, on the contrary was trembling on the verge of landing a Permanent Secretaryship in some outlying department, still had an untamed look to him, something about the way the lapels of his double-breasted suit with its curious brown stripe flapped around his ill-ironed shirt, or the way his hair, though smarmed down in a Fifties style, escaped into iron-grey whorls round his high-lobed ears. The faint look of surprise in his dark oyster eyes was unsettling too and could lead even the most insensitive minister to pause in mid flow, wondering whether he had said something more interesting than he intended.

'Well, well, so it's come to this. It is a sad day, indeed it is, the old place won't be the same.' He burbled on like this for a minute or two, before leaning closer and whispering in my ear, in the solicitous tones of one funeral-goer commiserating with another, 'Did you know that Alan screwed the Minister without Portfolio when they were at the LSE together? He claims she mewed like a seagull.' From years of sitting next to him in meetings I had learnt that the way to cope with these lubricious murmurings was to nod vigorously as though he had just offered a stimulating sidelight on the Private Finance Initiative, because for some reason the nodding prevented your mouth breaking out into an unseemly smirk.

Thus my features were nicely composed as I turned to greet Sir Wilfred, my first boss if you didn't count Roddy Bowle who had died, of cirrhosis as it turned out, in the Permanent Secretary's toilet in the Permanent Secretary's arms barely five minutes after he had delivered the most graceful and lucid summary of the graduated pension scheme to a fractious Cabinet committee – an achievement still spoken of with awe in the Service.

'You look wonderful, Wilfred.'

'It's the bell-ringing, Gus. Exercises the whole upper body. When you've rung Whitlock's Triple, you feel like a wet rag.'

Ten years into retirement he was alert as a whippet, with a crushing handshake and a suit of a crusted silvery cloth that suggested Dorset. But then they all looked wonderful, for example, the man who I had worked with when Wilfred sent me off to Agriculture and who was always so cross when people got his name wrong, which I, of course, now did as I introduced him to the little Air Marshal whom I remembered on the eve of hostilities twenty years ago apologising for wearing battledress but he had to be at Lyneham by first light.

'Alistair,' the man from MAFF was saying, 'and it's Dorran, not Dorrell.'

And then there was Theo from the MoD who remembered the Air Marshal too and who still had the stutter. Theo also looked pretty good, eager in a plump, appealing sort of way just as Dorran not Dorrell was eager in a craggy, impatient way. How did they keep it up, this eagerness, through all the years of mind-boggling detail, the patronising slights of ignorant politicians, the lino in the corridors, the stultifying hours, and then the utter frustration when the government changed and half the stuff you had been working on was chucked in the bin.

The room was two-thirds full now and vibrating with all this appalling eagerness, this relish for fresh challenges, this unquenchable zest. It wasn't a bit like those scenes at the end of famous novels when all the characters are gathered together and the narrator can scarcely recognise any of them because they all look as though they have been paralysed in a snowstorm. On the contrary, they all looked exactly the same as they always had. In this gathering, with the possible exception of Anona and Limping Lionel, time had been made to stand still. The statutory age of retirement was exposed as nothing more than a bureaucratic whim. You felt they could have run the reel backwards with Sir Wilfred starting tomorrow as an assistant principal and the nice young man who worked for Ian Riley-Jones and who Riley-Jones claimed had a cock ten inches long could have taken over Hilary's desk without thinking. You almost felt sorry for death, making repeated house calls with nothing to show for it, endlessly rebuffed by the vigour of his intended targets, his scythe swishing on empty air. You didn't need to go to some isolated mountain village in the Caucasus or a rocky island in southern Japan. Right here on the doorstep was a race that never grew old. How did they do it? What was their elixir? After thirty years' fieldwork I fancied I had cracked it. Their secret was, quite simply, that they were indifferent to experience, impervious to the stuff. Whatever height you pitched it at them, it just flew harmlessly past. Was this an innate quality, something that selectors could spot at first interview, or was it – more probably – a natural indifference developed and hardened by repeatedly watching your work shot down in flames?

'My dear Gus. How good of you, what a splendid occasion.' Hilary welcomed himself to his own office, looking around with what he would no doubt have described as huge pleasure at the room he sat in every day as though he had never seen the place before and couldn't believe his good fortune in being in such surroundings among such tremendous, first-rate, able, charming people. If zest had been an Olympic discipline he would have struck gold, probably at successive Games.

'You know, I rather envy you, Gus, getting a head start on the rest of us. I feel Ambrogio waiting for me with some impatience.'

'Ambrogio?' Was Hilary in the flush of the moment revealing a quite unexpected side to him, some boatman on the Brenta or waiter on the Via Veneto counting the minutes to the return of the big Englishman with the chequebook?

'Ambrogio Lorenzetti. You remember, my thesis was to have been on him had I chosen the art historian's path, on "Rhetoric and Harmony in Lorenzetti, the Iconography of Early Renaissance Political Theory" to be precise . . .'

I did remember now. One lunchtime in the Two Chairmen years ago, he had expounded his theory of the allegory of *Good and Bad Government* in the Palazzo Pubblico in Siena, had talked me through every figure in the fresco. In the intervening years, he had developed the irritating biographer's trick of first-naming his subject. I wonder if Lorenzetti would have responded by calling him Hilary, but then perhaps Lorenzetti had spent his leisure time in the Sienese equivalent of the Two Chairmen mulling it over with fourteenth-century Hilary types. In fact, Hilary himself probably was a fourteenth-century type. For all their vigour, you did wonder whether these enormously able servants of the Crown with their Ambrogios and their Whitlock Triples were entirely suited to running this country of earrings and razor cuts.

'. . . will be a little late,' he went on. 'She is tied up in the Other Place.'

Surely you could not legitimately refer to the House of Lords as the other place unless you were in the first place, i.e. the House of Commons, but let this pass as being the kind of pedantry Hilary might have indulged in himself. Since I had watched the once beloved Helen walk up the aisle in her ermine to be introduced to that moth-eaten assembly, it seemed to me that she had forfeited any right to be taken seriously and her marrying Hilary was not nearly as bizarre as it seemed. After the second glass of Rioja, far from the sight of having my past paraded before me inducing mellow sensations of nostalgia and mortality, a sour rage was gathering, a kind of cosmic dyspepsia. This was naturally the moment that Hilary chose to tap his glass with a fork he had begged off Limping Lionel.

I had thought of paraphrasing Hilary's remarks here in a couple of sentences, or perhaps omitting all mention of them in the interests of avoiding any renewal of the pain. But then we are taught these days that we have to work through our pain, that it is only by rehearsing our humiliations that we can overcome the trauma and grow as a person, and so – but no, on third thoughts, I won't. He was so grudgingly crass, so oafishly patronising, so slimy, so self-congratulating, so dismally unwitty, that even to write down what he said would somehow do him a sort of undeserved credit. The performance called for total and permanent obliteration, which it shall have, apart from the reflection that there were no doubt good grey men in their sixties and seventies all over England still waking up in the middle of the night sweating at the recollection of the speech Hilary had made at their farewell parties.

He was oiling his way by inches towards his conclusion and my rage was making the interesting complex of varicose veins in my right calf throb so alarmingly that I was beginning to speculate whether I might at least be remembered as the first man who had actually been killed by one of Hilary's farewell speeches – and then she came in.

To be accurate, I did not see her come in. All I saw was that there she was, standing next to the craggy man from MAFF, Dorran not Dorrell or was it the other way round, and I went red in the face as though I had once again introduced Dorran/Dorrell wrongly. It was an absurd reaction in someone of my age but I couldn't help it.

'And I think it is not the least indication of that modesty we all know and love so well that even my poor halting remarks should bring a blush to Gus's cheeks. To some of us he will always be that blushing young Assistant Principal who asked dear old Roddy Bowle if he needed to bring his typewriter with him to morning prayers with the Minister.'

This was a complete travesty of what had happened and not at all funny in any case – though it scored a few sycophantic laughs in this retelling – and I had told Hilary so the first time he had told the story some years earlier.

There she was anyway, still tiny – barely up to the shoulder of Dorran not Dorrell who was not that tall himself – and standing in that motionless way of hers which would have made you look at her anyway even if she hadn't had the milky blonde hair, and I was flooded with a rush of what could only be described as love, on a scale roughly equivalent to one of those tidal waves that leaves villagers clinging to their roofs and watching their livestock float past. This may seem an exaggerated description, seeing that I had been happily married for thirty years and had in any case written her off as an absurd social climber, but there it is.

She nodded at me, one of those nods she gave just this side of curtness, the nod you give to someone who has come for an interview, and then smiled at me in the way she did of not wishing to be conspicuous or interrupt the proceedings but, for me, interrupting everything.

Then, before turning her face to her husband who was now only about two-thirds of the way through my career and not nearly as close to finishing as I had hoped, she did a curious thing, something I couldn't remember her ever doing as long as I had known her.

She winked. Quite deliberately, neatly as she did everything, not at all saucily or jovially, but she winked.

Perhaps this was a well-known form of acknowledgement among her clapped-out colleagues, many of them no doubt too decayed to manage a verbal greeting. Or, a more hideous thought yet, maybe it was an economical salute they deployed on encountering the lower orders, to show they weren't stuck-up.

I was still musing on these dismal possibilities when she did it once more, this time to her husband. Again, only the quickest of flickers, the upper lid scarcely brushing the lower before she resumed that steady disconcerting gaze just short of a stare – in fact, not like a stare at all because she didn't seem to be looking hard at the object of her gaze but rather a look that made you stare back at her.

Still, the wink was odd and it wasn't really convincing to blame it on her fellow peers because I couldn't imagine her, even now, imitating them in a habit so alien to her.

Then she winked a third time and I became aware of the regular intervals she was doing it at, and even in my bemused state, groggy with adoration stirred up after so long and gawping with embarrassment as Hilary's long valedictory left its slimy trail all over me, and of course groggy with drink too, even in this state I was not too far gone to recognise that what she had was a tic, perhaps even a palsy.

And for the first time in this grisly event I was overcome by intimations of age and mortality. The wink happened at intervals of about forty seconds – I know because I began to count in my head to distract me from the unending agony of Hilary's speech, a distraction probably superior to going through the alphabet of composers while being prodded by the doctor, a gloomy pastime nonetheless, not one you are likely to envisage in the first throes of love, although an outcome not beyond the imagining of sexually frustrated poets: yield to me now because a time will come when my only pleasure will be counting the intervals between your twitches.

The vigorous applause which broke in upon my musings showed that at least they had kept me occupied until Hilary was done.

'That was wonderful, darling. Wasn't it wonderful, Gus?'

'Wonderful,' I said. 'Quite wonderful. There's no way of thanking you.'

'I meant every word, Gus, every word.'

He patted his chest as though to draw attention to some sincerity-generating device implanted there. He was much moved.

So were several of the girls. Even Limping Lionel seemed to be swallowing hard. Riley-Jones sloped over to me and muttered in my ear that he had heard hot throbbing cock in his time but never hot throbbing cock quite like that. I smiled benignly as though receiving the most Augustan felicitations and turned to face Helen again, determined not to be mesmerised by the tic.

'Is your wife here?' she asked.

'No, I'm afraid not. It was all arranged at short notice and she'd already fixed to go away.' I certainly wasn't going to tell her that Nellie was only collating some stuff with the Bug up in Mablethorpe and could perfectly well have come if she had fancied it.

'That's sad. She's quite an independent sort of person, isn't she?'

'I didn't know you'd met her.'

'I haven't,' Helen said, 'but I'm sure she is.'

This one was a little hard to work out. Did she mean that being married to someone like me would be intolerable unless you had a life of your own or that she knew this was the sort of woman I was attracted to, she herself being a good example?

'It sounds so brilliant, your project,' she said.

'My project?'

'And incredibly kind of you to bring in people who would otherwise find it so hard to plug in again after all they had been through. It's one of those things we social workers whinge on about.'

'What . . .' How had she got hold of the news . . . if she had got hold of it?

'But then you are kind, Gus, not everybody realises it because you have this manner which is so laid-back and cynical but you are.'

'Look . . .'

'And I am sure you're going to be rewarded, because it's such a far-sighted thing to do.'

'Are you . . .'

'It's so wonderful you'll be working with Beryl. She really needs someone to guide her.'

'*Beryl!*'

A flash so blinding it was odd that the room failed to explode. Beryl was Helen's only daughter, by her ill-starred first marriage to the ill-starred Bobs Moonman, carried off by cancer four, no more like six, years before. I hadn't seen Beryl since she was in her mid-teens, must be ten years ago and she had her hair done differently now and girls do change a lot, but even so.

'You mean.' Helen looked at me so intently I thought the tic had stopped, but no, there it was again. 'I don't believe it, you mean you didn't recognise her?'

'No, I didn't, I'm afraid. I did think there was something familiar about her, but Jade Treviso – you wouldn't instantly think, would you?'

'And she didn't tell you – when she saw you hadn't recognised her, I mean?'

'No. Amused to see how long it took me, I suppose.'

'She's been in a bad way, you know, she hasn't got much confidence.'

'I'm very sorry.'

'But then she is a naughty girl.' Helen chuckled for the first time, now deciding to treat the incident as a piece of Beryl/Jade's skittishness.

'Hilary,' she called – no, this was too much, she was going to betray me. He'd probably tap the glass again and begin afresh – 'And there's another thing about Gus you may not know, he's completely hopeless at recognising people, only the other day he . . .' But Hilary was off at the far end of the room, talking to Sir Wilfred in that eager posture, simultaneously assertive and ingratiating (for mere retirement did not break the great chain of authority: once a chief, always a chief), and so she had to turn back to me, with a kindly/pitying smile which persisted through the next wink.

'But why did she change her name?'

'Well, Treviso's her married name of course. She could have dropped it when they split, but she didn't, just to show him, I think.'

'Show him what?'

'That she took marriage seriously even if he didn't. But then he was still in treatment when he took up with Lada. I think he was angry that Beryl had managed to kick it and he hadn't.'

'And the Beryl bit?'

'She never liked the name. So I said why don't you choose another precious stone?'

'I never liked the name either.'

'You could have said.'

'I did, but she's not my daughter.'

She laughed not because it was funny, but at the thought of our old intimacy.

'How did she get involved?' I persisted.

'Oh, she met him at a disco, like they do. He was very good-looking.'

'No, I meant, in our . . . project.'

'She doesn't tell you much, does she?' Helen was now quite at ease with this notion of me being the total klutz in the Hollywood comedy, the mere man who understood nothing and was told nothing. Perhaps that was how she had always thought of me.

'I've only just seen her again,' I bleated.

'Anyway, she met this man, your friend Mr Troll.'

'Trull.'

'When they were in therapy together. Actually, he was in prison at the time but he was on day release for this course. He's a fascinating person apparently, more or less took over the course from the facilitator whom Beryl didn't think much of. And did you know? The most amazing thing, he's also very religious, like you used to be.'

A little smile spread over her, I suppose at the thought of how she used to rough me up for my churchy leanings, not a subject I wished to return to.

'Not at all like me,' I said firmly. But there was no point in trying to tell her why it wasn't. If people weren't interested in a subject, what they particularly were not interested in were the fine distinctions within it, the difference between baroque and rococo, between seam and swing. And so it would have been a waste of breath to explain to Helen that there was a world of difference between Trull's new enthusiasm and my own solitary excursions, now long suspended, to ill-attended services in dusty Victorian churches hidden away in shabby inner suburbs. Mine had been a furtive homage to something that was gone, not just mislaid, irretrievably gone – that was why it was so quiet sitting in the ruined choirs. In fact, its being gone had been the source of the serenity it had spooned out to me. If there had been any life left in it, being there might have been unsettling, repugnant even, but then it was also because there wasn't any life in it that in the end I reluctantly had to sidle out of the pew, not disillusioned – there had never been much illusion to start with – but suffering from the kind of mutual exhaustion you suddenly become aware of when you have stayed too long with an old friend and you have both said everything you have to say.

Whereas Trull – if I had taken in properly half of what he and Malc had said – Trull was in the resurrection game, he wasn't just watching the dying embers. On the contrary, they were going to turn up the flame to white heat, out-ortho the orthodox, throw themselves into every rite and rubric with as much awe and brio as if the whole lot had been tossed down to them yesterday. But, as I say, she wouldn't have wanted to hear about that either. To her we were just practising different varieties of the same exploded mumbo-jumbo, there was nothing to choose between us.

'Well, anyway,' she said, leaving the subject with reluctance – she was the kind of atheist for whom it is both a duty and a pleasure to smite the believers. 'He's been very good to Beryl and she does need support because she's still so vulnerable. You will be kind to her, won't you?'

She didn't need to ask and I was about to say so, but before I had time she stretched out her hands to me, rather close together but not quite, and I did the same to her so that our hands interleaved, just, but they were not clasped – we might have been playing some old-fashioned children's game.

'Please, Gus, can you come? It's Mr Riley-Jones, he's ill.'

For some reason Limping Lionel always called me Gus, but Riley-Jones was sir to him, which, we had once agreed, put us both down. I shouldered my way through the suits and *imprimés*, all by now creditably boisterous, to the black leather sofa at the end of the room – a Boltraffio design, Hilary had boasted when it was new (unlike Helen who was indifferent to her physical surroundings, he had an unexpected weakness for *The World of Interiors*). It was a deeply squashy sofa, so that Ian Riley-Jones was only intermittently visible. In fact, I had to lean over the arm to get a proper look at his face, which always had the look of a bruised fruit and was now dark purple and twisted around the mouth. His breathing was heavy, an unhappy snore. Lying there awkwardly curled up in the black squabs, he looked like a Francis Bacon, only somehow less three-dimensional.

'Shall I see if I can find Mrs Riley-Jones?'

'She's not here.' Pam never came to these dos. She preferred to stay in Much Benham with her flat-haired retrievers – 'the flats take a lot of coddling,' she had told me the last time we met, which had been ages ago.

'Here's the CMO.' Limping Lionel seemed to have taken charge and was ushering to the sofaside a tall, scaly-looking man whom I didn't recognise.

'I hope you'll forgive the gatecrashing. Dorrell and I were halfway through a session on Gulf War Syndrome and he thought you wouldn't mind if he brought me along.' As he spoke, he was kneeling at Ian's side (the Boltraffio was inhumanly low-slung) unbuttoning his collar and loosening his flashy tie.

'In fact,' he continued while examining the patient's pulpy face, 'you won't remember me but we met years ago when MAFF was in a flap about whether humans could catch foot-and-mouth.'

'Ah,' I said, '1967,' but thinking perhaps we could postpone these minutiae and then dimly beginning to remember him but as not being quite so scaly-looking. Had he in the line of duty as a government medical officer later contracted some nasty skin complaint, possibly while attempting to demonstrate to a nervous public that there was no risk to health?

'Looks like an ischaemic incident of some sort.'

'A stroke?'

'Mm,' he gave a beautifully tuned hum, indicating a smidgeon of approval, not to say surprise, at my knowing what he was talking about (which I had some fragmentary grasp of from Joe's stroke years before) but also a proper professional caution. 'Could be, let's get him into hospital first.'

'The ambulance is on its way, Doctor.' Limping Lionel spoke as though all his life had been a preparation for this moment, and it was only a couple of minutes before he and Smudger had Ian on a stretcher and were gently off with him down the stairs to the front waiting room.

I went down to see him into the ambulance and patted his shoulder as they took him down the steps, expecting never to see him again. As I trotted back up the stairs, I reflected that once again Ian had beaten me to it, first to make full Principal, first to Under-Secretary and then Deputy Secretary and now it seemed he might even beat me if not to retirement at least to the ultimate promotion.

I returned to a chastened gathering. Several of the guests had taken the opportunity to slip away. I met little Dorran/Dorrell at the door. He had an unholy glint in his eye as he thanked me and said how sad it was, and I could see he thought Ian's post (which he had been mentioned for before Ian got it) was as good as his. Among those who had gone was Helen, to an alas unbreakable engagement, Hilary said. He himself was now on his knees, in almost exactly the same spot as the Chief Medical Officer had been, shaking out some broken glass from the cushions while Anona was trying to make him get up and go away so she could use the dustpan and brush. But he liked doing things like that; in fact, he grabbed the dustpan and brush from her and made a thorough job of it. These successive scenes – Ian on the sofa with the doctor, Hilary and Anona with the dustpan and brush – were like little panels in one of those Italian Lives of the Saints which Hilary was apparently such an expert on.

While Hilary was finishing off sweeping under the Boltraffio, first a trickle then a stream of my guests came up to say goodbye. Hilary's flossying had signalled that the party was over, one of the wittier among them quipping that he didn't want to be swept out by the Permanent Secretary. The circumstances made the farewell a tricky business: there had to be an anxious, sympathetic word about Ian, along with saying how rewarding it had been to work with me all these years and how much fun the party had been, despite – all this after more Rioja than was sensible. But these were not ordinary guests; saying goodbye in tricky circumstances was what they had been trained for. The Foreign Office even gave parties 'to say goodbye' – a goodbye which might be caused by anything from a routine transfer to fatal illness or the fall of a government or the outbreak of bloody revolution. So they were well able in the briefest sentence or two to weld regret, congratulation, concern and a terrific sense of fun. I bathed in their courtesies while trying to hurry them on because I wanted to look in on the hospital and at the same time signalling to Anona and Limping Lionel that it was time to start collecting the glasses.

So that was it, at least it was a party they would remember, or perhaps they would only remember it for Ian's ischaemic incident, in only a year or two having to rack their brains to remember whose leaving party it had happened at.

All the same, it wasn't at all a melancholy feeling. On the contrary, my feet seemed to skip along the remorseless lino and out down the Goschen Steps, called for some reason I can't remember after the Chancellor who succeeded Lord Randolph Churchill, to Lord Randolph's chagrin, leading him to say 'I forgot Goschen' – perhaps it was these once famous words which had prompted some wag to call these little out-of-the-way steps down the side of the building after him. But of course it was a stupid way out to take because the side door was locked after 6.30 and I had to go back up again and turn right towards the main staircase. It was a mistake I normally wouldn't have made, which showed how drunk and distracted I was – and tired, too, because going up back the Goschen Steps my legs almost melted under me and the weight of the building, and all the other buildings like it which I had spent my life in, seemed suddenly intolerably oppressive, and it was impossible not to think with a rush of panic of all those days which had passed one after another until there were hundreds and then thousands of them, and nothing achieved, nothing at all in most of them, and nothing that would be remembered in any of them. And then I had my breath back and was recovered enough to tell myself how everyone thought such thoughts looking back on their lives and there was no point at all in thinking them. And down the great broad front steps I was skipping again and demob-happy once more. But then I had to stop and put my head round the glass door of the porter's lodge to say goodbye to Greg, the Armenian night porter who Ian said couldn't give you good morning without making it sound as if he was about to sell you a carpet amazingly cheap.

'Terrible about Mr Riley-Jones, he looked very bad.'

'He did, I'm afraid.'

'Still I'm sure he'll be back.'

'Unlike me.'

'You're well out of it, sir, I'll tell you that for a fact.'

Perversely, his confiding manner swung my mood back again and I began to feel that I wasn't well out of it at all and how much I would have loved even the smallest stay of execution before I passed out of those high swing doors and into the unsafe world beyond, how much better – but no, surely this couldn't be me thinking this, but it was – if we could somehow stall my departure just for a month or two so that I could have a crack at Ian's job, assuming, which of course wasn't to be assumed at all, that he wasn't going to be fit enough to carry on. There were precedents, Roddy Bowles's successor, a frightful shyster, had been levered out and was about to settle his knees under a City desk when the comeback call came.

God, how could I be thinking like this, how low could I sink? The damp cold of the night air made me shudder and these scurvy thoughts fled. I had stayed there too long, the sooner I got out the better. Joining a company of ex-cons and drug addicts would be decency itself by comparison. And I hailed the taxi which was bowling along Birdcage Walk.

V

Hillcrest

'So where do we start?'

'We start with the shoot.'

'What shoot?'

'Wake up, Gus, the photo shoot, xandre will be coming at eleven.'

I spell xandre in this fashion because it was written like that on his car – xandre – in lower-case cursive script in a place where you wouldn't expect, just below the rear-door handles of his jet-black, smoked-glass-windowed turbo 4WD. He was a sleepy-eyed fawn in combat trousers with only a charming whisper of a French accent. He looked around the long, low garret and shook his head. 'No, no, too retro. Outside is better.'

The sun was beating on the little patch of quay between No. 9 and the next warehouse. Behind us the river suddenly took a big sweep past Canary Wharf with the new towers rising beside it and the postmodern penthouses reflected in the glittering water. To me the scene was putting out all the right messages – opportunity, optimism, regeneration. The others thought so too. We sat on the bollards and thought we looked just the ticket.

'No, is kitsch, picture postcard. We go down here.'

We helped him lug his equipment down a dank alleyway on the other side of the street, some of us casting longing looks back at the sunlit quay.

'Here is perfect,' xandre said.

He lined the four of us up in order of height with me at the back and Jade (as I'll call her from now on) lounging against the wall at the front. Her back view looked sulky. Joe behind her had his arms folded in an uncompromising four-square posture. In front of me, Trull was leaning against the opposite wall from Jade. Even in profile he still had something of that spoilt cherub's look which had led so many good (or goodish) people astray over the years. Surely we must look as unappetising a crew as ever you'd hope not to meet up a dark alley and I said as much.

'Ssh, you, big one at the back,' xandre crooned as he squinted into his camera. 'And don't smile. This is business' (I notice that he didn't say anything like 'beezneez' and I began to lose confidence in his Frenchness).

The alley smelled of old food and dogshit and human piss – on winter nights it must have given shelter against the chill winds off the river. How odd we would seem to passers-by, cowering out of the sunlight like this. How could anyone think of putting his career in the hands of such a mob? Would any paper even want to print the pictures?

'What do we do now?' I asked after xandre had finished his interminable clicking.

'We go for lunch. There's a table booked at the Waterworks.'

'Jade,' I said, picking the wan leaves of artichoke out of their searing pesto, 'why didn't you say who you were?'

'Oh, Mum told you, did she? You still seeing her, then?'

'Don't be saucy. She naturally came with Hilary to my leaving party – of course she told me.'

'Oh, you had to invite Mr Bouncy didn't you? Sir Bouncy now I suppose.'

'So why didn't you?' I persisted, resisting the temptation to be diverted.

'Tell you? Well, it was awfully rude of you, wasn't it, not to recognise me?'

'Was that truly what you thought?'

'Of course.'

She really did have the most melting smile, partly because it stole up on you out of this solemn face. Not quite like her mother but in the same line.

'I don't think you were actually hurt, I think it was just a tease, to see how long it took me.'

'Think what you like.' That was like her mother, the way she could say something that would sound offensive coming from most people, but didn't at all from her; in fact, seemed to draw you into some subtle complicity which you must be part of because you didn't need to have it explained.

At four o'clock, no later, after the fourth bottle (Jade, of course, was on the elderflower and Joe was supposed to be, so the rest of us had done ourselves nicely) Joe said, 'Time for a zizz. Can I give anyone a lift?'

It would be pathetic to ask whether anyone was thinking of going back to the office, so I got on my bike and pedalled home, weaving a drowsy course through Banglatown past dark-eyed young men pushing racks of clothes and veiled women taking their children home. Their world seemed familiar, homely even, beside the strange *demi-monde* of commerce I had stumbled into.

To my amazement, the photographs turned out to be captivating. The brick alleyway gave the shots an intense focusing effect, so that you couldn't help staring back at Jade's dark eyes and Joe's entrepreneurial jaw and Trull's worldly roguish come-hither. And behind them there was this taller man with a look that was somehow both mild and grim, one of nature's accountants. But it was Jade who really bewitched you. A minute before she had been humping xandre's lights with this fed-up expression on her face which close up had a porridgy texture. Her hair looked like a hank of brackish seaweed and she scowled when xandre tossed her a brush and told her to tidy it up. She consented to pull the brush through only a couple of times before she slouched over to take up her position. Yet here she was in the photos, alert and brimming with life, nothing at all bolshie or self-regarding about her. You could trust her with your secrets, your savings, your life. She was so young, so lovely, but you didn't need her CV to see that she had already experienced a good deal more than some people would ever experience.

'She's a natural,' Joe breathed over my shoulder, 'xandre has really cracked it.'

To me it still seemed improbable that a set of photos, however nicely done, could have any impact on our commercial prospects, even assuming that any paper bothered to print them. But as I had been wrong about xandre's talents, I didn't say anything.

Which was just as well, because it was only a couple of days before Jade's dark eyes were staring out of every newspaper, and not just out of the business sections either. There were interviews in the features pages, mostly with Jade but also with Joe about how it felt to come back from the dead. Trull began to get mail from old admirers of his books, saying how much they had loved *Cybertyphoon* or *One-Eyed Dwarf* and how they had been with the company for thirty years before the people in Cleveland downsized the UK operation and closed Dunstable, so that now they were looking for a fresh challenge. Joe got calls from old business associates who said they were glad to see he was back and they must lunch and they'd quite forgiven him for that business with the leaseback. But Jade ... everyone wanted to talk to Jade. She had her own corner table in the Waterworks, just by the big pipes, where with her legs draped over the arm of her chair she talked all day long about the time she touched bottom. The detail of this varied a bit: sometimes it was when she had been vomiting in the toilets at Newport Pagnell services and she realised she had no idea how she had got there; sometimes it was when she worked in a club and gave herself to the bouncers because she needed money for booze or drugs.

'Jade, I don't know how you managed to find the time for it all,' I remarked, as I passed her one of the colour supplement pieces which she was pasting in the office scrap book, a pastime she enjoyed hugely. It was a pleasure to watch her shake her untidy hair clear of the album or purse her plum lips in concentration as she larded the cuttings with Pritt and straightened them up on the page. Then it came to me how years before I had watched her doing her homework as a child, but then there had been something cold, impersonal almost, about the way she concentrated, as though she was trying to show us, her mother in particular, how she could give her mind completely to the work without having much enthusiasm for it. Which was an appealing sight and I felt great sympathy for her. But now she seemed strange in her elation, unfamiliar in a way she hadn't been before I had recognised her.

'That's why they call it life in the fast lane.'

'Sometimes I think you make it all up,' I said.

'You are rude. Hey, don't you think this is a cool picture?'

Unlike xandre, the photographers from the supplements had no worries about being kitsch. They used the river backdrop mercilessly. Sometimes Jade was twined round a bollard, sometimes she was sitting in an old dredger with her feet dangling over the side. Sometimes one of us was drafted in to be snapped gazing on her with a fatherly eye. And always the theme was redemption, the second chance. A biblical tone began to creep into Trull's responses to the press. The parables of the lost sheep and the prodigal son were mentioned more than once. I was passing through the office where he was giving an interview to a squinny-looking girl from one of the tabloids and I thought I heard him say 'Valerie, the thing is we're really fishers of men', but he denied it when I challenged him later and said that anyway the girl was too thick to pick up the reference.

And where was I all this time, what was my contribution to the strange enterprise? I was out and about, working up the client base, in my view the only one of the four who was doing anything that could be described as work. Most days I set off early to register in good time for some conference, seminar or company bonding session, dunking the digestive biscuit in the muddy coffee, clipping on to my breast pocket the little slip of plastic which said *Gus Cotton, Heads You Win*, passing out my card with the website address www.headsyouwin.co.uk and the e-mail address Gus@headsyouwin.co.uk, and sitting meekly at the back of the hall marking the speakers with my own quality code: pl for plodder, ga for garrulous, gg for go-getter, ts for total shit, nbd for nice but dim. In these weeks I endured an ocean of business rhetoric. Half a dozen times a day I was exhorted to focus on core objectives, to incentivise my salary structure, to reshape my stock options package to reward high performers, to enhance compliance and commitment, to build my customer base, improve brand recognition, to grow the business by driving an integrated change strategy. It didn't matter what the conference was supposed to be about – pulp and paper, advertising, quantity surveying, hotel management, Internet banking, real-time wireless technology, cement and quarrying, asset management, e-business of every conceivable sort – the language was always the same. It drizzled over the audience like olive oil on a nouveau salad, unvarying, tepid, relentless. Nobody complained of the tedium any more than medieval monks thought of complaining about the repetition of their offices.

What I couldn't get over was how pleased they all were to meet me. They pocketed my card with unfeigned gratitude and said how much they had heard about us, and although they were of course absolutely happy in their present job we must keep in touch and what fun it must be to work with such interesting people. To start with, I expected to have to explain away the chequered past of my colleagues, even to endure some brutal ribbing. I had prepared a couple of jovial ripostes along the lines of how I at least had managed to keep out of jail so far. But nobody gave me the opening. Instead, they told me, with some solemnity, how much they admired what we were doing. The furthest even the most roguish young thrusters would go was to say they were ready for a one-on-one with that Jade Treviso any day.

'I don't understand it,' I said to Trull after coming back with another fistful of cards from directors and middle managers who couldn't wait to get on our books. 'I would be nervous as hell putting my future in our hands, but they're all queuing up for it.'

'Same at the other end, dear boy.' Trull yawned. 'Joe has his hands full. The head of human resources in every firm you ever heard of wants to give us a whirl. To start with I was all for letting them in on soft terms, but now we're going to go for the full monty: 10 per cent of the first year's salary plus a signing-on fee, non-returnable after six months.'

'But there are dozens of established headhunters with a hundred times as many people to choose from.'

'Ever see any of them on *television*? Ever see any who looked like Jade?'

'But don't they want discretion, track record, proven honesty, all the qualities we haven't got, especially proven honesty?'

Trull sighed and leant back in his chair.

'You still don't see it, Gus, do you? Tell me, what are you thinking about as you sit through those ghastly interminable seminars – sex, drink, death, anything not to listen to all that boring stuff? Well, they're all in the same boat. Bored rigid. And with us they have a chance to have a little adventure entirely in the line of business. Our colourful pasts aren't an obstacle, they're the main attraction. One of the things that's wrong with modern life is that it doesn't offer enough chances to show your compassionate nature. By going to Heads You Win you're handing out a mass pardon. You can boast to your other clients how you got this first-rate guy through us, some of the other directors were a bit nervous but you knew it was the right way to go. Heads offers you the chance to access unusual talent and to feel good about yourself at the same time. True, you might have hired exactly the same guy if you hadn't done it through us, more than likely if it's a techno job, metals, oils and so on, but by logging on to Heads you showed just a flicker of moral daring. After all, forgiving is just about the last grand gesture on the market these days.'

'But isn't it God who's supposed to do the pardoning? When you're on your knees with your friends, you're praying to be forgiven by Him, not by the Director of Human Resources at Unilever or some young executive who wants to take Jade out.'

'My dear Gus, God's grace may act through any one of us.'

He smiled his seraphic smile. I wasn't sure he was theologically sound, but it couldn't be denied that he had the psychology right.

There was an eerie eagerness about the way people approached us. They sounded somehow pent-up, as if they needed to be released from something. We seemed to be fulfilling a long-suffered want, watering a dry place deep inside them. Then it came to me that there was one of us whom they would have read about ten years or so earlier and might perhaps retain some dim memory of. Yet Joe's kidnapping was hardly mentioned. It certainly didn't lead off the profiles of him, and I flipped back through our prospectus and leaflets and saw that in our catalogue of crimes and misfortunes there was no mention of it either. And it had to be admitted that I had never noticed the omission myself. So the conspiracy to ignore the whole episode went on. There appeared to be some kind of tacit agreement that this wasn't part of the ritual, this strange ritual of confession and contrition on our part and absolution followed by enthusiastic support on the part of our customers. It was as though Joe (and by extension Gillian too) had been napped and brutalised while still in an unshriven state and so could expect to win no sympathy from that particular experience. It was precisely because the napping wasn't his fault that he couldn't be forgiven for it. The whole experience was a disconcerting blip on the radar that tracked his progress from shyster down to redemption. Not exactly logical; in fact, absurdly, self-indulgently illogical, but we weren't dealing with rational minds here, we were dealing with hidden longings and surging desires. You could almost feel the tremble of excitement at the other end of the line when they heard Jade apologising for calling out of the blue and saying she hoped it wasn't an inconvenient time, but she had just had particulars of a fascinating opportunity which she thought might be exactly up the callee's street and did he feel like meeting her to discuss it. She gave 'particulars' a husky emphasis that sent her clients scurrying to their desk diaries.

When Joe heard her in action for the first time, he claimed to be shocked. 'Jade, we aren't supposed to be offering phone sex.'

'Oh, do you think I'm overdoing it? But I thought we wanted to sound friendly.'

'There's a happy medium between sounding friendly and sounding as if you're lying on your back with your legs apart.'

'You're the one who's being disgusting.'

But the whole thing still worried me. 'What about shame? It all seems too easy somehow.'

'My dear Gus, shame is so over, blame is the thing. Everyone is responsible except us. It's a one-way thing. If we all started feeling ashamed again it would undermine the blaming. We blame, we forgive, we feel good about ourselves.'

So many people wanted to be on our books now that we all had to help with the interviewing. There was no chance of me sliding out of it anyway. You must have spent half your life interviewing people, they said. I suppose I had, but it seemed a long time ago.

At the start all we had for an interview room was a place at the back up yet another rickety ladder, the sort of eyrie Fagin might have made his last stand in. Even after we had it painted buttermilk it wasn't exactly imposing.

This is fantastic, my first client said. He was called Miles Morpurgo. He was a little goblin in his early thirties dressed all in black with a merry expression on his round face like someone who is still smiling while sucking a boiled sweet. He immediately sensed my nervousness and rushed to help me out.

'Are you using Myers-Gough?'

'Not at the moment,' I said cautiously.

Not many people knew about it, he said, but M-G was simply the best psychometric test on the market. 'Much better than Morrisby. Refines out the negatives and rolls out a high-res profile that you can use for pretty much anything.'

'Ah,' I said, 'but is it really a good idea to give our own candidates these tests? I mean, if we find out all their weak spots we might, you know, find it harder to recommend them.'

Morpurgo gave a disbelieving chortle. 'No, no, Gus if I may, customer confidence is the name of the game here. You need to show the client that you've really taken your candidates apart. Slip an M-G profile in with their CV and the HR people at the other end will know they're on a winner.'

'But supposing the profile shows our man is indecisive or bad with people?'

'It won't. That's what I mean by refining out the negs. How else do you think Paddy Gough paid for that *estancia* in Puerto Cruz? Look, here's mine.'

He threw me a flimsy blue folder across the table. I couldn't help being impressed. After two years as an account exec at Clarkson Savage he had moved over to the marketing side at McSherry's, where he had headed up media buying and had launched a bulk booking programme which was ongoing after he left to start up the New Products division at Divertico, which he was now leaving because of an incompatibility of management style with the CEO. His M-G profile rated him AMB-9, CRE-8 and INF a full 10.

'Ambitious, Creative and Imaginative, Influencing and Persuading, and do call me Miles,' Morpurgo said.

'There's a post here, Miles. Long-established manufacturer of toys and novelties, you can probably guess who it is, branching out in a new line of executive toys and gizmos. They need an MD for the whole shebang, design, production, marketing, 95k. Does that sound like you?'

'Perfect,' Miles Morpurgo said, 'just perfect. Lead me to it. You must be my guardian angel.'

'They've got a couple of interview slots tomorrow.'

Morpurgo waltzed into the job and a little tremor of pleasure shot through me when the firm rang and said how delighted they were. 'You'll find your first placement's like a tiny orgasm,' Trull had told me and he wasn't far wrong.

Patsy Hepple, my second candidate, turned out to be harder to place. She was all right on paper, had an even better M-G rating than Morpurgo, in fact, scoring a maximum on Patient and Persistent which for some reason had not figured on Miles's flimsy. But she did not interview well. She was bony and square-shouldered, and her apple-green suit hung loosely on her, which didn't make her look mannish so much as that she needed room to carry a concealed weapon. She had a short mop of fair hair, which she tossed out of her eyes whenever my line of questioning began to annoy her. We must have sent her to half a dozen places. Most times she called us back before they did, to let us know that the job was a no-no because the MD was a third-rater or because she could see the glass ceiling the moment she walked in the door. The HR people usually said that of course they *liked* Patsy but they didn't think her management style would quite fit in with theirs which was, you know, more consensual.

We slotted her in on about the seventh go with a cheerful MD who rang me himself to say that he was looking for a battleaxe to sort out those buggers down at Chorleywood and by God they'd got one now.

I rang Patsy to congratulate her. 'It isn't exactly what I had in mind,' she said, 'but it seems to be the best you can do.'

Despite this I was pleased with myself for having shifted her off the books. But then the next day I had the call about Morpurgo.

'That chap you sent us.'

'Miles Morpurgo, yes, I'm so glad we were able –'

'Could you come and take him away.'

'Oh dear, I'm so sorry, has he not –'

'Just take him away, please.'

'I'll send you the cancellation form straight away.'

'No, I mean it literally. He says he won't go unless you come.'

I had just started interviewing a sad man with a faint speech impediment who had been fired after twenty years with a security alarm firm that had been taken over, so it must have been an hour and a half before I got up to the far side of the North Circular. The Director of Human Resources was hopping about on the windswept tarmac as I jumped out of the taxi.

'He's in there.' He pointed to the widest of three doors at the back of the dispatch hall.

'The disabled one?'

'Yes, there's only one woman who uses it and she was away at her sister's wedding so we didn't know he was in there till this morning.'

I rattled the doorknob.

There was a mewling sort of groan from inside: 'Go away.'

'Miles, it's Gus, from Heads.'

'Oh, Gus.' Another mewling groan.

He still showed no signs of wanting to unlock the door. But then the security man appeared with his key.

Miles Morpurgo was curled up in a foetal crouch in the narrow space to the right of the disabled toilet. He was cradling a bottle which looked like Martell Three Star.

'He must have been there since Friday. That's when we picked him up going in on the CCTV.'

I held out a hand and said I'd come to take him home. But he merely shuddered and snuggled closer to the wall.

The security man held out a blanket like a nervous bullfighter but Miles shied away from that too. In the end the two of us had to squeeze in together and pull him out between us trying hard not to breathe in. We managed to wrap him in the blanket and shuffle him out to the security man's car.

Once he was in the back seat Miles seemed to cheer up and settled the blanket over his knees like a dowager accustomed to such cosseting. 'You were sweet to come,' he said.

One of my problems was to keep my personal feelings out of my assessments. Just because you took to someone didn't mean you could slot him in anywhere. Rather the opposite, in fact, those were the ones you had to be extra careful with. I had liked Miles Morpurgo and though Graham Ellis-Turner was a very different type I liked him too.

E.T. as he insisted we call him was bald, getting on a bit, with old-fashioned moustaches, superficially not an easy one to place, but I wanted to do our best for him.

'We've spoken, old boy.'

'Oh, how stupid of me, I can't –'

'I was the guy you contacted when you sent us Patsy.'

'Oh yes, you said she was going to sharpen up your people, at Chorleywood was it?'

'She did that all right. Sharpened up head office too. That's why I'm here.'

'You mean –'

'Had my job off me within six weeks – and persuaded the board she needed a sodding pay rise to add insult to injury. "E.T.," she said, "if this firm is going to go anywhere we shall have to let you go."'

'Oh dear.'

'So I reckon you owe me one.'

I thought he was going to sob like Miles Morpurgo had when we dropped him off at his flat. But he cheered up and starting enquiring about jobs that were way out of his league, and I happily ran through a couple before gently bringing him down to earth with a job as a warehouse manager for a timber firm in Gravesend which slightly to my surprise he landed. Unfortunately E.T. turned out to be one of those people who was better at landing jobs than doing them and he came back to us a couple of times after that. On average, though, we all agreed the work gave us a buzz.

'You must understand, Gus,' Trull explained. 'The world is full of people who feel undervalued. We are just about the only place that takes people at their own valuation. It's a unique sort of social service. That's really what they pay us for. Finding them a job as well is just a bonus.'

In our first full quarter, April–June 1999, we grossed just over thirty-seven grand, mostly from the modest registration fees. It was enough to pay the overheads – rent and rates, electricity, George's wages, phone, accountancy, computer leasing and servicing. In the next quarter when we got the first 20 per cents of the salaries of the people we had placed, we pulled in £189,000. That figure was expected to pretty well double every quarter as we crossed over into the new millennium – 350, 700, 1.2 million, who says there's no poetry in numbers?

'Next year we can even think about paying you,' Joe chortled as he took the new set of figures from David the Maltese accountant, who was a perfectly genuine accountant with a passion for early music and without a stain on his record – he reminded me of my old colleagues in the Civil Service.

'I'm glad to hear it,' I said, 'but Joe, isn't there someone else you should be thinking about first?'

The letter had arrived at the weekend, so this was my first opportunity to tackle him. 'Dear Goodster,' it began in the time-honoured fashion of Gillian's letters to me,

How are you getting on at United Con Artists? Defrauded any widows and orphans lately? Talking of which, this bog widow is a bit short of dosh herself. You may recall that my saintly husband promised to send me to the LBJ Memorial Hospital for a dear little miracle cure. At the moment the price of the bus fare to Sligo City would be nice. The weekly highlight in these parts is the visit of Dr O'Kelly Mahon who comes now to inspect his bungalow rather than the temple of my body.

Hillcrest has its charms, I'm sure, but so far they are cruelly hidden from me, mostly because it isn't on the crest of the hill at all but halfway down and all the rain from the mountain comes whooshing through our storm porch. Isn't the air just grand up here, says OK as I hand him the rent. He seems to have lost interest in my complaint, just taps my chest like people tap a barometer which they know doesn't work. He gives me hot news of the improvements the Tooleys are making at Drishill Abbey – underfloor heating, double glazing in the conservatory, a sauna – and oh, the cruel tarmac everywhere. You wouldn't know the place, but I dare say they paid a fair old price for it, he murmurs enquiringly as he takes my blood pressure which is rising to danger level, because not a penny of that money have I seen, the whole caboodle having been invested in Sharks and Shysters plc. I am sorry to dump this on you, but I need to get it off my cankered chest to someone and Himself isn't exactly the perfect audience as he only rings me on the mobile once a week and he always seems to be going through a tunnel at the time and can't hear my pitiful entreaties. So as you

*toy with your caviare roulade in a champagne-and-guinea-fowl coulis,
spare an occasional thought for your old sparring partner,*
    Deirdre the Hag of the Bogs

'Is this true?' I enquired.

'Well,' said Joe, 'we had a bit of trouble with the loan for this place,
so I needed some cash in a hurry and I haven't got around to paying
Gillian her share, but —'

'Presumably she needs to get to Texas rather soon, ideally.'

'Oh, I don't think a month or two will make much odds. I'll be
sending her some spending money this week, but the treatment is
pricey, you know, not much change out of 50k, and in any case most of
what we're earning at the moment is already committed in the business
plan. We have to get the website up and running at the same time as
the ad campaign, which is going to be fiendishly expensive.'

'Couldn't all that wait?'

'You have to catch the tide while it's turning, Gus.'

It didn't seem worth arguing with him, so I took myself off to a
seminar on depreciation at the Institute of Electrical Engineers, where
I spilled the salmon mayonnaise off the peculiar saucer-shaped lunch
tray on to my new linen shirt from Caesura which Jade had advised me
to buy because my wardrobe needed lightening up to fit in with the
firm's dress-down style.

The ad campaign was based on xandre's photos, mostly because time
was short, but the agency had cropped them in some cunning way, so
that the four of us gave off a hint of menace not present in the original
pictures. The viewer was left with the feeling that any job he or she got
through some other agency would be just a little flat, unlikely to lead
anywhere a real person would want to go. The voice-overs on Classic
FM, done by Jade in a voice that somehow managed to be cute and
desultory at the same time, also provoked this frisson. The whole pitch
hovered just this side of shady, but you were left with the impression
that the partners knew their way around.

And the ads were everywhere. At the peak of the campaign you
couldn't look at a bus or a business section or watch Channel 4 for
more than ten minutes without seeing us. And that is not taking into

account the banner ads on every website you ever heard of, or the inserts in junk mail from the banks and credit card firms. It cost millions. Every penny we expected to earn for the next two years was swallowed up, as was two-thirds of the venture capital package Joe had managed to string together. We were famous but if you took an old-fashioned view of the situation we were also still more or less broke. And an old-fashioned view of the situation was what I liked to take. In no time at all – well before the ad campaign – I had established my role as the resident Eeyore, pourer of cold water, knight of the doleful countenance. Every organisation needs one to make the positive thinkers feel even better about themselves.

'Don't be such a Cassandra, Gus.'

'Cassandra turned out to be right.'

'Only because she brought them down and they lost it.'

'Lost what?'

'Oh, you know, whatever keeps you going.'

'I don't –'

'Gus,' Joe interrupted, leaning forward from the depths of one of the low squashy sofas we had recently acquired – for all I knew another Boltraffio piece, Trull ordered the office furniture. 'Gus, would you do me a favour?'

'If I can.'

'Well, you know you were talking about Gillian being temporarily short of cash. I don't mind you mentioning it, not in the least, we're old friends and what are friends for? But I want you to know how bad I've been feeling about the whole thing. Anyway, as I promised, I've managed to put a little package together.'

'Good, good.'

'And naturally I would dearly love to take it over myself and make sure she's all right. We talk on the phone every evening, of course, but it's not the same, is it?'

'No, no,' I murmured, refraining from also murmuring that every evening wasn't what she had said in her letter.

'I was planning to go over next week, but we've got those bankers coming over all week and I don't think Keith can handle them all on his own.' Joe was the only person who called Trull by his first name, which paradoxically made it sound as if he didn't know him at all well. But then that was how Joe often sounded, his rather breathy way of talking to people – and about them, too – suggesting that he had only recently arrived on the scene but was eager to get to know them better.

'So I wondered if you could possibly find time to pop over and make a flying visit, just to see she's OK and do the other thing.'

'Other thing?'

'Hand her the whatsit.'

'Oh, fine, right. Yes, well, I'd love to see her, but surely you could get the bank to transfer the money.'

'In theory, yes, but in practice, well, I'm sure you understand.'

'Yes, yes, of course,' I said, not understanding at all but deducing from his furtive manner that the last thing he wanted was my further questions on the subject. In fact, he sounded not only furtive but tetchy, so much so that it seemed quite possible he might abandon the whole idea if interrogated any further.

'Great, fantastic. I've booked you on the first flight to Knock.'

'Knock?'

'It's the airport for the pilgrims. Much less fuss than Shannon or Belfast and half the price. Tuesday, ten thirty and wear something loose.'

'Loose?'

'Don't worry, yours is not to reason why.' He gave me one of his broad schoolboy smiles. 'I'll see you off.' The tetchiness had gone out of his voice and there was now a distinct excitement about him, which was more unsettling still.

It was slow going in the departure lounge. There was a queue snaking all the way back to the automatic doors which clunked to and fro crossly as another flurry of nuns, priests and figures hunched in wheelchairs came in from the rain. At first I couldn't see Joe at all but then there he was, looking rather at home hemmed in by a cluster of sisters in grey habits. To my surprise he embraced me in a tight hug, which he then loosened in order to give himself room to slip me a solid package, about the size and shape of a brick.

'It's on a belt,' he said, standing back and surveying me in the way people do after embracing long-lost dear ones. 'I suggest you nip into the gents and pop it on before you go through security.'

'Is all this really necessary?'

'Better be safe than sorry. Look, I must run.'

In fact, running was still beyond him and he disappeared into a gently heaving mass of old ladies at a limping strut, speedy enough but not exactly graceful, suggesting one of the more obscure Olympic events which imposed complex restrictions on leg movements.

I stood for a moment irresolute, the brick-package slapping against my thigh. Perhaps it would be more comfortable if strapped round me as Joe had suggested, although his implication was that the belt was for security purposes, to keep its contents from official scrutiny. I slipped into the gents and with some difficulty buckled it on under my Rainman. The tapes scarcely met at the back and even with the Rainman belted up the thing still stuck out a good six inches and made me look not so much pregnant as condemned to wear a cumbersome but life-saving piece of medical apparatus. Carrying this monstrous succubus before me, I waddled over to Security Control, tossing my keys and coins into the plastic tray with the nonchalance of a man with a million air miles behind him. As I stepped through the door frame, the machine squawked its disapproval.

'I should take off the money belt if I were you, sir. It's probably got a metal buckle.'

Which it had, and I stood there holding the brick while he felt me up and down. The nonchalance I was aiming for this time was that of the international entrepreneur who always takes a money belt the size of a brick with him wherever he goes. Not a complete success, but the security man had lost interest in me and was already talking to his colleague about why somebody had been late on shift the night before.

'It looks quite a weight, that parcel. You wouldn't like me to put it up in the rack now, would you?' said the sister with bifocals and short grey hair who had the aisle seat next to me.

'No, it's fine.'

'Present for the family, is it?'

'No, my family's over here.'

'Ah, off on holiday then, are we? The West's just grand at this time of year.' She seemed to have taken a vow of curiosity in addition to the usual ones of poverty and chastity.

'No, I'm going to see a sick friend.'

'A visit to Knock will put her right as rain in no time.'

'I'm afraid she's got terminal cancer,' I said irritably.

'We'll pray for her at the centre and then Father Tripp can put her on the priority list for the shrine. Would you like to write her name down for me?'

She plonked a blue card down on the money brick. There were already half a dozen names on it. What could she lose? I wrote Gillian Follows, Hillcrest, Cockburnstown with the ballpoint that the nun stuck in my hand and resolved not to tell Gillian about it but of course did the moment I saw her, not calculating whether she would be amused or annoyed.

In fact, she was neither, appearing to take in the news without much interest as she clasped the money brick to her bosom and sighed. 'Readies, what bliss. Joe still knows the way to a girl's heart.'

The effort of turning the Frontera in the narrow ranks of the car park made her pink in the face and her greeting was so warm that I thought – hoped would be more accurate – that she wasn't as bad as she was supposed to be. But as we got out into the byroad that took us up from the boggy pasture on to stony empty fields with the gorse past its best I saw how weak she was.

'You wouldn't like me to drive?'

'No, I need to have something to concentrate on. Driving's fine, just keeps my mind ticking over.'

'You don't think you should come over to London?'

'Oh no, that would be too much. Anyway Joe's probably got A. N. Other by now.'

'Not as far as I know he hasn't,' I said, not knowing at all and not having considered the possibility at all.

'I don't think you'd be the first person I'd ask,' she said.

'No, I suppose not.'

'Don't look so mournful, you're lucky, really. It's worse than the demon drink, you know, being the sort of person who has to think about fucking all the time.'

'Yes,' I said.

'Even if you're past it yourself. I don't mean you personally. But Joe, even when he was a total hemiplegic –'

'Yes, I bet,' I said, cutting her short. She spoke more slowly than she used to, not breathlessly, but elegiacally, almost as though she was reading out some sad piece of verse. Even so, she still had the trick of saying things that embarrassed you but at the same time tickled your fancy. Written down, her words sound raw, even irritating, but they always gave me a weird type of pleasure, well, almost always.

The road, single-track like Joe's mind as Gillian said, was winding up the side of a steep hill.

We still passed the occasional bungalow, glowing white with a scrubby paddock and the odd pony cropping what grass there was. As we came to the top of the hill, more of a mountain, there were no more bungalows and the stone walls were broken down.

'This is the hillcrest that Hillcrest isn't on the crest of.'

It was a couple of miles the other side of the pass that we came to the cottage flanked by a big rowan tree and a corrugated-iron shed that was the same rusty colour as the bracken. There was a tussocky paddock behind with a washing line, some cabbages that looked as if they were fending for themselves and a sturdy fifteen-foot TV aerial pointing down the valley which was now full of mist.

As I got out, the damp and the chill and the wind went through me and I shuddered so visibly that she laughed and put her hand on my arm to steady herself.

'Come on inside and let's count the money.'

We sat at the oilcloth kitchen table while I thawed out (she had the heaters on full blast) and she put the kettle on and then took the brown paper brick out of the money belt and began unpeeling the £50 notes, licking her finger at the same time and then licking her dry lips afterwards. By the end of the counting there were thirty piles of ten, which we contemplated with shared pleasure like a couple of train robbers.

'Fifteen Gs. Nice one, Joe. Which bank do you think he robbed this week?'

'I'm not really in on the financial side, but we are doing amazingly well.'

'You mean he's just nicked it out of the till?'

'Well, the salary arrangements are a bit rough and ready at the moment, so I suppose –'

'You think he'll put it all back and square up the accounts? Oh, my dear Gus. Or are you going to tell me he's a reformed character?'

'He does go to that church they all go to, St Thomas Didymus. I'm going myself, next Thursday, just to see what it's like.'

'They all?'

'The other partners, Trull and Jade.'

'Trull, Christ, and who's Jade?'

'She used to be called Beryl, she's Helen's daughter. Helen Hardress, who –'

'Oh, I know about her. The Golden Calf we used to call her.'

'Calf? She doesn't look particularly –'

'Because you all worshipped her. She only had to shake her yellow mop, like that, and you all came running.'

As Gillian shook her head, her thin dark hair conspicuously failed to flounce, making the gesture seem like a minor convulsion.

'I didn't know you knew her,' I said, reflecting uncomfortably on the thought.

'Knew of, more. So that's her daughter. Joe said they were getting a woman in to look after the IT side; he made her sound like an elderly boffin. I should have guessed.'

'Guessed what? No, I really don't think –'

'Don't you? Well, keep your eyes open and you might think differently. When you're all sitting comfortably in your pew, watch out for a hand sliding up someone's skirt while Brother Trull is taking round the plate.'

She spoke not bitterly but with a certain bleached gaiety, enhanced perhaps by the thought of me in the middle of this scene in the now familiar role of the klutz who is wholly unaware of any vibrations or complications around him. She packed up the money into the belt, still chuckling, and put it into one of the drawers in the dresser, then went out to the scullery at the back to bring in some vegetables which had the same bleached, if not blasted, look as she had herself – potatoes, a cabbage and something that might have been a swede – and began chopping as she talked.

'He still thinks I'm going to that Texas place, sent me a whole lot of bumf last week, that's what the money's supposed to be for mostly, but I'm not going, you know. The money will come in handy for getting the clutch fixed and I can get Dermot to build me a hen-coop. There's a man in Cockburnstown who took my hens, that was the worst moment leaving Drishill, you know, and I could get some of them back.'

'Why won't you go?'

'Why does anyone do anything or not do anything? Because I don't want to and he can't make me.'

'But mightn't it —?'

'Cure me?' She gave the word cure a sensuous, almost lascivious curl, as though it was an improbable, expensive pleasure of the flesh.

'Yeah.'

'Well, it might, so might Sister Nutburga's prayers. Or if you all wished very hard and held each other's hands in your little pew in St Whatever's, I might be right as rain. Or I might not. Not is just a little bit more likely.'

'You don't think that a —'

'Don't say second opinion, please don't say second opinion.'

'Second opinion might —'

'I may be wrong, but I don't think there's a great deal of point in getting a second opinion on a thing the size of a football.'

'Oh.'

'Oh is right. Oh is really all that needs to be said. So can we now forget all about that tiresome subject and concentrate on getting pissed, which is what I thought you came all the way here for?'

Only now did I take in how welcoming the little sitting room at Hillcrest was, with its warm dark-red walls, which Gillian claimed the colour chart called rhesus-negative and the twisting staircase leading directly up from the corner of the room, and the undulating old chintz sofa where she lay nesting in the kilim cushions. And though she was pleased to see me – you could believe her when she said so, because she couldn't fake – she also seemed rather good at being on her own, which at first I thought surprising because she was so friendly and didn't even have her hens to cluck at out here. But then ending up on your own was probably just as much of an accident as anything else in life – it certainly was in her case – and a warm heart might cope better with solitude, just as cold people were often happiest at parties. She poured me a slip of some local whisky, as distilled for Aengus the Red she said, and an unexpected feeling that we were in for a good evening passed through me, more than unexpected, faintly indecent in fact.

'You're not having one?'

'I'm on something a little stronger,' she said and she went over to the dresser and reached down a flattish box or case from an upper shelf. She was wearing a loose cotton dress, her favourite fuchsia, knee-length, and as she reached up I could see how stringy her calves were. And I remembered how broad and strong she had looked when I followed her out on to the fire escape and she kissed me, a gin-scented, smoky kiss, which I thought at the time I'd always remember and had.

She stayed with her back turned to me while she fiddled with the box and didn't turn round until she had finished, but I caught the glint of the syringe in the overhead light as she raised it.

'What bliss, OK is a real goodster to let me do it myself. Such a pity one has to be corpsing before they allow you, isn't it? You've got that funny look on. You know what it reminds me of? When I used to drag you round the boutiques and you'd sit in the passage pretending to look bored and really straining your eyes to see if you could see my pubes.'

'Not the same look at all.'

'How would you know? I remember once in Avanti turning round without a stitch on and your eyes piercing me like lasers.'

I'm not at all sure why she suddenly reminded me of a John Buchan heroine because physically she couldn't be less like, as the Buchan heroines all had hips like a boy's and were clean-run and sang 'Cherry Ripe' in a voice like a choirboy's, and she was foul-mouthed and sensuous-looking, and had a gurgly mezzo voice to go with it. Yet that is what she reminded me of.

'Perhaps I will have one after all. OK told me not to mix it with the demon, so I immediately did and had the most delicious high. But sometimes I overdo it and just pass out, so do forgive me and don't fret if I do. The rack of lamb's in the oven and the veg just need heating up.'

But she didn't pass out, at the most began to sound a little woozy as she lay back in the cushions, almost beautiful now she was so thin, at last coming to look as fine and elegant as her mother who had always been so embarrassed by her cheerful, clumsy daughter.

'Yes, I've noticed it too,' she said, when I ventured something along these lines, only putting it more delicately. 'Giving satisfaction rather late in the day on all fronts. She'd be so proud to know I was on drugs, as long as I didn't tell her it was because I was a tiny bit off colour. She couldn't bear illness, beautiful people can't, can they? Makes life so exhausting, having to pretend to be well all the time. You know the first time you came to see us, not the time recently, but when Joe was just recovering from his stroke, I expect you thought we were a pathetic couple.'

'No, of course not.'

'I bet you did, you must have. A bankrupt hemiplegic being looked after by his endlessly betrayed childfree wife, on the run from the law and hard up, not as hard up as we were later but hard up, and we hadn't even been kidnapped then, but the thing was, we were happy in a stupid sort of way. At least I was, and I think Joe was too, although he was driven mad not being able to do things. But we were weirdly content, because, oh, I suppose we knew we were at the end of the line, which isn't such a ghastly place to be when you get there. We didn't have to pretend anything any more.'

She then wandered off on to something else, but it occurred to me that she was really talking about her situation now and transferring this weird contentment back to a time when it had seemed to me (she was right about that) they had both been miserable, and why not.

'Suddenly I don't feel so sparky,' she said. 'Would you mind if I buggered off?'

'Can I help?'

'Oh no, as I said when we met in the passage at Drishill, it's a bit too late for – but wasn't that funny, you being all –'

She sketched a rude gesture and laughed, as she levered herself out of the cushions and walked, swaying a little, towards the stairs, turning to tell me not to forget the rack.

The lamb already had the herbs and seasoning on it, and the bottle of Fleurie was open by the cooker, and I tucked in, feeling quite sure that I was doing the right thing, feeling rather lighthearted, in fact. After dinner I needed to pee and so as not to disturb her I went out the back door and peed over the cabbage stalks, rocking on my heels a little and staring up at the huge night sky full of stars. And I remembered feeling so awash with melancholy when I had pissed in the bog at Thursby and wondered why I felt so lighthearted now.

VI

Tommy Ds

I must have walked past it a hundred times without noticing. A great barn built of that deathly greyish-yellow brick that makes you think of the Fens. There was a crude wooden cross stuck on the blank façade, once lit up by dusty bulbs at night perhaps, or Christmas, but now with several bulbs missing. Either side of the church the edges of the Ackroyd Estate, big Thirties blocks in the same dingy brick, reared over Sinclair Street, a noisy cut-through parallel to the railway. I wondered why Ortho hadn't chosen some more inspiring church for its base, like St Wulfstan's, the so-called Cathedral of the Docks, with its soaring twin bell towers, its spiralling crockets and finials, and its thrilling preachers. That was just the point, Jade explained to me, Malc got the job because nobody else would take it and the only alternative was to demolish the place. But what was great about it was it was only seven minutes' walk from Liffe and you could be back on the trading floor by 2.15.

'What are they like?'

'Who?'

'The people who come.'

'They're not animals, you know. They're OK. I expect you'll think they're creepy, well, they are a bit, but it's all very relaxed. You don't feel pressured at all.'

Jade looked at me as though expecting a reaction of the sort St Thomas must have given on first being told about the Resurrection, an incredulous snort, perhaps, or a sigh with eyes raised to the ceiling in a slightly theatrical, even camp fashion. But I wasn't feeling confident enough to make any gesture of incredulity. Unease, amounting to alarm, at the thought of seeing an army of believers, their eyes as clear and bright as the bulbs on the cross were not – that was my main sensation.

And there were a lot of them – the word multitude could not be suppressed. They crowded the narrow pavement, were pressed against the chain-link fencing by the thundering artics pelting in from the Tunnel, they spilled over the cycle lane, dodging the high-saddled cyclists swinging out of Wapping Lane. It was eerie to see such a crowd – there must have been three hundred at least – so soberly dressed and with such smart clacking shoes. They made you realise how quiet people usually were on the streets in their trainers and headsets. As we fell into step, I could not help staring at them just as Jade had accused me, as though I had been transported into the best viewing place in a safari park in some vehicle that not only kept me safe but rendered me more or less invisible to the grazing herds. But of course I wasn't invisible and they returned my glassy stare by smiling, or to be precise, since they were already smiling in a mild open-mouthed way, by intensifying the smile and making it focused and personal. Which meant it was impossible to avoid smiling back. After a hundred yards I was nodding and grinning in all directions, so that by the time we reached the steps of the church, any observer would have assumed I was quite at home with these people, perhaps a long-standing member of the congregation, even a helper who might assist the infirm or comfort those who were overcome by emotion, which was to be expected, because Jade had warned 'it can get quite heavy'.

She was sitting handing out leaflets at a table set up in the corner of the dusty screens that tried to keep out the noise and the litter from the street. The screens and the little folding table gave her the look of a pupil who had had to be isolated from the rest of the class while sitting some exam, perhaps to avoid cheating or because she was still infectious. She was smiling too, but in an inward way, not at the people coming in, rather as if handing out leaflets were an occupation that was much more fun than you might have expected.

'Hi, Gus, I didn't recognise you at first, you looked so cheerful.'

This was breaking my cover and I didn't care for it, but the bosomy chestnut-haired girl in specs standing behind me said, 'Oh, Jade cheers us all up, don't you, Jade? It's so great to have her with us. We've got such a lot of celebs, there's Tikha from Insulation, that's a pop group, and Decla D from Six of One and loads from the City of course. I'm afraid I don't –'

'This is Gus,' Jade said, waving a hand at me. 'He runs the firm, but he's such a dreadful cynic so I –'

'Thought you should bring him along and show him we haven't all got two heads. Brilliant.'

She took off her specs and gave me a smile of melting friendliness which was somehow at the same time remarkably keen. You might have thought smiling was a method of permanently imprinting someone's face on your memory. Gracia with a 'c', she told me, led me to one of the few empty chairs, spindly plastic things that appeared to be coated in anti-climb black paint.

We sat in silence for a few minutes to allow the stragglers time to find seats. The silence was intense. There was none of that bustle and whispering to be expected at social occasions in church or at a concert. Perhaps even if you did happen to know your next-door neighbour, this was a time for reflection and prayer. But what made the atmosphere so weird was the fact that most of them still had the half-smile loitering about their lips. And this huge collective smile began to work upon my nerves, not to irritate but to induce a deepening sadness. Their all being here together seemed to be the result not of some delusion or weakness but, on the contrary, a response to some terrible knowledge, a piece of knowledge that they had perhaps not fully grasped themselves but that those who were contemptuous of them had not grasped at all. They appeared to share some huge tragic secret which they had resolved to put the best face on, perhaps even to deny the existence of.

It was a relief when Malcolm Tedder-Brown came out on to the chancel steps and bade us all an intensely warm and toothy welcome. Everyone else in the church was in a city suit of dull hue, a few of them without ties and some of the women having squeezed in a bit of shopping before the service but all unmistakably dressed up for work. Malc by contrast was in an unzipped blue fleece with a purple T-shirt and he was wearing trainers. He ambled down the aisle as though he had nothing much to do with the service, in fact, might just be finishing off some maintenance work before popping out for a drink. When he was halfway to the door he turned round sharply and began reciting a prayer in a resonant baritone. I could not make out what he was saying but then I realised the prayer was in some dead language, conceivably Greek.

'That,' he said, slipping back not only into English but into a conversational tone, 'was a prayer that St Cosmo of Alexandria prayed before the merchant bankers of Ephesus in AD 331. And now I shall hand you over to Ian.'

A lean man in his late thirties appeared from nowhere, exchanged high-fives with Malc like a substitute running on to the pitch, and skipped up the steps to the functional metal pulpit (more like a cage for cleaning the windows of high buildings). He started by telling us to switch off our mobile phones because we were expecting a much more important call, a call from Head Office. But first we would sing a hymn. It was an old hymn, by Wesley the service sheet said, and I began to recover my composure as we sang it: '. . . a heart that's sprinkled with the blood so freely shed for me.'

What would be the point of sprinkling a heart with blood, especially with blood which had presumably been shed some time earlier, thus dousing a still-beating pump with a stale coulis that would do nothing for it? I was getting on quite well with this line of thought when I became aware of a warm, chubby-feeling hand closing itself over mine.

'Some of you today have come from the futures trading floor. You don't need me to tell you what a complicated business that is. At Liffe you have to work out the odds, you have to check out the prospects, and then you have to place your bet this way or that. Well, what we're into here is a kind of futures trading, but it's very simple, you don't need any A-levels to succeed and there's no pressure, no stress. All bets are on and you've got nothing to lose. No, I'm wrong, you've got plenty to lose. You can lose that sense of emptiness for a start, because God will fill you with life. You can lose that feeling of worthlessness, because God always puts the top valuation on each and every one of you . . .'

The chubby grip tightened a fraction. The warmth of it was comforting, not embarrassing at all and as long as you looked straight ahead at the speaker the contact felt pleasantly businesslike, as though we had needed to clasp hands for some practical purpose, like shifting a piece of furniture.

The lean man finished by introducing another lean man of about the same age, rather handsome in a way that had gone out of style, crinkly hair, confident mouth, not at all brooding. He told us his name, a Welsh name I think, might have been Alan Williams, but it didn't stay in my head because what he then did was to invite us to hold hands because he was going to talk about the healing power of the Holy Spirit and the first thing you had to understand was that the strength of that power was infinitely multiplied if we all joined together and thought of ourselves as one body. 'All of you here are brilliant with figures,' he said, 'and so you know that when I say two to the power of three or four or whatever, that means two multiplied by itself three times or four times and so on until you come to an absolutely astronomical number.' Well, it was the same with prayer. So anyway we were to hold hands.

But Gracia and I were already holding hands, in this businesslike way. So, in order to progress into the healing/prayer mode we somehow had to signal a change in the nature of the contact, which we did by looking at each other, exchanging smiles and then gently raising and lowering our clasped hands as a salute to the new phase.

Alan(?) Williams(?) then began to talk about prayer and the purposes and people we might pray for: cleanliness of heart, purity in thought, word and deed on the one hand; the City of London, the Stock Exchange, Tony Blair, world peace on the other. All this sounded familiar and I was on the edge of slipping into a doze when he began to talk, quite gently and without much emphasis, about getting rid of the devils inside us, about chasing out the unclean spirits. He was now using more or less traditional language, with no financial or business allusions. But all quite piano, even flat, there wasn't any throbbing undertone to prepare you for a great surge of passion. At the same time it wasn't exactly matter-of-fact either. The quietness of his voice in the great chilly barn was eerie, like the person who tells you very quietly, scarcely moving their lips, not to look now but just behind the third pillar on the right there is a man with a gun. He went on talking about the devils within and how persuasive they could be and how difficult it was to get rid of them, like friends who weren't really friends and who wanted to crash out on your sofa and you didn't actually want them there, and – but there I began to lose the thread of what he was saying, because the noise started.

At first I thought that it might be the throb of emotion which he was at last allowing to creep into his voice, or perhaps a trick of the amplifier if there was one, or even just some reverberation in this great hollow space. But quite soon the noise separated itself from his voice – which went on as quiet and level as it had started – and you could identify for sure that what it was was the noise of sobbing – quiet at first, almost reflective, then a little louder, though never loud, except that there were more people doing the sobbing, among them Gracia.

In her case I felt her sob before I could be sure of hearing her. There was a vibration transmitted through the touch of her shoulder and then down her arm to the hand that was clasped into mine. Then I could hear her making the same noise that I heard across the whole church, a slow, low, jerky moan.

Not everyone was sobbing, nowhere near, perhaps only one in half a dozen, it was hard to tell, but you could separate the individual moans, they didn't blend. So there might be others like me, perhaps dozens of us, who were bewildered, not disturbed or repelled, just bewildered, because nothing that had been said so far touched in us the depths that had been touched in the people sitting next to us. Perhaps we had no such depths.

I sneaked a look at Gracia. Her mouth was open and she had begun to breathe rather chokily. It occurred to me that she might be asthmatic, though this seemed to be one stimulus that did not affect my own tubes – dust and feathers yes, cats and dogs possibly, but the Word of the Holy Spirit not a bit.

On the contrary, a frigid detachment took hold of me and I looked as long as was decent at her pale face and her frizzy chestnut hair, and wondered whether it was dyed, whether she was married, or really rather intelligent, or came from Australia which something about her – her name, her voice – had suggested. She had her specs off and there were tears in her grey-green eyes.

And yes, it has to be admitted, there is no point in pretending otherwise, now I was moved too, not quite moved actually to make a sound – but certainly carried off the ground, with heart unquiet and tears queuing at the back of my eyes. There wasn't time to wonder how this had happened. A few seconds earlier I had been the dry-eyed observer, the Charles Addams ghoul in the cinema audience, and then in no time what I can only call osmosis had done its work – the moaning all around me, the firm warm grasp of Gracia's hand. Even in this state, this peculiar mixture of embarrassment and something approaching rapture, I could not help wondering how Trull would be taking it. I needed a minute or two to locate him – his duties, whatever they were, seemed to involve a certain amount of moving about, so that when we came in he had been standing by the far door beyond Jade's little table. Later on I had spotted him opening a door at the side of the pulpit to let in the new preacher.

Now, there he was, standing by the last pillar before the choir, in front of the bulbous brass lectern. Standing very still with his hands folded in front of him, not swaying as several of the congregation had begun to do. His head was still shaven and he had taken off the tinted Ray-Bans that he had on when we were beating the reed beds at HM Prison Thursby. There his appearance had given the impression that he was an East End villain of long lineage, well known to the Krays, perhaps even a distant cousin. Standing by the pillar in Tommy Ds he still looked professional. If it had been a funeral, you would have said he was part of the undertaker's team, keeping a watchful eye out to make sure everything was being done properly, the black gloves being worn as a mark of respect. As it was, without his shades he gave off an aura of austerity, of having attained a level of spirituality a rung or two higher than the rest of us, even of belonging to some religious order whose members continued to bear witness in the secular world, some no doubt working as bond traders or in foreign exchange.

But the extraordinary thing was that Trull's mouth was open, not just gaping vacantly but unmistakably engaged in making a noise, his rude cherub lips half-stretched and moving in a faint vibrating motion as though his teeth were chattering with cold.

And this sight, too, touched me. I know it should not have. Derision, or perhaps mere amazement, would have been a more suitable reaction. But in my unanchored state, floating among all these fellow lost souls, it seemed like a sort of unexpected grace that Trull should have joined us.

Just behind Trull I suddenly caught sight of the Reverend Malcolm Tedder-Brown. Perhaps he had always been there. If so it was odd that I had failed to notice him, not just because he was dressed unlike anyone else in the church but because he had this uninvolved look. It was now as though he had just returned from his lunch break and was waiting for the congregation to disperse so he could get on with replacing the light bulbs or hoovering the chancel carpet. His lips were parted in a negligent half-smile, his canines wolfishly exposed as he contemplated the proceedings with a detached indulgence, perhaps looking forward to healthy takings from the collection.

But at this moment my attention was drawn back from this ill-assorted couple to Gracia who had ceased moaning and was now being shaken by a series of mild convulsions, shivers would perhaps be a better word. This led, but only briefly, into a snuffling, snorting sound which I thought would develop into renewed sobbing but didn't. On the contrary, it seemed to be a prelude to coming down to earth and in a moment she was looking in the green A&M to find the closing hymn which was sung in a spiritless dirge-like fashion. I cannot remember what hymn it was. Perhaps it had been chosen for its dimness, allowing the congregation time to resume their ordinary selves without strain.

Then, quickly, without hanging about, we were out in the street, with the lorries rattling by over the broken tarmac and the litter swirling up in our faces.

'Isn't there, you know, coffee?'

'They're busy people, Gus. You wouldn't believe how hard it is for them to snatch the full hour off the floor. You hit it off with Gracia, I think.'

'Well,' I said, but at that moment there was a 'bye-ee' from a bike the other side of the road and Gracia giving us a huge wave, her long pink scarf trailing after her as she pedalled off back to the office, Palgrave and Sweetenham, where she was in confectionery and soft drinks analysis, all of which she had managed to tell me as we came down the aisle and I had realised that she was still holding my hand.

'So?' Trull queried.

'So what? Oh, all right then, I don't quite know what to say. I admit I was moved.'

'But then you're easily moved, Gus, aren't you? Underneath that carapace, you're a soft touch. But that doesn't stop you having, what shall we say, reservations? Which means you can have it both ways, can't you? You can be carried away by cheap music but still go on knowing it's cheap.'

'I'm not alone in that.'

'Not quite alone, I agree. But most of the people there today aren't like you. They don't have that luxury. When they let themselves go, they let it all go. When they open up to the Lord they don't keep anything back, because they can't. They *commit*, Gus, they have to. Now you tell me, are they lucky or unlucky? Are you so much better off than they are?'

'And what about you?'

'Oh Gus, really, I don't come into it. You know me, just trying to help things along.'

The sun had come out and he had put his Ray-Bans on, and he looked like an East End hood again. As so often before in our long on-and-off acquaintance, I felt no urge to press him. Why was that? I suppose because I knew I would only be led through a labyrinth of defence mechanisms until I became too hot and bothered to continue.

My eyes followed the last of the congregation now dispersing up Ackroyd Street back towards the City.

'They look fucked out, don't they?' Trull said.

'They? Not we?'

'You're so sharp these days it's disturbing. You used to let me get away with anything. Whatever became of that nice, easygoing Gus?'

'He took early retirement.'

'Perhaps that was an error.'

'Probably was.'

'No, seriously, I'm really glad you're with us, my dear. And it's all going so well it's weird.'

It was. We couldn't believe our luck – at least I couldn't and though my associates pretended that there was nothing in the world less surprising than that everything should be going according to the business plan, every now and then there was a dazed look they could not quite keep out of their eyes. I have seen that look on other people when they have just made it. They are not putting it on to show that they haven't forgotten where they came from, still less to persuade you that they never intended anything like this (absurd, after all, when they have been intriguing night and day for it since they were about twelve years old). No, it is simply an instinctive awareness that comes on them, just for an instant or two, that along with everything else they needed luck. It passes and they settle into the comfortable acceptance that the bottom line is that they deserved it, and the less comfortable insistence that everyone ought to recognise this, and the even less comfortable suspicion that they don't. But before all the conceit and arrogance and paranoia that go with success settle in for the duration, there is this golden, happy, dazed moment and you would have to be stony-hearted not to share in it just a fraction.

Jade looked and sounded dreamy – that was the way it took her. When she was on the phone to potential new clients her voice seemed to be a semitone lower. Joe had given up telling her not to talk to them as if she were offering phone sex, but then Joe was not in the office much, and when he passed through he was brisk, almost military in the orders he barked out to anyone who happened to be in his way, George, me, the new girl, Sally, we had got in to help with Systems. Only an occasional hand tremor betrayed his disability, and this simply added to the air of purposeful impatience, as though he was liable to fly into a rage if he was held up.

And Trull? Trull just looked serene and knowing. True, that was how he always looked, ever since I had first met him, thirty, nearly forty years earlier, hauling up his boat on the beach at Shorewinds and he had told me, quite unprompted, that he had been Junior Firefly Champion at Burnham the year before; not, of course, something I had enquired about or particularly wanted to know but a fact he managed to impart without seeming to drag it in, as though it was an unlikely thing that I needed to know because it was so unlikely. But if he had been serene and knowing then, now he was like a gnostic who had just discovered the final secret of the universe, the kind of way you would feel after completing the human genome and were putting on your coat to go out for a quiet glass.

Fee income was increasing by 5 or 6 per cent each month and had just passed the £100,000 mark (in August), while the only extra cost we were incurring was Systems Sally. We had a dozen of the

FTSE-100 on our books, a couple of them already on their second postings. The absurdly stiff terms we were insisting on they took like lambs. In fact, the exorbitance of it seemed to be an added attraction. Other headhunters who had been in the business for years were happy with a lower signing-on fee and would give the salary money back if the placement didn't work out after a year or even in some cases eighteen months.

'What happens when they get a dud from us? Won't they put the word around that Heads is a no-no, costs twice as much and they send you an idiot?'

'Gus, did you ever hear of Joe Duveen?' Trull enquired.

'Duveen the art dealer?'

'Exactly. Now Duveen would invite one of these elderly millionaires to call at his picture shop, some grocer who'd made all the money in the world and now wanted a little slice of immortality to go with it, and he'd draw back these velvet curtains and there would be this picture on an easel, a Rembrandt or a Titian or whatever, unframed so it looked as if the artist had just finished it, beautifully lit and he'd say to him, "Fred," or "Cy, this is one of the most expensive pictures in the world. I could let you have a cheaper picture, there's a fine picture in the next room that's half the price, but I think you're ready for this one. I could let it go to Kress or Huntington but I think this one's got your name on it." That's the principle we're operating on here.'

'But suppose the picture turns out to be no good, or at any rate not what it's supposed to be?'

'Well, that happens and of course you have genuinely done your best to make sure that it doesn't happen. Berenson's looked the picture over, the people at the Louvre have done an analysis. But even if it does happen, and once in a hundred times it's bound to, well you refund the money or perhaps the owner now really likes the picture, he doesn't want to admit he's been taken for a ride, he keeps on the label that says Rembrandt or Botticelli and you only refund half the money. Anyway, the point is he keeps the picture twice as long as if he'd only paid half as much for it.'

'Really?'

'Seemed to work for Duveen. He managed to build half the Tate with his spare cash. And in our own business the Suckling Centre's done some analysis which proves that executives recruited through headhunters stay in their jobs nearly twice as long as those recruited internally or by direct ads, by factors of 1.8 and 1.73 respectively. Now of course we use the numbers to prove that we're twice as efficient as the old steam methods, our pegs really do fit better in the holes. But you could argue that people are just more reluctant to junk what they have paid good money for.'

Trull's voice – and his vocabulary too – seemed to be shifting with success in a transatlantic or perhaps mid-Atlantic direction. He didn't really sound American, more like an Englishman who just happened to like the way being American sounded – Cary Grant would be the nearest equivalent.

Joe, by contrast, was becoming almost intolerably brisk and alert. He had difficulty taking off his overcoat, which was now too tight round the armpits after the relentless business lunches that fell to him. And he was still tugging at the sleeve of it while he breathlessly growled at me, 'Gus, a word.'

I was the only other person in the room but he used my name, they all did now. Perhaps that too was something to do with success: you had the self-confidence, even the duty, to name things, a category now including human beings. There was something about this in Genesis. Did God give Adam the assignment to name things before or after the Fall? In fact, I see it's Genesis 2.xix, and Eve hasn't even been created yet, which may explain why women don't go in for twitching and trainspotting.

'Sorry about the Ingrams debacle,' I said.

'Don't give it another thought. I've had a talk with Neil and he's still promising us a piece of the action on the next round.'

'I'm afraid I was rather snowed under when it came up. E.T. was back again, the Hatfield Galleria thing didn't work out, and there were a couple more that Patsy Hepple let go who I thought deserved priority because she's sort of our responsibility. And Miles Morpurgo insisted on having another long talk, although I'd made it clear we really couldn't do anything more for him after last time.'

Ah yes, yes, he said, not listening to a word. 'Actually I didn't want to talk shop.'

He sounded wheezy and looked flushed. I wondered whether the asthma we had once shared was coming back because he was overdoing it. Nobody could ever have recommended running a million-pound business as therapy for a hemiplegic.

'We're virtually a million-pound business now, did you know that?' he said, echoing part of my thoughts. 'Fee income for the first calendar year is on track for the Big M.'

'Gross,' I said.

'Gross,' he repeated but mechanically, not putting in the usual homily about thinking positively, because he was thinking about something else.

'Gus,' he said, 'are you on net, do you catch the gossip around the office?'

'What do you mean? These days there's usually nobody here but Sally and George.'

'Well, they've got tongues, haven't they? You know this is a fantastic business. I promised you one last big throw, didn't I? You didn't believe me, but this really is – it's the ultimate Journey to the Inferior.'

'Interior,' I said, thinking he was right the first time and wondering why he was so nervous because that was when the word fluffs tended to come these days, when he was trying to sound ebullient and fretting about something else, as though the closure of several regional branches in his brain had left the organisation a little short of capacity.

'Randy, you know Wirefree's personnel man over here, was saying last night that he had half a mind just to give us all their business and go home to St Louis and get some fishing.'

'Did he?'

'But even a great business can be shredded if the personalities involved start fighting. And it's usually some silly scrap of gossip that sets it off.'

'Like what?'

'You haven't heard anything?'

'Not a thing.'

'Because if you haven't there's no point in telling you.'

'No,' I said, meaning yes, even my laggard curiosity now somewhat aquiver.

'But you're probably bound to, so I might as well make it clear to you now that there's nothing in it, it's all complete balls.'

'What is?'

'You really haven't heard?'

He turned his head to the window and closed his eyes, as though seeking some kind of external guidance. The light from the barred attic window caught his cheeks and seemed to drain what life there was out of them. He looked waxen, like a dolled-up corpse.

'All right, then. There's talk going around that I'm going out with Jade.'

He paused and I couldn't think of anything to say.

'Having a thing with her, that we're an item.'

'I know what going out with means,' I said, before he exhausted the alternative ways of saying it.

'It's total nonsense, as I say. But that's the sort of thing you're bound to hear, in a small office like this, bound to.'

'Well, I haven't,' I said, coming in my mind, almost simultaneously, to two separate conclusions: that the rumour was true and that Joe was disappointed I had not yet heard it. Perhaps no such rumour existed but only the fact, and this laborious manoeuvre was, for some reason, the only way Joe thought he could nudge the fact into the public domain. Still, it seemed the polite thing to go along with the manoeuvre so I said, in a lightish way, 'People will say anything to amuse themselves, the more improbable the better I suppose. I mean, the age gap would be, what, thirty years.'

'Well, such things have been known,' Joe said. 'Some girls, God knows why, do seem to prefer much older men.'

'Anyway, not in this case.'

'No, absolutely not. I know you're in touch with Gillian, almost as much as I am in fact, and I'd hate it if she were told anything of the sort. It would be just awful for her to –'

This was a sentence better not completed, but Joe was fully capable of completing it, so I interrupted and told him it was the last thing on earth I would dream of telling her, even if I had heard it in the first place, which I hadn't.

'No, I mean, if she heard it from another source, I hope you'd, you know –'

'Set her fears at rest.'

'Yes, that's it exactly. Thank you, Gus.'

My head was teeming with unsavoury thoughts as we sat down for the exec meeting at four o'clock – Joe's freckly thighs pumping away and Jade's enigmatic face on the pillow, at first frowning, perplexed-looking, then dissolving into a slow ... well hardly a smile, just a relaxed look, as close as perhaps she ever came to satisfaction. So, although I had been told about the people from Hellman Drax coming and there it was on the agenda that Sally had typed up for us, at first I didn't really take in the two men unfurling their briefcases at the end of the refectory table that Jade had found in Junket just off the Portobello and which she said was just right for us. One was youngish with not much fair hair on top and he thrust out a hand like a traffic policeman.

'Tim Stoyt-Smith,' he said. 'As investment banks go we're only a boutique, but we like to think we've got heat.'

Then the other man shook hands and said how much Hellman Drax was looking forward to working with us and what a fantastic job we were doing. His voice was low and gravelly, but also unnaturally slow, like a sports car in a traffic jam. Mike Gurwitz, he added, bringing out his card in a synchronised manoeuvre as slick as a muscular reflex. But his eyes were already on Jade who was curled up in her bendy Boltraffio chair with her legs tucked under her.

You couldn't help looking at her, not only because she was so lovely but because she had this catlike self-absorption, so that every time she stretched or pushed the hair out of her eyes you imagined the two of you together somewhere miles way, undisturbed. Tim Stoyt-Smith went a little pink as if worried that we could guess what he was thinking. Even Trull was looking at her but not in quite the same way, more as though he was her personal manager who had brought her along and was unobtrusively pleased she was doing so well.

The only person who wasn't looking at her was Joe who had his eyes fixed on the pages in front of him and was reading aloud from them rather erratically, which was quite unlike him as I couldn't ever remember his reading aloud, or for that matter silently.

Even when he looked up to address the Hellman Drax duo, his eyes travelled along the other side of the table from Jade. This confirmed my hunch that his denial about having an affair with her was not only a complete lie, but also a kind of submerged boast. All the same, it remained an unsettling thought and I still found it hard to listen as he outlined the plan. Despite all the recovery he had made from the stroke, his voice had not shaken off that leaden, stressless tone. Mike Gurwitz's voice in a different way had the same numbing effect.

So it took me some time to haul in the exact nature of the proposal or even whose proposal it was. And it was only when Stoyt-Smith said perhaps it might be helpful if he summarised the position so far that I began to get the hang of it.

'The sense of the meeting, then, is that we should go for a float in the spring, pricing the offer at, let's say, 250p, to bring in 50 mill, max 60 mill, if the markets are looking good. We'd keep 30 per cent of the £1 shares for the founding partners, to be taken up at par. That should enable you to raise another 20 to 25 mill from the banks to reach the funding target of 75 as a minimum. We'd have our people carry out due diligence over the coming months with a view to getting a prospectus out in early Feb.'

'Target,' I said, in a voice I scarcely recognised as my own, 'what target?'

Stoyt-Smith looked at me in some surprise. 'I thought,' he said, 'that it was agreed that we should go for 75.'

'What target?' I said again. 'Target for what?'

'The business plan indicates that we need to raise seventy-five million pounds in two or possibly three tranches,' Trull said in a very patient voice. 'That, we calculate, will enable us to meet our objectives in Years One and Two, and leave room for moving into Phase Two in Year Three if the market place looks right.'

'But we've just spent millions on that ad campaign,' I bleated, for some reason wanting to stand up but knowing I shouldn't.

'Perhaps I should say,' Trull interjected with a cherubic twitch of his lips, 'that Gus here has been out on the road almost continuously these past weeks building our client base and shamefully we haven't brought him up to speed with the financial planning.'

'Good for you, Gus,' Mike Gurwitz said with the kindly look that is reserved on these occasions for those who are hopelessly out of the loop.

'The idea is, Gus,' Joe said, leaning forward, '– and I really must apologise for not putting you in the picture earlier – is that we should break out from our core business to offer services across a wide range – insurance, house purchase, legal services, then asset management, pensions, health care, you name it – all just by logging on to Heads You Win, the Service Station to the Nation.'

'And that's going to cost 75 million?'

'Sounds a lot, I know, but unless you saturate the media you won't get it moving, and media rates have gone through the roof.'

'Is it all decided? I mean, don't we have a vote on it or something?'

'These are only exploratory talks, I thought I'd made that clear. We need to go back to our numbers people and have them crawl all over it.' Mike Gurwitz sounded as nettled as someone so slow and gravelly was capable of sounding. My shrill question had offended against his sense of what was fitting. However divided you might be, you presented a united front to the outside world. The Hellman Drax duo busied themselves with their papers, Tim pointing out some figure of crucial importance to Mike who pointed to another figure on the other half of the spreadsheet. After a decent interval Mike Gurwitz said, his gravel tones soused in honey, 'The founding partners contacted us some months ago and we've had a series of useful meetings. If there's any problem, I'm sure –'

'As you recall, Gus, the partnership was set up just before you joined us. So, although you are a key figure in all our literature, legally you are still an associate, but of course you'll participate fully in the IPO on the same terms as the rest of us.' Trull was almost cooing in his anxiety to calm me down.

'So I don't have a say?'

'Not as such in legal terms, but of course your input will be immensely valuable to us. Any reservations you may have will be taken on board by Mike and Tim here, and factored into their calculations.'

'Absolutely.'

'No problem.'

'But that's what you're going to do anyway? Raise 75 million quid when you've already got a perfectly good business going.'

'A *small* business, Gus. One which is painfully short of capital to expand. We can't go on crouching in this attic indefinitely.'

'That reminds me, have you thought about space at all?' Tim Stoyt-Smith put in.

'We were thinking Docklands, Mudchute Tower perhaps.'

'How about Beckton? Only £8 per. Beckton's the new Docklands. How much footage do you need?'

'Hundred, hundred and twenty k.'

'Or you could try out of town for the back office, Dagenham or Luton, anywhere the car people are relocating.'

Suddenly this long low room with its barred windows – and the distant squint you got of the river and the elderly Bangladeshis shuffling along the broken cobbles outside – all seemed infinitely precious, part of an adventure that had come to an end and even in that instant, when I had not yet regained my temper and was still trying to think what I could possibly say that wouldn't sound even more petulant, it came to me that I had been happy with this grisly crew in a way which was not going to come again.

'Oh, Gus,' Jade said, 'go with the flow, you'll enjoy it.'

After the Hellman Drax team had gone home I pleaded a migraine and set off home too.

In the street outside a man with a bristling skull was fiddling with the hood of his open BMW. He had a radio on the bonnet thumping out garage music. I paused for a second, faintly envying his absorbed state, then heard more music – the same thumping – coming down the street. It was an old black car, I couldn't be sure of the make, a Mazda perhaps, and it was open too, with four youths in baseball caps sitting in it. A couple of yards down the road the car stopped and three of them got out, and came over to the bristle-skulled man and began hitting him with baseball bats. In fact, they only had two bats between them, so one of them had to wait till one of the others was out of breath and passed him the bat. The whole thing cannot have lasted more than a minute, but seemed to go on for ever. Not a word was spoken by either side. The bristlehead seemed unsurprised by the assault and didn't appear to utter a word of protest, though he did put up his arm to defend himself, but one of the boys was on the other side of him and started thumping him under his guard, giving his ribs a battering. Both radios were still thumping away too. When they had finished the three boys jumped back into the car and the fourth one drove them off. They were Asian in appearance and very young, not more than sixteen, I would guess. The bristle-skulled man did not stop to count his wounds but jumped into the BMW with unimpaired agility, and drove off after them with foot hard down and the fat tyres tearing at the cobbles. Soon even the thump of the garage music had faded.

Well, perhaps it wasn't the Garden of Eden, but I still couldn't see that an office block in Beckton would be much improvement.

In my distracted state it had completely slipped my mind that there would be nobody at home. My wife had reached a climactic moment in her excavation of the Scrope Diaries. Sir Scrope Dudgeon was laying claim to the Lincolnshire estates of his cousin Prosperous Dudgeon (who had been carried off by the plague) on the grounds that his daughter Anne (who was either a hunchback or a simpleton, the wording was ambiguous) was illegitimate, Prosperous having contracted a marriage with a woman of dubious character from Haverfordwest whose husband was still alive – or so Sir Scrope claimed, but then most things about him were dubious, including his knighthood. The County Record Office had to be consulted in Pembrokeshire no less than in Lincoln. She would be gone for weeks. I thought of the dusty Peugeot bumping across country with her long pale face peering through the smeary windscreen (the rubber had gone on the wipers), her mind abuzz with the comings and goings, mostly comings, of long-dead Scropes and Dudgeons, and her absorption too I envied and wished I were at her side instead of the Bug.

Not a lot in the post, only a note from Dr Playfair to inform me that my latest PSA was in fact a little elevated and perhaps I could make an appointment at my convenience, nothing to worry about.

So I sat down, slumped would be nearer the mark, and contemplated extinction. Not with the clear head and stoical resolve that came so easily to Sir Edward Leithen. No, this was a deep, sagging, cold despair, a dragged-down feeling, so all-inclusive and unremitting that you could see no end to it. When the thought of death had come to me before, as it had at intervals ever since that first consultation with Playfair, there was somehow room to summon up comforting thoughts, even if you knew they were false, recollections of happy moments, things that had gone well, friends, the children, the sheer length of the innings, not enormous perhaps, but nothing to complain of. But now there was no room for any of that.

Then the telephone rang and the possibility of talking to another human even if it was only a wrong number got me out of my chair with such alacrity that my despair began even in that instant to seem misplaced, the result of some puzzling delusion.

'Oh, there you are. They said you'd gone home.'

The voice was friendly, almost bubbly, with a trace of – what? – Australian in it.

'You don't recognise me? Oh, that is a disappointment. I thought I had such a distinctive voice.'

'Oh, I do, Gracia,' I said, pulling myself together. 'I just couldn't remember how you say Gracia.'

'You do it beautifully. Now listen, great news, P&S have moved me to HR, so you and I can do business. Isn't that lovely?'

'Yes, lovely.'

'Lots of little one-to-ones. Some of the girls think HR is like outer darkness but I think it's fantastic. You get to know everybody's innermost secrets and those you don't you can make up. And you sit in on all the interviews and make life hell for everybody.'

'I wonder if you've quite got the right idea. You sound like a dangerous character to be let loose in Human Resources.'

'Oh Gus, you mustn't be solemn. I once dated a guy from HR and he was just the most fun.'

'What happened to him?'

'He got fired.' She laughed, more of a chuckle, a friendly gurgling sound, somehow giving the impression that it was I who had made a good joke.

'Look,' she said, in that peculiar friendly way Aussies have of saying 'Look', encouraging rather than the reproving way we say it in England, 'come round tomorrow night for a business cocktail.'

'Where's round?'

'Padstow Mansions. I bet you know it, everyone does. They say every Englishman has spent at least one night there.'

'Half a night, in my case. I came to see a friend who lived there and was trying to kill himself.'

'Yeah, that's what living there does to you. Did he succeed?'

'No.'

'Well, perhaps he'd like to come along too?'

'He's no longer with us, died of cancer a few years ago. In fact,' I added, the thought only just coming to me, 'he was Jade's father.'

'He must have been an amazing person.'

'Well, no, he wasn't actually, he was really quite unamazing, Bobs, rather an irritating character in fact, though I liked him,' I added in a flustered way which must have sounded guilty, though it was true.

'You must have known him quite well if you came round to try and stop him killing himself.'

'Well, he asked me to.'

'Come round and stop him?'

'Yes, more or less.'

'He doesn't sound as ordinary as all that.'

'Well, he was. He always got the wrong end of the stick.'

'Perhaps it was Jade's mother who was the amazing one.'

'Yes, she was.' But I didn't want to talk about Helen, or indeed to go into anything that had happened at Padders all those years ago. All I wanted was to have a quiet drink with Gracia and discuss future vacancies at Palgrave and Sweetenham. And then I realised I wanted to do this quite a lot and couldn't stop thinking about the idea when the phone rang again.

'You were on the telephone a long time, very unlike you,' my wife said. 'It's quite annoying having to stand in the passage so long because Mrs Brigg doesn't have phones in her rooms.'

'Sorry,' I said, 'business,' and she began talking about her days burrowing in the archives and the fresh complications in Sir Scrope's amorous dealings which were coming to light by the bushel. And I thought of her standing in the corridor at the B&B in – where was it this time? – Wisbech, her shoulders hunched against the cold, and then I thought of Gracia again.

It would have been a surprise if much had changed at Padders in half a lifetime and nothing much had. There was a superior entryphone now, but dust still rose from the brown carpet in the hall and the same letters on the little hall table looked as if they had been there for months; the light on the landing still only stayed on for a few seconds before needing to be pressed again on the next floor and it was hard to see where the button was in the floral incrustations of the wallpaper. If I looked up the stairs coming up to the second floor in the old days I sometimes caught just a glimpse of Bobs's naked buttocks because the bell usually wasn't working properly so he had to come down to let me in and he was always in the bath because he was so chaotic and the bath towel always came adrift as he scampered up to the next floor to press the button.

Gracia liked all that. She wasn't one of those people who can't summon any interest in any story which doesn't concern themselves. There was a generosity about her which you were aware of the moment she started talking.

She sat opposite me on an upright old-fashioned chair that looked out of place in her minimalist sitting room with its square-edged squashy sofas one of which I was lolling on and an op-art poster on the otherwise bare walls. It was odd, I thought, that this was the first time I had had the chance to look at her full face, because in Tommy Ds we had been sitting side by side and when we came out hand in hand that was how we still were.

She seemed lovely to me, which is a clumsy way of putting it, but it is the way I put it to myself as though I were being asked to comment on the quality of some species I didn't know much about, like cocker spaniels or carrier pigeons. Come to think of it, that was more or less the case.

Her face was full, creamy, not fine but exotic like a flower you see only at night in vases or corsages. But she wasn't unnerving, her tangle of chestnut hair hadn't been brushed recently and she was wearing an old Yankees sweatshirt.

Yes, she was Australian, in fact very Australian because she was one-eighth Abo and what did I think of that? That's wonderful, I said, but she wasn't really asking. Anyway, she had been in London so long most of her friends from home thought she had lost her accent, which was quite something because she came from North Queensland. Her father had kept a small hotel on the Gold Coast, not the fashionable bit though. They had to close it for a couple of months in the year when the poisonous jellyfish came inshore, but it wasn't doing very well anyway because it was when Australia was having its own private

recession while the rest of the world was booming, and unfortunately
that also happened to be the year the jellyfish chose to hang around for
an extra month, nearly two, and the banks ran out of patience and her
dad ran out of road, and her mother just ran off and Gracia hadn't seen
her since. There was talk that she had gone back to her own people but
that was rubbish because she was only a quarter Aboriginal and even
that wasn't certain. In fact, she hated Queensland and had probably
gone back to Newcastle where she had been raised, or even Sydney.

'Didn't you look for her?'

'Didn't want to. If she couldn't stick with us when we were in
trouble, why should we bother to go running after her? Anyway she
was one of those women who can't get along with her daughter
because she doesn't want to get along, you know?'

She was quick, but only to forestall pain, not to put me down. She
said, for example, that I wasn't to be nasty about Tommy Ds, because
she could see I was only there to see what it was like and it wouldn't be
my thing at all.

'No, well, it isn't, but I was, well, moved. You saw that, I'm sure.'

'Yes, I did I think, but you were probably only moved because the
rest of us were. That's all.'

'I expect you're right.'

'Still, you could have been disgusted.'

'Disgusted – that would be a bit strong.'

'You probably are underneath, after the Alan effect has worn off.'

'Alan?'

'The preacher, the second one.'

'Oh, the preacher; well, he really wasn't my type.'

'You didn't like his talk?'

'No, not really.'

She looked sad. 'I suppose it's just aimed at idiots like me.'

'It's part of a series, isn't it? You probably need to hear the whole lot
to catch the thread.'

'No, you don't,' she said, still looking sad, 'you think it's just cheap
evangelism, exploiting lonely and vulnerable people.'

'No, no, I don't.'

'But there are a lot of lonely people, you know. Not everyone has a
wife and kids and all that.'

'I didn't say –'

'That's what a lot of people do say. But I don't think we're being exploited. I think we can do what we fucking well like.'

For me the sudden swear word was the equivalent of hitting one's head on an unexpectedly low door. On her it had the effect of cheering her up.

'That's part of its appeal, you know, going against the grain. I like being laughed at in the office.'

'Blessed are you when men shall revile you . . .'

'Yeah, they don't usually tell you how much fun that is, how you really get a kick out of it when some slimy toerag says here comes Mother Gracia and genuflects or crosses himself or some other bollocks.'

Her cheeks had flushed at the thought and she was quite unconvincing when she added, 'Of course, that's spiritual pride which is the worst sort.'

'The very worst.'

'Something nobody could ever accuse you of.'

'I am a byword for my humility.'

We smiled at each other. On her little upright chair she was enough above me for her downward look to seem quizzical or even flirtatious. She was wearing a black skirt, perhaps the one she had worn at work, and although it was not tight it had rucked up three or four inches above her knees and when she leant forward to pour me another drink (she didn't drink herself but she liked to have decent plonk in the house, she said), it was a struggle not to gaze up at the creamy wolds she so carelessly exposed.

Three or four minutes later we had both risen to our feet, rather awkwardly like worshippers who have been on their knees for a long stint of prayer, and we were kissing voluptuously, starved kisses, hurried as though there were only a few minutes to closing time.

'Oh, Gracia.'

'Yes,' she said, 'you do say my name so nicely.'

It was ridiculous, of course, utterly and totally absurd. I had always wondered what betrayal would feel like, perhaps most faithful people do, but at this moment it felt like the most natural thing in the world to feel Gracia's body against mine, her quick-beating heart, her warm damp cheek – it seemed much too simple to qualify for such an ugly word. And when we stumbled, still stuck together in a clumsy conga, towards the door to the bedroom the move was no more than a continuation which had been bound to happen from the moment I first felt her hand clasp my hand at Tommy Ds. We were going for it, we were full of life, we were young, or rather she was young and I was young again, no, young for the first time. How hesitant and awkward it had all been then, how free and easy now.

That was how it was, whatever it may look like written down, and nothing was going to stop it, certainly not banging my hip hard on the edge of the door as we two-stepped into the little white room. And as she tugged the Yankees sweatshirt over her head and I helped her to free her hair from it, I exulted in the certainty, the uncovenanted decisiveness which had come to me, come so late, too late but it was exhilarating to know that my lacklustre half-cock life still had room for surprise. All the old difficulties seemed to have happened to someone else – all those terrified fumblings, the one abortive night with, or as it turned out not with, Helen, the long knockabout but somehow also low-key affair with Gillian so rudely cut off and devalued by Joe's appearance on the scene, then marriage and all its private quiet pleasures. It was a career like many another, I suppose, not unusual for its time and place, but there had been nothing in it like this exuberant bustle.

She was negligently unhooking her bra and I was kissing her bare white shoulder when my eye caught the mirror on the dressing table behind her and I saw two things in the same instant: my face reflected in the mirror and a photograph stuck in the corner of the mirror. Let us start with the face: it was flushed and there were bags under the eyes, but what took me aback was that the face was so tired, so hangdog, so furtive. None of the zest, the freedom, the sheer exhilaration that I felt was there. All right then, if you must, an old face.

And then there was the photograph. It was a colour photograph, largish, nine inches by seven perhaps, she must have taken the trouble to have it enlarged. It was of two people climbing a sheer grey rockface against a brilliant blue sky, a man and a woman. They were in ragged shorts and skimpy tops with climbers' gear strapped round their waists and helmets on their heads. They were both deeply sunburnt, although the man was so hairy that you noticed it less on him. He had hair everywhere, it sprouted out from under his singlet and down his biceps. The woman had a red helmet and she was laughing as she called up to the man in the blue helmet who had turned his head from his hold in the crevasse to look down at her. The woman was Gracia. And the hairy ape with monstrous teeth who was calling down to her was Malc, the insatiable Reverend Malcolm Tedder-Brown.

One or the other – the photograph or the sight of my face in the mirror – I might have taken in my stride or at any rate survived to carry on the business, and how dearly I wished I could, if only to be kind to Gracia. But the combination stopped me in my tracks, lifeless, limp, catapulted from exhilaration to the lower depths in a moment.

I did try to be nice to her. What did I say? I don't really like to recall the tame, dismal words. Was it her or me who said perhaps, after all, we didn't quite know each other well enough yet, each of us being clear that after this we never would because this was something that had to be rushed into if it was ever to leave the ground?

We kissed a little more and said how fond we were and other things too which are too dim and false to be repeated. Then I left.

VII

Much Benham

The first time I had dropped in on Ian R-J at St Elmo's, three or four days after his seizure at my envoi, he was scarcely conscious, so I should not have expected too much. Even so, I was not prepared to see his old prune face lying so still and waxy on the eau-de-nil hospital pillow with a cock-eyed white turban protecting the spot where they had operated. If he hadn't shifted his head a fraction as I sat down beside him, he could have passed not merely for a goner but one who had already been tidied up for the rest of us to file past and pay our respects to.

'Ah, Gus, yes, yes,' he said in a sweet, faint voice, as though speaking of someone he had known a long time ago.

'How are you?'

'Oh, dying I think, don't you?'

'No, I don't believe it for a second. It's probably the drugs making you feel woozy.'

'Oh yes I am. Are you dying too, Gus?'

'Not that I know of,' I said.

'I expect you are. That's why you've come.'

His lips uncoiled a slow, seraphic expression, quite unlike his usual grim smile, and he closed his eyes.

'Of course he isn't,' the nurse said, 'he's doing very well.'

I dreaded going down there again, fearing that I might find the bed empty or the screens drawn up round it. Nothing of the sort. On the contrary, the next time he was wide awake and tetchy, complaining that the food was pigswill and the nurses were bitches from hell. He had come out the other side of the tunnel or returned to earth and I should have been pleased to see him back to his old form, except that this wasn't his old form. His ill humour was still raw, he had regained none of his languid, sardonic, confidential way of talking. He sounded as though he was pretending to be cross because he could not quite remember how to talk normally.

'It will be hell going back to those dogs,' he said.

Yet I remembered him trotting along behind the flat-haired retrievers as they squeezed through the iron kissing gate up to the Chiltern ridge and him showing every sign of enjoying the run as much as they were.

'I don't know why you've come,' he said abruptly, 'I've got no news. What could I have to say, stuck here?'

'Oh, I just wanted to see how you were getting on.'

'Well, now you can see I'm not getting anywhere. What did you expect? I'm finished, if I ever started.'

I didn't feel like listening to much more of this, so murmured how pleased I was to see him back firing on all cylinders and dropped the novel I had brought him on the bedside table (stopped reading years ago, he grunted, not even pretending to look at it).

'He's trouble, that Mr Riley-Jones,' the staff nurse said when I looked in on her on the way out. 'Can't keep a civil tongue in his head; a couple of my nurses won't go near him.'

'Strange,' I said, 'he used to be so easy.'

'It takes them in all sorts of ways. They can go through a total personality change. Dr Morfa believes that the new personality is often the real one, you know.'

'But physically?'

'Oh, he's right as rain. Had the haemorrhage in the best possible place. We'll have him up and running around in no time.'

Still, his abrasive manner did put me off repeating the experience. He was getting better anyway, I told myself. The whole ordeal must have been shattering, literally so. The old Ian would take time to put back together. I would go down and see him in a few weeks when he was ready for visitors.

So there was a little prick of guilt when the phone rang a couple of months later and Systems Sally said, 'Call for you. Someone called Riley-Jones.'

'He's an old friend.'

'Sounded more like a woman.'

'Must be his PA.'

Though I wondered what Ian would need a PA for, now he was retired, not to say half-dead. Still, perhaps he really had made an amazing recovery, as the staff nurse had promised.

But it wasn't Ian, it was his wife, Pam. She announced herself briskly as such in one of those telephone voices that proclaims a fixed dislike of the instrument and a determination not to be kept gassing for hours on it.

As soon as she heard it was me, though, her voice relaxed, rather charmingly. Would I like to come down to lunch very soon, next Saturday or Sunday, for instance. It would be just me, I said, because Nellie was away. She didn't trouble to hide her relief. Sad not to see Eleanor, of course, she felt dreadfully guilty that they hadn't seen each other for such ages, the dogs kept her a complete prisoner but as it happened Ian wanted to consult me about something, a professional thing, so it would be mixing business with pleasure.

'Does he want to be headhunted?'

'Something like that, but not exactly.' She laughed in a gruff sort of way and then I noticed that her voice wasn't relaxed at all.

Anyway, I said yes, vaguely wondering why Ian hadn't made the call himself. Perhaps she was keener on the scheme, whatever it might be, than he was. Or maybe he still couldn't be bothered to make his own calls. He always had been adept at getting other people to do things for him.

After I put the phone down, I found I was looking forward to the outing. By now he would surely be back to his old self. His foul talk and his lugubrious mien had always heartened me. Besides, anything to stop thinking about my disastrous evening with Gracia. My mind ran to and fro between the memory of getting dressed and bumping into each other as we did so, and trying to pretend it was funny and me just saying 'God, I'm so sorry' over and over again, and her saying 'No, I'm sorry, it was so wrong'. That was on the one hand and on the other nightmarish images of her blissful rock-climbing holiday (or holidays) with Malc, the hearty evenings in a real-ale pub, then the creaking bed in the B&B and the stifled laughter and the also stifled gasps of passion with the landlady down the corridor. And the next morning Malc looking out of the window and saying in his breezy way, 'Which do you fancy, pet, Helvellyn north face or an all-day bonk?'

No, a walk at the expiring Hertfordshire end of the Chilterns after a couple of drinks with Ian and Pam in the pub at the end of the footpath would be some kind of therapy, certainly the sort that Sir Edward Leithen would have approved of.

The normal routine when we were younger had been to take the Metropolitan train to the village halt and walk up to the pub, the Old Ben, where Ian and Pam would already be sitting in the corner of the snug, he with a large Scotch, she with a double vodka and tonic. So that's what we arranged.

But when I walked into the pub there was only Pam.

'Ian late as usual?' I said, I don't know why, nerves I expect. He wasn't a late person, rather unnervingly prompt, in fact. You would see his great gloomy face already bent over the file looking sage and knowing as you came into the meeting.

'No,' she said. 'He's not here, he's not coming.'

'Not ill again, is he?'

'I don't know. The thing is, Gus, he's disappeared and I don't know what to do.'

'So you –'

'I rang you pretending it was about a job because nobody must know he's disappeared because if he's temporarily lost his mind or something he'll never get another job and he'll never forgive me for letting it out.'

'But surely he's retired anyway. You must at least let the police know. They can ring round the hospitals and find out if he's had an accident.'

'No. He'll have had cards on him, he always does. I'd have heard by now. It's been seven days. And I want you to help me, because you know his mind.'

'Only the dirty bits of it. I don't really know what makes him tick. Who does, I mean, about anybody?'

'Well, if you don't, nobody else does. I certainly don't, never have. Gus, you're the only person who can do it. You can find him for me.'

'Look, Pam, I'm terribly sorry, it must be absolutely awful and I'll do whatever I possibly can to help, but I really don't want to get your hopes up and I have to say I think it would be much better if you went straight to the police.'

'No. I want you to give me a week of your time, full-time, and you'll find him. I'll pay any expenses of course.'

'Don't be silly.'

'I'm not being silly. That's what I want you to do. And you must promise not to get in touch with his office either.' She was speaking with some command now. Having given these instructions, some of the strain had gone out of her voice.

'And if I don't succeed, you will get in touch with the police?'

'The day after you come back to me, I promise. It's a lot to ask, I know, because you must be very busy. But I do ask it.'

There was something so fine and downright about her last words that it would have been impossible to turn her down even if I had wanted to, which I didn't. I could no more disobey her command than any of her flat-haired retrievers could.

'All right, I'll have a go, but it's an understatement to say I can't promise anything. I can't even think where to begin. Perhaps you could tell me a bit about how he's been recently.'

But she couldn't, at least nothing that seemed to lead anywhere. He had been rather quiet and depressed after he had come home, even more depressed when the doctor told him firmly that he really did have to take early retirement, enough to depress anyone. More recently, though, he had looked better and was bounding about in his old style (she might have been referring to one of the dogs which had been a bit off colour). They had planned to go walking in the Dolomites next summer. No, he didn't seem to mind being at home so much. He had painted the spare bedroom and he had joined a local investors' club, just an excuse for boozing and getting away from their wives, probably. And there was the bridge and the golf.

Suddenly I didn't want to hear any more of this and as we had finished our poached bream (the Ben had gone up in the world since my last visit) I suggested we take the walk as we always used to. First we went down the lane to pick up the dogs.

They started barking as we came up the gravel path, and you could see a couple of them jumping up and down at the bow window of the sitting room. As she let us in, the barking was deafening and we were festooned in leaping, wagging, panting retrievers.

'No need to worry about burglars,' I shouted.

'Oh, they're all soft as butter, this lot.'

While she was collecting dog leads, I looked round the sitting room. There were ornaments on top of the bookcase either side of the fireplace and a couple of landscapes on the wall. The room was perfectly comfortable. All the same, it was strangely impersonal. It might have been a place that was rented out to visiting executives, the owners themselves being overseas.

'No, no, you can't come with us, Kingsley, not until your paw is better. I can only manage three of you at a time.'

More barking as the rejected ones hurled themselves at the front door while we were sidling through it.

The low winter sun was only just above the hedge along the lane and it caught her face as we turned to go through the iron kissing gate that led up to the Chiltern path. She was a little flushed after sorting out the dogs and her hair was blown about, and for a moment she looked young and blithe and pretty, and although we did not have such a lot in common I felt fondly for her and wanted to do my best to protect her.

We came round the brow of the hill, skirting the last clump of beech trees, our boots stumbling on the sticky ground. There was now a golden light spreading across the long slope. The huge plain below us was beginning to fade into the afternoon mist, though the tops of some distant town were still sparkling near the horizon.

'How could he want to go away?' she said, holding back a sob in the middle of the question.

'Did he want to?'

'You think he was kidnapped? Oh, grow up, Gus.'

'No, no, I'm just trying to keep an open mind, for the moment.'

'I'm sorry that I – oh stop it, Basil, leave him alone. Basil, heel.'

We walked on in silence. Her sadness stretched out and enveloped me.

'Would you like to look through his papers?' she said, as she let me back into the house to a renewed chorus of yelps, growls and howls.

She led me into the study, a tiny box of a room with a leaded window looking out on to the laurel hedge that divided Broomiebank from the next-door house. It wasn't just that the room was tidy and dusted. It seemed immediately obvious that Ian had never spent much time in it. The bookshelf on the wall contained only a couple of dictionaries, and an old *Who's Who* and the first volume of the life of Field-Marshal Montgomery. On the desk there was a calendar from a local estate agent and the fixture programme for the Civil Service Golf Club and some bills, none of them very large and a couple of them receipted: dentist, tree surgery, garage for a recent car service on the Volvo. Wherever the centre of Ian Riley-Jones's world lay, or had lain, it wasn't here.

'This is as he left it?' I asked.

'Well, I've searched it for hours. But as you can see, it wasn't the sort of den that some men have. If he wanted to get away from me, he would go to the Ben, or he'd stay up in town at the Jordan.'

'Yes, the Jordan,' I muttered to myself as though she wasn't in the room. Up in town at the Jordan – what an old-fashioned phrase it was. You might have heard it half a century earlier, or even earlier than that when these villas were first built and you would go by dogcart through the bluebell woods to catch the steam train hissing down in the valley.

Ian had taken me to the Jordan a couple of times. It was an old establishment named after William IV's mistress, the indomitable actress Mrs Jordan, but founded years after her death. It lurked apart from the rest of the clubs, in a backstreet behind Hanover Square. As you came into its dirty cream hall with the porter behind his glass window, the smell of cabbage and overdone meat from the dining room met the smell of disinfectant – some old type no longer used anywhere else – creeping up from the gents, which had a grubby little barber's salon attached to it, though I never saw anyone having their hair cut there.

Ian told me it had always been like that, except for the first few years when the stars of stage and Fleet Street really did stroll in for a nightcap, and the waiters used to bring in the first editions hot from the presses and some famous actor had punched a critic for the review he had just written. But that had been only the briefest flash of glamour. In no time at all the place was invaded by unsuccessful businessmen and briefless barristers and public officials who wanted a club that was cheaper and a bit more raffish than the Reform. In fact, its dimness was what Ian had liked about it from the first, and he liked it even more when the dimness turned to seediness and the unsuccessful businessmen became unemployed businessmen and the barristers gave up their chambers and you could spend a whole evening playing bridge for low stakes, by which time most of them were fully cut because they had been there all afternoon, and he reckoned that on balance he made quite a few bob over the years, and he didn't mind their conversation either, although it wouldn't be everyone's cup of tea.

I set off for the Jordan at dusk. My plan was to burst through the creaky old glass double doors and stride on past the porter's lodge with a self-confidence which would repel questioning and so up the stairs to the card room before the porter could ask me my business. Luckily he was on the phone with his back to me, so by the time he turned round I was past him, flipping him a half-wave and a negligent 'good evening'.

The card room was a long dark room at the back on the second floor, smelling of stale tobacco and something like varnish, although there could have been no varnishing done there since World War Two. On the wall there were photographs and caricatures of men in suits and waistcoats, often with cigars sprouting from their lips or pipes cupped in their hand. Two men were playing backgammon by a spluttering fire with a third man, a little bald man, sitting on the arm of the chair, watching.

'Good evening,' I said with the same clubman's negligence, 'I'm Ian Riley-Jones's guest. You haven't seen him by any chance?'

'They shouldn't have let you in, you know?' the little bald man said. 'Not without your host.'

'Oh, I am sorry, I thought we were meant to meet up here.'

There was a frosty, hanging sort of pause, during which I became aware that all of them were drunk, soddenly so.

'You were going to play *bridge*, were you?' said the little bald man, as if he had made a brilliant deduction, worth at least a share of the Nobel Prize.

'That was the general idea.'

'Well, actually we were looking for a *fourth*.' Again this bizarre emphasis, suggesting that a fourth player at the bridge table was an unusual extra feature, perhaps deployed only at this particular club.

'I could sign him in, Geoff, couldn't I? We have to sign guests in, you know? There's a book' – he waved vaguely at a round table in the far corner of the room on which there was indeed an object answering that description.

'Silly rule,' said one of the backgammon players, 'but there it is. It'll cost you five pounds, table money. I can't think what they do with the money.'

'It was a compromise,' the little bald man said.

'What was?'

'The fiver. Some people wanted ten. Some people wanted nothing.'

'Did they?'

'Where do I pay?'

'You put it in the box,' the little bald man said as though this was a fact known to the entire population of the United Kingdom. 'Over there. Next to the book.'

'I'm sorry to break in on you like this,' I said, as we shuffled over to the green baize table in the other corner of the room.

'No, we need a fourth. If R-J's late again, that's his own bloody fault.'

'His hard cheese,' said the taller of the two backgammon players, a man who managed to be both cadaverous and red-faced.

'He's always late, that bugger.'

'You were expecting him, then?' I ventured.

'R-J? Not at all, not at all. Haven't played with him for ages, months. Not here anyway. Not anywhere, in fact.'

'Which one is Riley-Jones?' said the other backgammon player.

'Tall fellow, looks like a prune, needs a haircut.'

'Oh, him. No, haven't seen him for years. Cut for partners. What do you play?'

It was so long since I had played the game that I couldn't think of a convincing answer.

'We play no conventions here,' the little bald man said.

'That's fine by me.'

'And it's five shillings a hundred as usual,' he added.

'Shillings?'

'We stick to old money up here. Not downstairs, not in the bar. They caved in.'

'Bloody pathetic,' said the cadaverous red-faced man.

'They'll be doing it in euros next,' said the other man who had not yet spoken. He was skinny with a light-bulb forehead and specs on a string, and he chuckled to himself after he had spoken, a little stertorous mournful chuckle which didn't seem to expect much.

'My name's Grimwade, would you like a drink?' the little bald man enquired in a meaningful way that suggested there might be some linkage between the two utterances, the revealing of his name a necessary preliminary before the offering of a drink, perhaps required by club rules.

'Yes, thanks, I'd love a gin and tonic.'

Grimwade tore a page off the bridge scorer and wrote Gin and Tonic RPG in an upright rather elegant hand. Underneath he wrote XRPG, then passed the piece of paper to the other two who each scrawled an X and their initials. Then the tall cadaverous man limped over to the corner behind the table and opened a hatch in the panelling. He put the paper into the hatch and tugged at a rope. There was a distant creaking.

'Saves waiting for the bloody waiter to come up.'

'Truth is, they won't come up here any more.'

'Not after Glad left.'

'You could rely on Glad but with this lot ...'

A sense of infinite remoteness stole over me. We might have been becalmed at sea a thousand miles from land. The flip of the cards on the worn baize suggested the negligent flap of the sails, the noise of the dumb waiter the creak of the mast in a light breeze. No one was out there looking for us, even the vanished Glad would never waste a thought on this desolate crew. I imagined her safely back at home somewhere in Essex with a nice job at the local supermarket where there were human beings to talk to.

'You in the same line of business?'

'Same as what?'

'Same as that other fellow, what was his name?'

'Ian Riley-Jones.'

'Yes, him.'

'I am, or rather I was. Civil Service. I'm retired, now, we both are, in fact.'

It was, I think, the first time I had ever used the word, about myself at any rate, and it struck with cruel force. Originally I suppose it was meant to be hopeful. You retired for the night hoping to rise again the next morning, an army retired to regroup before launching a fresh attack. But that was whistling in the wind. We all knew perfectly well what we were retiring to get ready for.

'Funny he hasn't shown up yet.' Grimwade had drawn me as his partner and gave me a suspicious look that seemed to contain a glimmer of human intelligence. When all other mental faculties have entirely calcified, a little twitch of suspicion can still switch the lights on and I wondered if he was at least a quarter of the way towards blowing my cover.

'He doesn't owe you money, does he?'

'Good Lord, no.'

'Because that's a lost cause.'

'Why, did he owe you?'

'No, not a penny. But getting money back from him, you might as well –' He paused searching for a simile strong enough.

'Getting money back from whom?' said the cadaverous man with a good deal of lip pressure on the whom.

'Riley-Jones, fellow who hasn't turned up.'

'Oh, him.'

'A legend for it, was he?' I pursued.

'What, who?'

'Riley-Jones, borrowing money and not paying it back.'

'Oh yes, yes, one diamond, I think.' Grimwade's bald head was deep in his cards.

'You understand that as a Grimwade Diamond?' enquired the fourth man turning to me.

'Um, I'm not sure what a Grimwade Diamond is,' I said. 'I thought we weren't playing any conventions.'

'It's not a convention as such. He just plays it, nobody else does.' Grimwade looked immensely pleased at this attention.

'Well, what is it exactly?'

'I could not possibly comment,' Grimwade said.

'It means you have to go on to game in a major suit if you have more than twelve points.' The cadaverous man spoke with some weariness as though the Grimwade Diamond had caused trouble before.

Although I could barely remember the rules, it seemed rude not to respond to my host's invitation and I seemed to have enough court cards to qualify, so I bid on in a spirited fashion and we finished in Six Hearts and I went four down doubled.

'Thirty-five shillings down the plughole,' Grimwade said. 'I wasn't playing my Diamond. I only play it when we're vulnerable and we aren't.'

'Oh, I see. Sorry.'

'You could always try a detective agency, you know.'

'A detective agency?'

'To get your money back.'

'He doesn't owe me any money.'

'I say, you aren't a detective yourself, are you?'

'Certainly not, I'm a retired civil servant as I said.'

'I mean, you come in here, you're not a member, and you say you're meeting a chap to play bridge and he doesn't show up and you can't play bridge and you start asking all these questions.'

'You should have told him about your Diamond,' the fourth man said mildly.

'It didn't arise, we weren't vulnerable.'

There was a trundling, creaking noise in the corner of the room and the ropes visible through the still open hatch began to quiver and dance.

'Ah, here comes the cavalry,' said the fourth man. 'Same again while we're at it,' and he tore another sheet off the pad and scribbled down more Xs and initials, before going over to collect the tray.

They took their drinks from the tray with ceremonious gravity as though this were a rare event, one which perhaps occurred only once a year and demanded their full attention. Meanwhile the fourth man had sent the dumb waiter back down again with the fresh orders, which in view of the time it had taken for this round to come up was not such an absurdly premature move.

It was time to go. I waited until I was dummy, then explained that I was going to pop down to the porter's lodge to see if there was any message from Ian. As I went down the stairs, I was brought to a crawl behind a very old man who was clinging on to the banister. His foot seemed to hover for an age over each tread, as though he had perfected some drill for slow-marching downstairs, and after three or four such steps he would pause to review progress, catching his breath with a slow, rattling gasp. After a year or two he reached the bottom and stopped in his tracks possibly to give thanks, but I managed to dodge round him and strode on past the porter's little glassed-in box and out through the double doors into the night. After I had gone a few yards down the street, I paused to catch my breath; in fact, to take several breaths of the cold night air. It was faintly scented, I could not tell by what. I looked up at the leafless trees and down the street at the figure of a woman in a long flappy coat walking towards the square. And a feeling of being intensely alive, a feeling that was at once exhilarating and melancholy, swept over me and I thought of my father, both because he exemplified both sensations more than anyone else I had ever come across but also because he had a habit of stopping stock still when something caught his attention. In the country that was not such an odd thing to do – other people would often stop to catch their breath and admire the view or identify the bird that was singing in the hawthorn – but in London other pedestrians had to brake and dodge round him and some also wanted to stop and see what he was staring at, further jamming up the pavement before walking on rather puzzled because what he had been staring at might well be nothing more than an ugly vase in a shop or the woman on the zebra crossing who reminded him of a girl he used to know before the war. And that habit of dwelling on things, everyday experiences that slipped out of most people's minds as soon as they were over – cashing a cheque in Barclays Bank, a conversation with the man who kept the watercress beds down the valley – the recollection of that habit made me realise how much of life I had carelessly walked through.

Which made me think of another quirk of my father's. This was his insistence that there was always something to be gained from the most tedious encounters, however dull the company or unpromising the occasion. It might be some practical piece of advice – about preheating the oven or not planting a rose where another rose had been – or it might be some maxim about women and their old lovers or the bad manners of diplomats. And then I realised why I was thinking this. My hour at the Jordan Club had not been as wasted as I thought, Grimwade was right. Why not try employing a private detective to track down Riley-Jones? Odd, perhaps, that this thought had not cropped up earlier, but Pam had been so insistent about not alerting the police or doing anything that could let loose the impression that Ian had gone off the rails. But a private detective would be trained to the utmost delicacy and discretion, and even if the fact that he was making enquiries did by some mischance leak out, the impression given would be not so much that Ian had gone mad or defected (not that there was anywhere to defect to these days) but rather that he was mixed up in some minor domestic or financial squabble which might easily be sorted out. Pam might still not care for the idea but then, unlike with going to the police, Pam would not find out.

Better still, in the same instant that I remembered Grimwade's advice I remembered also that I did in fact know a reliable private detective, or at any rate someone who had seemed reliable and was now a private detective. Jervoise, the neat dark man from the Fraud Squad who had investigated the kidnapping of Joe and Gillian, had sent me his card when he had gone into business after retiring from the force. True, he had been on the creepy side, and his manner of knowing the whole case backwards before you had said a word was at best unnerving and more often annoying. But he knew his stuff, there was no denying that.

In his little office high above Regent Street I gave him the sheet of names and numbers that were all Pam could dredge up. It wasn't much and Jervoise looked at it with that faintly pitying air that I remembered from our previous meetings.

At the same time, he himself seemed to have undergone some buffeting. While he was still thin, he did not look quite so sharp. It was hard to tell whether the blow was a physical one – a major operation perhaps – or the familiar slackening and deflating that you saw in people who had lost the official position that had given them their edge.

'Shouldn't be too difficult,' he said. 'My terms are £80 an hour. Sounds a lot, but I'm quick, damned quick. You won't be disappointed.'

He peered out of the window with a suspicious look, as though he was already working on a couple of leads. It might have been this intensity that had made him seem creepy before. Now he gave me confidence.

'And expenses, of course, there'll be expenses.' That warning too gave me confidence with its echoes of private eyes in books. 'You'll receive a full accounting. Your old office is out of bounds, no way round that, I suppose?'

'None, she was very specific on that point.'

'Pity, it would be a doddle if we knew where they were paying his pension. Even so, it won't be long. When I find out where he is, what do you want me to do, finger his collar or just inform you?'

'Inform me, please.'

'You're sure about that?' He looked at me with that concentrated look and I thought I was right the first time: he was creepy.

'Quite sure.'

'Because sometimes the last thing on earth they want to see is an old mate and it's easier if a stranger makes the first contact, someone who's acting in what you might call a professional capacity.'

'No, just tell me when you've got a lead and we'll think what to do.'

As he had promised, it wasn't long: five days or so.

'He's been using two credit cards almost entirely in the Andover area. Petrol stations, a supermarket and a couple of pub restaurants, and he's drawn out a maximum at three cashpoints, so that's what he's probably living on. It's possible he hasn't given any fresh instructions to his bank or to the pension people.'

'So he can't go on like that for ever.'

'Well, he's got quite a bit of credit to use up on each of them, nearly three thousand quid. So he could hold out quite a bit longer. But in any case we had better get down there sharpish.'

'Because he might move on?'

'Well, there's nothing on either card in the last few days. So either he's using some other source of finance, or he's pushed off somewhere else, or . . .'

'He's dead?'

'Or taken ill again. We'll have to ring round the hospitals if we run out of leads.'

'I see,' I said. 'I'd better get down there as soon as possible.'

'You, sir? I think it might be better if –'

'No,' I said, with a certainty that surprised me.

'You sure, sir?'

'Yes, I'll call you if I need you.'

'It's your decision.' He was miffed and I couldn't blame him. My eagerness to take over did not come entirely from my concern for Ian and his fragile state of health, mental or physical. Even to my nostrils dulled by age and habit there came the distant smell of the chase, as acrid as the scent of a fox at the bottom of the garden.

The night before I set off for Andover I phoned Pam.

'Oh, I'm so pleased you rang. A dreadful thing has just happened, at least I think it must be dreadful and I wanted to know what you thought.'

'Pam,' I said, 'are you all right? You sound awful.'

'I was away at this dog show all day judging, which is about the only thing that keeps me sane, and when I got back there was this letter from the pension people, you know, in your office, telling me that acting on Ian's instructions in future they're going to be paying his pension into my bank account.'

'Is that awful? I mean, it shows he's thinking of you.'

'No, don't you see? It means he's, well, signing off, taking care of the little woman, while he goes off to whatever, I don't know, kill himself, live with some silly squit of a girl.'

I hadn't heard the word squit in twenty years and it affected me deeply.

'It could be just a thoughtful thing to do while he's sorting out whatever he's sorting out,' I said.

'But he planned it all in advance, they had my account number and everything. He's getting away for good.'

There was no disputing that this was what it sounded like. And I realised for the first time how much we had been placing our hopes in his disappearance being unpremeditated, a temporary excursion, a fugue which might end as suddenly as it had started, not a long planned, long dreamed of change of life.

I checked in to the motel next to a Little Chef off one of the roundabouts on the Andover bypass. It was drizzling but warm verging on muggy.

Pam had given me two photos of Ian. In the first he was laughing like a maniac in a dinner jacket. She could not remember what do it had been, but she was in the other half of the picture which she had cut off, she told me, wearing a strange purple dress which didn't really fit. In the other, a studio portrait, he was sitting sideways on in a chair with scrolled arms, pretending to read a book. Neither gave much impression of what he was like in action, but they would do.

What I had not bargained for was the way people looked at me when I asked them if they had ever seen this man. When they took the photograph from me, they gave me this piercing look as though to make sure they wouldn't forget me in a hurry. By comparison their inspection of the photograph was not exactly cursory but rather unenthusiastic, as though this was the kind of thing they were always being asked to do and it was a complete waste of time but they had to go through the motions. Then, handing it back to me, they would give me another piercing look to make sure they had me sized up. I started with the girl at reception who relieved the routine with a friendly half-giggle before and after looking at the photo. Even so, when she handed it back to me the meaningful look she gave me would have done credit to a TV detective. It was the same in the three or four pubs I tried on the way into the town centre and the two hotels in the high street: no, never clapped eyes on him; no, what an ugly mug, what do you want to go looking for him for, if I was his wife I'd be glad to be shot of him, and so on. One or two of my non-informants asked 'you from the police?' and were disappointed when I said I wasn't. The woman behind the counter at HSBC said she was not authorised to deal with this type of enquiry. The man at the Star garage told me he wasn't one for grassing up his mates.

It was a dispiriting day. And I wondered whether the whole thing had not been one of Ian's elaborate jokes. After all, would anyone starting a secret new life seriously choose Andover? Perhaps I had gone about it the wrong way. It might have been better after all to leave this section of the chase to Jervoise.

I rang him from my bedroom to report my lack of success.

He sounded unbearably bullish. 'Just as I expected, sir. The trail has gone cold. He was probably out of there after six or seven days. It all fits in.'

'Fits in with what?'

'I must warn you that my expenses will be rather higher than I had anticipated. My friend in Cardsearch is being most helpful. He tells me there's been no recent movement on any of the accounts, with one very interesting exception.'

He paused, waiting for me to ask what it was. I remained silent.

'A week ago he spent £23.10 at Swansea West Motorway Services.'

This seemed to me one of the less interesting pieces of information he had given me, so I said nothing.

'You don't get it, do you, sir? Swansea. Think. *Swansea.* What does that say to you?'

'Not a lot. Rugby, I suppose. Ferry to Ireland. Dylan Thomas. Didn't Kingsley Amis teach there?'

'Forget about your famous friends.'

'They aren't – weren't – friends.'

'Come on, sir. Swansea.'

'I give up.'

'Don't the initials DVLA mean anything to you?'

'Ohh.' It was a long oh that I exhaled, longer, perhaps, than Jervoise had been expecting but then it wasn't exhaled for the reasons he was expecting. Anyway, he was gratified.

'So you see.'

'I don't see at all.'

'He went there to get a new driving licence.'

But my mind was still musing on the coincidence, or the peculiar possibility that I might have been lording it on, let's say, the sixteenth floor with extensive views of whatever you have extensive views of from the heights of Swansea while down below Riley-Jones – frantic, desperate or perhaps even happy – was asking directions, filling in forms, queuing, doing all the things that mortals did in the DVLA. But then, on the other hand, why did he have to go to Swansea? Couldn't he have got one at the local post office?

'Come along now, sir.' Jervoise spoke as one herding a sheep through an open gate. 'He didn't want a driving licence saying Ian Edward Riley-Jones, Broomiebank, Much Benham, Herts, did he? He wanted a new identity and the best place to start these days is with a driving licence. Once you've got one of those new digi-cards in your wallet, you can open a bank account, get a credit card, rent a house, anything you fancy. And what else does Swansea tell us?'

'I don't know.'

'It tells us he's not going abroad, doesn't it, sir? Because if he was going abroad, he'd get a fake passport first and then the driving licence on the back of that. Whereas you can't get a passport on the back of a driving licence, you need a birth certificate.'

'I still don't see why he has to go all the way down to Swansea. Couldn't he just go to someone in Soho or somewhere?'

'Oh dear, you are out of it, sir. You can't get anything in Soho now except a dose of the clap. No, there's a little firm down there will do it for you, out towards the Mumbles they operate. You need to fix the software, see. Police thought they were going to nick them last Christmas, but they'd moved on. Five hundred quid for a forty-eight-hour job, sounds a lot, but it's the genuine article, so if you're done for speeding, you show up in the records, all proper and correct.'

'How would Riley-Jones find them?'

'Oh, everyone knows them, they're practically in the Yellow Pages.'

I felt a surprising little stab of envy at the thought of Riley-Jones setting out to get a false driving licence. Becoming someone else was a kind of resurrection, especially when you were getting on a bit. And the more upright a person you were, the more it must revive you. Buchan heroes used to do it and were always a little taken aback by how well they slipped into the new personality, and the reader was too because he had been told over and over again what a dry stick the hero was. Riley-Jones wasn't exactly like Sir Edward Leithen but he was fifty-eight years old with a wife and six flat-haired retrievers in Much Benham. And then I noticed that I had started thinking of him as Riley-Jones instead of Ian. Was that how hunters always thought of their quarry?

'Sir, are you still there?'

'Yes. So what do we do now?'

'You sit down for half an hour, longer if you can, and think about our friend, think forwards, backwards, sideways about everything you've ever heard him say or do, the clothes he wears, the people he likes and dislikes, hobbies, anything. Somewhere in there is the answer to where he is now.'

I lay on the bed, not bothering to draw the curtains when it grew dark outside. It was a strange exercise, like being a psychoanalyst (perhaps it was lying on the bed that made me think so). But after a few minutes I did succeed in bringing Ian to mind, quite vividly, in fact: that long, stooping figure, or not so much stooping as leaning his whole body to one side as though to get a better look at an object that was half hidden. And then his long face, like a prune was a crude way of putting it. In fact, there was something almost noble about it, dark and gloomy and a bit out of perspective like a Spanish grandee in the background of an El Greco, except that his sprouting black tangle of broccoliesque hair destroyed any possibility of the solemn.

I had the file to help me out too. Only s. of Mr and Mrs Godfrey Riley-Jones, educ. Eastbourne and St Edmund Hall, m. Pamela Stoddart, dau. of Dr and Mrs J. Stoddart, Wimbledon, no c. Then the dates of his Civil Service postings, the date of his CB, his secretaryship of the Wickham Commission on the future of the Rate Support Grant. What could be more blameless or give less away? Apart from the *Who's Who* entry, there was not much else in the file. Indeed, to call it a file was absurd. I had fitted it all into a single envelope: the details of his bank accounts, club memberships and so on that I had jotted down on my visit to Much Benham, two or three press clippings about evidence he had given to a select committee and – the only thing I had in his own hand – a note pointing out a filthy double entendre in what the Secretary of State had just said which he had slid across to me and I had kept because it made me laugh. Still, even these unyielding items began to lubricate my mind. 'Lubricate' – Ian would have done something with that.

VIII

Llandiwedd

'Darling.' It was my wife on the mobile, using the endearment in her awkward way as she always did, as though it was an unfamiliar word, possibly foreign, and she wasn't quite sure when it was correct to use it. 'Just to say hello and to say I've finally said goodbye to Scroopie; he's got another five years to live of course before he dies in dreadful agony, some sort of cancer I think, but I've wrapped up the diary. The last entries are really rather touching, but some of the references are a bit obscure and I'll have to go back to the BL.'

'That's great,' I said. I didn't want to hear any more about the Dudgeon Diaries, least of all when they were interrupting my important meditations.

'Longing to see you.'

'Longing to see you too,' I said.

'You're still chasing Ian, are you? It all sounds very odd. I don't quite see why you should have to waste all your time on someone you used to complain about.'

'Did I? I had forgotten' – which I had. My recollection was of endless jokes and asides and shared grumbles.

'You did indeed.'

'What about?'

'Oh, I can't remember, usual office moans.' She wasn't interested in my quest, but then I wasn't interested in hers.

'So when will you be back, darling?'

'Oh, next week, I expect,' I said, without thinking much about it.

'I don't think it's good for you roaming about the country in this peculiar way, not at your age.'

I didn't point out that I could have said the same of her, because if we went on talking about all this I could not trust myself not to give away how much pleasure I was getting out of it, a pleasure which she would surely diagnose as unhealthy and how could I hope to convince her it wasn't. So I said again how much I was longing to see her and she said the same, and we put our telephones down.

I sat on the bed and tried to let my mind return to the likely whereabouts of I. R-J. But instead of thinking about Ian, I began thinking about Nellie. How hard it was to remember what someone had been like when you first met if you had lived together so long. When I described her to other people – and it seemed odd somehow that other people were so eager to know what she was like, as though there was some mystery about her – the description I gave sounded not inaccurate exactly but as though it was being given by someone who didn't really know her. How did you meet, I had been asked, by Jonquil Fincher. Oh, at a party, I said, one summer in Norfolk. It was a barbecue, but it had come on to rain and they had had to move the barbecue indoors, into a barn. The place was owned by these cousins of Joe's who were cousins of Nellie's too, so they were distantly related – but then Jonquil broke in to ask me whether it was love at first sight and I gave some embarrassed answer and the thread was lost. Because to explain the whole thing it was necessary to set up the scene with some exactness.

The rain coming down outside. There was a row of poplars the other side of the track I remember and the rain was swishing through their leaves. And inside you could smell the damp wool of our serious sweaters drying off by the fire, and the sickly sizzle of the first lamb chops. We sat on straw bales in the mouldy half-light from the couple of bulbs strung overhead. Gillian had told me a fortnight earlier the news that I had been expecting anyway, that she was going to marry Joe, and they were not at the barbecue, because they had gone down to Devon to tell her father the Colonel.

So there I was, not knowing anyone much because the invitation had really come through Gillian and Joe, and sitting on this bale nursing my paper plate with a couple of blackened chops on it and one of Joe's or Nellie's Anglo-Catholic cousins with a big Adam's apple was trying to shake the congealed barbecue sauce out of the bottle. And this tall girl in an old mac sitting on the next bale said to me, the first thing she said to me, 'Do you know who invented barbecues, because I think it was a very bad idea.' I said it sounded French, so we invented Monsieur Barbecue who had been a doctor in Marseilles and who happened one day to leave a kilo of lamb chops out on his patio on top of some sticks which caught fire in the fierce sun of the Midi and the rest was history.

I liked her looks – the long face, the goofy grin, the sad eyes which she said were doggy but weren't really. Yet the way she looked was not the point, nor was that unusual gurgly voice, which sometimes sounded seductive and sometimes like the bubbling of a coffee percolator. What she had – and has – was a quality of being there, which is somehow a comfort, although ironically one of the social skills she lacks is that of knowing how to offer comfort in bad situations. Presence is, I suppose, the word for what she has, except that sounds too much like someone who sets out to create an effect. And nobody could be less domineering, either deliberately or unconsciously. In any case, she does not have the effect on everyone that she has on me. I am sometimes surprised – affronted would be a better word – when someone scarcely takes her in, treats her as if she is unremarkable. Because it seems to me that you could be wholly uninterested in the things she is interested in – children, old diaries, architecture (Gothic) and, an odd thing that never ceases to surprise me, sex – and still you would have to register her extraordinary quality. But then perhaps what I am describing so tortuously is a feeling that has a shorter name.

I came to with a jump. It wasn't my wife I was supposed to be thinking about. Her phone call had distracted me, or had it? There was something in my sentimental recollections which seemed relevant, some connection with the quest. Not a direct one, I fancied, because Nellie and Ian had not seen much of each other in the last few years. He and I both preferred to separate home and office life, an arrangement which seemed to suit both our wives. In fact, what she had just said suggested not merely that I had been in the habit of complaining about Ian but that she did not much care for him either. No, this connection, whatever it was, was unlikely to be a personal one, more an association of ideas.

It was something to do with the barbecue, that was it, the lamb chops. Years ago Ian had said something about lamb chops. We were sitting in the Cabinet Office canteen, we were only principals then, and Ian had said that the trouble with the Welsh was that they couldn't cook to save their lives not even a bloody Welsh lamb chop. Whenever he went to visit his aunties in Pontypool it took his digestion weeks to recover. But he had said more and then I remembered. Surprising it hadn't come back to me earlier, but then it was more than thirty years ago. What Ian had said was that when he retired he was going to take over a restaurant somewhere in west Wales where you could see the sea from and show his fellow countrymen how to do it. I remember laughing and saying something about him drinking the place dry and him being quite nettled and saying that he was perfectly serious.

That would explain Swansea, rather than Jervoise's convoluted theory about a fake driving licence. So it was partly the pleasure of proving Jervoise wrong that instantly decided me to head west without updating him.

The next morning I bought the *Good Food Guide* in the local Waterstone's, half-price because it was last year's, and set off for the Severn Bridge. The girl at Reception gave me a special smile when I checked out. As I was picking up my luggage, I saw her nod to the other girl further down the counter.

After I passed Cardiff the rain came on, a series of fierce squalls driven on by a gusting westerly gale, which sent the car bucketing out of its lane on the exposed stretches. I paused in a layby to have a look at the book. Luckily west Wales was still mostly a gastronomic desert. There seemed to be only half a dozen entries that might lure my quarry. He would be looking to take over an existing restaurant, I thought, one which might have three or four rooms as well, a place where you could leave your fishing rod in the hall and there would be a bookshelf in the lounge with mouldering guidebooks and tattered Agatha Christie paperbacks. If these were the right criteria – and somehow I knew they would be – then the only possibles I could see were:

Tir-Nan-Og, *Little Mussel Bay, the Gower Peninsula: Meaning land of dreams, these converted lime kilns nestle deep in woods full of bluebells and wild garlic. Locally landed fish and seafood are served in a large oak-beamed space hung with colourful paintings by Inge Trollson who also does the cooking together with her husband Lars, a former Norwegian marine biologist.*

Cliff Richard, *Govanston: Fulmars, guillemots and the occasional RAF helicopter from the nearby Rescue Station circle above Trevor Richard's former lighthouse perched perilously close to the edge of the 300ft cliff. From the seaward rooms there are spectacular views of Lundy Island. You eat sea bass and mackerel from the little bay, beneath photographs of the eponymous pop star. One inspector found the sauces 'samey' and there have been complaints about the noise levels (Mr Richard's resident guitarist is not to everyone's taste). More reports please.*

The Jackdaw's Nest: *Walls eight feet thick guard this old fort from the gales of St Brides Bay. Commander 'Tommo' Thomson presides over an extensive wine list, while his wife Alvilda cooks a surprising variety of Spanish dishes she learnt when they lived in Andalusia. The welcome is 'large and gruff' and the kitchen 'spotlessly clean'. The decor is eccentric, but the tapas are described as 'tempting'.*

By now the squalls had gone and the sun came out over Carmarthen Bay. Tir-Nan-Og wasn't at all hard to find. In fact, there were neat blue signs to it over the heathland and in the network of lanes leading down to the shore through the wind-bitten sycamores. The lime kilns were old grey blockhouses built into the low cliff. Their walls were decorated with pottery sculptures: grimacing masks, lumpy Easter Island heads and several baskets with flowers growing out of them. On the terrace in front a man with a pipe was sitting at one of the tables looking out at the sea.

'You're early,' he said in a husky, rather stifled voice.

'I'm sorry, I –'

'Don't worry. This is a pleasant time to sit and watch the oystercatchers.' He gestured with his pipe at the birds skittering about on the wet sand beyond the rocks. 'We open at seven,' he added after some thought, as though this was information he wouldn't release to all and sundry.

I sat down opposite him and, by now quite practised in the art, set about the build-up to showing him Ian's photograph.

'I wonder –'

'The bladderwrack is plentiful just now. They say that means a storm, but marine biologists cannot account for the phenomenon.'

'You must –'

'It may be something to do with the undercurrents, but there are many things we marine biologists do not know.'

Sometimes he spoke with his pipe in his mouth, sometimes he took it out. Neither seemed to inhibit his ability to hold the conversation.

'You like my wife's sculptures? There, on the wall, they are all by Inge. They are most popular. Sometimes I say she should leave the cooking to me and devote herself to her art. It is only a joke. Inside there are some of her paintings. Occasionally she sells them to regular customers, the paintings and the sculptures too.'

His eyes were clear speedwell-blue. His hair was tawny-silver. He must have been in his late fifties and become accustomed to mesmerising people.

'Look,' I said, 'I am searching for an old friend who has gone missing and we believe he may be somewhere near here.'

'Gone missing,' he said, 'that is a strange phrase. You find it in the newspapers, I think. But surely if you are missing, you must also be gone.'

'I have a photograph,' I said.

He slowly took the photograph and then slowly looked at it, in two separate actions as though instructing a subnormal class in how to perform this feat. 'No, I have not seen him, he looks troubled. Why should he have come here?'

'Because he loves food.'

'Ah, then he has come to the right place. You will dine here tonight. You may gather some clues but in any case you will eat well. There is no menu. I always say if you trust us to cook for you you must also trust us to choose for you.'

Inge's paintings were mostly landscapes with a few flower pieces. Prussian blue, orange and viridian were her preferred colours. She did not appear until the end of the meal, wiping her yellow-silver hair away from her sweaty cheek. She was even friendlier than Lars and asked each of the fifteen people in the restaurant whether they had enjoyed the meal. I went round after her saying I was sorry to bother them but had any of them seen a man looking like this? Everyone said they had enjoyed the meal. Nobody recognised Ian.

What we had for dinner was Carmarthen Bay prawns with a pepper-and-passionfruit coulis, roast guinea fowl with a guava and pineapple stuffing, and a swede-and-blueberry soufflé. Several guests, including me, commented on the interesting mixture of flavours.

There were more of Inge's paintings in my bedroom, notably one of Lars, or rather of a lion with Lars's head in a heraldic pose, passant rampant I think is the technical term. The paintings in the dining room showed a strong Van Gogh influence, the one in my bedroom was more Douanier Rousseau.

The diners had weakened my confidence. They were so happy and bustling and absorbed in their own affairs that it seemed impossible they or anyone dining there should ever have bothered to notice a lugubrious elderly civil servant sitting by himself in a corner, or not by himself as the case might be. The trail, if trail there was, seemed to be growing cold. But I had started, so I would finish.

In the morning I asked Lars the way to Cliff Richard.

He gave me directions with his pipe. 'You will find a very different establishment from this one. Mr Richard is Welsh, of course.'

The last bit of the road ran along the top of a bare limestone cliff between low shivering hedges of blackthorn and gorse. In the distance there was a helicopter hovering over an RAF installation. Through the open window I could hear the seabirds mewing overhead. Outside the back door of the low white extension to the lighthouse there was a man in shorts and wellies feeding a plastic tube into a bucket.

'Fucking drain's blocked again. I'm buggered if I'm going to get those Dyno-Rod boys out this time, cost you an arm and a leg, they do. You haven't got a set of rods, by any chance?'

'I'm afraid not.'

'Have you come about the estimate, then? Only I thought you were coming tomorrow.'

'No, no, nothing like that. I'm looking for a friend of mine.'

'Missing Persons Act, is it? Let's have a look.'

He wiped his hands on his shorts and grabbed the photo. 'Oh yes, yes, dear me, know him anywhere. Had lunch here last week he did, or the week before. Came with the Solihull Ramblers he did, or was he with that woman who complained about the toilets? Can't be sure exactly which party he was with, but I do remember him asking about the way we do the sea bass. Nothing to it, I said. Just bake it in foil with a few herbs, then dish it up with a sorrel sauce, but he insisted on having the recipe. And as it happens I've got most of the recipes on-line now because we're planning to publish them, the Cliff Richard cookbook with a foreword by the man himself. He's been here twice, you know, just loves it he said, you know for the peace and solitude. Anyway, the bloody printer was on the blink, so I had to write it out for him by hand. I can see him now standing by reception, waiting for me, tall fellow, last week or the week before it was.'

'Did he give you his name?'

'Well, you'd know his name yourself, wouldn't you? Oh, I see, could be travelling under an assumed name, nudge nudge, wink wink, say no more. Well, what I do remember is him saying you're a good deed in a very naughty world, Trevor – he called me Trevor. Said he hadn't had food like it anywhere in west Wales, not that that's saying much to be honest.'

'You don't know where he was heading?'

'I think he said he was going to try the Commander, you know, over at the Fort. I told him to take his tin helmet with him because if you get the old boy in one of his moods, whoo-err.'

'Thank you,' I said, 'thanks a million,' not bothering to keep the excitement out of my voice; in fact, starting off towards the car as I spoke.

'My pleasure, sorry you can't stop for a bite.'

The Fort was visible from a couple of miles away, a squat, greyish, many-sided box on the flat clifftop. Closer up the place was no more welcoming. Its cement flanks had half-effaced graffiti and were waist-deep in brambles. There was a muddy causeway leading over a ditch, also overgrown with brambles, up to a big door wide enough for an armoured car, with the green paint blistering off most of it but not off the square black and white notice which said The Jackdaw's Nest

Restaurant. There was a piece of paper attached to the notice flapping in the raw wind. I was trying to read what was written on it when I became aware of an elderly man in corduroys in the ditch below me. He was wearing protective headgear and directing the nozzle of a bulbous spray gun at the invading brambles. He shouted something at me which was inaudible until he pushed up his visor and shouted again, 'Can't you read?'

'I was trying to.'

'It says closed. C-L-O-S-E-D. Got it?'

'Yes, I'm sorry. I was looking for someone who recommended this restaurant.'

'Well, you won't find him here. We shut up shop when my wife first went into hospital.'

'Nothing serious, I hope.'

'Course it's serious. You don't stay in hospital for two whole bloody months if you've got an ingrowing toenail.'

'No.'

'Not that you can expect the bloody bank to understand. Little pipsqueak turned up without warning, found the place closed and told us they'd call in the loan unless we came up with another hundred thousand security. Where the hell do they expect us to find that kind of money in a place like this?'

He waved the spray nozzle at the line of gulfs and chasms that stretched away from us towards the distant point where Trevor's unwinking lighthouse or another just like it stood watch, or rather didn't stand watch, over the unforgiving sea.

'It doesn't grow on trees,' I said weakly.

'What's that?' While he had taken off his visor, his earmuffs were still half clamped on his flabby red ears. I suddenly noticed that he was on the verge of tears, perhaps had been since we started talking.

'Doesn't grow on trees.'

'Trees, what trees?'

'Money.'

'No, of course it doesn't.'

'I was wondering whether —'

'Look, if you'd like a place to eat, I suggest a place up the valley, Llandiwedd Farmhouse. Plain cooking, not too bad of its sort. Kept by a local couple. Welsh, of course,' he added, as though I needed guidance, or perhaps warning, on this point.

Somehow it seemed too intrusive to show him the now crumpled photo, also likely to lead to further misunderstandings, so I thanked him and followed the direction of his pointing dripping nozzle along a single-track lane going inland between high hedgerows showing the first of the blackthorn blossom – the season on this bleak peninsula being a fortnight behind at least – until we came down off the cliff plateau through steep twists and muddy farm crossings to an overshadowed valley and an old stone bridge over a stream with another lane beyond it leading upstream. There was water running down both sides of the lane, eating away at the eroded asphalt and grass and buttercups growing down the middle of it, and ancient trees, windswept oak and ash and thorn, entangled overhead.

For a mile or two which seemed like ten, the road led steadily upwards, crossing the stream and then crossing back again, until it came out of the trees and traversed a rushy meadow beneath a line of crumbly grey crags. At the end of the meadow there was a little village, surprisingly neat and painted-up considering the primeval scrub we had come through, and at the far end of the village there was a grey farmhouse, not much bigger than the other cottages, with yellow encaustic tiles framing the windows and a sign with a crossed knife and fork painted on it, rather crudely, and tulips and forget-me-nots flopping out over the path leading up to the porch. Some building work was going on. There was a small cement mixer perched at the top of the front steps and pots of paint huddled just outside the door.

The young man in paint-stained overalls was taking a breather sitting on the steps reading the *Sun*. 'Sorry, we're closed, for a bit of refurbishment, as you can see. Under new ownership, so we thought we'd do the place up a bit like.'

He had one of those strong metallic Welsh voices and a friendly look in his bright black eyes.

'It seems to be catching,' I said. 'I tried at the Jackdaw's Nest first and they were closed too. I think it was the Commander, he sent me up here.'

'Ah, poor bugger, he's really up shit creek. We were going after his place first, but he wanted too much. Anyway, turned out for the best, it's great up here.'

With a sweep of his arm he indicated the immense panorama, the woodland below sparkling green from our vantage point, then the widening valley and the cliffs and headlands beyond all glistening in the sun, even the Jackdaw's Nest looking passably romantic from this distance, and the sea glinting all the way to the horizon.

I sat down beside this friendly character to admire the view together, instantly drawn to him by his easy way, and it seemed perfectly natural to slip out the photo of Ian and ask if he had come across this old friend of mine who I knew was somewhere in the neighbourhood but I had lost the phone number of.

I had scarcely begun my spiel when he went dead white and his face set in a completely different expression, which even I could see was panic masquerading as indifference. 'No,' he said, 'never set eyes on him, to my knowledge that is. But then, the camera's deceiving, isn't it? I could have met him in totally different circumstances when the light was bad.'

At this moment there was a call from inside the farmhouse, it sounded as if from somewhere upstairs. 'Gladdy, you couldn't come up and give me a hand, could you?'

The young man made a startled sound, halfway between a gasp and a grunt, but couldn't utter a word.

I knew the voice immediately, had a strange, violent, thumping feeling which told my brain, quite falsely, that this was the very place, the exact moment where I had expected to hear it.

Receiving no answer, or none he could make any sense of, Ian Riley-Jones clattered down the stairs and came out into the sunlight of the porch.

If his voice was just the same, his appearance certainly wasn't. He was sunburnt, the creosote-brown of a Welshman in summer, and he had shaved his hair, not quite down to the scalp but enough to give his face a lean nobility you would never have suspected back in Whitehall. The scoop neck of his scarlet T-shirt made his head seem sculpted, almost imperial. Hard to imagine it could ever have been compared to a prune. Sunglasses were propped on his bristly crown and he was blinking partly because he was coming from the dark farmhouse out into the sunlight, but mostly because he was looking at me.

'God. You. I never imagined, well no, oddly enough I did half imagine that it would be someone like you. How did you do it? You bribe one of those hoods in Swansea?'

'No, no, I just followed the *Good Food Guide.*'

'Undone by gastronomy? But why this part of the world?' He sat down on the threshold and stretched his long legs out into the little flowerbeds.

'Well, you said once years ago you wanted to run a restaurant in Wales, somewhere near the sea I think you said, and the Swansea thing must have put the thought into my mind.' It sounded lame when spelled out and even as I said it I marvelled that I could have had confidence in such gossamer clues.

'Christ, did I? Actually it was Mr Gladwyn Williams who insisted on being near the sea, didn't you, Glad?'

'All the time I was working at the Jordan, see, I was dreaming of a little place down here. We're Cardiff, really, but we always went to Tenby or Aberporth for the holidays because my mam couldn't be doing with Barry Island.'

'We tried to find somewhere in Hampshire first, but then I saw – do you remember that little Air Marshal who came to your leaving do? – well, I saw him in Sainsbury's in Andover and I realised we'd have to move on a lot further.'

As he described their westward odyssey, I became aware that he was watching me, but not with any sign of anxiety or tension. On the contrary, the more he described their adventures, the more relaxed he seemed with his legs stretched out in front of him, carelessly crushing the tulips. He had the amused curiosity of a zoo visitor who has thrown a few scraps into the cage and is waiting to see what happens. The mention of my leaving party made me notice that any after-effects of his seizure that evening had completely gone. He had the carefree look of someone who has escaped from time, a honeymoon look you might say, except honeymoons don't usually turn out so easy.

'So,' he said, after he had finished explaining how they had taken over the lease from a retired couple who had run out of money because there was no passing trade.

'So what, exactly?'

'Now you've found us, what have you in mind? What's the next step?'

He spoke gently, but in the way he said it there was a little undercurrent – polite derision was how I would describe it. And it also had to be said that his relaxed *bienséance* was unsettling and somehow, without being unfriendly, established a kind of distance between us, a distance which had never been there before.

'I'll go and make a cup of tea.' The young man – I couldn't yet quite think of him as Glad – got up and stepped over Ian, patting him lightly on the head as you might pat a dog that was in your way but not inconveniently so.

'Do you have a posse down in the valley waiting for the signal to come and take me alive? God,' he added by way of afterthought, 'I hope you haven't got Pam with you.'

Yet curiously when he said this he did not sound at all panicky. It was more that this was the prospect he might be expected to be panicky about and he was going through the motions.

'No, no, nothing like that.'

'She did send you to come and get me, though, didn't she?'

'She asked me to see if I could find out what had happened to you, yes.'

'Well, it would have been rather unflattering if she hadn't, after thirty-five years of marriage. But somehow I didn't expect her to choose you.'

'Oh, why not?'

'I suppose I expected the police.' He spoke reflectively, almost wistfully.

'She didn't want it to be known that you had – whatever you had done. Thought it would damage your chances.'

'How sweet. Chances of what, do you think? I'm afraid she was still thinking of the K that never came. "We are much honoured to have Lady Riley-Jones with us to judge the flat-haired retriever class again this year." If she kept my disappearance dark, I might yet be called back and appointed director of, what, the DVLA.'

I did not feel strong enough to tell him that I had actually been offered this post. In the old days it would have amused him. Perhaps it would amuse him still. All the same I didn't want to tell him.

'Of course, coming out is bound to be covered by our equal opportunities policy. In fact, I'm sure it says somewhere that at least ten per cent of G1 posts must be reserved for registered poofs. So she could have saved you all this trouble and gone straight to the police and done my career no harm at all. Still, Plod might have taken longer, not being capable of your imaginative leaps. I wonder who gets the widow's pension, though. Do they split it down the middle, or is it so much per year of service, which would leave poor Glad penniless, unless the restaurant turns out to be a money-spinner, which I somehow doubt, don't you? One feels rather like Don Quixote up here, mistaking the sheep for an advancing army of customers.'

He waved at the bright meadow below us with the scattered sheep scarcely needing to move, the grass was so thick and green.

'But you've already made over the pension to her, haven't you? At least that's what she said.'

'So I have, now I come to think of it.' He spoke as of a trivial piece of business conducted years ago, on another planet.

'Anyway, I suppose I had better tell her you're all right.'

'You will, whether I want you to or not, won't you? You couldn't not.' For the first time, there was a petulant, almost sour note in his voice. 'I suppose it would be too much to ask you to restrict yourself to telling her *how* I am, not *where* I am.'

'You could tell her yourself,' I retorted, with the same hint of petulance.

'Yes, you're right, of course you are,' he said, suddenly friendly as though he had needed to get a rise out of me first. 'I was going to, obviously, at some stage. It wasn't simply that I couldn't face it. I wanted us to get settled first, to become a fait accompli, but we had so many false starts.'

Glad returned with the tea things on a pretty little wickerwork tray, hopping over Ian, who absent-mindedly stroked his leg as he passed.

'Well, anyway you've found us. In a way I'm glad,' Ian said.

'No, no you're not, I'm Glad. You're Ivor. Oy.' Glad did a comedian's freeze with outstretched palms.

'Ivor?'

'Ivor Rowan Jeffreys,' Ian said wearily. 'Had to be the same initials because I had all these monogrammed shirts. Don't know why I bothered.'

'Expressing your repressed personality, that's what it was.'

'Thank you, Dr Freud.'

As they bantered to and fro and even bickered a little, or pretended to, I puzzled over the change in Ian/Ivor. At first I thought that it was mostly an illusion, my own reactions – shock, prudishness, call it what you will – pushing me to discern alterations in him that weren't really there. And there was a touch of injured pride to be reckoned with, too. Here was a friend I had seen most days for thirty years and more, and all the time I hadn't had a clue what he was really like, what lay behind the filthy jokes, the rueful poker face. But it wasn't long before I decided that it wasn't simply my own jumbled emotions that were blurring my view of him. He *was* different, and different in a way that most people would have approved of: he was more open, less guarded. What you saw was all there was to get. And I was calm enough now to find this sad, because it was his wound-up, guarded persona which had made him so deliciously funny. Coming out hadn't cost him his sense of humour, but it somehow meant he wasn't funny any more. Or to put it another way, he was happy.

Happiness breaks up friendships. We notice other reasons for drifting apart – an unsympathetic new wife, a sudden absorbing interest in something that doesn't much interest you – but sometimes it is simply that the old friend is too happy for his company to give either of you the old pleasure. Perhaps it is an imperfection, dissatisfaction, even resentment in another person that draws you to them in the first place, some way of being ill at ease which you share or which somehow fits in with your own dissatisfaction and makes you allies against the world. To be happy is to go over to the other side.

Looking at Ian sprawled out on the doorstep among the wallflowers and blinking into the hot noon sun, I could see that he had taken his second chance with both hands and that one of the minor, very minor, consequences would be that we wouldn't be seeing each other much in future. At that moment it was Glad who seemed to be more on my wavelength, more sensitive to my situation as, curiously, I found I was to his.

Glad told me about the structural problems of the farmhouse and their difficulties with the planners because although it didn't look much it was Grade Two listed. Then he asked about my wife and where the children were, and gave every appearance of caring about my answers.

It wasn't until we had gone on to talk about the sort of menu that would work in a place like this – local produce obviously and not too much choice – that I became aware that Ian was bored. Not just bored with our conversation but bored with me, with my presence, my mission, with the thought of Pam and how he was going to have to deal with her. And he wanted nothing more in the world than for me to go. At that particular moment this was the only thing in the world he wanted and he wanted it very badly and, in his new, open, T-shirted existence, he didn't mind showing it. In fact, after a lifetime of suppressing his views and inclinations in front of everyone he met from ministers of the Crown to his wife and no doubt her flat-haired retrievers as well, he exulted in showing it.

So when Glad said he'd just go and cook up something to eat for us if I didn't mind a bog-standard pub lunch, I said that it was incredibly kind but I honestly felt that if I was to be in the office the next day as I had promised I really ought to be making tracks, because it was nearly three hundred miles.

'Anyway, ten out of ten, my dear,' said Ian, for the first time edging into camp. 'You've found the love nest and tagged the birds. Mission accomplished, I'd say.'

'It's not like that.'

'No?'

'So what shall I tell Pam?'

'Oh, anything you like.' He sighed. 'Tell her she'll be very welcome to come and sample our pigeon pie any time after Whitsun – that is our new target date for opening, isn't it, Glad? No, on second thoughts don't tell her that, I couldn't quite face it. Tell her anything except that I'm desperately sorry about the whole situation.'

'Why –'

'Because if I were, I wouldn't be here, would I? You could say I'm desperately sorry for her, which I ought to be, but she'd hate that because she can't stand being patronised. I've always rather liked being patronised myself, it's so restful.'

'If you're sure you won't stay?' Glad persisted.

'Quite sure, I'm afraid.'

'At least have a quick look around before you go.'

He showed me the long low dining room with the bare stone walls freshly rendered, and the curvy bar in the corner with the varnish still sticky-gleaming and the prints of local scenes – girls in Welsh bonnets by a waterfall, goats/sheep in a mountain landscape – not yet hung and stacked in a corner. From the little windows you could catch a sidelong glimpse of the far-off sea.

'Fantastic,' I said.

'We can't really get going until we've got the bedrooms up and running. At the moment they're still cowsheds and really grotty. They've got to be up to Tourist Board standard, otherwise the guides won't let you in. Once you're in the guides you're made. Takings here dropped fifty per cent after they got left out of this year's AA.'

'You'll be doing all the cooking, then?'

'Yes, I'm really looking forward to it. They never gave me a chance at the Jordan, said you couldn't go from being a waiter to a commis chef. It's been so great being with Ian. He really encourages me, you know, keeps telling me to experiment.'

'That's good,' I said.

'Well, what do you think, isn't it all splendid?' Ian said, leaning against the doorpost watching Glad give me the tour.

'Splendid,' I echoed, finding the word as odd on my own lips as I did on his. It was flung out with enthusiasm, an epithet as gleaming and sticky as the varnish on the bar. Not how the old Ian spoke at all.

So I trundled away over the hillside across the broad bright valley, zigzagging through the ancient woods. There was a breeze, in fact quite a wind getting up and the long ash branches rattled against the car, and now and then flicked through the open sunroof and brushed against the top of my head.

As I hit the coast road again near the bleak battlements of the Jackdaw's Nest the mobile rang. I assumed it must be Nellie. She had rung earlier that day and I thought she was on again to add something she had forgotten to say, about collecting some stuff from the cleaners or arranging some delivery. She was like that when she was away, often needing three or four calls to complete her messages.

But it wasn't her. It was Joe, though it took me a few seconds to identify his voice, which was thick and blurry as though he had a cold or was drunk or a bit of both.

'Where are you? Why aren't you in the office?'

'I'm in darkest Wales, by the sea.'

'You ought to be here, I can't get through this without you.'

'Get through what?'

'You haven't heard, you must have heard.'

'No, I haven't, I —'

'Gillian, you —'

'Oh no, I am so sorry.'

'She died early yesterday morning, about five-thirty or six, the doctor said, you know, OK.'

For a second, I thought Joe was trying in his slurry growl to tell me he was OK and rallying, then I remembered that the doctor was called OK after his uncle the priest.

The reception wasn't too good anyway and so I had pulled the car off the road, which was just as well because it was difficult to breathe and I felt faint as though I had not eaten for a long while. And then there rolled over me that great wave of sadness which only comes a few times in most people's lives, in my life anyway, a sadness which so drowns your mind that while it is passing you are not thinking about the person who has died, not thinking at all, but only being carried along tumbling and choking until it has finally passed. And when I did think of Gillian it was not of her recent sad and final days in Ireland, not of the glint of the syringe, or even of meeting her in her nightie in the passage at Drishill, but of the early days, the kiss on the fire escape, the bright pink woollen suit which we had laughed at, and her saying 'oh fuck this zip' as she tugged at it, then looking up as she was taking off her tights and saying, 'I'm not used to this kind of thing, you know.' And then later on, 'oh yes, you can, if you like' and the little hesitation before the 'if you like' as though even to suggest that anyone might like was presuming too much.

Joe was still talking, about the arrangements for the funeral and so on, and I wasn't catching all of it because the reception had faded again, but I did catch the word launch and thought for a moment that he was planning a burial at sea, which I would have told him wasn't a good idea, but then I gathered he was talking about the launch party for the new company, which was fixed for the same day and it was going to be a bit of a tight squeeze.

'You can't,' I said.

'Why not?' he said. 'It's the only day they can manage at the church.'

'Wouldn't it be too much for you, I mean?'

'I'll have to handle it.' There was a touch of complacency about the stoicism, I thought, but then he began to sob and cough again, so perhaps that was misjudging him. Still, he deserved a bit of misjudging and as he went on talking about his feelings I felt less and less sorry for him.

'Sorry,' I said, 'we seem to be losing the signal. I'll call you back as soon as I get on to higher ground,' though as a matter of fact I must have been parked at 500–600 feet above sea level. I started the car and roared off down the coast road with my heart knocking against my ribs, but this time pumped up with rage, not sorrow.

But then, as my anger eased, it came to me that there was Pam not knowing whether her husband was alive or dead and this was what I had driven 300 miles to find out. So I stopped again. By now I had reached the head of some narrow valley where the black scree tumbled down to the edge of the road, or perhaps it wasn't scree but the spoil from old mineworkings, because there was a bleak row of derelict miners' cottages just opposite me and a chapel with sludge-coloured streaks from the rain down its cement façade. It had come on to rain a few minutes earlier and the scree was shining wet already.

Naturally I told her first that he was alive and extremely well, and she tried to sound merely cheerful at the news, no more ecstatic than if she were hearing that one of her dogs had won Highly Commended at a show, but she couldn't quite manage it. In fact, her voice quavered and then broke. It seemed an age before she could control herself to ask for more. I had decided to do this whole bit in one breath, to avoid a drawn-out Q and A session.

'He's running a restaurant up in the hills in west Wales, or rather they haven't opened yet because it needs a lot of doing up. He's in partnership with a chap from Cardiff who knows the area well,

Gladwyn Williams, who used to be a waiter at the Jordan but has always longed to be a chef; he seemed very nice, full of enthusiasm.'

It has to be admitted that it came out oddly as though I was playing one of those party games in which you have to smuggle in a particular word or phrase without the other players noticing. Even so, I was unprepared for her reaction.

'Gus, don't be so bloody stupid. Do you imagine I didn't know? You must think I'm a complete halfwit.'

She was fully back in control and in a fury.

'Pam, I wasn't trying to hold anything back, I really wasn't.'

'People like you think because you're so sophisticated that nobody else has a clue what's going on.'

'No, honestly, I assure you.'

'You don't have any idea what some women have to put up with. Just because that goofy wife of yours has her head buried in the library the whole time, you can lead the life of Riley – or Riley-Jones, ha. Were you in on it? I expect you were, being all sympathetic and helpful and knowing all along what he was up to.'

'I certainly was not,' I said, catching a gust of her rage, 'and if you knew all along yourself, why the hell didn't you tell me?'

'Firstly because there are thirty million men in this country so how on earth am I meant to know which one he's buggered off with – buggered, ha – and secondly because it's so humiliating. Even you must see how humiliating it is.'

'Yes, of course it is, I'm so sorry,' and I began seriously trying to appease her, all the while gaining the curious feeling that she had not really known or that if she had ever had any inkling about Ian it had been long buried under the vast debris of their life together. Perhaps he had said something to her when they were first married, assuring her that it was a stage he had grown out of, and she had found it easy to believe him, thinking that most men who had been to English boarding schools had to make similar confessions when they got married.

'Could you give me the details?' She sounded calmer now though still unforgiving, continuing to give the impression that I was, if not in cahoots, at least indirectly responsible for Ian's defection.

'Well, I never got the phone number.'

'I don't want the phone number, he'd just put me off, say it would be inconvenient at the moment but perhaps at a more propitious time. God, you can't live with a civil servant this long and not know how they can put anything off if they don't fancy it. What I want is the address, please.'

'If you're thinking of going up there, I'm not sure that's such a good idea. They're not quite ready for ...' I tried to think of a phrase to describe their unreadiness.

'Of course they're not ready for me. That's why I'm going. Do you expect me to sit at home and wait for their lordships to finish their canoodling?'

'No, no, I don't.'

And it was true, I didn't, although I had only just realised it. I had not the least desire to prevent her from storming up through the valleys and invading their Shangri-La. I had nothing against Glad, knew nothing of what tribulations he had been through before he reached the old stone farmhouse on the bright green hillside. But I didn't see what special right Ian had to enjoy his great good place unmolested. I felt no duty and even less inclination to act as the guardian of his privacy. It was easy to be sentimental about someone who had seized his second chance and found that green place high up in the hills, but lower down, back in the smoke, there were casualties who had their rights too. I was almost as angry with Pam as she had been with me, but I was now angry with Ian as well and wished she would stop displacing her rage and direct it back at its proper target.

'All right, then,' I said with immense weariness, 'you go up there and fight it out between you. It's in the Upper Cwch Valley, it's called Llandiwedd Farmhouse and it's in last year's AA guide but under different management.'

The rain was coming down hard now and there were more sludge streaks down the front of the chapel. It must rain a lot in Ian's Shangri-La too, I thought with satisfaction. In fact, it must have rained a lot in the original Shangri-La and in that green valley of Buchan's as well. The two words 'earthly' and 'paradise' didn't go together, they were a contradiction in terms, the oldest oxymoron in the book, look at the Garden of Eden.

IX

Snakes

'Who's Gracia?'

'Gracia?'

'Don't pretend you don't know.'

'Of course I know. She's a girl who works in personnel, not with us, at a place called Palgrave and Sweetenham.'

'She doesn't sound like a girl in personnel.'

'Well, she is. Anyway, how do girls in personnel sound?'

'Why does she keep ringing you at home? Just tell him it's Gracia, she says. She doesn't say anything about Palgrave and Sweetenham. She just says it's Gracia, he'll know what it's about.'

'As it happens, I met her with Joe and the rest, at this church they all go to.'

'She doesn't sound churchy either. She's all breathy, like Marlene Dietrich.'

'She's not at all like Marlene Dietrich. She's probably never heard of her.'

'I didn't say she'd heard of her. I just said she sounded like her.'

'Anyway, she doesn't look like her, not at all.'

'Well, there's her number.' Nell held out the yellow Post-it with a jerky, almost violent distaste, adding, 'But I expect you know it already.'

Nell doesn't often display common resentments and when she does she acts as if some evil homuncula had seized control of her body. Her voice, which is normally fluid, even gurgly, becomes dry and awkward, close to barking, and her movements which are so careless and sprawly go stiff. It is not a pretty sight and I try to edge her out of her suspicions especially when, as here, they are not all that misplaced. But something else was already on her mind which prevented any such sly manoeuvre.

'You don't expect me to go to this funeral, do you?' she said.

'No, no, of course not. You scarcely knew her.'

'I didn't know her *at all*. I don't know when you thought I could have met her.'

'No, of course, they were in Ireland for years really, I keep on forgetting.'

'Didn't stop you zooming over to see her three times,' Nell said.

'The first time was so long ago, just after he'd been ill. And the second time it wasn't her I went to see. The Finchers fixed it without asking me, I told you. Then the last time it was because she was ill, to give her the money.'

'You can't have forgotten where they lived, you're so good at geography.'

'I didn't realise it was quite so close to Francie's. Anyway –' I trailed away, not quite able to finish whatever further lie I had in mind.

'Anyway what?'

'Well, I won't see her again at any rate.'

'No, you won't. It must have been a sad end.'

'Yes, it was, very.'

'She was the sort of person who always gets badly treated. From what you say, I mean.'

'Yes, it seems so.'

'Not my sort, you said once.'

'Did I? I don't remember. Why did I think that?'

'You said she was too hearty for me.'

That had the ring of truth, that I could have said it, I mean, not that it was the right way to describe her. The last few times I had seen her I would have used quite different words: eager and heroic, for instance.

'Did I?'

'As a matter of fact I'm rather good with hearty people,' she said. 'I'm a sort of suppressed hearty myself, really.'

That might have been true too and at another time, a cooler time, it might have been pleasant to muse on the possible similarities between

Nell and Gillian which had attracted me, the awkwardness in the way they moved and how they started talking with an eager rush, though what they talked about was not at all the same. But this was not the time for that kind of musing. In fact, I didn't think it was the time for Nell to be musing about Gillian at all, or about herself, come to that. She might have thought so too – we thought the same about a lot of things, which was why she went on doing it, irritated by the sight of my gloomy face. And you couldn't blame her either. Old lovers should be mourned privately or not at all. There is no way of being sad about them which does not suggest that something was lost all those years ago that has never been quite repeated or repaired.

'Well, you had better be going,' she said grimly. 'Is that tie really all right?'

'We were told to wear something pink. It was her favourite colour.'

'Was it? I still think black's better for funerals.'

'So do I.'

My agreeing did not much mollify her. I slunk out the front door with a curious sense of shame.

Joe had chosen St Thomas Didymus for the send-off, which I thought was a mistake because it was such a draughty great barn and after living so long in Ireland she was unlikely to have that many friends. Also, I could not see why he had fixed it for a quarter to one when any marginal mourner might be setting off for a lunch date. But to my surprise, when I swung open the great door there was quite a throng, not so many as at the normal services but still something approaching seventy or eighty people and all of them decked out in the recommended pink or what they thought of as pink.

It was not so often now that the lectures of the philosopher W. R. Scrannel (1911–1966) – vulgarly known as Scrannelogues – floated through my head, but his discourse on colour had always stuck in my mind. I remember him leaning forward, clutching the lectern with his gown sleeves hunched round him like eagle's wings and his dry voice rasping out the word 'colour' in that way of his that suggested both amusement and contempt. Why is it, he continued – at least so my memory roughly reconstructs his words – that philosophers are so eager to dabble in those treacherous waters? What is it that leads them to baffle their brains – and ours – with such questions as 'what colour is an apple really'? For what could be at once clearer to us and more mutable than the colour of a thing? An apple may be ripe or unripe, it may be seen in shade or sunlight, it may be impregnated with chemicals to enhance or alter its colour, it may be a Worcester, or a Cox's or a Granny Smith. And the way we talk takes full account of all these possibilities: we will say 'it looked reddish but the sun was on it at the time', or 'I believe they are naturally green but these days they put arsenic in them to make them redder', or even 'that's not what I call red'. But we do not despair because we cannot find certainty in these matters. On the contrary, we would chafe at the limits of our language if it could not permit us to say all the things we mean. It seems also to escape the attention of my colleagues – Ayer being by no means the only offender – that we do not fume impotently when we encounter some impediment to express our meaning. On the contrary, we devise, often rapidly and with a remarkable fertility, a whole host of alternative routes: we build new grammatical and syntactical devices to modify or complicate the bald statement, we lard it with adverbs, and we pluck nouns and adjectives from that abundant orchard which offers an endless supply of analogy and metaphor. At the dawn of language we are already hard at work: the sea is wine-dark, the dawn is rosy-fingered. And as for defining redness, why dally on such an unrewarding task when we have rose, pink, scarlet, crimson, vermilion, mauve, madder, fuchsia, cerise, even lobster to choose from?

Scrannel would have been delighted to see what a various response the simple command 'please wear something pink' had had on the congregation and I, too, was happy to see such a garish array and felt ashamed that I had been so prim when Joe first told me about the plan. The clash of colours did, after all, convey something of Gillian's awkward vivacity. Some of the women were wearing hats she might have worn – great strawberry-mousse cartwheel brims which you had to duck under and twist your head round to kiss the wearer of or pert blood-red toques with a mangy feather sticking up. And just in front of the seat I took there was a big girl wearing an old-fashioned hairy wool suit of blush-pink which was eerily like the suit G had worn the day she had come down to see those gangling cousins of hers with their Adam's apples and their boomy laughs, the day we first met and had that smoky kiss on the fire escape (how smoky kisses were then, before purity got to us). The big girl turned to say something to the man sitting next to her and for the smallest possible moment in my dazed state something about her, perhaps the way she nodded as she smiled a greeting, her exuberance held back by the sadness of the occasion, I thought that it was actually Gillian – no, not thought, it didn't qualify as a thought, it was one of those missed heartbeats during which some weird illusion leaps and blazes inside you until reality douses it again.

But even when I had managed to get hold of myself I was still much moved by the sight of this congregation in all its ruby and salmon and brick and raspberry dazzle. How young and fresh they looked. What a gift for friendship she must have had. It was extraordinary to be tucked away in the bog and to be remembered by so many people.

Across the aisle, just at that moment, I saw a woman give a little wave in my direction. For a second I thought she must be waving at someone else, then realised that under the prawn-pink beret crushing her chestnut curls it was Gracia. I did not feel embarrassed in being so slow to recognise her since there was no reason to expect her to be there. So far as I knew she had never met Gillian. I was about to get up and go over to her, but she was quicker and was squeezing in beside me before I had time to move up along the pew.

'Isn't it a brilliant idea everyone wearing pink?' she said. 'I was a bit doubtful when they told us, but it looks so cool.'

'Us?'

'Oh, Malc said at the study group. Everyone was so keen to come, you know, to support Joe.'

'You mean, these people didn't actually know Gillian?'

'Well, she lived in Ireland, didn't she? She sounds such a nice person and Joe's fantastic, so we wanted to do what we could, to be solid.'

'I see,' I said.

'You're unhappy, I can tell,' Gracia said, with a sweet, furrowed look. 'It's awful to lose a really good friend, isn't it? Joe said you used to go out together, before he came along.'

'He didn't.' I was unable to stop myself gasping these words out.

'Yes, he did. What's wrong with that? I mean, it was a long time ago, before everything.' She trailed away a bit, not wanting to specify the everything and looked expectantly up at me. But there seemed no way of explaining to her how indecent I found his telling her.

'Anyway,' she said, 'what's wrong with people coming to funerals of people they don't happen to know? We're all brothers and sisters in Christ, aren't we?'

At that moment they brought the coffin in and to my surprise I found Gracia's piety a comfort, because it somehow drew me away from the thought of the body inside being all the things it so conspicuously wasn't in life, such as cold and silent.

It also distracted me from the sight of the Reverend Malcolm Tedder-Brown leading the coffin up the aisle. I had not seen Malc in surplice, gown and dog collar before. He looked sombre, Victorian, the sort of rugged, undaunted priest who could have brought God to lesser breeds without the law (which I suppose is what he was still doing). In theory, Gillian might have got on with Malc – their language was equally filthy for one thing – but it suddenly came back to me that she had a quiet but settled loathing of organised religion and vicars too, so it was odd that Joe should have arranged for us all to be standing here with heads bowed while Malc told us that we brought nothing into this world and it was certain we could carry nothing out, though she herself would not have thought it odd because she said it was the one thing her mother and her husband had in common: that they never listened to a word she said.

Talking of which, there was the blubbing husband following the coffin, his freckled stubby fingers clutching a hankie to his swollen red face, and his gait stumbling again as it had been just after his stroke, or perhaps that was just how it seemed to me by comparison with the measured tread of the undertaker's men. His puffy chin nestled in a kipper tie of flagrant puce. He would have liked to wear his old salmon-and-cucumber Garrick Club tie, he told me, because he and Gilly used to have such great dinners there but they asked him to resign when he fled to Ireland and he didn't feel like asking if they would have him back now.

Thinking about this curious pudeur of his (in the old days, if he had wanted to wear the tie he wouldn't have given a damn whether he was still a member or not), I failed to notice until he was halfway up the aisle that he had a companion on his far side, her slight figure mostly blotted out by his stumbling bulk. He paused for a moment, to catch his breath perhaps, and she went on half a pace so that I could see it was Jade. Almost alone in this congregation she was wearing black, a long shiny mac the colour of wet coal. In this desperately cheerful clash of a dozen shades from coral to near-crimson, she stood out for both chic and seriousness. It was as though she alone was up to confronting death while the rest of us were merely making clumsy efforts to keep our spirits up.

Well, he needed support and she was his business partner – more than that, she was our public face. The name Jade – just the one word, like a Brazilian footballer – as well as that soft enigmatic oval visage was what people thought of when you mentioned the company name. She was the partner of partners and it was only natural that without any other family around it was she whom he should choose to lean on at this sad moment. Perhaps it was only because I had had so much of his talk about her and had believed so little of what he said that I found the sight of them together so repellent. Even if he was telling the truth – that he was much distressed by all the gossip that he was having an affair with her – then they should not have been parading up the aisle together, putting the thought into the minds of people who would not otherwise have thought it.

But that was not the worst of it. As the funeral service released its terrible messages – the messages of hope were scarcely less alarming than the dust-to-dust and ashes-to-ashes – my own thoughts would not stick to the text but ran off into old paths that were better blocked off, sweet indecencies that had not been revisited for years like the time Gillian and I had been driving through the high lanes above her father's damp old house in Devon and her hand was absent-mindedly stroking my thigh and happened to stray across and start stroking there instead, and a van coming the other way nearly hit us and I said we had better stop and she said I had to go on because this was the Advanced Driving Test and she was determined I should pass it.

The wake was in the church hall next door, another draughty barn. What it had, which the church didn't, was a smell, not the usual church hall smell like polish or disinfectant, but stale-sweet and a little heady like the smell from a distant brewery.

'Ah, there you are, a friendly face, we were looking for you in the church.' Jonquil Fincher smacked me with a kiss and cuddled me to her warm bosom. Francie too gave me a hug. There was nothing of Mr Justice Fincher about him now, the tears were scarcely dry on his ruddy cheeks.

'So sad, so sad, pity we didn't know about wearing pink, she'd have liked that, so she would.' The words rushed out of him.

'It's wonderful you came over,' I said and it was. The two of them standing there so grief-stricken reduced me to tears again but also cheered me up.

'We wouldn't have missed it for the world. She was going to come over herself, you know, if her health would stand it, said she wasn't going to miss out on the great day.'

'What great day?'

'Oh, come on, Gus, don't be so modest. The floating or launch or whatever you call it. I've never seen the like of it. You can't turn the page in the Irish papers without seeing a picture of that girl, what's her name, Jade? She's just as lovely in the flesh, isn't she? Such a nice touch her walking up the aisle with Joe, wasn't it?'

'Yes.'

'And it's today isn't it? What a terrible irony it is that you should be burying the poor soul the very same morning.'

'Cremating, actually.'

'Oh, yes, I remember now, she told me she'd prefer to be a puff of smoke floating through the air, because I had said I'd rather be laid in good old peat so they could dig me up in two thousand years and put me in a museum perfectly preserved only with my figure improved as the Bogwoman of Ballyturbet.'

'Jon, dear, you're being morbid.'

'That's what funerals are for, Francie Fincher.'

'One very nice thing Gillian did for us was to ring up Joe and get him to reserve us a block of the shares. With luck he thought he might be able to let us have 20,000 and, as it so happens, the lump sum from my pension scheme turned up last week, so we'll be able to take them all up.'

'Capitalists at last, isn't it wonderful?' She struck a haughty pose beside her husband and he smiled at her, that patient, kindly smile I remembered so well.

'Now, now, we mustn't keep you. You must have a hundred friends to talk to, what a charming young crowd it is. She had such a gift for friendship, you could see that the moment you met her.'

I didn't feel like explaining how the congregation had been recruited. Some of them were already leaving to get back to their offices. One or two nodded or smiled at me as they shook hands with Joe, recognising me perhaps from the couple of times I had been to Tommy Ds, but they were all strangers to me. I drifted back towards the table at the far end where the coffee and sausage rolls were being dispensed.

'Didn't they look sweet going up the aisle together?'

'Oh, Trull.'

'I didn't see you in church,' he said.

'I was at the back.'

'There was a place reserved for you at the front, next to me, as it happens. Apart from Joe, there were only a few cousins up from Devon and an aunt of sorts, so as an ex-stepfather I was almost the next of kin. In fact, Joe asked me to read something but I thought better not. We didn't exactly see eye to eye, my wife's daughter and I, and in any case he wanted that piece about the departed only being in the next room and I suspect she's gone quite a long way away, don't you?'

'I had forgotten you didn't get on with Gillian.'

'Well, towards the end we did agree on one thing which was that her mother was quite impossible, but it wasn't enough of a bond to cement a lasting friendship. I never think cement is exactly the right material for bonding, do you? It sounds so awfully heavy.'

It would take more than a stepdaughter's funeral to suppress Trull – even a stepdaughter who was probably only five years younger than he was. All the same, he seemed less than his usual self. Perhaps it was the pale-pink tie he had on, or because he had taken to wearing contacts, but he had a bruised and shifty look which reminded me of how he had looked just after coming out of Thursby. I asked him something about the evening's arrangements, but he didn't appear to take it in, then said he had to be going for precisely the reason that I had asked him about and left me almost in mid-sentence, which was even more unlike him, his habit being to finish a conversation with a rounded *mot* of some description.

But by now most of the mourners had left or were leaving. Quite soon there was nobody much in the hall except Jade and Joe and me, with the caterers collecting up the glasses and disposing of the uneaten sandwiches with a certain lack of delicacy that seemed in keeping with the bleak proceedings.

'Well,' Jade said, 'it must be very sad for you too.'

'It is. Very.'

'Does it happen a lot, do you think, two guys taking out the same woman and staying friends for ever? I mean, you're sad together now because it's so awful, but there must have been times when you resented Joe, or perhaps he resented you because you were first? I know I shouldn't be saying this, but somehow funerals make you say things you wouldn't normally say.'

'So I see.'

'I'm sorry, didn't mean to upset you. Don't pay any attention to me.'

'I won't.'

But it was difficult not to, as she stood there gazing at me with her steady big eyes, holding her glass of mineral water in front of her with both hands as though taking part in some religious ritual, not in the slightest embarrassed by the effect her chatter had had on me.

'Please don't clam up on me. I know men are from Mars and all that crap, but I do want to help, I really do. She sounds such an unusual person and Joe is so desperately sad, you know, about everything.'

I couldn't miss it now, the proprietorial note. She was the authorised interpreter, the one with the inside track if you wanted an update on Joe's innermost thoughts and feelings. Certain parts of the terrain might require further mapping, such as why he had stayed married so long to this strange ill person in Ireland and, come to that, if there was research time available, how this strange person had managed to bewitch at least two men known to her, when she sounded rather boring, but then bewitching men was not rocket science.

And conversely she couldn't miss my annoyance and my thinking that she was too intrusive and pleased with herself (weren't recovering addicts supposed to suffer from low self-esteem?). But I don't think my reaction upset her much. On the contrary, annoying someone was one way of checking that both of you were alive.

For once in my life I longed to be rescued by Joe. He was over by the drinks table, counting out £20 notes to tip the waiters. When he had finished he stumped over to us, quite briskly.

'God, that was hell,' he said. 'I don't know if I could have got through it without you two.'

'Are you all right?' Jade asked in a low, meaningful way which somehow conveyed that there were ways of being all right or not all right that only she could understand.

'Surviving,' he said.

'I'm afraid we'll have to go. We promised to meet the PR people at three and there won't be time to change after.' She smiled at me, the kindly excluding smile women give you to show they are part of something special you aren't part of.

'See you at Serpents,' Joe said.

'Snakes,' she said. 'It's called Snakes.'

The launch pad was in Soho, a few doors up from the Lexington Street car park and next to a strip joint which seemed to specialise in women looking like belly dancers though not actually dancing, at least not in their photographs. A large pasty-faced bouncer in a black fleece with a black T-shirt underneath scrutinised my invitation as though it was written in tiny Sanskrit characters before moving his bulk fractionally to one side of the door and giving a grunt of welcome. Inside, the place was much bigger than I expected with a large circular floor and a sinuous balcony running round it supported by gleaming steel pillars with glittering green and yellow snakes twirling round them. There were snakes everywhere, inlaid in the shiny floor, swirling in the gilt chandeliers above us and, I saw as I moved in under the balconies, in tanks at the back of the alcoves, in this case real live snakes. These were sitting coiled and morose amid the sand and rocks or in those tanks that had water in them swimming very slowly through the weeds. They didn't look as exotic as the decorative snakes on the pillars, let alone the tangle of purple vipers which had begun to whirl around the ceiling.

There were already a dozen or so helpers moving chairs on to the floor, setting up the screen for the visuals, putting out the name cards – Joseph D. Follows Managing Director, Keith Trull Chief Executive, Jade Treviso Deputy Chief Executive, Aldous Cotton CB.

'I haven't got the CB,' I whispered fiercely to Joe.

'You said all civil servants got the CB when they left.'

'Well, I didn't.'

'Oh well, nobody will notice.'

'But we' – but Joe had lost interest because he had caught sight of the bankers who were advising on the float coming in looking nervously about them.

'Who chose this place?' I muttered to Jade.

'I did,' she said sweetly, smiling at the gawping bankers who were all longing to rush over to her but had to listen to Joe's welcoming spiel first.

'But really, *snakes*?'

'That's just the point. It's so contrarian. We're attracting the City to the snakes, not the usual way round.'

This time it was me she smiled at and I was melted all over again.

Soon the rest of the crowd began to come in – the financial journos and the investment analysts and the asset managers, and the waitresses began circulating the cocktails: there was a choice of Coiled Cobra, which was basically a souped-up daiquiri, Viper on the Rocks which was like a champagne cocktail but with a shot of yellow chartreuse, and the Rattler which packed such venom that we were told no customer was to be allowed more than two. The waitresses were wearing slinky black dresses of fake snakeskin. In fact, everyone was wearing black or blackish, not merely the City people who always had but the PR team and the technicians who were setting up the display, and they were all talking in low serious voices because after all this was not just business but serious business, being the moment at which one group of people was to be persuaded to part with large sums of money to another group of people, namely us. There was a buzz, but it was a sombre absorbed buzz and if you had just arrived from another planet you would have identified this as some ceremony of the local snake culture, possibly connected with the afterlife. In retrospect, the explosion of pink at G's funeral seemed positively festive.

The money men – no, money people, half of them were women now in their sharp-shouldered black suits and little satiny tops with the scooped neckline and thick gold chain or billowy scarf to help with the neck – the money people settled themselves in their seats and the ritual began. It was a ritual I knew more or less by heart now: the short introductory talk (three to four minutes max) about how they had first conceived the concept and how they had started off in a loft or garage or somebody's empty flat, and how they had only an old Mac which was on the blink (there was always a machine that was on the blink), and how they had been amazed by the response and a little humbled too, and how they now wanted to expand the concept and offer the wider investment community an opportunity to be part of it, and this was where the good people at Goldman Sachs, or Trotter Held, or as in this case Hellman Drax came in, and he'd now like to ask Mike Gurwitz to come forward and take us through the business plan, which he personally found very exciting.

Mike Gurwitz's low gravelly voice was hard to listen to for more than a minute or two. But this did not matter too much because he was only there to provide the background music to the charts and tables with their bright highlights that flipped up on the screen just a bit too quickly for you to take them in. It was irresistible, even hypnotic, the story told in those cascading columns. Year One would be a grim Dunkirk sort of year in which the gallant little band of initial investors watched the cash haemorrhage in all directions: property search, launch costs (pause for a sly jest about the modesty of the fees Hellman Drax were charging), recruitment advertising, acquisition and development. Then Year Two, a hold-your-breath year as the first revenue streams began to come through, but the costs were still rising and the minus figures were still soaring in every column. It would not be until Year Three that the first pluses crept into the P & L columns, only to be wiped out again by depreciation and central overheads and bank charges by the time you got to the bottom of the chart. Then Year –

'What about Dudgeonvest?'

'Excuse me, sir, but we'll be taking questions at the end of this presentation.'

'What about Dudgeonvest? I want an explanation.'

He was a short man, in his late sixties, bald except for a wisp of tow curled round the back of his scalp. He was holding a carrier bag as he stood up and his hands were shaking.

'I'm sorry, sir, but I think you must be in the wrong meeting.'

'There's no mistake, we put three-quarters of our savings into the company because Mr Follows told us it was a sure thing. My wife's dead now, it was twenty years ago, but –'

'I'm afraid I can't help you.'

'I know you can't help me, but he –'

'Could you sit down, sir.'

'Why should I sit down?'

'I'm afraid I'll have to ask the stewards to remove you if you refuse.'

The short man stood there, his whole body shaking now, pointing his finger at the platform, or to be precise at Joseph Dudgeon Follows who remained magnificently impassive, until the bouncers, moving with remarkable agility along the packed row, removed the short man, lifting him gently over the knees of the people in between as if he were no heavier than an overcoat.

'There's always one,' Joe muttered to me and that was the view the audience seemed to take too, there being a spattering of applause as the short man was led away. If anything, they now seemed even more rapt by the beauties of the business plan as Mike Gurwitz droned on. I remembered a little about Dudgeonvest. It was one of Joe's property companies, pitched to the smaller investor. There was a rather good slogan – 'Stake your Claim' was it? – with a series of ads in places like *Money Mail* and the money came rolling in but it all went up the spout in the property smash of 'seventy-four and the reason I remembered that much was that Joe told me it was the only thing that as a friend he was ever going to advise me to have a punt on, but luckily I had nothing to punt with at the time.

By we were on to Year Five or Six and Gurwitz's voice was as mellow as a cello as he pointed to the income streams now flooding in from every division of the great enterprise, the first dividend and the projections of market valuation, strictly hypothetical, of course, but based on the most conservative assumptions, but even if you put that aside, the Investor Rate of Return would be climbing inexorably year by year. Year Seven, IRR 233 per cent, Year Eight IRR 276 per cent, Year Nine IRR . . .

By now he was gurgling out IRR as though it was some triumphant tribal ululation, some gloria without which the cermonial could not conclude. But it was hot sitting there under the platform lights and though I tried to stay looking alert, my mind drifted off again and I started thinking back to my father's love of custom and ceremony. He liked parades, processions, fêtes, protest marches – anything involving ritual and costume. At the sound of horses trotting, or a band playing, or people chanting he would jump to his feet and rush to the window or the door. Did he like form because his own life was so formless, so unchannelled? It had been odd to be brought up to love ritual at a time when everyone else was rebelling against it. All my life I had remained faithful to my father's enthusiasm. Like him, when I heard the clump and jingle of Morris men dancing on a pub forecourt, I would stop and stare, not in a derisive mood as most other people did, but with something approaching sympathy or even wonder.

Yet now, rather late in the day, I began to feel a faint revulsion, even to see what people had meant when they said they found such-and-such an occasion a relief because it was so informal. I could have wished that there had only been three or four of us at Gillian's graveside and that we had simply thrown a bunch of flowers on her coffin and gone round the corner and got drunk. But then after the presentation when I was crushed into a corner with my Viper I remembered how my father had liked formality so much that once when we were clipping the front hedge from the roadside and a funeral procession passed by, he had made me join it although we had no idea whose funeral it was and I was wearing a bright red sweater and gym shoes. Perhaps the people at Tommy Ds had been right after all to turn out for G's funeral even if they had never clapped eyes on her.

'Ask not for whom the bell tolls,' I found myself muttering.

'Come again, didn't quite catch that one,' the man standing next to me said in a cheery tone. 'I'm Ari Aristides, I'm with Swynnerton Asset Management. I didn't quite catch your name – oh, of course, you were on the platform. Well, I must say it's a fantastic prospectus.'

'Fantastic.'

'Pity about that nutter. There's always one.'

'Yes.'

'Don't know why they let him in. You could see just by looking at him.'

'I suppose you could.'

'I mean, I knew that company. We handled some of the underwriting, I was a stockbroker at the time. Well, we all have a skeleton in our cupboard, don't we? But you can't spend the rest of your life moaning over spilt milk. You've got to move on.'

Ari Aristides was a bright-eyed slender man, disconcertingly handsome, with a head made for someone a bit larger.

'You don't look old enough to have been around then,' I said.

'It's the worrying that keeps me young.' He laughed and I laughed too, against all my nature finding this moving on rather agreeable, like some game that sounds silly when it is described to you but somehow catches your fancy as soon as you try it.

But then it would have been hard not to be swung along by the whole thing. No sooner had Ari Aristides told me that personally he was going to see to it that Swynnerton filled their boots with this one and if they couldn't get enough of the allocation they would be into the grey market first thing, than a couple of brokers came up and told me what a good relationship they had always had with Joe in the old days and how they hoped I could put in a word now before we'd fixed the price as they had a heap of clients who had the hots for it. And then a man with a shaven head and a chirpy smile from one of the tabloids said he thought it was a terrific issue, just the kind of thing his editor really went for, and he assumed we would be keeping a few shares back for personal allocation and – he was obviously used to not finishing sentences like this, except with his chirpy smile. And so I said that the Daily Thing had always been my favourite paper and we parted, patting each other's backs gently, just below the armpit, as if we had been doing this sort of thing for years, which no doubt he had.

And Jade was standing there in the middle of the floor just under the purple laser snakes, which were now writhing in a remorseless, frantic motion, casting a purple glow upon her still, oval face. In fact, the more jovial and voluble the men around her became, the stiller and calmer she seemed to be, responding to their chaff with only a half-smile as if to say they would have to do better than that.

'283, that's the figure Macpherson's are betting on – but Jimmy the Greek at UDB thinks it might be as high as 305. He's my cousin, Jimmy. Our grandparents jumped into the burning water together at Smyrna in 'twenty-two, nearly fried. Came over in the clothes the Red Cross gave them, not a penny between the lot of them.'

Ari Aristides was at my side again, almost dancing on his toes with reckless pleasure. 'I must introduce you to one of my investors and he's still one of my best friends too, would you believe.'

He pushed forward a bald man with old-fashioned moustaches who looked a little the worse for wear in this pristine throng.

'Remember me,' the bald man said. 'You ought to. I've been on and off your books like a yoyo.'

'E.T.,' I said. 'Great to see you.'

'Well, it's a great occasion,' Graham Ellis-Turner said beamingly (suddenly you could see why he always landed jobs). 'I collected a fair whack of redundo from my last gig, so I'm wading in up to my neck on this one.'

'It's a goer, this one, believe you me,' Ari Aristides said urgently, as though I were the one who needed convincing. 'I tell you, my old dad will go for it, he's my barometer. Lives in Winchmore Hill, eighty-three, just recovering from prostate cancer and he still plays the market every day, and he always calls it right.'

'I thought I had prostate cancer myself, but they got the biopsy back today and it's all clear.'

'Really? That's fantastic news. We deserve another of those Cobras to celebrate.'

The phone call had come that morning just before I went off to the funeral and I had told no one except this complete stranger. To have been given this reprieve had seemed too marvellous to announce without looking as if I were crowing. But Ari Aristides took the news with ease and pleasure. After all, this was a day for second chances all round, a time for fresh drinks and fresh wagers.

We both had a couple of Cobras and the shaven-headed journo said anyone who wasn't a total wimp had to try a Rattler. So when I got home and finally guided the key, which was beginning to stick anyway, into the front door, I nearly missed the long white envelope on the doormat. It had some firm's logo on it, not a firm I knew, and inside there was another envelope also addressed to me in a hand that I did know.

'*Dear Goodster*' (why this strange term of endearment? I think she babbled it long ago, in a moment of abandonment, Gus/good/ Goodster, something like that, or was it a general greeting, not for me only? How odd that I cannot now recall),

By the time you read this I shall be ashed out. In fact, my remains will be sailing on the prevailing wind in the general direction of Stevenage. I know this because my lord and master is being especially masterful about the funeral arrangements. (Curious how very attentive he is being about it all, like a man who hasn't said a word to you all evening and then makes a big thing of helping you on with your coat.) There will be a private cremation at Golders Green after the State funeral at that strange church he goes to down in the docks with a whole lot of City sharks who wish to be shriven of their sins and made pure. Seems hardly worth the trip for someone like me who's already pure in thought, word and deed but he said it would be a comfort to him and that's the main thing after all, isn't it? Anyway, I'm not quite sure who's going to be crowding the pews since my circle of friends is rather exclusive these days, consisting of Jonquil Fincher, Mrs Quin who keeps the draper's shop in Ballyturbet and three or four well-bred hens who simply don't travel. It does not include my medical adviser Dr O'Kelly Mahon who couldn't cure a broken fingernail nor my legal adviser Mr Dermot Sperrin who is equally useless and perfectly foul and probably reading this letter although I told him not to because there's nothing legal in it (Hi Dermot!). He has a lecherous eye and little slimy hands that wander and the only comfort is that I haven't paid his bill in this life and won't be paying it in the next one if I can help it.

Oh, how I miss your hot throbbing cock, my nipples are hard for you and I am rotten ripe and ready you know where – this bit is for Dermot's benefit while I try and get my thoughts into some order to say what I mean to say because the lovely H seems to be wearing off rather quickly these last few days.

Well, I could start by asking if you will look after Joe for me when I'm passing over Stevenage. Perhaps that's a silly thing to say because Joe always looks after Number One and in case of difficulty A. N. Other usually comes along to help him out. The incumbent A. N. Other has long dark hair I believe and a moony sort of expression and won't look at any man who isn't twice her age. I don't know where they breed them. In my day going out with a fifty-nine-year-old stroke victim was social death. All the same, he'll need help when she gets bored of him. (Notice total absence of jealousy in betrayed wife, only deep concern for faithless husband's welfare.)

And anyway, what I really want to say is what that man you told me about said at the end – you know, I've had a happy life or words to that effect, because in spite of all the miseries he really did think he had. And that's what I feel like and I don't think Joe ever has or ever will, because that sort of unsatisfied person is always driving on to the next big thing, and even when he's purring along he knows he's not going to be contented when he gets there. He's like a spoilt child (well, he is a spoilt child). It doesn't matter how many goes you give him on the merry-go-round he always wants another one.

Oh, how I wish I could see you all again one more time. But then that would be just as sad as not seeing you, sadder perhaps. You can't put off the solitude bit indefinitely and it's probably better to be in practice, like setting up the tent in the back garden before you go on a camping holiday.

Remembering things is the best comfort at this stage and I was going to recall a few of our choice moments (Dermot, are you still with us?) but Jones is wearing off again (did you know in the army now they call it Jones after H. Jones VC?) and I must get this letter off before I'm posted myself.

xxxx G

I put the letter away at the back of a drawer in the big brown envelope marked Electricity Bills which contained one or two things that I liked to keep to myself. Nell never stirred when I came up to bed and in the morning she said only that I must have had a tiring day. She seemed more interested in the launch than in the funeral.

But then you would have had to be deadish not to catch something of the excitement. Hellman Drax had soared beyond Jimmy the Greek's estimate and advised us to fix the offer price at 330p. We held our breath but only for a couple of days. In no time it was clear that the offer was going to be massively oversubscribed, eight or nine times according to X's early calculations, in the outturn almost eleven times. The money just kept on rolling in. Instead of raising the original target of 50 million, we had raised something nearer 75 million, so we didn't need to borrow a penny from the bank. Joe's personal stake was worth nearly 10 million, Trull's only a little less, Jade a little less again, and even I – well, on paper I too was a millionaire. Even to write out the word makes me giggle nervously. Nellie looked at me nervously too. She was delighted, of course, but she couldn't really believe it or, to be more precise, couldn't believe that it was I who was in this extraordinary condition. It was as though she had woken up and found herself married to a centaur or a merman.

Of course, we could not actually dip into these crocks of gold. To reassure the other investors we were legally bound not to sell our stakes for at least two years and we advised any other investor to do the same, because the stock was bound to keep on rising steadily as the business came on stream. This was one for the long haul, we told anyone who asked us, and most people seemed to take our advice because when the market opened there were very few sellers and a flock of buyers. Even the professional stags who made their money by selling as soon as they saw a clear profit were moved by market sentiment and most of them hung on to a good half of their allocation. All of which sent the price soaring, within a fortnight it was over 450 and from then on it continued to climb steadily towards the 700 mark. All this before we had sold a single house or insurance policy or any of the dozen other things we were going to do with the money. All we were doing was spending the whole time talking to Mike Gurwitz and Tim Stoyt-Smith and the other people at Hellman's, while there was a queue of clients at our old business which, even if we had had time to attend to it, had begun to seem a trifle vieux jeu. In fact, we were beginning very secretly to interview one or two other headhunters who we thought might take over the work while we embarked on our new adventure.

Something else happened too, something which I had not anticipated at all. Far from being forgotten in the rush, Gillian was discovered – or rediscovered – by the media – a bit late in the day, as she herself would surely have remarked. All the details of their kidnapping twenty years earlier were now rehearsed, not in that iffy suspicious way in which they had been reported at the time but with full-hearted sympathy. How tragic it had been that this brave victim of foul IRA barbarism had discovered she had cancer just as she and her husband were on the verge of hitting the jackpot, and how doubly tragic it was that her funeral should have been on the very day that her mercurial maverick husband had finally made it. A huge congregation of showbiz and City celebrities had paid their respects at St Thomas Didymus, the Cathedral of the Docks (which, of course, it wasn't, see above).

'Showbiz?' I queried.

'Well, there was that man who used to be in *The Bill* and his partner does the scripts for something on Channel 4. But isn't it great how they've really forgiven Joe at last?'

Jade was right. Even when our enterprise had been getting the most favourable coverage generally, you would still occasionally read references to Joe as a disgraced financier and the kidnapping was hardly referred to at all. But now his past was simply described as 'colourful' and he himself as a buccaneer and even a kidnap hero. Somehow the money flooding in had persuaded people that he was, after all, blessed, and worthy to be blessed. People scurried to put money into the new company because they thought the gods were with us. It was an act of worship.

Though we couldn't cash in our shares, Mike Gurwitz pointed out, we could pay ourselves decent salaries commensurate with our increased responsibilities. There was something especially mellow and reassuring about the way he said 'commensurate'.

'What, roughly double what we're getting now?' Joe enquired.

'Treble,' Mike said, 'at least.'

And so at last there was real money gurgling into my Nat West account, which had never seen the like. I bought a new car for Nellie, a Ford Focus – she didn't want anything bigger – and sent some money to the children who were still abroad, Thomas continuing in New York and Elspeth having gone to Chile to teach. And I bought a new carpet from one of the Oriental rug places on the Highgate Road but when I got it home it was too bright for our sitting room, which is predominantly russet-brown.

'You ought to get a new motor,' Joe said.

'I have, but it's really Nellie's.'

'You ought to have something flash of your own. It's not right you coming in by bike. Doesn't fit the image.'

'Couldn't I be the new sort of businessman, you know, ecofriendly and all that?'

'Jade could get away with it – but you just look like an old civil servant on a bike. You need a Merc; in fact, you need one more than any of us.'

'Oh, all right, then.'

So I bought a small silver Mercedes which virtually did all the driving for you and I purred down to Bagge's Head Wharf, or rather sat stuck in the Commercial Road listening to Albinoni on Classic FM and drumming my fingers on the leather-clad armrest.

When I finally reached the in-house car park at Bagge's Head Wharf and left the car with the other Mercs and Beamers, and trotted up the new wrought-iron spiral staircase (based on a Victorian model), I usually found the office empty. Even George, who had been upgraded to office manager, would be out inspecting the larger offices which we were moving into or the other premises out beyond the M25 which were to house some of our new satellite enterprises. Trull would be with the bankers or the brokers, or talking to some company we might be contracting work out to, and Joe and Jade – well, they would be out giving presentations and interviews and being photographed, especially being photographed. It was noticeable how often the magazines and colour supplements now asked for them as a double act. Jade would be in the foreground, of course, sometimes looking soulful, sometimes smiling thoughtfully, occasionally even with a mischievous grin, but standing behind her there would be Joe, gruff, bulky, used-looking, unmistakably a man who had been through it. You were left to enjoy the contrast: there was youth and, no, not innocence, for it was part of Jade's appeal that she too had been through it, but freshness, and behind her was this rough ancient, an emeritus professor in the university of life, Tiresias as played by Albert Finney. Beauty and the bloody Beast, as Joe himself put it. They did one shoot with xandre on the old spot by the river, with Jade sitting on a bollard and Joe standing by the next bollard.

'The last time we came here, xandre, you said it was too kitsch.'

'Kitsch is the new black, darling.'

xandre looked leaner and harder now, the soft angelic bloom had gone and so had the foreign accent. He spoke, these days, in a slightly nasal voice with occasional flat vowels that seemed to have come from someone else's voice, but he was as relaxed as ever.

'You're looking too charming, Joe. I don't want charming, I want strong. Try folding your arms like before.'

Soon the 'people' columns started joining them up. The irresistible Jade was comforting the distraught Joe, they were constant companions, adversity had thrown them together, though she still kept her penthouse in Marylebone and he still lived in his £4 million house in Kensington. There was no hint of criticism, not even when the more daring columns went the final hundred yards and revealed that the comforting had started when Joe had been so desperately worried about his sick wife across the water. In fact, the earlier the comforting had started, the more tragic the whole story came to seem. That, after all, was what tragedy was when you stopped to think. It wasn't about people behaving well and doing the decent thing, it was about people being swept away by their emotions when under enormous pressure, it was a titanic struggle between passion and fate. From Tristan and Isolde to Joe and Jade, always the same story.

It was on that overcast September day (xandre kept complaining about the light) that I noticed something else. Joe and Jade never touched each other, at least not in any way to suggest that they were anything more than friends and colleagues. This was odd, seeing that there was no need to hide it. They were now an accredited item and, if anything, it would be good for business if they at least made a show of being unable to keep their hands off each other.

Had they made some peculiar compact between them that they would give no public sign of being gone on one another, to elevate them above the sloppy run of lovers? There were couples like that, weren't there, who found that a public froideur helped to excite the private passion, to bank up the fires, not least because of the thrilling secrecy and the fun of pretending that you hardly knew one another (even if in reality everyone else knew what was going on). But in my experience at least, Joe had never been like that. He was an impulsive hugger and kisser.

Was it conceivable that he had asked her to play it so cool because he felt guilty about Gillian? With most men in his position that would be possible, even probable, but then deducing how Joe would behave from the way most men behaved would be like predicting the life cycle of the cuckoo from a general study of nesting birds.

We sold the lease on Bagge's Head Wharf. It had been a perfect place to jump off from and it photographed so well – the spiral staircase that Jade poked her dark head through for the snappers, the low beams and trusses that had once sent Pevsner into rhapsodies and now seduced the woman from *The World of Interiors*, the squint of the river through the attic windows with their original iron bars, now claimed to have sheltered French prisoners during the Revolutionary wars – it was all delightful but it was a little too unstructured for a major corporation. So we were taking a couple of floors in Mudchute Tower, that vertiginous silver cylinder you could just see from the attic windows because the river took a big sweep to the south below the Wharf. The new offices were on Levels Twelve and Thirteen, six floors below the substantial footage occupied by Hellman Drax who had negotiated our lease and claimed to have got a fantastic deal. The disadvantage was that, as well as bumping into Mike Gurwitz and Tim Stoyt-Smith in the express lift which took you from Twelve to Twenty-four, they never stopped popping their heads round the door. There's a buzz about this place, they kept saying.

We must have seemed exotic enough to them when we were sharing three phone lines and a single old fax machine under the low ceilings of Bagge's Head Wharf, looking like some remedial project for ex-cons, with George making the tea and doing the odd bit of carpentry, and Joe keeping up his exercises to forestall another stroke. He had abandoned the exercise bike and had installed a second-hand walking machine in the corner of the office, which he tramped on for twenty minutes morning and evening while dictating to Systems Sally who couldn't really do shorthand, which was no loss because Joe still spoke fitfully. Perhaps it was this atmosphere of penal rehabilitation that had bred the legend of the French prisoners of war, as though our landing up here with our chequered pasts must be part of a long tradition.

But we were a different proposition now. We were the lost sheep who suddenly found themselves in clover. The money was all in the bank, several banks to be precise (to have just one bank account was a low-rent kind of thing, apparently), and our investors expected us to start spending. We would win no Brownie points for letting it pile up on deposit, Trull explained, look what happened to Arnold Weinstock when he sat on his cash mountain. So Joe had been sent to America to look for business opportunities.

'It was great,' he said when he came back, 'absolutely fanta.'

He looked as some English people do when they come back from

America, elated and pitying at the same time, like people who have just seen the light at a revival meeting. The glow of the experience is still on them and they have this duty to explain it all to those who still sit in darkness.

'We identified four or five great propositions. Mike and Tim had a couple more in view, which I didn't see as fitting into our portfolio. But I'll tell you more at the meeting. There was something else I wanted to talk to you about. A personal thing.'

He stood up and went over to the huge window and looked out at the view of Greenwich and Blackheath before turning round to face me again, in the way people do in films when they have some embarrassing lines to deliver.

'You remember,' he said, 'some time ago, it must have been three or four months, no perhaps it was longer, when I said to you that there was this gossip going round the office, about me and Jade, that we were having a thing. You remember that?' He looked at me rather sharply as though I was trying to pretend I didn't. Joe's speech was so jerky that you quite often found yourself starting to reply when it turned out he hadn't finished, so I left the usual pause before answering, yes, of course I remembered.

'Well, I told you then that there was nothing in the story. It was all just idle gossip, nothing in it at all.'

'Yes, I remember.'

'Well, that was absolutely true, Gus, there was no consonance in it.'

Some of the next bit I didn't take in fully because I was distracted by trying to work out what was the word he meant instead of consonance. By the time I gave up this struggle he had moved on and was emphasising a couple of his points with a strange jabbing of his stubby forefinger, a rather uncertain movement like someone looking for the right button to push.

'Well,' he was saying, 'it's a funny old world and no mistake because the gossip has just gone on running and there doesn't seem to be a blind thing we can do about it. Even you must be aware of it. I mean, it's got into this rag' – he gave another wavering jab at the copy of *Frag* magazine that I now saw lying on his desk – 'and there have been insinuendoes, in a couple of other newspapers – I don't see them, of course. Jade cuts them out, you know, for that cuttings book she's kept ever since we started. I told her the agency would be handling all that now, but she just likes doing it.'

He paused and this time I thought he wanted me to say something, so I said, 'Well, once a rumour gets going it's always hard to stop. Why don't you put a counter-rumour round, like saying you're gay or something?'

'Don't be so fucking stupid.' He gave me one of those glares I knew so well, the glares that had made him look especially freckled when he was young but now merely made him look mottled. Yet even so there was something urchinlike about it still. 'You don't see the point at all. Well, how could you?' He paused and looked at the ceiling as though taking a moment out to confer with someone up there who might have the wit, the insight to grasp what he was on about.

'The thing is,' he said, refocusing on me, 'that while there was nothing in it then, nothing at all, well, now there is.'

He stopped there, so I exhaled in a non-committal sort of way and he carried on. 'You see, she was so kind to me after G died, a real comfort. She understood absolutely about the guilt thing. I mean, you'd think she wouldn't because she's so young but she's been through a lot so she isn't really jejune at all.'

'No,' I said, 'I know.'

'I could tell her everything, all the things you are too bloody embarrassed to tell anyone.'

I resisted the temptation to ask him what things might those be in his case, and then came the sudden painful thought that this willingness to spill it all out was probably what had kept him and Gillian together all those years, including the parts of it most recently when they were physically separated. For all her teasing him, that quality must have appealed to her. He was so unguarded, always bursting to tell you his latest. And although she was more composed, more stoical (as well as being a better person on almost anyone's scorecard), she had that confiding zest too and if you had it surely you would find those who didn't a little mean-spirited, defective. If all you could think of to say as this apologia proceeded was that he obviously didn't know what jejune meant, then you were clearly out of the running in some important department of being human. This being my situation, I continued to breathe out now and again, making this pianissimo noise somewhere between an oh and a mm.

'I knew, of course, that every man within five miles was after her, so I wasn't even thinking of her in that way. We used just to sit together on the sofa over there after you'd all gone home and we'd put our arms round each other, you know, like an old married couple, and we'd just talk. And it went on like that for ages until one evening she suddenly said this is ridiculous and she gave me a kiss, a proper kiss, and we took it from there. I mean, there on the sofa just like we were teenagers.'

He pointed at the low, frog-coloured sofa which he had brought with him to Mudchute Tower although it was an ugly piece and didn't fit in with the Boltraffio make-over which had cost a bomb. This had seemed a mildly peculiar insistence of Joe's, but now it was revealed as being a sacred site.

'It was extraordinary, you know, Gus,' he said, leaning forward and speaking in a stertorous near-whisper, 'but she's brought me back to life, not the first time, you wouldn't expect that, but very soon afterwards. You know what I'm saying, I got my full potential back, felt like I was twenty-five again. Amazing,' he added after a pause, as though he were someone else who had been called in to comment.

'Amazing,' I echoed and found myself looking at the sofa with something of the reverence he had himself displayed. It appeared to have miraculous powers, a combination of the Golden Bough and the Great Bed of Ware.

'I think you know that Gillian would have been pleased to think I wasn't going to be alone. When you've been married as long as we have, you do begin to understand how the other person ticks, not completely, of course, but you get a pretty good idea of how he or she would react in a given situation, don't you think so, Gus? The partner who isn't going to be around takes it as a kind of compliment.'

'Takes what?'

'When the other partner gets married again. No, no, hang on, we're nowhere near that stage yet, may never get to it for all I know. All I can say is it isn't totally impossible but we need time.'

'Yes,' I said.

'I thought you'd like to be put in the picture. After all, although we're growing like the clappers we're still a small management team and we need to stay open with each other. Anyway, I know how fond you always were of Gillian, and she of you let me add, and so I wanted you to be the first to know, know properly, I mean, not just rely on all that garbage they print.'

'That's very kind of you.'

'It hasn't been easy, believe you me, because of the G factor, but I'm glad to have got it out. I think it was the right thing, don't you?'

He stared at me in a way which wasn't entirely friendly, either sensing some lack of wholehearted approval in my dead-bat responses or perhaps displaying a certain resentment in having to go through the whole business for my benefit.

Still, the news was out in the open and Joe and Jade began to be spoken of officially as partners or even by the more sycophantic scribes as the dream team. They were to be seen together in the sassier restaurants clearly dining for pleasure and not because they were hatching some new deal. The other change was that they now permitted themselves outward and visible signs of affection. They would hold hands as they walked down the street to pick up Joe's huge Merc. In the office, during a meeting he would put his arm round her shoulder as he bent over to look at the figures she had in front of her.

'When did you first know?' I asked Trull.

'About forty-five minutes later, and that was only because I was on a long call from the States and he couldn't get through. He was like a schoolboy, but then he always is.'

'And how long ago was that?'

'You seem strangely prurient this morning, my dear Gus. Why is it so important to you to establish exactly when our dear colleagues first achieved sexual union? About three months ago, I think is the answer. Ah, I see. Yes, I fear you are right in your suspicions. He was not yet a widower. The flesh is awfully weak, Gus, that's what's so sweet about it.'

Trull was no longer in that fretful uneasy mood I had met him in at the time of Gillian's funeral. He was every bit his old self, like I remembered him from years ago long before his prison spell. Of all of us, having money agreed with him the most. He didn't seem to spend much of it, still lived in a large flat off the Chelsea Embankment which he never asked anyone to. For all I knew (and I was supposed to know him as well as anyone), it could have been elegantly furnished with classical antiquities and a Sheraton sideboard, or on the contrary, minimalist and vaguely Japanese, or then again, a complete tip. Nor had I any idea what he did for company outside office hours. He was certainly always available for lunch or dinner to entertain a new client. I did wonder whether he might be lonely but his self-confidence seemed too brimming to wonder that for very long. It occurred to me too, in the wake of my Riley-Jones experience, that Trull might have been gay all along: the camp manner, the marriage to Peggy, a retired femme fatale a good fifteen years older than him (perhaps more), the feeling he sometimes gave off that despite his unwavering *bienséance* he didn't care much for people and/or that the world had somehow played a trick on him. Yet I had never come across any evidence of this and he didn't seem to light up noticeably when a handsome young man came into the room. What did light him up was having money.

He spent some of it on clothes. Not that what he wore changed much – a pale suit, greenish or blue-grey and a tie to match – but the cut had a new distinction that even I couldn't miss and the material faintly shimmered but not so as to come close to being flashy. He had the clean, wise look of a Swiss banker. Of the three of them, he was now the most regular attender at St Thomas Didymus. Joe was away so much and Jade – well, she said nothing, yet somehow I gathered that she had moved on. As for myself, there were several reasons for not going, but avoiding Gracia was the best.

Tommy Ds was not the only source of spiritual nourishment for Trull. Sally McFee, no longer known as Systems Sally since she had been promoted to Head of Personnel and Training, revealed that she was a qualified yoga teacher and started regular classes in the lunch hour down in the training room. But Trull insisted on private one-to-one lessons for himself to be held in his office.

'I used to be a fair enough gymnast, only county level, of course, but it would be nice to stretch one's old limbs, don't you think?'

Trull was inclined to reveal such accomplishments. Apart from telling me the first time we ever met that he had been Junior Firefly champion at Burnham-on-Crouch, he later revealed that he had done a cordon bleu course and was a qualified car mechanic. I pictured his parents – both elderly schoolteachers in Ipswich – wearing themselves to a frazzle as they ferried him to and fro for these extramural activities and exhausted their savings on paying for them. In later life, he never displayed these accomplishments in action, at least not when I was around, but somehow I never doubted that he was telling the truth about them. It was as though these varied dexterities had somehow been fused into his poise, much as an opera singer may need to acquire all sorts of skills – breath control, foreign languages, understanding of musical style – in order to qualify to sing a simple love song.

Anyway, it was a new distraction to hear through the partition Sally's harsh Belfast contralto crooning encouragement to Trull as he flexed and reclined on the oatmeal Cotswold shagpile. Sometimes when the sun was at a certain angle you could see their shadows faintly through the flimsy eau-de-nil wall suggesting by their slow, mannered movements some genre of Japanese theatre which was only allowed to be seen in this delicate refracted guise.

Trull would emerge from these sessions looking as near flushed as he was capable of and intimating some erotic aspect to Sally's exercises which I had not associated with yoga as taught in these parts. But I don't think he really expected us to believe him. He was simply keeping in shape.

By contrast, Joe was a terrible colour, blotchy and purple around the eyes and definitely wheezing, which I didn't ask him about because there is nothing that annoys an asthmatic more.

'Utterly shagged out,' Trull said. 'I must say I'm impressed.'

'Well, he has crossed the Atlantic six times in the past three weeks.'

Now at last we were to see the results of his incessant travels. Joe was to unveil the preferred options for investment, the businesses that he and the Hellman team had decided to buy with the money that was still sitting in the banks – all £63 million of it. Decided was the *mot juste*, although for form's sake we were invited to contribute.

'Well, we have three triple-A contenders,' Joe began. 'I'll begin with the Della Robbia Cleaning Co. This is an old-established firm in Pittsburgh, started as a backstreet family cleaning business in 1908, now has branches in a dozen cities across the central and eastern states as well as an industrial cleaning business in upstate Pennsylvania, the shares currently stand at a depressed level of $7.50 but they're worth three times that at a conservative valuation, Mike thinks, a great people company which we can see expanding into a comprehensive domestic services group from its existing client base.'

On the screen he had an old sepia photograph of, presumably, the della Robbia family standing in white uniform and straw boaters outside a rather small, dingy shop, *circa* 1910. Then he switched to a more modern picture of a low white factory building with a chimney. There were no people in this one and the premises looked strangely desolate.

The next candidate for our investors' millions was Hi There Inc., an Internet games company that had expanded from its Florida base at a totally fantastic rate since 1998. They started off as a small greetings card business in the Everglades, hence the name, but moved smartly into the fun end of the Internet and now held the franchise for the Vargon Destroyer games.

'We believe Hi There has the potential to become a major player, if not *the* major player, in this sector which as you know is one of the most rapidly growing in the whole IT field.'

We nodded, but only on a small scale, the merest nictitation, making it clear that we did indeed know this and a lot more besides. Trull stirred, feeling his professional expertise as the author of *Cybermonsters* and *Humanoidosis* called into action.

'Vargon's a rather feeble pastiche of early Asimov, but then people seem to like that sort of thing, don't they?'

We passed on to the third triple-A candidate, Harkmore Assurance, a small retail insurance business, based in upstate New York, Buffalo to be precise, which provided services to the rich at irresistibly low premiums. This too was a steal, apparently.

'The thing about high net worth individuals is that the risks are really lower than for plain folks,' Mike Gurwitz explained, his voice even more gravelly at the thought of these admirable beings. 'They live longer because they look after themselves, they have better security, their wiring is in better shape and so on.'

'But don't they get robbed more often?'

'Actuarially speaking, no, that's a popular fallacy based on what you read in the papers. The chances of an ordinary joe getting his stereo or his wife's necklace lifted are about a hundred times the chances of some big shot losing his Renoir. So Harkmore can afford to offer premium rates that in ordinary circumstances would be criminal. Added to which, their client list is a fantastic base camp for us.'

We sat listening in a state of vaporous bliss as Mike and Tim expanded on the beauties of these exemplary companies and the other only marginally less alluring ones – a lively little mobile phone business on the East Coast, and a couple of growing realtors in Virginia and North Carolina. It was magical, the way our money empowered us to roam the world, so that blameless strangers in suits insuring the lives and goods of high net worth individuals thousands of miles away beneath the spray of Niagara Falls could suddenly fall into the hands of people they had never heard of, namely us. Thoughts of Marco Polo and the Silk Route – all those old ventures based on travellers' tales, King Solomon's mines, there's gold in them thar hills . . . My attention was wandering again. It had become a habit, this drifting off in meetings. Could it have some physical basis, some imperfection in the supply of blood to the brain – an ischaemic incident such as seemed to come to all my friends sooner or later? Was this perhaps an early warning sign of that ultimate wandering? Should I go and see Dr Playfair again?

Then somebody said something which snapped me back to attention. At first I was too dozy to be quite sure that I had heard right but then Tim S-S helpfully said the word again.

'I understand that Dodo's people are doing due diligence as we speak.'

You had to be getting on a bit to remember Waldo R. Wilmot in his heyday. But it was a long heyday and in it Dodo – everyone called him Dodo, even people who had never met him, especially people who had never met him because he was someone you wanted a piece of – had made millions in anything there was to make millions in: real estate, hogs, oil, farm machinery, minerals, especially minerals. He had gone more or less bust a couple of times and people liked that too and were inclined to say Dodo's not extinct yet, and because they were inclined to say it he never was and as soon as he started up again the investors came running. He weighed in at twenty stone plus when I first met him on a French racecourse when I was eighteen and he showered me with 10,000-franc notes for betting money although he had never set eyes on me before and I was only the tutor (nanny, really) to the children of some American friends of his. I was captivated by his generosity, by his elephant bulk and his strange light eyes the colour of beryls, if you know what colour beryls are, and the way they didn't miss a trick, especially tricks you didn't think he would be interested in taking.

So far, so good, but the word beryl takes us on to Dodo's other side, the side that even now all these years later I didn't care to dwell on – the time, for example, when I almost thought that Helen Hardress might be in love with me and it turned out she was being screwed (the appropriate technical verb, I think) by Waldo R. Wilmot who was employing her as a geologist for one of his African mining companies and incidentally deceiving her, not to mention the UN sanctions people, as to the destination of the beryllium she was helping him to mine. Then there was the way he treated his wife who shot herself when he took up with her best friend. And there was his friend the mobster, Sting Ray Rawston, who had a yacht the size of a house moored on the Lower East Side which I couldn't wait to get off when Dodo lured me on it. All of which had pretty well de-captivated me, though you could never be sure that he wouldn't somehow worm his way back. Look at Helen, as steely a moralist in her way as ever I came across, and when she had a daughter what did she call her despite my protests? Beryl, in memory of her happy days in Africa, and nothing I could say would change her mind.

'The background to this,' Mike said, 'is that Dodo is planning to wind down a tad, the guy's in his late seventies now, though you wouldn't think it, so he's concentrating on his core interests and of course that stud farm down in old Virginny. But he fancies playing one more hand with you guys.'

'So the die is cast,' Trull purred as he studied the figures that Mike had pushed in front of him.

'Yeah, it's a done deal, we signed an outline agreement, but of course completion's a helluva way down the road, so if you see anything you don't like the look of –'

'No, no, it all looks admirable. And you say Mr Wilmot is happy to join us as a non-executive director?' In these gatherings Trull had now adopted a mellow, detached mien, somewhere between an old-fashioned family solicitor and a member of some contemplative order. I could not make out whether this apparent lack of concern was a by-product of

Sally's yoga lessons or he had something else on his mind. Perhaps he was simply becoming bored. A short attention span had accompanied him through life like a faithful dachshund.

'He's just thrilled at the idea of working with Heads, though like most Americans he thinks non-execs aren't worth a pitcher of warm piss.'

Trull laughed heartily at this, usually a sign that he was not amused and was becoming impatient.

As for me, the news that Dodo was not only selling us three of his companies – for it seemed he had the controlling interest in all three of them – but was also coming over to join us on the board threw me into an unvarnished panic. So, talking a little faster than I intended, I said, 'I used to know Dodo a bit and I'm sure you're aware that his reputation has been, well, patchy in the past.'

'Listen, Gus, there isn't an investor either side of the Atlantic who hasn't been following Waldo Wilmot up and down that old roller-coaster. They know all about the guy and they just love him for it. Having him on board is worth another 30, 40 per cent on the share price. They'll follow him anywhere.'

'Gus, you're a worrier,' Joe said. 'Having someone like Dodo on our team will make people like you stop worrying.'

Being patronised by Mike Gurwitz was bad enough but I wasn't going to take it from Joe. 'Look,' I said, 'the truth is he's a crook, he drove his wife to shoot herself and –'

'Perhaps it would be better if that comment were not minuted,' Mike interrupted, leaning over to place a fatherly paw on the sleeve of David, the Maltese accountant now promoted company secretary.

'We don't need to bring anyone's private life into this,' Joe said, 'after all, we have all had our internal skeletons.'

This last bizarre phrase somehow distracted me enough to stop me carrying on – that and the feeling that further warning would be futile.

'I prefer to look on your previous acquaintance with Dodo as a building block for cementing our relationship with the group,' Mike added in that rueful rumble which was as near as he ever came to a rebuke.

As we came out of the meeting room (nice coffin-shaped table in dark bannoko wood from renewable forests, big Caulfield prints on walls which had the new wet-sand look), Jade pulled at my sleeve and tugged me into her snug little office.

'Fantastic, isn't it, about Mum having an affair with him and me being named after that stone?'

'She told you all about Dodo?'

'Yeah, we have no secrets, Mum and me. And she told me about the stuff he was selling to make bombs with without telling her and how she was so furious but afterwards how she thought of it as a crazy adventure. Oh yes, and how you were so shocked. You're still shocked, aren't you?'

'About which?' I played for time.

'Oh, her letting him screw her, and cheating on her, and the whole thing, really.'

'Shocked isn't exactly the word,' I said, though it was.

'For a bit I thought how great it would be if Dodo was actually my father instead of poor old Bobs. But Mum said the dates didn't fit.'

'I despair of you,' I said, trying to sound relaxed.

'Lighten up,' Jade said, 'it'll be cool. By the way, George has got your combat gear ready down in the storeroom.'

'Combat gear?'

'For the war games. Gus, where have you been?'

'Oh,' I said, and remembered.

X

The Great Plain

I got up at half six, befuddled and in low spirits. Morning glooms deepened as I put on the kit we had been issued with. The overall smelled of some chemical cleaning agent and was clammy against the skin. The camouflage was the darker end of the range – slate, umber and black with only a streak of sage, designed for inching unobserved across some forbidding terrain of rock and scree. From under the bedclothes came a derisive gurgle as Nell caught sight of me against the gap in the new check curtains which didn't quite meet.

'Good hunting,' I think was what she said, but I pretended not to hear.

We weren't told where we were going. Tim Stoyt-Smith, who had been in the Territorials and was directing our group, or platoon as he insisted on calling it, merely handed an envelope containing a grid reference to George who was to be our navigator and told him not to break the seal until D-Day minus one and to rendezvous at 0900 hours, allowing a good two hours to get there. George took this assignment seriously, refusing to open the envelope, let alone allow me to look at the map, saying only that he would pick me up at seven.

'Where exactly is it, George?'

'You'll find out soon enough,' he said, grinning under his forage cap, his red Vectra already transformed in his imagination into a jeep bouncing over the Western Desert. At least he had not yet blackened his face. He drove along the flyover as though he had to reach Alex before dawn. In the back, Jade was asleep and David the accountant was talking on his mobile, but quietly so as not to wake her.

I had thought it would be some heathland, perhaps on the Surrey–Hampshire border, and imagined us dodging through the pines and sinking thankfully into the deep cover of dripping rhododendrons. But George drove on out to the west, until the M3 turned into the A303 and we came on to the edge of the plain.

We were in open country now, but the morning fog had hung on here. At first the stray wisps seemed like vestiges lingering in the scoops and hollows of the downs. But they turned out to be the edge of a great mist that stretched for miles. Soon the visibility was so bad that the old railway sleepers stuck upright in the ground to guide the tanks off the road on to the chalky trails came at us abruptly out of the fog.

George took a sharp right off the main road up a byroad which was not much better than a track and although I did not remember this turning I knew that it must be taking us up over the downs towards the scenes of my childhood. In a mile or two we would be passing somewhere near the head of the little valley where my father used to take me shooting, an odd, remote, boggy, narrow place in that country of broad dry bottoms and chalky hills. And I thought again of those winter afternoons when my father had tried to teach me the elements of the sport and we had hopped and splashed from one sedgy tuft to another, with the snipe or duck keeping just out of shot ahead of us. The light always seemed to be fading, although we would start soon after midday, with or without sandwiches. We had the farmer's permission but I always felt that somehow we were trespassing and was glad when we reached the valley head and came up against the old WD Keep Out signs. And I thought again of the time I had shot the lapwing by mistake and wondered whether I would recognise the place when we passed it.

But I must have miscalculated because of the fog and we were still driving through military land on both sides with MoD signs every hundred yards. The land was nearly flat, only a little undulating, and I peered through the thick mist for where it began to fall away into the valley of my youth. No sign of that, but, startling in the extreme, what there did seem to be a couple of hundred yards away was some sort of building, quite large, more like a house, certainly bigger than a shelter for cattle or one of those old shepherd's huts on wheels that used to be dumped in the remote ends of the downs. Then behind it but at an angle there was another, much the same, neither of them at all like any local house. They had (and so did the others which were visible now that my eyes had got used to the mist) high-hipped roofs, a dull rusty orange colour and a foreign look, not Italian, Dutch perhaps. There was a whole ghostly village of them clustered together in this misty downland. At the back of them I could see the silver-grey shape of a church spire. There seemed to be no road to this place, at least not from the road we were on. I was certain there had never been a village there nor anywhere within five miles of it. Even if my memories of the landscape were awry and I had got my bearings a little muddled after forty years, there still was not and could not be a village there.

George took us slowly along the narrow road with us staring again and again at this apparition, which came no closer but did not dwindle back into the fog either. (In any case the fog was beginning to melt away now.) The village was larger than it had seemed at first, there must have been four or five streets in it and thirty or forty houses, but it was oddly compact, again not like the local villages, which were all strung out with the occasional infilled bungalow. Still I could see no ordinary road leading to or from it, and still it had this foreign look, definitely northern European yet impersonal, unlived in. As the mist lifted and hazy sunshine began to come through, the place seemed more unreal, not less, as though the mist had been sprayed on to deceive our senses while we were being translated into this other world.

'George, what is this place?'

'Tim says it's where they practise guerrilla stuff. It was meant to look like somewhere in Poland or Germany for when the Russians come and there's a bit of hand-to-hand fighting. So now they don't need it, they rent it out.'

'You mean it's not a real village?'

'No, mostly breeze-block and hardboard. Tim says the locals call it Eldorado.'

'Eldorado?' I looked again as we approached the cluster of orange dwellings on the desolate plain. We had turned out of the lane on to a concrete-slab military road.

'Like the TV serial they built a whole village for, in Spain somewhere, and it bloody flopped so the village was surplus to requirements.'

He laughed at the thought. 'I'll let you off here.'

'Won't the place be full of unexploded bombs and stuff?'

'We are assured that the bomb disposal people have swept it thoroughly,' David added, 'otherwise we couldn't get the accident insurance.' They all seemed to know more about it than I did.

'Ever heard of the peace dividend, Gus?' Jade said. 'It's all a lovely game now.'

She looked lovely herself in her combat fatigues, with her long black hair swept rather casually under her cap and her skin glowing in the hazy morning light of late summer. She began applying the camouflage stick making long slow smears of black down her brown cheek. This was one indignity I was determined to hold out against.

'Oh Gus, don't be such a Meldrew. Your great pink face will be visible for miles if you don't.'

And so with my face blackened and my heart heavy I led my little platoon over to Tim's briefing. He stood on some sort of pretend monument in the fake village square. All around were the tall ginger and cream fake houses looking pretty much like the small town in north Germany that was the intended killing field of that third great war which had been called off for the time being. Close up, the houses looked so flimsy you felt you could knock them down by leaning your shoulder against them. All the same, under these familiar skies they did succeed in conveying a strange alien environment and standing round this fountain or whatever it was the rest of our forces, some forty of us allocated to the Blue team, mostly from Finance and Marketing, were on a high state of alert, our faces so thoroughly blackened that some of them were nearly unrecognisable.

'Now, have you all got the picture?' Tim said, his voice getting crisper by the minute. 'Our mission is to fan out and let the enemy move in to occupy the town at 0945 hours. They may sit tight or they may conduct search-and-destroy sorties out into the country, but our mission remains the same, to recapture Redtown by 1300 hours, at which time the operation will cease. Walking wounded must attend the casualty station over there to the east, the tent with the Blue Flag, before returning to operational duties. Those who have been killed can of course take no further part and must go straight to the lunch tent. If we are still engaged in hand-to-hand combat when the siren goes at 0100, victory will be decided on a casualty count, two wounded personnel to equal one dead, officers to count double. Is that clear?' By the end, his normally mild voice had risen to something close to a bark.

George then formed us into an orderly queue at the back of the old army lorry from which he chucked us down our weapons. These were surprisingly heavy, much more like real AK-47s than the plastic replicas I had expected.

'Remember, don't unlock the trigger unless you mean to fire. Don't point your weapon at a fellow soldier, you could cause a nasty accident. The paint's non-toxic, of course, but you don't want to get it in your eyes. You've got a full canister there, but remember there are no refills, so only fire when the target's within range. And bring it up to the shoulder, like this, don't fire from the hip like they do in the films.'

To begin with we crouched like hares in the stubble no more than four hundred yards from the fake village, our eyes level with the stray scarlet poppies and the cornstalks tickling our nostrils. There was a strange sickly smell, too, from some low frothy herb which lay crushed beneath us. I could feel the sun, quite hot now, on the back of my neck. In the distance we could hear the droning of vehicles up and down the disused tank tracks. Then the droning became louder and was coming from overhead, and with a fierce whirr a helicopter passed overhead, no more than forty yards above our heads.

'Christ, choppers, we can't stay here. We're dead ducks.' George, assuming the command which, by tacit agreement, I seemed to have surrendered, took off at a leopard crawl towards the longer grass beyond the fence. The other half-dozen of us creaked after him, some of us finding an arthritic low lope easier than going on all fours.

The only refuge we could see was a clump of trees at ten o'clock which George said was marked on the map as Claypits Wood, so we made off in that direction, none of us troubling to crawl now that we were a fair distance from the village but merely bending a little as we trotted through the high wispy grass. Going along out of breath at this reverent crouch with the grass flicking my bare arms, a tremor of pleasure took hold of me, unbidden, unexpected. The exercise was suddenly appealing, all the more appealing because so absurd. When the Middle Ages had petered out, people probably felt the same about jousting. What was jousting anyway but a management team-building exercise like this one?

We paused for a moment to regroup. The back markers in our group, three young men and an older woman from New Zealand, all in Media Buying, took a bit of time to catch up and flounced down in the high grasses behind us, one of them saying he was knackered already.

There was a rustling in the grass somewhere ahead of us and what looked like two young deer came into view about thirty yards away, one rather taller than the other. They seemed to walk in an awkward strutting fashion, not like deer at all, and raising myself cautiously I could see that in fact they were immensely tall birds, like giant pheasants or partridges. The taller of the two – he must have been four foot high or more – stopped and then made a curious retracting motion of his head so that it almost disappeared into his neck which at the same time began to swell. Within a minute it was like a dirty-grey balloon and you could scarcely see his dark imperious eye at all. Then, in a weirdly synchronised motion his wings and tail fanned out and began to display great snow-white froths almost entirely covering his chestnut-buff body. In no time the whole bird seemed to be buried in a white foam bath. The smaller bird, presumably the female, watched the remarkable process with a stony gaze, both birds silent in the tall grass and the light breeze.

'Ostriches,' George breathed, 'Christ.'

'You sure?'

'They're Great Bustards,' Jade whispered, 'but you're right, they used to call them the Wiltshire Ostrich before they died out in the nineteenth century. Look, she knows we're talking about them.'

The female turned from contemplating the giant snow-white puffball and glared at us.

'They keep on reintroducing them,' Jade said, 'but they never survive long, nobody's quite sure why. Habitat probably.'

The male was now slowly deflating. When he was back to his normal shape he gave a sharp little nod to his mate and they strutted off. We watched them until they were lost in the high grasses. For a minute or so none of us felt much inclined to move on, feeling a little deflated ourselves, a little fragile, as though our prospects were as uncertain as the birds'.

George must have been right about Claypits because inside the clump of trees there was a hollow half overgrown by brambles, and one or two wild box bushes but with the muddy white of the clay showing through and a pool of dank water at the bottom of it. A single shaft of sunlight came through the treetops and flicked the flies hovering over the water. We found a place in the bushes where there were the least prickles and the ancient smell of box, fresh and yet sour too, began to arouse in me memories of very early childhood, crawling along the edge of the lawn under the box hedge and playing with the cupped buds, running my fingers through the clippings that fell from my father's shears.

Jade had lit up a Silk Cut and was lying on her back, blowing smoke at the sky. George was consulting the map again. Our first meeting had been when we were thrashing through brambles like this, I reflected, but did not say as much to him. Did he have dreams about being back in Thursby, perhaps wake trembling in the small hours to find himself safely in his cosy two-bedroom flat overlooking the Limehouse Basin? The quartet from Media Relations were playing some word game that the men were better at than the woman was, which was making her cross. Apart from the flies, which had just discovered us, it was a peaceful scene.

'Why don't we stay here all day?' Jade said.

'Tim said there'd be no lunch for non-combatants,' George retorted.

'Anyway, we can't do much corporate bonding here,' I said.

'Oh, I'm sure we can,' Jade said. 'I think we could bond brilliantly, just the eight of us.'

'Seven,' George corrected. 'Young Ron's got to stay up that tree, otherwise we're buggered.'

We looked at the leafy ash tree in the corner of the clump, in the Y-junction of whose trunk Ronny from the post room was keeping watch.

In the end, it was the flies that drove us out, that and having finished our two thermoses of coffee. We rose and clambered through the brambles and out of the little copse, feeling dozier than when we went in, any hint of combat readiness having melted in that torporous glade. George led us single file through the tall grass. He alone held his weapon at a threatening military angle. The rest of us dangled them like shopping bags. Behind us the quartet from Media Relations were playing another word game and I thought I had almost got the hang of it when there was a sudden rumble and roar of engines to our left and a blizzard of some wet stuff hit us in the face, on the chest and legs, everywhere in fact.

I fell back into the grass struggling to clear my eyes with my dripping hands. When I got my sight back I was covered with red paint from head to toe and so were the rest of us.

'Yaoo, Alamo, remember the Alamo. Boy oh boy, we got the whole bunch of them.'

Rearing over us in a red field buggy with bulbous tyres was a huge man in a red overall with a red baseball cap and goggles on his fleshy face.

'Hey Joe, come take a look at this. Number Three platoon's a wipe-out. Like shooting turkey in the hill country. We had you guys under observation ever since we saw you from the big bird.'

'Wasn't it a bit out of order using a chopper?'

'All's fair in war and the other thing, my boy.'

He had removed his goggles now and there he was. He took off his leather gauntlets and offered a paw the size of a ham to George who shook it warmly.

'Waldo Wilmot, my friends call me Dodo because they all think I'm extinct or damn well ought to be. Why, there's a familiar face if I'm not mistaken. Gus, my boy, you look perfectly bloody.'

He hadn't shrivelled in old age as I had expected. On the contrary, he had somehow ballooned again so that although mountainous and monstrous he also looked like a small boy, no doubt particularly so at this moment when he was aglow with delight at having liquidated the lot of us with one burst from his automatic weapon which, I now noted, was considerably larger than ours and was mounted on a swivel platform on the front of a buggy that also had a windscreen, thus offering a 180-degree field of fire and protection for the gunner.

'And hey, you must be Jade. Let me give you guys a lift back to the field hospital. You hang on the tow bar, Gus.'

Jade laughed and jumped up on the seat beside him, not bothering to wipe off the red paint from her face or hair, wearing these scarlet streaks as proudly as a squaw in her warpaint. Hanging on the tow bar was easier said than done, as my trainers kept slipping and I had to put my arms round Dodo's massive belly to keep my balance as we bumped across the rough ground with the tall grasses whipping my wet face. Even with all the distractions of clinging on and surviving the jolts and sudden turns Dodo took to avoid obstacles, I couldn't help wondering whether he knew who Jade's mother was and if he did how long it would be before he brought up the subject. About a minute and a half was the answer. And of course he knew, he knew everything, especially the things you thought he wouldn't know.

'I'd have recognised you any place any time,' he roared above the puttering and jolting of the buggy. 'You got that look of your mother's, like no other girl I ever met. Being dark don't make no difference, like as if it was a wig. It's the look.'

'I don't think we look alike at all,' Jade said.

'Course *you* don't think so. No girl wants to look like her ma.'

'*He* didn't recognise me,' she said, nodding back in my direction, which wasn't so far to nod because I had learnt that the only way to reduce the jolting was to bury my chin in Dodo's shoulder.

'Oh, Gus. What a guy.' And he laughed the kind of laugh people laugh when words fail them.

Out in the open now, I could see other buggies crawling about the plain and every now and then you could hear the plunk-splat of the paint guns but there seemed no pattern to the action, nor to the stray figures in overalls limping or crawling across the grassy veld.

'The poor bloody infantry.' Dodo chuckled as we passed Tish from Customer Services sitting exhausted on a tussock. She was covered with blue paint, a rare score for Us. She gave us a plucky smile, recognising Management even thus bedizened.

Further on we saw a buggy capsized at the side of a ditch, with its bulbous wheels in the air like a dead insect. Two young men were trying to heave it back on to the track. I didn't recognise them because they were so blacked up, but they were probably from Finance because their efforts were being directed by Trull who was technically Head of Finance. Trull was not in regulation camouflage but was wearing a silvered siren suit with a red-and-white kerchief knotted round his neck and a pair of goggles pushed up above his forehead. Clearly he thought he looked like Rommel with a hint of Churchill. In fact, he looked more like a juvenile lead from some Thirties musical, perhaps an actor who persisted in playing juvenile leads beyond his expiry date. He greeted us cheerfully, saying wasn't this fun in a way that suggested he had capsized the buggy on purpose.

'Those pesky things won't stay upright. Centre of gravity's too damn high,' Dodo clucked sympathetically, at the same time letting in the clutch and bumping off down the track.

The fake village – Redsville as Dodo called it – had a sentry posted at the way in.

'It's OK, these guys are with me, they're POWs,' Dodo called out to him and the sentry (also from Finance, I think, but there were so many new faces around now) came to something resembling attention and gave a casual salute with fingers bent in the American style.

We stopped at a gap in the flimsy houses where there was a view of the plain. Below us lay a broad hollow I had not suspected, quite steep, and the few remaining Blue troops out in the field were tramping across it towards us. The two other young men from Finance were pushing the buggy while Trull strolled behind them. As these bedraggled remnants began clambering up the slope, unseen Red snipers perched in the houses opened fire. A couple of the Blues – already splattered with red paint – raised their hands in surrender. One waved his weapon, tapping the canister to indicate that he was out of ammo. But the remorseless snipers continued blazing away until the supposed besiegers were soaked in scarlet.

'They certainly aren't taking any prisoners,' Dodo wheezed with pleasure. 'Pity there won't be any hand-to-hand combat. These fellows are finished already.'

I walked over and stood behind the Head of Media Buying, a mild figure generally assumed to be gay, who was sitting on a buggy parked alongside us and kept his finger pressed on the trigger until the last slurps of paint began to lose range and leave a scarlet trail back to the buggy. He sat back on the moulded plastic seat with an expression of infinite contentment on his blacked-up face.

'It's orgasmic,' Jade murmured. 'Do you remember that experiment they did, at Yale or somewhere, when they got these students in a room and told them that if they turned up these dials the more pain they would inflict on the people the other side of the screen and they all turned them up to maximum?'

'Most folks have a high tolerance of other folks' pain. I got a pretty good idea of that when we were going through the *bocage* in 'forty-four. You'd see these guys pumping dead men full of enough lead to kill a regiment. Say, you guys had better report to Tim. I want my kills in the gamebook.'

Just outside the village Tim had set up a circular area marked out with stakes and string, which he designated the Holding Area where the wounded (splashed on arms and legs) were to be separated from the fatalities (serious splashes on face and chest). Already there were small groups sitting inside the grass compound sucking at bottles of beer or sipping plastic cartons of coffee. Tim was moving among them with a clipboard on which he was drawing up a casualty list. Jade and I slipped off the buggy and sat down with them to be counted. The atmosphere was rather less jovial than might have been expected on what was after all supposed to be a day out. There were one or two complaints that the rules had not been properly explained and that it was unfair to be hunted down by the buggies like natives being massacred. And why hadn't our buggies come to help us?

These little circles of bedraggled, paint-splattered colleagues seemed genuinely demoralised. Their failure to survive, or at least to take a few of the enemy with them, had seriously upset them. Their dejection was the most realistic aspect of the whole shooting match.

'After you've been logged, you can shower in the facilities behind the lunch tent.'

I followed Tim's pointing hand and trudged over to the rickety canvas contraption weary to the bottom of my old trainers, although we could not have crawled and crouched more than a mile or so to the Claypits before Dodo zapped us. I too was beginning to feel the weight of failure as if the exercise had been for real.

Circling under the erratic jet of the makeshift showers, I began to feel slightly human again (how odd to equate being human with feeling confident and well when so much of that particular state was spent being dejected and knackered). But it was soothing to feel the red paint running down off my chest and back and the occasional brush of the rough canvas against my bare shoulder as I turned under the shower, but only half-turned out of a certain prudishness which had never left me since puberty, so that it took a vigorous splashing behind me to let me know that I was no longer alone.

'Jeez, isn't this great?' I turned properly now to see the huge form of Dodo under the next jet, slapping soap all over himself, under his pits, between his buttocks and thrusting up his massive privates as he soaped round them.

'Not a scrap of paint on me,' he said, 'but I never pass up a good old shower.'

His pale-green eyes stared at me, his best/least bad feature but also his most disconcerting because his gaze was so cool and appraising, and had no connection with his menacing exuberance. I had seen him naked before, well, we had seen each other naked, out in Africa when we swam in a rock pool with Helen and the sight of her diving in, rather awkwardly, had stayed in my head. But I also couldn't forget his great body plunging in like a seal returning to its proper element, his privates then swinging below his sleek fuzzy belly like a medieval purse. Naked or clothed, he never stopped throwing his weight about, to intimidate, to amuse, to wheedle, to charm, to alarm.

And when, freshened up in a crisp sky-blue polo shirt and chinos, he sat down with us at the long trestle table for the cold lunch and a Chardonnay, his bottom bulging over the bench, his great forearms swelling over the salmon salad, he was still working at it.

He told us the story of the three companies he was letting us take over. They were his babies, he had dandled them when they were so high. He would never forget the day when he'd stopped for gas in downtown Pittsburgh and he'd seen this little cleaner's, neat as a tack, with this china statue over the door just like the ones he and Tucker had seen when they were in Florence that fall, 'and there was old Gianluca della Robbia, Robbie they all called him, standing outside, all in white like a deck steward and he said "Hi, nice day", and something about him made me ask could we come in and take a look around and there was this place all white tiles, cleanest place you ever saw, and he told me about how he got started and how all his kids and his nephews wanted a piece of the business, but there wasn't room for them all and they hadn't got the capital to expand and so, well, you could guess the rest'. So we had to take good care of his baby and he gave Jade a hug, saying, you know, he kind of had a little inkling that she was really his daughter after all, but perhaps it was only wishful thinking. And Jade didn't mind a bit. Nor did Joe who was sitting opposite and was normally resentful at anyone paying attention to his girl or, now I came to think of it, at anyone paying attention of that sort to anyone, as though all such displays of affection should be reserved for him and when anyone else indulged in them it somehow depleted the available store. It was an interesting illusion, this, that sexual energy was really like oil or some other fossil fuel, there were only finite reserves of it and access to continuous supplies was crucial for survival.

'Anyway, you'll be there to keep an eye on us,' Joe said slavishly.

'Well, you know, Joe, there's nothing in the world I'd like more and that was my first instinct, I didn't want to let go and though my rule in life is that the non-executive director is like a bull without a prick – oh, Jade, you mustn't mind me, I'm just a good old Texas boy – I wanted to stay alongside you guys for the duration. But then the truth is that in this life you better fish or cut bait and you'll find out soon enough you don't want a fat old guy second-guessing you on every pitch.'

We whimpered that this was exactly what we did want, but Dodo was adamant. It was just great that he was leaving his babies in such great hands but he was a restless sort of guy, his daddy had been a riverboat gambler and he took after him, and he had to be moving on to see which way the grass grew in the next field. So he was just going to climb back in that old big bird and say adios with a tear in his eye and a goodbye kiss for his honorary daughter.

He gave Jade a long sucking kiss on her lips, which again she didn't dislike a bit and responded to. Then, turning to me, he added, 'Gus, it's a goddam shame this has to be only a flying visit. How about you taking a ride back with me and we shoot the breeze a little?'

I could have given half a dozen excuses, some of them genuine. There was no real need, after all, to suck up to Dodo since our dealings with him were all but completed. I had no illusions about him and my memories of our previous meetings were mostly humiliating. Yet somehow I found myself saying yes. He was old now, I'd probably not see him again. After all, he had been a part of my life and if he was a monster he was the kind of monster you could tell your grandchildren about. It would be feeble to duck out of it. The truth was that I wanted a little more of his company. Which was his secret, that you were always drawn on a little further, promising yourself that this really would be the last time.

And so when the big red helicopter dropped out of the cloudless sky again, it was I who scurried after Dodo crouching under the whirring blades. In a couple of minutes we had lifted off and the fake village was only a bunch of orange dots on the great plain. In a couple more minutes Dodo was fast asleep, his great baby's head lolling across on to my shoulder, his huge stomach pushing against the safety belt. He was breathing in a jerky, gravelly way, more like an asthmatic wheeze than a snore.

Then, just as we were coming into Northolt, there he was, awake, with his beryl eyes gazing at me as though it was I who had nodded off and he who had been watching me. 'Great days, weren't they,' he said, putting his giant paw on my sleeve. 'Seeing Jade brought it all back. They're two of a kind, those two. They don't make it easy for you but, you know something, you wouldn't want it any other way. Hey, I've been neglecting you. Pray join me in a cocktail.' He hoicked out a silver flask from a metal box under his seat and as we landed I felt the delicious chill of the vodka hit the back of my throat. The green Lexus was waiting at the edge of the runway and we hadn't reached the Hanger Lane underpass before he had talked me into having a few more drinks together and then dinner, and I had rung Nell on the mobile to say I'd be late. 'And how did D-Day go?' she asked, but I pretended I hadn't heard.

'Now first we're going to meet a very old and dear friend of mine who I'm sure you'll remember. Ray Rawston, one of the best. *The* best in my book.'

'Ray Rawston?' I gasped. We were going up in the lift at Claridge's by now and there were other people in the lift, so it was a muted gasp.

'Yeah, the old Sting Ray, you remember him? He's the kinda guy you don't forget. We're doing a little business together in London, just a couple of old-timers having ourselves some fun.'

'But.' Well, it was too late to get out of it. Anyway, the fact that Ray Rawston was a convicted racketeer who ought to have done a lot more time than the three or four years he had served didn't seem so alarming now that I had three vodkatinis inside me. In fact, I was surprised to hear that he was still alive. He had seemed pretty ancient all those years ago when Dodo had first introduced me to him on his boat in New York harbour.

But there he was, sitting in a peach-coloured armchair by the fireplace in his suite, almost dwarfed by the huge vase of flowers on the little table beside him. He had been yellow and lizardlike when I first saw him. Now he was shrivelled and maggot-white.

'Yeah, sure I remember. You're the Brit who couldn't wait to get off my boat. I was mortally offended. Most guys would have sold their mothers for an invitation. I had to let her go when I broke up with Tara. Hurt like hell, I really loved her.'

'She was just the greatest thing, Ray.'

I murmured assent, not clear whether we were talking about the boat or the ex.

'So how've you been, Ray?'

'This angina's hell on wheels, you know that, Dodo. Every time I call my broker, I feel like some guy's stuck a couple of knives in my chest.'

'Old age is a tough call.'

'Better than the other thing, though.'

'You're goddamn right it is, Sting.'

We had finished the flask in the car but Rawston waved us to his drinks tray where there was a shaker already charged and soon we were most of the way through that, with Rawston drinking only a small glass of red wine, for his heart, he said.

He seemed infinitely fragile except for the flicker of malice in his eye. His suite was kept at blood heat, like a giant incubator or a reptile house.

What with the heat and the vodkatinis and the gruelling day we had been through, I began to sink into a drowse and listened with only half an ear to their business talk, which was none of my business in any case.

'It's a great institution, the British Stock Exchange, you know that, Gus,' Rawston said sharply as though I ought to be paying closer attention.

'Mm,' I said.

'You can do things there quite legitimately you can't do in New

York or Chicago. There's nothing tight-assed about the way you Brits do business.'

'Glad to hear it.'

'You follow my meaning. I'm talking shorting here.'

'Yes,' I said.

'Ray, do we need to be quite so specific? Gus here is just about my oldest friend, but we did agree there were certain confidential aspects that –'

'Dodo, forgive me, I'm an old man. We tend to be a little indiscreet at times because we figure what the hell we won't be here to watch the stuff hit the fan.'

'Excuse *me*, Ray, I brought the subject up in the first place. And let me tell you you've got a good few miles left in you yet.'

'Six months, Dodo, that's what the Harley Street fellow gave me. Saw him yesterday.'

'Does he say it straight out like that?' I enquired, suddenly interested and emboldened by the vodkatinis. 'You know, I give you six months?'

'What makes you so curious, young man? You take out some life insurance on me?' Rawston cackled.

It would have taken too long to explain that I had suddenly thought of the passage in *Sick Heart River* when Sir Edward Leithen asks Dr Croke how long he's got and I had always wondered whether people actually did ask and, if they did, whether the doctor gave a straight answer. Behind the cackle Rawston seemed affronted by my enquiry. Perhaps he didn't care for personal questions, preferring to set the terms of conversation himself.

'You think I'm some kinda phoney? Hang around a few minutes and see the shots that nurse pumps into my bony ass and you can ask her.'

'No, no, I'm sorry, I only meant –'

'Forget it, baby. Life's too short already.'

Rawston sank back into his chair and pressed an old-fashioned ivory bell push that was hanging over the arm. For a moment I thought my questioning might have brought on a seizure and he was ringing the bell for the nurse. But it was only the waiter who came in and, at a weary wave from Rawston, started freshening our drinks.

'No, Sting, time to get going. We got a table at Gando's upstairs.'

'You won't keep an old man company?'

'Listen, Sting, I know what you get up to with those nurses and you don't want no voyeurs for that unless your tastes have changed since my day.'

Rawston gave a feeble cackle and sank deeper into the peach armchair, as white as the bones of a medieval saint in a reliquary.

'Listen, Gus,' Dodo expounded, waving one of Gandolfi's famous ribs across the table at me, 'you don't like that guy, am I right?'

'Sting Ray Rawston? Well, he wouldn't be my ideal companion on a desert island.'

'I could tell, I could hear you thinking what's Dodo doing with this old crook, I wouldn't touch him with a bargepole. Well, let me tell you something, me and that Sting go back a helluva way. We've been together in good times and bad, and we've always been there for each other.' The juice from the rib had spread around his lips as though he had slapped on lipstick in a hurry. 'He stood by me when I had a cashflow problem back in the Seventies and then I used to go visit him in Albany, and I had a couple of friends on the Parole Board who did the right thing. And when Tara threw him out he came to Turkey Creek for a month until the new house was ready. So there's a lot of back history there. You don't throw it all down the garbage chute just because the guy ran into a little trouble, especially when the federal witnesses were a bunch of lowlifes who –'

'I didn't mean –'

'And let me tell you another thing. In America we don't give up on people. The system always gives you a second chance. Hell, that was why most of us went there, because no place else wanted us. It's programmed into our DNA. If you're an American, you always want to see the guy get up at the count of eight and come off the ropes and start over slugging his heart out again. Doesn't matter where he's been, or what he's done. He has that right, constitutionally. Now you're going to come right back at me and say where the heck in the Constitution does it say that every sucker shall be entitled to a second chance. And you know something, you're damn right.' He finished his last rib and sat back in his chair, chuckling as he wiped away the deep-red juice from his lips. 'Because it isn't in the Constitution per se, it's in the Declaration of Independence where Jefferson says, We are endowed by our Creator with certain unalienable rights and among them are Life, Liberty and the Pursuit of Happiness. Not the pursuit of happiness until they send you to the slammer after which you are to remain an outcast condemned to suffer for the rest of your time on this earth. No, the Pursuit of Happiness, period. Unalienable. In America, you're still a citizen even if you're doing ten years on a chain gang in Alabama and you're just as entitled to a second chance as Bill Clinton or Teddy Kennedy. You know something, over here you talk about some terrible criminal by his surname, Sutcliffe or Brady or whatever, but we call them Charlie or Tommy because, what the hell, they're still fellow Americans.'

'What about Myra?'

'That's because she's a woman. It don't affect my point. And I'll tell you one more thing before I'm done. What America thinks today the world thinks tomorrow, or maybe next month or next year. I know you folks over here don't much believe in God, but you do believe in rehabilitation, which is only a kind of earthly redemption. You're gonna find quite soon that's the one thing you really do believe in, that everyone deserves another pitch, whether they have just been unlucky or whether they're guilty as hell. Am I right or am I wrong?'

'You're right,' I said. 'We're halfway there already.'

'Talking of lucky, let's go play some chemmy. We can get ourselves coffee over there.'

He rose to his full height, which was still monumental despite his age – what was he, seventy-seven, seventy-eight – flicking the crumbs from his enormous stomach which hung over his belt-buckle like the ice cream melting over the rim of a giant's cone. I followed him, waddling through the glass doors to the casino, bobbing in the wash of his exuberance.

The Vegas Room at the Gando was done up like a fancy saloon on the Strip and you had to thread your way down a promenade of punters grappling with fruit machines before you got to the tables. There was none of the usual chilly ennui around the tables either. The players were jostling one another and when Dodo had collected his chips from the girl cashier with her frilly scarlet top, and waddled over to the high chemin-de-fer table at the end of the room, he was greeted with cries of 'Hey Fat Man', 'Come to drop another bundle?' and other such comments and enquiries. Dodo took all this with great good humour, slapped his gloomy vaguely Levantine neighbour on the back and beckoned to me to take the empty chair two beyond him. But I knew I wasn't up to it and drifted off to the roulette tables to lose £100 and fill a respectable interval before I could go home. In fact, twenty minutes was long enough to drop the lot and remind me how little pleasure I took in the pastime. By the time I went back to the chemmy table, Dodo's pile of chips was less than half its original height and he had out in the middle three or four of the purple £5000 biscuits. His pale sea-green eyes stared impassively at the croupier's deft hand flipping cards out of the shoe. 'Card,' he said in that surprising, light, mild voice and then 'bust' in an equable tone, watching without a tremor as the rake scooped up the purple biscuits.

'I'm off,' I said, 'I haven't got your stamina.'

'Remember what I said, Gus, the guy upstairs always gives you a second chance. That's why I only quit when I'm ahead. Deal me in, Sergio.'

XI

A Bend in the River

'I love these first signs of autumn.'

'You're so perverse,' Nellie said.

'No, I do. The sun on those heavy dews and the first mushrooms. Then the blackberries.'

'Means winter's coming. Gives me the shivers.'

Even after however many years it was we had been married, I looked at her with surprise. Standing there in her long cardigan, with her translucent white plastic bowl nestled in the crook of one arm and the other arm reaching deep into the brambles, she did not seem like someone who would mind about the end of summer.

We had come here, to this bramble thicket just below the beeches, as a ritual act, a sort of thanksgiving or propitiation. Once, when the children were small – for us that phrase now had the same resonance as when my father used to say 'before the war' – we had rented a cottage just where the Chilterns began to steepen. We had taken it for the whole summer, one of those Seventies summers when it was hot as soon as you got up and the fields were white. And it was along this same path that we used to push Elspeth's buggy with Thomas on my shoulders tugging at my hair, not because he needed to cling on but because he enjoyed my yelps of pain. A couple of times since, we had tried to repeat that amazing month, but the cottage was already taken. It was taken this year, too, so instead we had booked rooms for the four of us at an Edwardian hotel on the river, all red-brick gables and white-wood balustrading. In the end, we only needed the one double room because, though the children were back in England now, Thomas had to go to some conference and Elspeth's boyfriend, a demanding schoolteacher, had insisted she go walking on the Pennine Way. But at our age one of the things to get used to was other people changing their plans to unsuit us. Even the time they had come a couple of years back and joined in our gentle amusements – the walk along the towpath, the shared crossword and now the blackberry hunt up the ridge – Nellie always worried that they were humouring us.

On the way up from the car Nell and I stopped at Easton Brett church, as we had done so often before. Nothing much to be seen there – reach-me-down late fourteenth-century flint and stone, redone to death by W. D. Caroe in 1897, font not bad – but stopping there was part of the ritual. Inside the church they were already gearing up for harvest festival. Crates of scabby russet apples and some hefty vegetables encumbered the aisles, and on the chancel steps an elderly woman was arranging a selection of canned foods interspersed with long-tasselled sweetcorn. 'Come ye thankful people come, raise the song of harvest home,' Nellie gurgled into my ear in her unexpectedly flat contralto. When we first went out together I had expected her to be musical, I don't know why. But she was right, this whole day was meant to be our harvest home.

At the top it always took us a minute to catch our breath, these days quite a few minutes, but the climb made us feel superior to the sloths who had driven up to the car park. There were few enough even in high summer and none, it seemed, today. From the top you could see the whole Oxfordshire plain, the motorway curving out of the precipitous cutting and then straightening again, and the cement works blowing white smoke at the far end of the ridge. Sometimes you could see the red kites planing and stooping above the traffic. The red kites had been reintroduced here like the great bustards on the plain. Even wildlife deserved a rerun. We were all entitled to a second chance.

The sun came rather quickly out of the clouds, as it always seemed to there, and the whole panorama was full of a pale golden gleam – the golden moment Nellie called it the first time we saw it – and we stood side by side and watched it come, hover for a few minutes, then fade again.

*

The stock had retreated a long way from its absurd peaks (653 had been the high point) and was now coasting towards the psychological 400 barrier (how quickly one picked up the jargon, coasting seemed to mean going down, but slowly). We still stood to make millions between us at the first moment we could legally sell the shares. We now had leases on forty-seven different premises across the country – our one-stop life-changing network where you could buy a house, take out life insurance, set up a self-invested pensions scheme, insure your car or lease one, and play the stock market with the aid of our unrivalled investment advisers (terms and conditions apply, stocks can go down as well as up etc.). And then there were our American interests. Johnny della Robbia, the old man's son, had just bought a string of dry cleaners and niche leisure complexes all the way down the river from the bend – St Louis, Cairo, Memphis, Little Rock, a couple of other places. 'Leisure complexes? Do you mean amusement arcades?' Trull had queried in his best Lady Bracknell manner.

'Well, not in the old style as you would understand it,' Joe had parried, 'these are more like Net cafés, places you can buy a latte, text your friends, play the latest games.'

But I don't think he knew that much about them (he had been carried away by Johnny's panache) and he was keener to discourse on how they were applying the one-stop Heads concept to commuter towns along the New England shore from Stamford up to Bar Harbor. He had done this spiel as a double act with Jade to half a dozen brokers and Hellman Drax said they had never had such feedback because these were businesses people could relate to in places they knew from living or vacationing in the neighbourhood. Now the two of them, Jade and Joe, were off touring the same double act to institutions and brokers across the Midwest and, according to early reports, getting the same fantastic reactions.

So despite the coasting there was still a sense of abundance in the air. We were on a roll, the ball kept on bouncing out of the trees back on to the fairway.

My basket was half full and I had paused to stretch my back, as Sally had told me to do every ten minutes at least, and was looking idly down the path where it turned from springy turf to muddy clay and dipped down into the beeches. The light was vague, uncertain there, shadowed and a little misty, and at first I did not see the woman pushing the buggy up the path and even then could not make her out clearly in the poor light (my eyes still a little dazzled by the golden moment). The woman seemed to be using all her strength to push the buggy through the half-light, as though she had to come up through the shadows in order to reach our world, she and the child in the buggy being ghosts trying to come back, which, we flatter ourselves, is what ghosts spend a lot of their time trying to do. The whole scene, the contrast between this darker, misty place and the gleaming plain beyond encouraged me to an even weirder fancy, that we might be seeing the ghosts of our younger selves, that here was Nellie with the pushchair and soon, very soon, only a few yards behind, I would see myself coming out of the trees with my son on my shoulders tugging at my hair.

But as they came up on to the grassy bit of the path, I saw that what the woman was pushing was not a child in a buggy at all but an old man in a wheelchair, which would explain why she was finding it such hard work. Even now that reality had reasserted itself and they were out of the muddy shadows moving more easily over the level turf, they still seemed connected to me in some way that was not entirely rational, familiar spirits of a queer sort (odd, that familiar should be the word we use for the most frightening apparition, or not odd at all if you consider who usually crops up in nightmares). That thought induced in me a passive, trancelike mood, so that my eyes glazed over and I wasn't really looking at them in the way you would ordinarily scrutinise a couple of strangers crossing your path. They had come up quite close to us before I recognised them and it was she who recognised me first, although I pride myself on my long sight.

'Gus, what on earth are you doing here?' Pam's voice clanged through the afternoon, dispelling any visionary skeins that might be lingering.

'I could say the same of you, except I suppose, no, of course you live only a few miles away, up that way,' I babbled, in my confusion pointing at what I assumed to be the direction of Much Benham, which she presumably knew well enough. But what had caused my total confusion was not meeting her on this brambled track – which was a legitimate place for flat-haired retrievers to revel and no doubt retrieve things – but the fact that the old man sitting in the wheelchair was her husband.

'And Ian,' I said, 'how ... amazing, what a ...'

He did not speak. I could not even see whether he was trying to, because as he saw me he raised his hand across his face. It was a strange and terrible gesture. At first I thought he was just giving me the casual salute he gave in the old days when he caught sight of me on the steps of the Cabinet Office or at the traffic lights by the Abbey. But instead of making a flipper with his hand like a naval officer and bringing it back down to his side as he used to, he splayed his fingers towards me, fending me off, no, forfending me as though I were an evil spirit sent to harrow him. Almost in the same instant he seemed to lose confidence again and his hand strayed tremulously across his face as though brushing off some insect that he couldn't quite locate. Then his hand fell back on to the plaid rug over his knees and for the first time I really saw his cold, desolate face, pale and waxy like a death mask, except that the eyes were staring out of it, bright and dark as if not part of the mask at all but staring through the waxy sockets.

'I'm afraid you won't get much out of him,' Pam said, 'he had a bad night.'

'When ... when did he ...' I could not think how to begin this, but it had to be begun.

'He was doing much better till my sister Flip came down from Pickering at the weekend. They never hit it off at the best of times.'

'It must be ...'

'It's nice to have the old boy back, but I was getting used to having the house to myself. Men make such a mess, don't they?' She turned to Nellie whom she had not yet greeted. Nellie, never quick on her feet in social situations, was still gawping at the figure in the wheelchair. 'I can't think how he ever thought he could run a restaurant. If he tries to boil an egg he burns the pan.'

'The restaurant is ...?'

'Utter shambles. Honestly, how many people are going to climb a mountain in the middle of nowhere? A nice little man from the Midlands has bought the place, thinks he can make a go of ponytrekking.'

She paused and bent down to retrieve the rug which had fallen off his knees. As her head came level with his, he croaked or mumbled something to her, but the sound was so broken that I could not tell whether he was thanking her or irritated by her fussing over him.

'That poor Welsh boy didn't know what he'd taken on. The whole thing was absurd. He had no money, none at all, but Ian insisted on giving him a half-share. Never works, you know, that sort of arrangement. Flip went halves with her cowman in the milking parlour and look what chaos that caused. I must say the boy's family were very good about it, said they wouldn't presume.'

'That was good,' Nellie said by way of vague encouragement.

'I mean, they could see instantly that they really had no claim.'

'No, of course not.'

'Anyway they hadn't found the body then. Like the rest of us, they thought he'd just buzzed off. Never stayed in one place for long, they said, couldn't settle to anything.'

'I didn't know, he seemed so –'

'Well . . .' She was about to carry on, then thought better of it and continued, not in a softer tone exactly, but speaking as though she did at least know us and we were not just strangers who had to be briefed on the situation. 'Well, no, I suppose you wouldn't, because I couldn't quite face telling you and I don't suppose anyone else would. I should have, I know, because you took such trouble, but it was hard.'

'So you went up there?'

'No, no, not after you told me where he was. I know when I'm not wanted, well, I thought I did until all this. But –' She was near breaking now, and Nellie walked over to her and put an arm round her, rather clumsily, as she was when making such a public show of affection, so that it looked more as if she was shielding Pam rather than hugging her.

'No, he summoned me, poor poppet. Said the boy had gone and he didn't know what to do. Which I didn't expect, not at all. I thought he'd gone that way for good. But old Pam has her uses.'

There was another broken croak from the wheelchair and a hand tried to get out from under the rug.

'Then they found him, the day I got there. Farmer looking for his sheep, down near the coast, saw something at the bottom of one of those blowholes and it was him. That's when he took the pills – Ian, I mean.'

Ian's hand had escaped from the rug and sought hers.

'Why did he do it?'

'Why not? Why does anyone do anything? He didn't leave a note. They said he was depressive. Most people seem to be these days.'

'No note.' For the first time Ian spoke clearly enough to be understood. But he spoke with immense effort, like someone learning to speak again after an operation.

'Well, you didn't leave me a note either, did you, poppet?'

'No note,' he said again.

'I don't expect he was much of a one for writing, a boy like that.'

'No note.'

'Yes, darling, we heard you the first time.'

How long ago had it been that he came skittering down the stairs at Llandiwedd, a nut-brown Welshman on holiday and with that light mocking tone that had so disconcerted me? Four or five months, if that. The pale, broken figure in the wheelchair looked thirty years older. Even when I knelt down beside him on Hilary's sofa after he had his turn at my leaving party, he still seemed full of unexhausted life, though he was in danger of dying on the way to hospital. Now he was drained, mummified almost.

To my surprise, his hand reached out and clutched my wrist. Quite a strong grip, clawlike, not entirely human, pulling me down to his level. He cleared his throat slowly, calling up phlegm from somewhere a long way down. 'Gus,' he managed, after a long, slow, whistling intake. 'Gus,' he said again, with rather less effort.

'Yes,' I said.

'Not long now,' he said. At least I think that was what he said, but his voice had begun to run out of juice again and he might have said 'not long enough'. Either way, the message clearly had to do with mortality, not a message I wished to hear. Luckily that was all he seemed to have to say on that or any other subject.

'It's getting cold,' Nellie said.

'And damp too.'

We gathered up our baskets, still only half full but we hadn't the heart to pick any more. Pam swung the wheelchair round in that brisk way she did most things. We walked alongside her back to the car park.

The natural thing, I suppose, as the mist began to come up from the valley would have been to think of Glad's body sprawled in the sycamore and brambles at the bottom of the deep cavern and the startled farmer peering down. But instead, all I could think of was Ian standing in his smart red T-shirt amid the empty tables waiting for the customers who never came. I wondered whether Glad had ever managed to get the place listed in the guides.

'Would you mind pushing the old boy for a minute?'

'Of course not,' I said and handed my blackberry basket to Nellie.

The women walked on ahead, at a faster clip than I cared for even when I wasn't pushing a wheelchair, but even so Pam's voice carried back to me through the thickening mist.

'I got the local clearance people to get rid of the restaurant stuff. I shouldn't think we'll get half what they paid for it. Stainless steel everywhere, but I suppose that's all EU regulations.'

'It must have been a lot of work,' I heard Nellie say. People like to confide in her. She is so awkward that she doesn't make them feel she is judging them or storing up their revelations to pass on. She just stares at them with her large shining eyes and says how awful or whatever else seems appropriate to her, which is not always what seems appropriate to the person doing the confiding. But somehow that doesn't seem to matter even when she said how awful to a friend of hers who was describing this extraordinary evening when the friend had been seduced on a Corfu beach by a man who later went into film and which had, in fact, been the greatest night of the friend's life.

'Not too bad, really,' Pam said. 'After all, Ian had done his flit with only enough to fill his suitcase, the one he took on business trips for the Ministry. And the boy's mother was happy to take the knick-knacks they'd bought together, which naturally I didn't want cluttering up the place. Ghastly taste anyway. Just shows how right I was never to let him do any of that ridiculous home decorating everyone goes in for now. There was some awful muck upstairs which I just chucked in a bin liner.'

'Oh dear, poor you.'

'I don't really want to go into detail, you know, French letters and that sort of thing. I did find a use for the ointment, though. Turns out to be just the thing for the dogs; they get so sore at this time of year.'

It was getting dark now and the plain was only just visible through the trees. It was a struggle helping Ian into the passenger seat. We waved them goodbye with frenzied smiles.

The house was dark and cold (Nellie couldn't get used to the idea that we could now afford to keep the heating on all the time) and the telephone was ringing, which is never good news, or perhaps it is only that those are the times you remember when you have not had time to put the light on and are still out of breath when you pick up the receiver, so the message that you did not want to hear comes to you out of the dark and you are in no state to respond to it.

Not that initially I was much bothered. By the time you get to our age you have heard more terrible things than that your share price is going down. Most of the agonising was on Tim Stoyt-Smith's side, him being twenty-five years younger.

'But surely it's been coasting for a month or two,' I said in my grown-up way.

'Coasting, not drifting.'

'Is there a difference?'

'Losing thirty points in a month is coasting, losing thirty points in a week is drifting. But on Friday we lost fifty points in a session, we closed at 293. I've been trying to reach you all weekend. Jade and Joe are taking a break somewhere and both their mobiles are off. Jesus.'

'I'm sorry but I don't see how I can help.'

'Get into the market, Gus, first thing tomorrow. Start buying. We can take some of the load at Hellman's but the best thing is if you buy on your own account. That's the real confidence booster.'

'How much would I need to ... ?'

'Fifty thousand minimum, a hundred would be fantastic.'

'It seems –'

'I know it sounds like a lot, but you need to break the flow. Once these runs get momentum, it's like stopping a raging bull, well, raging bear I suppose.'

By any rational calculation, one thing I had enough of in this world was shares in Headsyouwin plc. But this was not a moment for rational calculation, if TS-S's tremulous voice was anything to go by. It was a moment for acts of faith, not a commodity I specialised in but it was never too late to try. My voice sounded quite firm and manly as I said that we had better make it a hundred.

'Fantastic. I'm sure the guys will make it up to you.'

Oddly, I slept well that night, as untroubled by thoughts of the Riley-Joneses as by second thoughts about my reckless investment.

The newspapers the next day were the first, I think, in the history of our venture to be unanimous in casting serious doubts on its prospects. There had always been one or two professional sourpusses who made a living out of predicting disaster for any innovative enterprise but they could be safely disregarded, or so Tim and Mike had told us. Now the mainstream commentators were beginning to purse their lips: *Losing their Heads? ... Is the shine coming off the Jade-and-Joe show? ... Last night the glamorous duo could not be reached. They were said to be on holiday up the Grand Canyon – looking for their cash flow perhaps?*

'But David says we've got half our money in the bank still,' I said after I had rung the brokers.

'Yes, Gus, but, you see, you have to look at the burn rate. Some of the analysts are saying we'll be cinders by the third quarter of oh two. That's way off the spreadsheet of course, but you can't stop them saying it.'

'But they're still saying Hold the shares.'

'Hold means Sell, Gus, to the pros. And there's a couple of Weak Holds in there and that means Sell Fast before the small investor has got his socks on.'

'And –?'

'Yup. Down forty-two already. We've been in there twice this morning. Now we're going to wait for the plateau.'

Paradoxically, it was Mike Gurwitz's voice, that flow of honeyed gravel, that really put the wind up me.

'But what's behind it all? I mean, the trading results from all the UK branches sounded fine at the last executive meeting. I know it's early days but you can't expect miracles.'

'Look, Gus, these guys are operating two years down the track, which is a spooky place to operate because they don't have the numbers. All they have are our old friends Greed and Fear, and as of now Fear is knocking Greed all round the ring. And there's another thing. We're getting word of some shorting operations, major-league action. Don't know where it's coming from yet, but that is the very last thing we need.'

'Shorting?'

'You know, where the fellow borrows the shares to sell them now and agrees to buy them back at half the price in a couple of months. If you sell on a big enough scale, you can bring the price down all on your ownsome to just where you want it to be.'

'Yes, I've had it explained to me.'

'We know our fundamentals are robust but who wants to look at your fundament? It's going to be a rough ride, so hang on to your hats. Oh, and thanks for the hundred. Not many guys would have come through for us like that. We really appreciate it.'

That was when I realised what a huge mistake I had made, a huge, pathetic, elementary mistake. A year's supply of liquid funds had been splashed into the sand just as the sun was coming up over the dunes. In an hour or two there would be no trace of damp. By the time I got to the office, Heads You Win had dipped another thirty and the place was so quiet I could hear my own pulse. They were already sitting round the coffin-shaped boardroom table. There were scarcely any papers on the gleaming renewable surface. When you were falling out of the sky nobody had much time for paper. Paper didn't help. Only voices. This was the time when voice management came into its own. Sounding normal was what you aimed for in the first instance. In fact, sounding normal was brilliant. Not many of us could do it. What went first, I noticed, was pace. The most difficult trick was to go on talking at exactly the same speed as you did when asking for a cup of coffee or passing on the weather forecast. What happened in practice was that people overcompensated for the panic swilling inside them and talked in an exaggerated, almost parodic version of their normal tempo.

Mike Gurwitz, who seemed to be leading the meeting, slowed to lentissimo. 'We. Just. Tough. This. One. Out. Don't. Go. There. Don't. Play. Their. Game.' It was like a video of a lorry tipping gravel, but so slowly you could see the individual stones and pebbles falling through the air.

Tim Stoyt-Smith, whose normal speed was a peppy allegro, delivered in a zesty high tenor, speeded up to a manic presto: 'Yes, absolutely yeah, Mike's spot on, we do this our way. Plan A absolutely yeah I mean we've been in there twice already and we're forty-five down so that's it calmsville we stay with it put out a holding statement. Yeah put out a holding statement, fundamentals absolutely sound, no skeletons, no profits warning of course because we're not into profit yet – on course for trading profit in oh three-four absolutely on course for that.'

He went on like this for a bit until Joe, my old word-fluffing partner in crime, put up a hand in a stately, almost biblical gesture. 'You want me to say something to the press?'

Jade and Joe had got off the plane a couple of hours earlier and he hadn't shaved and looked rough. But it had to be admitted, there was authority about him, not least because his voice sounded exactly the same as usual. Having had a major stroke ten years earlier was perfect preparation for this hour. He could not alter his pace or his expression however hard he tried. Far from his disability diminishing him, he seemed more super- than subhuman. That impassive veil or screen which hid his feelings seemed for once enviable, as though the lingering of his paralysis had heightened the unknowableness we all had, that quality which we used to dignify by such names as spirit and soul.

The bankers babbled that it would be brilliant if Joe could say a few words.

'And Jade, too, would you like her to say something?'

Jade, too, of course, yes, obviously. Which made me look at her for the first time since I had come in. In fact, when I had come in she had been in one of her curled-up sideways-on postures with her hand gently curling and uncurling her long dark hair, not a nervous gesture at all, more part of some slow complex dance movement. Now she was sitting up straight next to Joe at the end of the table like a schoolgirl who has been ticked off for poor posture.

She looked, well, marvellous is the word, even if it is the word one actress says to another when all else fails. But then the glow about her was that of an actress who is still soaking up a standing ovation. She didn't look pale and mysterious any more. She was the goddess whose mysteries had been exposed, possibly profaned. It was extraordinary, I thought, how Joe even in his depleted state could still manage it.

'Oh, but guys, what do you want me to say?'

Now she was parodying the exploited sex icon, the much abused bimbo. She was Marilyn with the Kennedys, mocking herself but mocking her clumsy abusers too.

'Just give them the facts, Jade. The new trading figures which David is checking as we speak, the cash burn absolutely on schedule, and you can report first-hand on the picture in the States. You've got a great story to tell and nobody can tell it the way you do.'

A lubricious burble of agreement. Then, in the silence that followed – there were quite a few silences in this meeting, one of the things about these situations is how lost for words most people are – a discreet cough, the cough of an old-fashioned servant, a Jeeves cough. From Trull, so beautifully turned out in his light Italian weave from Lapello and his new tinted specs. 'Will they ask, do you think, about Johnny della Robbia?'

'We had a fantastic time with Johnny. I never knew dry cleaning could be such fun.'

'He didn't by any chance mention his difficulties with the FBI?' Trull persisted.

'No, he did say how we wouldn't believe the pressure the authorities still put on Italian Americans but that was all.'

'That's one way of describing it, I suppose,' said Trull, leaning back and looking down at us through his new glasses with their crude plastic frames, like children's toy specs.

'What exactly are you saying there, Keith?' Mike Gurwitz's seemed jolted out of his super-slow panic mode into something approaching normal human speech pace.

'Well, you rashly gave me oversight on compliance, so I thought we needed someone to do a little background work. On Joe's recommendation, I hired former Chief Inspector Jervoise, who I think is well known to you too, Gus. He has good US contacts and he's turned up some interesting stuff on your friend Johnny. Nothing indictable yet, but then it may come out the congressional route first. I'm told that's often the best way to get the evidence on the record and encourage the birds to start singing.'

'What the hell is all this, Trull?' As a sign of his agitation, Joe reverted to the surname he had always used in the old days. 'What on earth can be dodgy about a chain of dry cleaners?'

'The word is it's not only trousers they're laundering.'

'I don't believe it.'

'Well, when Heads bought those dear little shops, who did you make the cheque out to?'

'Oh, a holding company, Progressive Laundry Investments, some name like that. They asked if they could keep a minority stake in the business and we were very happy with that.'

'Ah yes, well, it appears that the money they were originally holding was a touch too progressive.'

'Christ. You mean they actually bought the shops with the unmentionable and then sold them on to us.'

'Something like that.'

'Well, we haven't done anything wrong.'

'But we still own a chain of shops the length of the Mississippi in partnership with persons who appear to be closely connected to that Italian-American organisation which has been, as you say, so pressurised by —'

'No, I don't think I want to know any more about it. We better get rid of them. And David, I don't want any of this minuted.'

'I defer to our learned friends from Hellman Drax,' Trull persisted, 'but I should have thought that the news we were disposing of such glittering assets only months after we had acquired them would hardly be likely to appeal to market sentiment.'

'Christ.'

'You are a bastard, Trull,' Jade said. 'Why didn't you tell us before we went?'

'I didn't want to prejudice you, my dears. Better to hear your own first impressions.'

'Well, I thought Johnny was a star. I expect it's just some jealous rival dissing him.'

'I do hope so.'

'How long have we got before —?'

'Oh, a couple of weeks, I'd say, though there is some journo who's said to have got hold of it already, Jervoise said Bob Woodward, but I think Jervoise is something of a star-fucker.'

'So we're damned if we sell and damned if we don't.'

'Nicely put.'

'Shit.' Now Joe did look seriously distraught. The bad news on top of the jet lag had unfrozen his face, giving it a mournful, dragged-down expression with a curious mouchy turn to his mouth. He looked like some hairy type of Highland cattle browsing on stony ground, a yak even. He also looked old, old like we all were except Jade who was still glowing. She seemed to have the recommended capacity to treat triumph and disaster just the same. And Trull, too, was still in good shape. Perhaps knowing things that other people did not know and then telling them kept your self-confidence inviolate. He remained dapper in a front-of-house way, not emotionally engaged in the disaster that was happening out on stage.

I wondered if we would get through the day, or even the morning. In the end, we decided to put out a statement: Headsyouwin plc remains puzzled by the turbulence surrounding the company's share price. Our revenue forecasts for the current year are unchanged, the company's acquisitions in the United States are trading satisfactorily, the cash position remains sound etc., etc.'

Didn't do a blind bit of good. We were down ninety-two on the day by the close, way below the launch price. If you had put some money in HYW at the peak, you would have lost two-thirds of it. The hundred I had so dumbly ventured shortly after breakfast had lost nearly a third of its value.

'Oh, so we're poor again,' Nellie said with one of her goofy smiles which was meant to be mocking but comforting at the same time and in my fragile state annoyed me hugely. She was chopping leeks and listening to some baroque tinkling on the radio. Everything about her said, here I am, a real person to come home to when that trumpery world has finished with you. In theory, I loved her indifference to designer labels and trendy chefs and everything electronic and flickery. But there were times when her contempt for the contemporary just seemed like old-fashioned snobbery and a dank variant at that – and it was the last thing I wanted to hear now. In fact, I would have preferred her to break down in helpless sobs and start throwing saucepans, but that was never on the cards.

In bed that night she put her long arms round me and I nestled against her, feeling infinitesimally small, not so much like a baby as like some tiny fleshy parasite which was liable to be squashed if she moved too abruptly in the bed, but by this stage my churning wits must finally have switched off for the night.

That was Wednesday. On Thursday morning the shares plateaued for an hour or two while the amateurs took advantage of what the poor fools saw as a buying opportunity. But our spirits kept on heading south.

Joe wasn't in the office.

'Jet lag I'm told,' Trull said. 'But Dr Trull diagnoses a touch of LMF.'

'LMF?'

'Lack of Moral Fibre. Still, it means we needn't have another one of those ghastly meetings. Without our leader we are but a demoralised rabble.'

'Trull, please.'

'I'm so sorry, I'm just the tiniest bit edgy this morning, I can't imagine why.'

He didn't seem edgy at all, except he had dropped into old high camp, which normally meant something was up, usually something that you could not be expected to see coming.

'Trull, I'm afraid we do need a quickie meeting. Won't take more than five minutes.' Jade was dressed in a boxy plum velvet jacket with black trimmings and a furry cap, like a hussar in a ballet.

In the event, the Hellman Drax duo also wanted to come down and update us. So down they came, chalk-faced, both of them looking as if they had just thrown up. Mike was still speaking at dictation speed, so he had got nowhere before Jade interrupted him, herself speaking rather quicker than usual.

'Do you mind, Mike, love? It's only a little personal news, but it really is business-relevant.'

'Jade please go right ahead.'

'Well, the news is I'm engaged to be married. Woo, doesn't that sound really retro, like Jane Austen or something. Anyway, we're getting married next June, so it's like a really long engagement, you know, Victorian.'

'No, *fan*tastic, congratulations.' Mike, as the latest person to speak clearly felt it his job to respond. But something about the announcement left him fazed, and not just him either. 'Can we, is Joe...' he stumbled on.

'Oh, Joe was the first to know.'

This struck us all as intolerably witty and we fell about. We hadn't had anything much to laugh at for some time and we were out of practice but we did our best.

'You've all met him, I think. Gus certainly and Trull, oh, and Mike and Timmy, he snapped us all at the launch, I'm sure you remember.'

'You mean,' I said, 'that you're going to marry xandre?'

'Yes, isn't it amazing? He's wanted to for ages. In fact, he's proposed to me on practically every shoot we've done this year. But I wasn't sure if I had, you know, the marriage gene in me. I mean, Gus, look at Mum. Then he ran out of petrol when we were going up to the NEC and he kicked that silly car of his and he looked so sweet and I thought he's not going to go on doing this for ever, proposing I mean, so I thought let's go for it.'

'Well, that's fantastic,' said Mike Gurwitz, looking even paler than when he came in. He reached for the carafe of Malvern and I saw his hand shake. 'He's one terrific guy, that xandre, and I wish you all the very best.'

'Thank you very much, Mike.' She got up and bent over and kissed him just above the eyebrow, which unmanned him further.

'I don't quite know how to say this,' Mike continued, examining his shaking hands with glazed eyes, 'but I do appreciate you telling us this wonderful news in this forum because, because...'

She bent her head at an angle and smiled sweet encouragement at him.

'It is a difficult matter but out there in the market there are certain expectations.'

'Yes, I know,' she said, keeping the smile going.

'Expectations which we in our own small way have encouraged, at any rate not discouraged.'

'Mm.'

'Expectations that you and Joe here, well, not here in person as it happens, you and Joe were shall we say an item. Naturally that would be a purely private matter if it were so, and Joe Public, the public anyway I had better say to avoid confusion, had no business poking its nose into your business. But there it is, that is how they have come to see this company and that is to some extent how we have marketed it, you know, the Jade and Joe show. And now you're telling us we have to go out there and tell them it just ain't so, and what are they going to think? I'll tell you what they are going to think. They'll think there's been the mother of all bust-ups between the two of you and you've – excuse me, I'm just saying what they'll think – you've flounced off and married the nearest guy who happens to be this two-bit paparazzo who takes all your pictures.'

'xandre is not a two-bit paparazzo.'

'I'm just giving you the reaction. Doesn't afford me pleasure, I wish it were otherwise, but I have to say it, this is just about the worst development you can think of for our share price. It completely destroys our market strategy.'

'Oh, and our strategy was going so swimmingly,' Trull murmured.

'Mike, Mike, he is not a paparazzo, you just don't –' Jade was leaning right across the table now, almost yelling at Gurwitz, who had turned the other way to yell back at Trull.

'No, but Keith you fucking well know what I'm telling you. This company was all about a unique mix of sound commercial propositions and kooky charm. It was a people company and the pitch was you just had to love the people. Now we're telling them the people don't love each other any more. You're telling me that's the good news?'

'Listen, just listen will you, xandre is *not* a two-bit paparazzo.' Jade was up on all fours now, halfway across the gleaming coffin top. Mike Gurwitz was recoiling from her and making a choking noise. He was also fumbling in his pocket and for a wild second I thought he might have a gun there, but what he brought out was a blue-and-grey inhaler. He took a couple of long gasps and while he was speechless Jade grabbed hold of him by the shoulders and shook him so hard that he nearly swallowed the inhaler and was choking even worse than before. In fact, it was hard to say whether it was Jade or the inhaler stuck halfway down his gullet that was contributing most to his desperate gasps.

Timmy Stoyt-Smith now came to his colleague's rescue, gripping Jade by the frogging on her hussar's jacket and trying to push her back, which caused her knees to skid across the shiny surface, and made her fall forward, loosening Stoyt-Smith's precarious grip, but he clutched again and now for a second he had her round the throat before he let go, blushing a sweaty smoked-salmon colour at the horror of having nearly throttled her. Jade crawled back to her chair feeling her neck and making a mewling sound which in no time broke out into sobs. Mike Gurwitz now had an uninterrupted pull at his Ventalin but he was a terrible pasty colour and I wondered if there wasn't something more serious amiss with him.

'Please, my friends, please,' Trull said. 'I think we all want to congratulate Jade and say how happy we are for her.'

'You nearly strangled me, you stupid cunt.'

'Jade, Jade, I'm so sorry,' Stoyt-Smith whimpered.

'I'm only engaged you know,' Jade sobbed, 'I haven't killed anyone.'

'And I'm sure,' Trull continued imperturbably, 'that our friends at Hellman Drax are as delighted as we are.'

'Excuse me, I need . . . bathroom.' Mike Hurwitz shot from his chair like a fighter pilot ejecting.

'That's a pity,' Trull remarked after he had gone, 'Mike's input would have been so valuable. Because we do need to think, rather urgently I suggest, about how we might handle the presentation of all this.'

'What presentation?' Jade asked fiercely. 'I'm just getting married, that's all. Why does everything around here have to be a fucking presentation? I'm sick of all this phoney PR crap.'

'But my dear, you are the queen of these black arts. It's like Raymond Blanc saying he's sick of sauces. You are the only person who can save us.'

'What do you mean?'

'You must realise that there was a good deal in what poor Mike said – Timmy, perhaps you should go and see if he's all right, you know where it is I'm sure – nothing was said explicitly, of course, but we did rather encourage the impression that there was at the very least, what shall I say, a *tendresse* between you and Joe. I am not suggesting that any such thing existed in reality and I would not dream of asking whether it did, none of us would, I am sure, but the fact remains that we never contradicted the press reports. Indeed, we rather wallowed in them, discreetly I like to think, but wallowed nonetheless. We allowed the thought of that supposed item to colour our image, to lend it, as Mike has said, a certain kooky charm. But now –'

He fluttered his hands in a stylised way to indicate a helplessness which he clearly did not feel.

'So what am I supposed to do? Get up and wriggle my bum and say sorry, I never screwed the old guy, this is the man of my dreams?'

'Jade, I don't think we are quite strong enough for the full-frontal approach. But it would be much appreciated if you invited the press to take a glass of wine to meet your fiancé. At San Lorenzo, say, or the Groucho, nothing too fancy.'

'But they all know xandre already. I mean they go on jobs together all the time.'

'Oh, I thought he wasn't a paparazzo.'

Jade had the grace to laugh, although the tears on her cheeks were still wet, but then she had the grace to do anything and if anyone could get us out of this quagmire she was the one.

Perhaps, I ventured, a little event of this sort might actually distract people from their obsession with our share price. This suggestion sounded so weak and improbable that I found myself floundering on to support it and was relieved when Sally came in and slipped a message in front of me that she said was urgent, which I believed as she was too grand now to bring in messages. On the badly folded bit of paper torn from a ring notepad it said, in Joe's trembly hand (never recovered from the original stroke): '*Come out NOW and meet me in S's room.*' He hadn't bothered to sign it.

I made my excuses.

'I seem to be doomed to the role of the boy upon the burning deck whence all but he had fled.' Trull was still loving it.

Sally's office was on the next floor down in the Technical Support Suite, a good place to hide from the armed struggle. She waved me in and disappeared on to her operating floor.

Joe was sitting hunched on the guest's chair. He had shaved but otherwise he looked worse than the day before, eyes red-rimmed and staring, and his face pouchy and slack as though it had come loose from his skull. And even with my sense of smell I could smell the drink as soon as I closed the door. Yesterday he had looked jet-lagged and old. Today he was terminally pitiable. Even so, when he looked up at me there was a terrible memory of boyishness in his look. It was like the way a beggar looks up at you from the pavement and something about the way the face has to twist up makes you think about how he must have looked as a boy and how much must have gone wrong. Perhaps beggars know about the effect of this upturning and pass on the secret to one another. Perhaps Joe knew it too. He had always traded on his freckles.

'You've heard, then?'

'About them getting married? Yes, she just told us.'

'She only told me on the plane back. Not much fucking warning.'

'But you must have known, known it was on the cards, I mean.'

'Not a clue. Not a fucking clue.'

'Oh. That's tough. Did you think that you and she might –?'

'Might what?'

'Eventually might –'

'Get married ourselves? Did you really think that, Gus? I don't believe it.'

'I don't understand.'

'You really thought that we –'

'Yes, of course I did. You told me you were. Quite distinctly. First you said you weren't and then you said you were.'

'I know I told you, but I didn't expect you to believe me.'

'Well, why did you tell me, then? And if you lied to me then, why should I believe you now?'

'Look, you still don't understand. The point is I was telling everyone, so I had to tell you too. You all had to sing from the same hymn sheet. It was her idea originally. Let's pretend we're having an affair, she said. It'll be brilliant for the business. Nobody will believe it, I said, for one thing look at the age difference. That's just what makes it so exciting, she said, anyway everyone always believes stories like that because they want to. Well, she was right about that. Nobody doubted it for a second, not even you, and you had background knowledge.' He grunted sourly at the thought.

'So it was entirely a put-up job – all the time?'

'Yes and no.' He was miserably hunched and twisted in the spindly chair like a tormented figure in a Francis Bacon. One thing about Bacons that I could never understand was where these tormented figures were actually supposed to be on these spindly chairs against a bare beige background and now I realised that what they were doing was having a bad day at the office.

'But it must have been fun, though, playing this game and fooling the rest of us.'

'Fun? It was hell, absolute bloody hell. Not at the start, I suppose, because I thought here's an angle, here's one way I can pull it off.'

'Pull it off?'

'Have her, get inside her knickers, fuck her. Can I make it any clearer? I thought you were supposed to be the clever one.'

'Oh, so you wanted –'

'Of course I wanted her. Every man for miles around wanted her. Everyone who saw her picture in the papers wanted her. For Christ's sake even the people she schmoozed on the phone wanted her. Do you think I would be the only exception in the entire sodding universe? Gus, come on.'

'Hi, how ya doing, mind if we park this little darling here?' Two young men, dressed almost the same in leather jackets and black T-shirts that said rap-something across the chest, came in bearing a large model of a human head.

'Sally just popped out, has she?' enquired the one with the spiked yellow hair, while the other one who was shaven-headed busied himself with settling the model on the table. The head was translucent and faintly glistening, made of perspex or some glassy plastic, and life-size, no, bigger, nearly two feet high in fact, and inside it you could see the works, the intestinal coiling of the brain and all the stems, veins and assorted ganglia.

'I hope she won't be long.'

'Because she promised to sign the project off today.'

'What the fuck is this?' Joe growled.

'It's for the Head Zone.'

'We're from Rapunzel Designs.' They talked in alternate sentences, each one giving a slightly aggrieved twist to the end of his bit, as though he would have preferred to handle the whole thing by himself.

Then I remembered – and I saw Joe did too – that Sally had cajoled us into doing something for the millennium and this must be it. Sally was Exhibitions and Events as well as Technical Support. In fact, Exhibitions and Events was the part she liked best now and her office was always cluttered with all the apparatus of the trade: billboards, dump bins, banners, flimsies, press packs, foldaway stands.

'He's called Brainbox. Didn't you see the Phase One Mock-up? He's so cute. You go in here, through the mouth, see, and the atmosphere's all sticky and humid and then you go on this little escalator that takes you up the nasal passage and now you're all red and gooey –'

'Get out.'

'The whole tour takes seventeen minutes, so that means a throughput –'

'Get out and take that fucking thing with you.'

'Could you give us any idea when Sally will –'

Joe got up in his stiff hemiplegic way that made him look more frightening and was about to seize the model, but the boy with golden spikes was too quick for him and clasped it to his chest, so Joe went over to the door and opened it, making stiff shoving motions like a traffic policeman, and they didn't hang about.

I hoped the interruption might break his flow and we could talk of something else but he sat down in the chair again in the tormented Bacon position and started from the beginning in the same agonised tone, just as though an unseen director had cut and told him to go again from the top. And although this was not what I wanted, as a performance it was certainly impressive. That was what will-power amounted to, after all, the capacity to repeat the performance until you had got whatever it was you needed, repeat it without hesitation or embarrassment, or in Joe's case, since his speech still had some of the jerkiness left over from the stroke, with hesitation but without embarrassment.

'You can't imagine what it was like. At first we had agreed not to paw each other in public but just let the rumour run – no snogging, she said – and that was bad enough because I just wanted to stroke her hair and kiss her neck and that would be enough, I thought. Do you remember those times, Gus, when you fancied a girl so much that all you could imagine doing was stuff like that?'

'Yes, of course I do, but I'm surprised that you –'

'Oh, I know what you think of me. You think I always want to go straight for the jugular.' Which wasn't exactly the phrase but I knew what he meant. 'You don't think guys like me have any romantic feelings.'

'No, I don't think that.' Which was true because although Joe's methods of going for a woman were certainly direct, even rough, I never doubted that for the period of engagement he was consumed with something that could only be called love. Certainly the women he went for – the ones I knew, anyway – seemed to think so and I don't believe they were duped because they were bright enough to be sure that he was incapable of putting it on. Denseness was his secret weapon.

'But then she said it was time to change because the punters would be getting bored of the don't-touch routine, so we ought to start pawing each other just a little. It was at breakfast in the Holiday Inn or whatever in Leeds and she said quite cool and down to earth that I should start putting my hand on hers and stroking her, discreetly, nothing too sexy but just enough to attract attention. Well, I hated it, the cold way she told me what to do, it was so automatic, but still I thought that, you know, it might lead to something more. So we went straight from breakfast, you know when you still feel the fry-up inside you, on to the platform for the presentation. And, you know, the strangest thing, I just couldn't do it. Touch her, I mean. I just sat there frozen. I don't know, perhaps it was because I had had to restrain myself so long or perhaps because of the stroke, it still does funny things to my reactions, but I just couldn't bring myself to. So she gave me this smouldering look and that made it even worse. Then afterwards she said "what the hell" and I said "oh sorry, Jade, I just forgot", which wasn't exactly tactful.'

'And then –'

'Well, in the afternoon we had another presentation, at Harrogate, and I had a couple of glasses at lunch, and I was relaxed and it all went like a breeze. I slipped my hand gently over hers like a real smoothie, and you could hear the intake of breath from the old dears and the local brokers told me afterwards that they were rushed off their feet with orders. So she was right, Jade, she's always right, really.'

'So it ended happily.'

'No, that was only the beginning of the bad time. Because of course I had another couple of glasses at dinner in the hotel and we were getting on brilliantly again, so after dinner you can imagine what happened.'

'You made a pass.'

'Well, I kissed her in the passage and she didn't mind it, it was just a good-night kiss, and then I tried to follow her into the room and she wouldn't have that but she didn't lock the door on me – I suppose she thought it would be common or something. So a bit later I went in and, well, she was very angry and so was I. You can imagine all the things we said, I said she was a pricktease and she said I was a pathetic old man and completely unprofessional, which I resented.'

'Pricktease is worse.'

'Anyway, she threw me out. I couldn't imagine she could ever speak to me again, but there she was the next morning bright as anything, little kiss on the cheek, told me not to take things so hard. And off we went, Newcastle, Edinburgh. She didn't seem to mind a bit.'

'But you –'

'I was in agony. Every time I went through our routine, patting her hand or stroking her hair, it was like an electric shock going through me, and then when she had to do her bit, smiling at me or putting her arm through mine, it was like, you know, jump leads. All I could do was try to carry things on in private but she didn't respond at all. When we were alone together it was like stroking a chair. At first I thought she was leading me on, trying to stoke me up, but then I saw she was completely uninterested. I couldn't sleep, I couldn't think and it made me so angry, Gus. I mean with her past when you think of all the men, why on earth won't she? No, don't answer, of course I can see why. All the time she was saving herself for this fucking photographer.'

He paused, his misery or his breath exhausted for the moment. I was still where I had been all the time, sitting on the corner of the desk. Outside I could see birds planing over the black water of the dock.

They, too, were black against the sullen sky and for a moment I fancied they were birds of prey but then I could see they were only gulls.

'Back to Sick Heart River, then,' I said.

'No, I told you,' he said, gesturing out of the window, 'this is Sick Heart bloody River and I've had enough of it.' For once he was right. But before I had time to protest that he wasn't finished yet the phone rang and it was Trull.

'Ah, there you are. Press conference and photocall for the happy couple in twenty minutes. We've got to catch the late editions.'

So there we were one more time being photographed, the four of us plus xandre, only this time xandre was not behind the camera but holding hands with Jade, while the three old codgers stood behind them and did their best to beam. There was a crowd of reporters and photographers crammed round the coffin table in the boardroom. It was too cold and wet to go out, which made me think of the happier photo shoots when we had squinted into the sun on the quayside and half believed that by some unsought miracle we had been given a second chance.

I didn't dare to look at Joe when the questions began flying. I just concentrated on smiling and facing front.

'Joe, how do you feel about losing out to a younger man?'

'Which is worse, seeing your share price go through the floor or losing Jade?'

'Jade, can you confirm that younger men make better lovers?'

'Joe, is this a case of Tails You Lose?'

Jade and Joe were brilliant. They teased the hacks back, Joe gave Jade a smacking kiss, he hugged the pair of them, we all swore that none of us had ever been happier, and we were all thinking about the wedding and couldn't give a damn about the market. It was agony. The whole business must have lasted no more than half an hour but it seemed a lifetime. Somehow, though, I thought, Joe had pulled it off. He had dredged up from somewhere a beguiling innocence, which had charmed the reporters and turned their sour intrusive questions into the most harmless banter.

After the reporters had gone, Joe came into my room and sat down and sobbed like a child. Then he went home to his big empty house, which had been a South American consulate or something and still felt like one. Jade and xandre went out to celebrate at the Waterworks and Trull called me into his office.

'You know Mr Jervoise, of course.'

I had not at first seen the mournful dark figure. He was sitting in the corner of the room hidden from the door.

'He has to be brief, because he has a plane to catch back to New York. But I wanted you to hear from him first-hand and under secure conditions. Would you mind sitting a little closer?'

I pulled my chair so close that I could inhale the delicate, minty scent of Jervoise's breath. Trull had pulled his chair closer too, so that our knees touched. Beside him on the desk there was an old-fashioned electric fan which he preferred to the air conditioning. He switched it on to full strength, which tousled our hair and made a brisk brrr.

'Right. Shoot.'

'Mr Trull, as you know, asked me to make some enquiries about the US businesses you purchased. I understand he's already told you something of Mr della Robbia's connections.'

'Yes.'

'Unfortunately that's not the worst of it. The dry cleaning businesses may be embarrassed by these links with organised crime, but they are at least solvent. The problem really arises with the insurance companies. The due diligence was conducted by auditors who were, shall we say, friendly to Mr Wilmot and they did not uncover the full extent of the group's liabilities. The truth is that the previous management has sucked them dry. The usual tricks, nothing fancy. Reinsuring the risks with stooge companies who then pass the premiums back to him as management fees, then go broke.'

'Has this got out?'

'No, not yet. My man says you've got a couple of weeks' grace, though I don't know exactly what you can do.'

'So that's not a reason for the shares to dive so violently over here?'

'As it happens I can help you there too. It came out quite accidentally. I asked my agent to track some of Wilmot's share dealings. And he turned out to be unusually active in the UK market, acting in parallel with an old associate of his, a former mobster by the name of Ray Rawston. The two of them appeared to be conducting large-scale shorting operations on the London market. And the shares they were concentrating on – nearly half their activity, in fact – were yours.'

'Christ.'

'In a strong bull market I'm told the shares would have a chance of riding out even operations on such a scale, but the market these days is rather uncertain, toppy I believe the technical term is, and by spreading their operations over the rest of the financial services sector they weaken the whole sector and thus further undermine their principal target. A new company like Heads You Win can be especially vulnerable, because so many of the shareholders are anxious to cash in the substantial profits they made in the bull market since flotation. After all, they are unlikely to see a dividend for a year or two.'

Well, I had warned them, nobody could say I hadn't, though this was not the moment to say so. The truth was that since that bootless warning I myself had become comfortable with our alliance with Dodo. He was a crook, I thought, but he was our crook. His fertile brain, his dealer's itch, his total ruthlessness were all at our service. Other British firms had come unstuck as soon as they put a toe into the American market, but we were going to be different, because we had the inside track smoothed and raked for us by the ultimate insider. Except that it turned out the only person he was raking for was himself. You couldn't accuse him of inconsistency.

We sat there, Trull and I, with the dull light of the Docklands sky blanching our faces which were pale enough already. Even Trull didn't seem to have much to say. The only noise in the room was the brrr of the fan. Perhaps it was my jittery state but it seemed to have switched to a clattery tone, like that of jackdaws in a distant chimney. With an abrupt movement, Trull switched it off and the room felt cold and empty although there were three of us in it.

'Would you like me to send in an interim report? I could get something to you by the weekend.'

'The less we have on paper the better.'

'I couldn't agree more, my dear sir. And if I might offer a further word of advice, I'd keep the phone on the hook. And no e-mails either.'

'Certainly no e-mails. Thank you, Jervoise.' I noticed that Trull and Jervoise liked this old-retainer style of talk, both of them deriving pleasure from playing stylised roles. The crisis seemed to have pumped up Trull. He responded to each new calamity with coherence and even élan.

'Word of mouth only, then. Could you tell Jade, Gus, while I go round to Joe. I thought he looked in a bad way and if I don't get a grip on him he might do anything.'

We broke up and I walked Jervoise to the lift.

'Oh, by the way, sir, I thought I'd kill two birds with one stone and bring along my account.'

I unfolded the grubby piece of paper which had Jervoise's address typed at the top and then, in his tidy handwriting, 'to professional services £5000'.

'That's for cash, you understand. Without VAT.'

'It seems rather a lot.'

'Well, your subject did a good job of hiding himself away.'

'I suppose so, but it was me who found him.'

'Groundwork, sir. You wouldn't have done it without the ground-work.'

'I haven't got that sort of money on me.'

'I don't mind waiting.'

'All right, you can wait in my office while I get it organised.'

'Good idea. You wouldn't want me walking down the street with you. Some of my old friends in these parts might get the wrong idea.' He gave a dry cluck, which was as near as I remembered him coming to a joke.

I put on my Rainman and went round the corner to the HSBC branch. The girl at the till didn't blink as she counted me the money out in fifties. How peculiar it was to be settling another brick of cash under my Rainman only a year after the first when in the rest of my life I had never seen such a pile of banknotes outside gangster films. When I got back Jade was sitting in my chair entertaining the ex-Chief Inspector.

'Oh, Gussie, I was just telling your friend about my wedding. It's going to be absolutely fantastic. The French church in Soho because of xandre. It turns out he's a Huguenot, isn't that amazing? And then a carriage absolutely splurged in flowers to take us to the hotel, I said Claridge's but xandre thinks the Dorchester because he so loves the Thirties and Paula's going to do the flowers because she's such a friend of xandre. The only downside is that Sir Bouncy's going to want to give me away. Would you do it, Gus? Or perhaps, no, I suppose Joe wouldn't, or if it has to be a relation Mum could do it. Does it say it has to be a man? Having Mum would be so cool.'

'You know we're going bust, don't you?'

'Bust?'

'Bust, broke, belly-up, heading south. They just touched seventy-five.'

'Oh, the shares will recover. Shares can go up as well as down, that's what it says.'

'Tell her.'

Jervoise told her.

All at once she crumpled and went as quickly as a child from insouciance to utter misery, not bothering to hide her sobbing.

'But Trull,' she said when she had half pulled herself together, 'Trull said we'd get through, it was just, you know, like a bad patch. I mean, we were big before we ever heard of Dodo Wilmot.'

'Trull must be on something,' I said. 'Nobody could be that calm.'

'Unless he was, shall we say, insured,' Jervoise said in that pregnant super-quiet way he had.

'How do you mean? He stands to lose millions, more than any of us, in fact.'

'In the course of my enquiries one of my professional informants pointed out to me that these days shorting is not the only way of profiting from a downturn in the market, or a particular sector thereof.' He paused at the 'thereof', savouring its antique slither on the palate. 'Indeed,' he continued, confident that he had us gripped, 'it is a rather cumbersome device, since getting hold of the shares in the first place is not cost-free and can be difficult to organise. How much easier simply to place a series of bets with one of the spread-betting agencies. For every point such-and-such an index or such-and-such a company goes down, you gain such-and-such a sum, and conversely, you lose if it goes up. As you can imagine, such bets are highly leveraged. If the stock market collapses, a modest stake will very quickly produce a huge return. Well, I thought, in my enquiries it would be helpful to know who was betting big in this particular area, since if news of large-scale spread betting gets around, it impacts upon the index and, of course, vice versa.' Another pause to let the hiss of 'versa' expire. Then he asked if we were following him and I said we were getting the general drift.

'These bets are highly confidential. Many of the punters are senior executives in multinational companies who stand to make substantial sums in share options and performance bonuses if the market keeps on rising. It would not be good for confidence if it were known that they were in effect betting against the success of their companies. The word is that spread betting is currently doing as much as the shorting to drag prices down, perhaps more. The details of the transactions are securely encrypted, there is very little possibility of hacking into them. However, there is another possible modus operandi.'

'Get on with it.'

'Their chief IT security officer is a former colleague of mine; he has a remarkable head for figures but no head at all for wine. We had not ordered the dessert before he was going on about how I wouldn't believe how many CEOs and suchlike were betting against their own sector. In his position I would have held out for some more substantial inducement than lunch at the Paradiso e Inferno in the Strand, a favourite of mine but not exactly the Caprice.'

'And?'

'Your Mr Trull and a couple of his nominees – transparent, they were, only took me half an hour to trace the connection – stand to make three or four million at the present market level, obviously a good deal more if it goes on sinking. So it's not surprising he looks so calm.'

'And if the market had gone up?'

'Oh, he'd have lost as much again, but then think how much more he'd have gained on his shares. As I say, it's just insurance.'

'So either way he's sitting pretty.'

'Snug as a bug in a rug.'

'And he hasn't done anything wrong?'

'It's not against the law. As far as I know, there's nothing on the subject from the Financial Services Authorities either, no *obiter dicta.*'

There was enough rage swilling inside me to spare a little for Jervoise's habit of deploying Latin phrases which seemed to have grown on him of late. What I felt for Trull was in any case not plain loathing but a mixture of resentment and fascination. How peculiar it was to have known someone so long, off and on, and yet still to be taken aback by what he was capable of. How regularly it came round, as regularly as a lighthouse beam, his eye for the main chance, so bright, so unblinking. Nothing could deflect it. And in a way you were almost glad to see it, to be reassured that business was still being carried on at that address. Once or twice in all the years I had known him I had seen him, only for a moment, look discomposed – a couple of times during my visit to the prison, then again in the early days of Heads You Win when he had seemed a little lonely – and those moments were weirdly unsettling. He had looked sad and empty, and my heart missed a beat, as though my happiness were bound up with his. Nellie would have said that I had a repressed crush on him – she often said such things, as though to show that she wasn't an unworldly scholarly type but just as interested in sex and gossip as the rest of us. But I don't honestly think that was so. It was more, I thought, that you couldn't help being mesmerised by the shimmer of his self-confidence, his iron-willed cool and you didn't want to see it crack because it reminded you how fragile we all were.

Anyway, there he was down the corridor sitting on a mat in the lotus position, making strange slow gestures with his arms under Sally's directions, without a care in the world.

'Well, you seem to be all right.'

'Oh yes, please do excuse me. Sally is most particular about tackling stress at source. You mustn't just carry on in the good old British tradition, isn't that right, Sal? Always take time to sort yourself out.'

Sally corrected the position of Trull's arms and smiled at us. 'Mr T gets so tense.'

'Really,' I said, 'I hadn't noticed.'

'Oh dear,' Trull said, 'I sense froideur. I do beseech you, don't let's have a tiff. The plight of our American investments can scarcely be laid at my door. If I remember rightly, it was Joe who was so gung-ho and even you, my dear Jade, thought it would be fantastic – or was it fab? – to go over to the States all the time.'

'Don't be so shitty, Trull.'

'We're not talking about America,' I said, 'we're talking about the spread betting.'

'Oh, that.' He smiled and very slowly with Sally sitting alongside him, extended his arms in a curve until his fingertips met. 'You have suddenly become opposed to gambling, then. You regard it as not quite cricket to insure one's little nest egg. You have become severe in your old age, Gus, but then I always knew there was a puritan streak in you.'

'Come off it, Trull,' Jade said, with a sudden briskness which wasn't like her but was exactly the way her mother spoke when nettled. 'You know perfectly well that betting against us destroys the share price if it gets out.'

'Prove it,' Trull said.

At this moment for the first time I became too angry to speak. In fact, it was unbearable to stay in the room a minute longer, especially when Sally began to guide Trull through a strange swaying exercise suggesting galley slaves operating in slow motion.

What I needed was not a stand-up fight but a refuge from this ghastly world. I wanted to go home and blot out everything in the long, yoga-free arms of my loving wife. All this week I had been working ten, twelve hours a day to prop up this doomed enterprise and all I had to show for it was another wad of worthless shares in it. The sooner I returned to the real world of flesh and blood, the better for my mind and probably my body too. A collapsing share price could probably give you cancer, most things seemed to. By the time I left the office Heads had touched 39p.

All the way home my head was flooded with homely images of escape, memories of the quiet times Nellie and I had not so much enjoyed together as taken for granted. This was the life we were made for: the little family dinners at the local trat, antipasto misto and the fegato veneziana with Giulio himself wielding the big pepper grinder, and the zabaglione for two I would share with Elspeth while Thomas had the tiramisu and Nellie had her herbal tea, and the Sunday trips to Easton Brett, or to Scrope Dudgeon's draughty house in Lincolnshire where you couldn't hear yourself speak because of the Harriers screaming overhead, or the visits to Nellie's Aunt Tab in her flint cottage behind Aldeburgh to chime with the first asparagus, or the films we used to see at the old Vista (which had just closed because of the new multiplex): all the Jean Vigos and Jean Renoirs (*L'Atalante* was my all-time favourite), and *Last Year in Marienbad* and Antonioni and Cassavetes, but we liked the Hollywood comedies and John Ford too. And it was sad that we never did any of these things now, and even sadder that I had scarcely noticed we didn't.

So as I ducked past the overgrown bushes and kneed open the squeaky front gate, I was filled with a melancholy that brimmed over into a resolve to make up for wasted time, to take up where we had left off.

The house was in darkness, the curtains not yet drawn, which was surprising because Nellie had said she would be coming back in the afternoon and would buy dinner on the way. But then the front door was not double locked, which suggested that she was already home. It was cold in the hall. When I switched on the light, there was her coat on the peg, the brown Tickway with the hood and the fluffy lining which made her look like a lanky woodland creature. I called but there was no answer. Instead of calling again, as I usually did if she was at the back of the house and hadn't heard, I stopped and listened to the breathy silence that seems to lap around your ears when you are fully alert. The apprehension which came over me was so powerful that my head had no room to think of plausible alternative explanations, such as that she had popped up the road to the shop or gone across to tell her friend Cath that she was back. Somehow it was clear that she was in the house and also clear that something was wrong, or the other way round: something was wrong which meant that she was in the house. I stood there listening for what felt like several minutes, as though the situation, whatever it was, demanded extreme caution, a sort of mental or even spiritual preparation, and rushing at it would certainly make things worse.

Then I started up the stairs, slowly, deliberately, like an old man. Halfway up at the landing I stopped and listened. The same breathy silence, or no – there was some kind of rhythm, or in fact broken rhythm, to it now, a very faint stumbling noise at the bottom of the silence. At the top of the stairs I stopped again. Now you could pick it out, clearly enough, although it was still faint. More like a sobbing that came and went, but definitely coming from a person.

The bedroom was dark but the curtains were not drawn here either and there was still enough light from the street to see the form huddled under the bedclothes. I called her name but she did not answer until I came to the bedside and stood over her, and then she told me to go away. I asked why and she just said again, go away, her face pressed into the pillow so that she was scarcely audible even from so close.

'What's wrong?'

'You can't help.'

'Didn't say I could, but –'

'Just go away, please. I'm too' – a word I couldn't hear – 'to talk.'

'Too what?'

'Ashamed. You see, you can't even listen.'

'Ashamed?' The word was so odd coming from her. It wasn't only that I had never known her to have anything to be ashamed of, it was not a feeling I associated with her at all. She could be gloomy, though not often, and sometimes she would be annoyed with herself, usually for some tiny practical error – forgetting to take something she needed or leaving her bag or her reading specs somewhere and not being able to remember where – but not ashamed, ever.

'Oh, go away.'

'No,' I said, 'I don't think I will, because I wanted to see you.'

'That makes a change.'

'Nellie, please.'

'I'm no good.'

'Don't, please don't say that. You know it isn't true.'

'It is, you don't know how true it is.'

I squeezed down next to her on the edge of the bed and tried to catch her in my arms but she squirmed away from me. The rough wool of her cardigan scraped against my cheek and I felt her shudder. She was fully dressed under the blanket and her breath had some sort of drink on it. It was hard to know where to begin.

'Why, please, why ashamed? I'm sure it's nothing, really, something you've got out of proportion.'

'I'm no good,' she moaned again, then more sharply, 'you don't think I'm capable of doing anything bad, do you? You don't want to think of me doing anything, really.'

'I don't understand what you mean.'

'You don't think of me having a life at all, do you? You just think of me doing these things, getting something for dinner, worrying about the children and then my little pastime, Nellie's diaries. I expect you make jokes about them, with that girl and that terrible Trull person. But that's it, that's all there is to me, that's supposed to be my life.'

'No, no, you know –'

'And of course you're quite right, you know you are. Because there isn't anything else. So when I start thinking about being old and dying and being dead, I haven't got anything else to think about. It's just a great big void and when I try and fill it up it's no good because I'm no good.'

'Nellie –'

'Good old Nellie, isn't she splendid? She takes everything in her stride. Don't worry about her, she'll be all right.'

'Look, you're terribly tired and we've all been under –'

'You haven't a clue what I'm talking about, have you? I could go on crying all night and you still wouldn't have a clue, would you? That's what's so pathetic.'

'All right then, give me a clue.'

But she was crying again and huddled up deeper under the bedclothes as though if she made herself really small she could disappear out of my clumsy clutches. There seemed nothing else to do but sit there helpless in the darkened room and wait for I didn't know quite what.

About ten minutes later, perhaps less, but it seemed as long as that, she sat up.

'Well,' she said, 'I meant to tell you, so I will, though it's probably a very stupid thing to do, but then everything I do is stupid. Anyway I want to tell you, I don't know why, I don't expect you'll be the slightest bit interested.'

'Tell me what?'

'I've been – oh, it does sound stupid – I've been having an affair.'

'Oh,' I said, 'oh.'

'I thought you might say, are you sure? I know you think I don't know much about that sort of thing.'

'Oh, well,' I said, 'um –'

'With Christopher,' she said quickly, as if I was about to suggest some other more embarrassing name, though it was difficult to conceive of a more embarrassing alternative.

'Christopher,' I said.

'Chris Alison. Yes.'

'The Bug. No.'

'Yes. I know you don't think much of him. Well, he doesn't think much of himself. That's what I like about him, I suppose.'

'The Bug,' I said again, not meaning to say anything much but it popped out.

'I could see you couldn't imagine, you know, that there was anything going on. If you had, I expect we wouldn't, or I wouldn't, anyway.'

'So it's my fault.'

'No, no, I didn't mean that, but it's true, isn't it? I can see you still can't believe it.'

But I had got beyond that and was sunk deep in the slough of humiliation. And as a matter of fact I found it perfectly easy to imagine and was already conjuring up little tableaux, of hands intertwined below the library desk and the soft glow of the library lamp upon the blushing cheek, then the first clumsy embrace on the landing of the B&B (they never stayed in hotels, because the Bug couldn't afford it on his librarian's pay and he wouldn't take a subsidy from her) and then the fumbling in the doorway and the frantic – no, I had no problem with thinking how all that would be, down to the languor of the intertwined legs and the stray, damp, frizzy tress falling across her face. That was all too easy to picture, or rather to remember.

'No,' I said, 'I can imagine it very easily.'

'You're not going to be patronising, are you? I can't bear it if you're going to be patronising.'

'You spent such a lot of time together, it's not surprising.'

'You mean I'd have gone off with anyone? You think I'm a sex-starved old crone.'

Other women might also have used the word crone but to me there was something especially characteristic of Nellie in the way she gurgled that word in her voice with its unique quality of sounding, at the best of times and at the worst too like now, both jumpy and self-confident. Anyway, she lived in a world of old-fashioned children's stories and medieval diaries where crone must be a standard noun.

'No, no,' I said, 'I just thought, well, I know from my own experience that when you're away from home in these places you do get lonely.'

'Oh? So it's happened to you hundreds of times? Every time you go off on some Civil Service course you think which one shall I screw this time? What about Rachel, oh no, I had her last year and she wasn't much good in bed. You're just laughing at my single sad little –'

'No, no, I'm not laughing at all. In fact, I'm crying.' Which, in a miserable halting way, I was. I had read in books of people crying tears of rage and had thought it was fanciful. But here I was, sobbing, almost barking with fury. Not fury alone perhaps, but jealousy, hurt and possibly even a touch of guilt. And I kept on blubbing in memory of the times when I waited so anxiously for that slow toothy grin to break over her face and her long fingers to start unbuttoning my shirt.

Somehow, in trying to find a better perch on the edge of the bed, my elbow caught the little fake marble button that put on the bedside light.

'Oh, you *are* crying. It makes you look like a baby, why's that, do you think? I suppose it's like them all looking like Churchill,' she said, drifting off at a tangent as she did.

She didn't look like a baby at all. She looked wild, dishevelled, her large eyes red-rimmed and blinking, her hair tossed all over the sheet, her cardigan rumpled up to her ear.

'What I don't see is why you're telling me now.'

'I said it was a mistake, didn't I? Because I'm no good at keeping secrets. You know that, don't you, or have you failed to notice that too?'

'I mean, is it –'

'Oh, I see, you haven't even grasped that much. It's over, of course it's over, that's why I'm telling you. I wouldn't have otherwise. I want to finish the whole thing off properly, do you see that?'

'Which of you –?'

'At least I've managed to rouse your curiosity. I stopped it, well, he probably would have quite soon, because he wasn't going to leave his family. Actually, it was him leaving his wallet out and me seeing the pictures of his children that made me. They don't look at all like him, much better-looking. I believe his wife is quite pretty but brainless. You can't see anything in him, can you?' she went on. 'You just think of him as a squinny little librarian; you can't see he could be attractive to women.'

I dutifully tried to think of Chris in this light, as though taking part in some thought experiment, but failed to summon him up in any detail. Small, dark, wiry I suppose would be the word for it. Was he rather bent, or was it only that I was always peering down at him in the little Peugeot? Did he have hair on the backs of his hands, was there perhaps even something a little satanic about him? And his voice – it had been mild, faintly Welsh, although Alison didn't sound very Welsh. It might have been his voice that had singled him out. Perhaps that was what had charmed his beautiful bird-brained wife. While he had wittered on about folios and variorum editions, she had scarcely been listening but just thinking nice voice, nice eyes. I found it much easier to think of Nellie standing naked at the dressing table and peering, without her reading glasses, at the snap of the handsome children. Then it came to me with an extra little stab how I hadn't even made it with Gracia before the dreadful photograph of her rock climbing with Malc had unmanned me. You kept photos around as mementos, but they were all too likely to act as grim sentinels, reminding you of things you were trying to forget. If you were out looking for a second chance it was best to leave the snaps in the bottom drawer. And looking for a second chance was, I suppose, the category Nellie's excursion fell into, and Chris's too, for that matter, not that I cared about his motives.

It seemed especially sad that Nellie too should feel that need because I had always thought of her as someone who was so unmistakably, not happy exactly but authentic, confident in herself for all her awkwardness. If I was to justify my neglect of her (which at the moment I was still too angry to think of doing), it would be that I had thought she did not seem to need worrying about. But now, much too late, it was clear to me that she was as hungry for a second chance as the rest of us, had the same sense of having missed out, of failure to seize or perhaps even to notice the opportunities as they flitted by. Because flit was what they did, like a wren darting from one bush to the next, too quick to allow you to think twice. There was no application form to fill in, no exhaustive interview or security checks. You either jumped at it or it was gone.

'Well,' I said, fumbling to re-establish some sort of sympathy, but certainly not intending to tell her about Gracia, 'I suppose we all want a second chance.'

She sat up in bed and in the same abrupt motion hit me, an odd little glancing blow just below the ear. 'I told you not to be patronising.'

Then she hit me again, harder this time. I tried to grip her and she tried to wriggle away but the sheets wound round her like a tourniquet so she couldn't move and I found myself embracing her, although at that moment I hated her.

'Get off me,' she said. 'Get off.' And she tried to free her pinioned arm and caught me on the side of my head with her elbow. I let go and then she hit me again to show she meant it, only a light swat across the face this time. So I hit her back, blindly, stinging her somewhere behind the ear, and she drummed her fists on my chest before I managed to get hold of her so that she couldn't move, though I could feel her trembling.

All week Trull had been mysteriously absent from the office. So had Sally. When he rang and invited me to come down to his new place in Essex, I asked where he had been and he said he just couldn't bear to miss the last of the sailing, which I didn't believe for a minute. Joe had fielded the calls as best he could, looking increasingly frantic and scrofulous. It was a miserable time and I couldn't refrain from reproaching Trull for not being there to share it.

'Well,' he said, taking my coat with mock deference, 'in our own small way we have not been idle down here.'

'How do you mean?'

But he didn't answer for the moment and silently led me through to the big sitting room overlooking the river.

'You've met my mother, haven't you? You haven't? How extraordinary. I thought everyone had met Momma.'

The old woman was sitting, rather upright, in an upright chair. She was pale and spry, and you could see Trull's keen eyes through her faintly tinted glasses. Her bony hands gripped the arms of the chair. She might have been an unusually ascetic doge.

'Haven't I heard a lot about you?' she said. Her voice was quiet but firm.

'I shouldn't think so.'

'Yes, I have. Keithie tells me everything and he tells Esmé too.'

She nodded towards the other old lady sitting across the room near the window looking out over the mudflats. Aunt Esmé was not quite so skinny or so severe, but her smile of greeting was also on the wintry side. The same went for the view, especially at low tide which it was, but it was the scene of Trull's triumphs in the Junior Firefly class and so, he said, sacred ground to him. In the office, he had shown me pictures of the house. He had bought it six months earlier. It was a big Thirties villa with huge windows. With the mooring and the paddock for Sally's horse it had cost £1.3 million. The boat had cost another 150k.

'Like an oven when the sun catches it,' Aunt Esmé said.

'Blinds,' Mrs Trull said, 'you need blinds.'

'I don't like blinds, Momma.'

He spoke to her in a way he didn't speak to anyone else, more direct, flatter, not ill-humoured – he was never ill-humoured – but without any campy twist on it. Almost in the same breath he turned back to me and began a tease.

'You are kind to come down, Gus. I don't expect you've ever been to Essex before, but I promise you we shan't tell a soul.'

I was protesting stoutly that on the contrary some of my happiest hours had been spent in the county, but Trull was already helping Sally to unload the tea tray. Back at Bagge's Head Wharf I had thought of Sally as, well, I suppose healthy would cover it. She glowed even when she was fixing one of the Macs. But out here she seemed to have gone pale too. Not that she looked unhappy. On the contrary, she was much more relaxed, but she too had begun to speak in this flat, clipped way that seemed to be almost a family language.

'You didn't want cake.' You couldn't quite tell whether it was a question or a statement, just as I hadn't been sure whether Mrs Trull had heard a lot about me or nothing at all.

'No,' said Trull. 'Momma's not a cake person.'

'Would you like some cake? It's really very light,' Sally said to me, in a cautious, polite voice as though we had never met before.

I didn't want any cake. And I didn't want to talk about cake either.

*

The rumours had started at the beginning of the week. The company was about to cease trading, there was a huge hole in the accounts, an administrator had been appointed. In short, the end was nigh. This hadn't made a huge difference to the shares, which were already nearly valueless and being hoovered up only by collectors of so-called penny shares who calculated that if one in ten of their investments came good they would be making serious money.

So they had all gone irretrievably west, that bright army of punters. Mr Justice Fincher and his lump sum, E.T. and his redundo, Ari Aristides and his old father in Winchmore Hill and his cousin Jimmy the Greek, and the man from the Daily Thing, and hundreds, perhaps thousands, more of them, all gone, the whole caboodle down the tubes, belly up, kaput. And Miles Morpurgo's body had been picked up over the weekend on the mucky shingle a few hundred yards downstream of Bagge's Head Wharf. I wondered if in his fuddled state he had been trying to make an appointment. We had closed his file months earlier but that hadn't stopped him ringing up and he would have forgotten we had moved.

'I suppose it's all true, then,' I said, 'there's nothing left?' I was appealing not so much for reassurance as for condolence. In so great a ruin we should surely pause for a moment's mourning, perhaps even a few muttered words of contrition. But I could see at once that this was not the mood Trull was in.

'Well, Gus,' he said, 'for some months now it has been obvious to the meanest intelligence, and your intelligence is anything but mean, that Heads in its present form is doomed. At the current burn rate we'll have used up the remaining cash within six to nine months. Even if we row back on the spend, we would only be putting off the evil day. The investments recommended by your dear friend Mr Wilmot have headed so far south they must be at the pole by now. A little more tea, Aunt Esmé?'

He got up and did the rounds, as silent and attentive as a waiter in an expensive hotel, pausing only to stroke the back of Sally's neck.

'So I wondered if there was anything I could do to help. One thing was clear. Our original enterprise, dear old Heads You Win, was and is sound as a bell. In fact, it is positively soaring. It would be a tragedy if we were to let it go down the tubes with the rest. So I thought that a

friendly bid might be in order. We could reverse the headhunting
business out of the group and carry on as before. I am glad to say that
Momma and Esmé and Sally, the three directors of our company, are
fully in agreement with my strategy.'

'What company would that be?'

'We have set up a little shell company, New Crouch Projects, on the
proceeds of some rather successful spread betting that we have
indulged in of late. I fear I have been leading my mother and my aunt
into evil ways.'

Aunt Esmé gave a slight smile and even Mrs Trull's stern features
relaxed a fraction.

'Why aren't you yourself –'

'You forget my lurid past. I have another eighteen months to go
before I may serve on even the tiniest board of directors, though I am,
of course, a shareholder. To avoid any conflict of interest, as of
yesterday I am no longer an employee of the group.'

'So you're going to buy it back.'

'You have grasped the point. Exact figures remain to be settled, but
the sum should cover most of the group's outstanding liabilities and
enable it to be wound up in an orderly manner.'

'But supposing they – we – don't agree?'

'I don't see there's much alternative, do you? Who else is going to
want to pay for the privilege of taking on such a can of worms – what a
strange phrase that is, presumably the worms must have been canned
for a purpose, as bait for fishing perhaps or some oriental delicacy.'

'So the rest of us lose the lot?'

'But your jobs will be protected, which otherwise one cannot see
much prospect of, can one? I need hardly say how much I hope you
personally will carry on with us. We would be lost without your sage
counsel. And Jade, too, of course. Jade will continue to adorn the
company, in a non-exec capacity for the time being. She's having a baby
as I expect you know. The advertising people see a lot of potential
there, but I always find those posters of pregnant women rather
offputting, don't you?'

'Joe won't like it. I can't see him going for it at all.'

'I'm afraid he won't have much choice in the matter. The Hellman
people have spoken to all the major creditors and they are happy.'

'At least Joe would carry on being chairman, if he agreed, that is.'

'Alas, that was one condition that we had to insist on, that there should be a new chairman. Mrs Trull was very insistent on that, weren't you, Momma? And so, indeed, was the second Mrs Trull – did you know that Sally and I were married in Ipswich on Wednesday? A rather small do and no honeymoon for the present because things are so hectic, but we'll make up for it later, won't we, darling?'

He leant over and laid his hand on hers, and she then raised her other hand so we could see the wedding ring flashing in the afternoon sun.

'Lovely,' said Esmé or possibly old Mrs Trull (my eyes were still on the bride who was really blushing and could reasonably be described as radiant).

'Well, I'm not doing it, certainly not without Joe.'

'This is the moment at which one normally says that your loyalty does you credit but you know, Gus, I'm not at all sure that it does. Surely your first loyalty should be to your colleagues, to the little people, if you will forgive so sentimental a phrase? I'm sorry about Joe, deeply sorry. He is, as you know, my oldest and dearest friend, and I owe him a great deal. But there comes a time to move on.'

'For him to move on, you mean.'

'If you prefer to put it that way. I can see you are still looking askance, which compels me, I think, to make myself a little clearer. Surely you must have noticed that for the last few months Joe has been rather . . . distracted.'

'Oh, that stupid thing with Jade you mean?'

'That, I fear, was only a symptom. The truth is that Joe is not what he was. Momma spotted it the moment she met him, didn't you, Momma?'

'Past it,' Mrs Trull said, 'he's past it.'

'Elderly people are so refreshingly forthright, don't you find, Gus? They say things that you or I shrink from and that can be awfully valuable, which is why I think our little board is so well balanced.'

'I don't –'

'Perhaps you may feel a little differently when I introduce you to our new CEO. Well, of course she's not exactly new to you. In fact, I'm sure you will be as delighted as I am at the prospect of working with such a valued old client of ours. At the moment she's next door sorting a few things but – ah, no, here she is. You remember Patsy, how could you not?'

Patsy Hepple came through the door and shook my hand, giving her mop of fair hair a brisk flip at the same time, as though some electric current had passed up her sinewy forearm to activate her follicles. She was wearing a smart red rollneck but somehow even this managed to give the same loose-fitting impression as her office suits, of allowing room for a concealed weapon. Since she had last been on our books Patsy had passed through several more boardrooms, leaving a trail of shattered careers, none of which seemed to have done her much harm. She had highlights in her hair now and dangly gold earrings, but the force of her will was as raw as the first time she had clumped up the stairs into our buttermilk attic.

'Gus,' she said, 'you're looking better than I would have expected. Have you learnt how to run an interview yet?'

Somehow this angle of attack made it even harder to duck out of the whole business without seeming terminally feeble.

'It's a fantastic team, don't you think, Gus?' Trull put in when I could manage no better response than a watery smile. He stood a little to one side, himself smiling gravely, his left hand spread out with a modest flourish to indicate the four women now arrayed in a shallow arc around the sitting room: Patsy Hepple leaning over the tea tray to take a cup from the new Mrs Trull and beyond them old Mrs Trull and Aunt Esmé in their upright armchairs with the cherrywood armrests. Trull was now in his MC mode, one of those MCs who specialises in being imperturbable especially when welcoming to the stage an act that has every chance of flopping.

Patsy took a gulp of tea and then began to outline the proposed arrangements for after the reverse-out. It seemed impossible to phrase my objections in front of this flinty jury. Now and then I was aware of one or other of their stony gazes coming to rest on me but only as it might have rested on one of the yachting scenes that hung on the walls. I was not expected to answer back.

'That's all beautifully clear, I think. If Gus has any thoughts, I'm sure he'll tell me on our walk. There's just time before the light goes.'

We put on green wellies – Trull knew my size, of course – and trudged out across the sodden lawn. There were no flowers, only a low cement balustrade separating the garden from the foreshore. Looking back at the house, I could see Mrs Trull and her sister sitting in the big picture window. They waved at us as though they never expected to see us again.

We came down from the rough grass to the mud and pebbles. By then I think I had already caved in. It was a mournful prospect either way. Certainly, I did not fancy answering to the Trull family cabal, but I had grown attached to the work and I kidded myself that I would only carry on for a year or two to see the business back on an even keel before . . . before what?

As I stumbled along behind Trull towards the estuary, it came to me with sudden violence how much I disliked – no, hated – him and almost in the same instant how odd it was that I should have spent so much of my life with him in a state of suppressed resentment. How – and more to the point why – had I taken such trouble to muffle my feelings, to pretend to myself that he stimulated me, when the truth was he generated a sort of numb dissatisfaction in me, so that I never left him without feeling that my inadequacies had been unfairly exposed? Yet I had never admitted even to myself, certainly not to other people, that I did not enjoy his company, never had; in fact, always dreaded it as some kind of test, one of those tests at school for which you could not prepare. An unseen, that was it, he was a human unseen, well, almost human.

Beyond the creek there was a scrubby wood, blackening now against the dusk and above it a sky flushed a bloody pink. Cerise? Fuchsia? I thought of the motley pinks sported at Gillian's funeral and a great sadness came over me. How had the idea ever taken hold that feelings faded as you grew older? On the contrary, each loss now seemed harder to bear. It was very quiet. The birds had settled down for the night. Only the splashing of our boots in the mud.

We came to a little spur of tussocky grass and Trull turned round to face me. The light was over the hill now and I could scarcely make out his face, though some last reflected gleam caught his lunettes.

'You know something, Gus?'

'What?' I said.

'I'm not normally at a loss for words as you know, but I'm really not sure quite how to say this.'

'What?' I said again. I was wheezing a little. I always did, now, as autumn came on.

'Perhaps I shouldn't say it, but I'm going to say it anyway. Look, I know you really don't like me very much, you haven't liked me for years, perhaps you never did. But what I wanted to say was how grateful I am that despite all that we've stuck together. I owe you a lot, Gus, and I'm not going to forget it.'

In the gloom I could see him adjusting his specs and then taking them off to polish them as people did when they were deeply moved. I was relieved to discover that I was not myself the least bit touched by this confession.

'Don't be silly,' I said, 'all old friends loathe each other, that's the point of having them.'

'You think so,' he said, putting on his earnest voice, 'we aren't freaks?'

'Completely normal,' I said. 'Do you think we could go back now? I'm getting a bit chilly.'

'Of course, of course,' he said. 'Look, Gus, it would be great if you could stay the night. Aunt Esmé's going back to the cottage and her bed's made up.'

'I'm afraid I can't,' I said coldly. 'I saw there was a train at seven.'

The silver Merc went back to the leasing company and I had to take the bike in to be serviced because the gears had got mangled while it was in the shed. I had been out of the domestic circuit too long. Almost everything in the house seemed to need servicing, including our marriage.

I knew Nellie would not complain directly about our reduced circumstances but I thought she might have an angle, and so she did. Her voice would take on this odd wistful quality and she would say things like 'I suppose we couldn't possibly afford a new duvet now' or 'it would have been nice to go to India before we're too old', although during our fleeting opulence she had shown no interest in splashing out on exotic travel or soft furnishings.

But the money or the lack of it was not the real issue. Nellie was too set in her unworldly ways to be swept off balance by a flash flood of cash. The real issue was the Bug, as I had gone back to thinking of him and occasionally when roused calling him though I had promised her I wouldn't.

I do not know how long it will go on, the anger between us. We had the first round of forgivings the day after she told me and we hit each other. We agreed that I had neglected her because I had been too wrapped up in Heads, and that it was only because she had spent such an unhealthy amount of time with Christopher that she had become obsessed with him and it would not have happened otherwise.

The real part of our lives would begin again, especially now that the children were homing in on London and there was a chance that Elpie's schoolteacher would marry her, though her own views on marriage were not to be relied on.

But the recriminations have not stopped. It would be comforting to think that each quarrel is not quite so bad as the one before and that the bitterness is fading, but I do not think it would be true. There is no longer that tacit understanding that deep down we are as fond of each other as ever. Or at least neither of us is sure that the other still feels that way. So our reconciliations are wary and inhibited, as though we had to be careful to say nothing that might be used against us in later proceedings.

I know that I am in no position to cast the first or even the second stone. Things would not be evened up if she knew about Gracia, they would be worse. The trouble is that I like casting stones, it's one of the few pastimes that doesn't pall with age; in fact, it gets better. And although my wife is a sweet-tempered person – you would see it the moment you met her – she too has tasted the savage pleasures of recrimination and won't give them up lightly.

The irony is that in every other way I have never felt better. Dr Playfair says he never wants to see me again, my prostate is no bigger than a walnut. Indeed, I have these strange spurts of energy, something I never remember happening when I was younger. They come over me quite without warning. Suddenly I feel muscles in my arms and legs that I have not been aware of for years, like Popeye after the spinach, and with the muscles (or the illusion of them) comes an impatient desire to take on some arduous physical task. I bought some

York stone half-price (or so he said) from a villain under the railway arches and laid the slabs myself, then stood there panting in a Chicago University T-shirt sodden with sweat waiting for Nellie's praise, but she had forgotten she had ever toyed with the idea and would only peer out of the window moaning about the mess.

These peculiar fits of activity have a disconcerting after-effect. I am dog-tired as you would expect but with the tiredness comes a sense of utter depletion, no, worse, of complete joylessness, as though the exertion had emptied the world of any conceivable purpose. The task seems pointless – perhaps it is – and my return to glowing health seems pointless too. I feel like an athlete who has trained his socks off for an event which has been abruptly cancelled.

During one of these energy spurts I felt compelled to tackle the teetering piles of books and papers that had been making my study a no-go area. After an hour rootling about and putting books back where they belonged, I came upon the stained and buffeted scarlet-bound copy of *Sick Heart River*. I must have pulled it out to read it properly when I got home after skimming it that night at Drishill and then wearied of the prospect and put it aside.

I knew where it belonged, with the other Buchans in the little bookshelf Thomas had made in carpentry and which was in the room that we still called his. But halfway up the stairs I stopped and came down again and took the book back into my study.

Ah yes, that was why it was called *Sick Heart River*, because an old Indian chief had been homesick for the place and pined away in exile and died. What a sentimental book it was after all. But once again I had got it wrong. The green and gracious place in the hills that Sir Edward Leithen remembers from his youth, the ultimate meadow as crisp as an English down with its bubbling spring fringed with flags, that isn't Sick Heart River at all. That is called Clairefontaine, and the Sick Heart lies far beyond it over the cruel glaciers and couloirs of ice, a pitiless country where no birds sing and there is no hope in the air. As he plods through these blanched barrens under a leaden sky, Leithen has a sensation that he is already dead, which he finds a queer comfort. That sensation did not sound so queer to me now. And the unexpected spurts of well-being that I had been having, something of the sort was in the book too. Most of the time Leithen is deathly weak, too feeble even to pull the Zeiss glass out of his pocket. Then, mysteriously, vitality floods back into his veins and he is able to cut ice steps in the couloirs and shin up the steepest gully. Perhaps that is how it always is when the batteries are on the blink. The power fades, then it surges briefly, then it fades again.

I took the book upstairs and put it on the shelf next to *John Macnab*, then tried to decide where to put the *Short Guide to Structuralism* and the third volume of the Eden memoirs. But the thought of the Buchan book and Joe's surprising passion for it would not go away and I wondered what Joe was up to.

There had not been a squeak out of him since he let the gloomy house in Kensington that had once been the embassy or consulate for some South American country, was it Paraguay? We had been on the phone a few times when Trull's plot was coming into operation. But he seemed reluctant to meet any of us. Not wanting to see Jade again ever I could understand, but Joe made no effort to fix up a confrontation with Trull either. In fact, he showed no wish to put up a fight at all, even through lawyers. When I asked him what his plans were he muttered something about going abroad to review things. He even wanted to give me a power of attorney over his affairs, but I said I had enough trouble as it was.

'At least you can persuade him to come to the Dome thing. Everyone would love to see him.' Jade was only a couple of months pregnant but she was already aglow.

'I mentioned it to him the last time we spoke but he said he wouldn't go near the bloody place if you paid him.'

'Oh dear, I'm afraid nobody's going to pay him, are they? I just hope I've stopped throwing up by then. I do hate working breakfasts at the best of times, don't you?'

It was a muggy morning with the mist steaming off the river, the weather no more uplifting on the Thames than it had been on the Crouch. There was a nasty little wind coming round the corner from Canary Wharf (somebody said the towers whipped it up) and there was an ugly swell on the river which sent the skirt of orange peel, driftwood and detergent bottles slapping up against the old wall. That lazy slap had been the rhythm accompaniment to our happy days when we had sauntered out from No. 9 for a long lunch at the Waterworks, Jade or Joe having snared another client or two and my own client book full to overflowing.

Four or five tables were laid under big umbrellas by the black bollards on the quayside where Jade had lolled and perched for the cameras. In between the tables there were tall helmeted heaters of the sort they set out in Italian cafés in the winter months. The PR girls were handing out champagne and scrambled eggs, and flustering around our guest of honour, a Junior Minister with a resolute profile and a pitted complexion, who said no toast please because he was on a wheat-free diet, worse luck. We sat down and Trull introduced the Minister, but I couldn't quite hear what he said because the heaters were spluttering. Sally was wearing an electric-blue suit with white piping and a hat to match. She was helping to dish out the scrambled eggs. There was nothing stuck-up about Sally. Trull didn't deserve her and I couldn't see what she saw in him. But, then, however did this idea of deserving creep into our heads? Whatever gave people the notion that fate handed out results on the basis of merit? Now I came to think of it, pausing to wonder at the same time whether I could really manage the whole mixed grill which, despite the best efforts of Sally and the team, was on the tepid side, our remote ancestors had had no such delusion. The whole point of the gods was that they were capricious and cruel, they put their own desires first. All we had achieved in three millennia or so was to rediscover the indifference of nature. Not a journey of discovery to boast about, really.

A shrill whistle broke into my musings. A motor launch with a ginger awning had drawn up at the quayside and a bearded man in naval uniform (the beard the same ginger as the awning) was putting out a gangplank for us to walk. As the Junior Minister (for work, training and information technology, I think) stepped aboard, the bearded man blew his bosun's whistle again and we followed the Minister along the plank.

'Sad, isn't it,' I said when we were settled under the awning and the launch was reversing out into the river, 'how little traffic there is on the river these days. In Pepys's day it would have been like Piccadilly in the rush hour.' I often said this sort of thing when on or near the river and people usually agreed with it but they did not often pursue the theme.

I was still facing the shore and so was taken aback when the Junior Minister contradicted me. 'Looks pretty busy to me this morning. Our Alternative Transport Initiative must be taking off.'

I turned round. Surprisingly, he was right. The Pool was unusually bustling for this time of morning, for any time of day, in fact. A big dredger with half a dozen men on deck was steaming down from Tower Bridge. A pleasure boat, two-thirds full, was just setting off from the next wharf downstream of us. Three or four white launches were bobbing across the brooding waters and further down at the next bend there were several other craft that I could only see indistinctly, lost in the brief glinting of the sun coming out between two banks of cloud.

'I was hoping to meet Jade Treviso,' the Junior Minister said.

'What, oh yes,' I said, still startled by the river traffic. 'You'll see her down there, she's been organising the show.'

We reversed engines and turned downriver. Most of the traffic seemed to be heading in the same direction, as though we were all off to some motley regatta. When we came to the bend past Canary Wharf, the dredger and a couple of the launches peeled off towards the north shore where they hove to as we went past them, except for one of the launches which set off downriver again, more or less keeping track of us from a distance of twenty or thirty yards.

'Don't look now but I think we're being followed.' The Junior Minister laughed. 'My last job was in Northern Ireland but I didn't think they'd lay on this sort of treatment for me today.'

'They?'

'Oh, it's a police launch, no markings, of course, but you can tell.'

The Junior Minister told us several stories about security precautions in the Province and how once you had been in the Northern Ireland Office you were told never to sit with your back to a window in a restaurant, which had turned out to be very good advice because once in the Brasserie St Quentin he had asked to be moved and a drunk in the Old Brompton Road had thrown a brick through the window and the people who had taken the table instead had been injured by the flying glass, quite badly, and his driver had to take them to casualty.

By now we had finished coming round the bend and we could see our destination squatting on the next promontory. And though I had seen it before, at closer range, when coming out of the road tunnel a few hundred yards away, it was only now in the grey morning light that I realised what it reminded me of. What was it we had compared those low grey rounded mountaintops with when we wandered on Cockburn's Pavement three, no, only two years ago – mushrooms, macaroons and a McDonald's bap? This thing had not been built then, although they had published the design for it, I think, and it hadn't occurred to us. Yet it was very like, so low and flattened, almost immediately making you think of other things that hadn't risen – an empty gasometer, a failed cake – somehow almost wilful in its lack of ambition.

'Amazing project,' the Junior Minister said. 'Fantastic synergy with the private sector.'

'Yes,' I said, thinking of Gillian cuddling her hens to her as Joe told us the plot of *Sick Heart River*. Then I thought of Francie Fincher and how Jonquil's gossipy letter a week earlier had reported, completely without rancour, that Francie had lost virtually the whole of his retirement lump sum when Heads went belly-up but there were plenty worse off than they were and how she hoped I hadn't been too badly scorched.

We were coming up to the quayside now, but we had to wait for one of the white launches to take on a couple of passengers before we could dock.

Jade was waiting for us, pale in the grey light. She was wearing a sheeny black catsuit which was both sinuous and reassuringly old-fashioned, *Avengers* vintage. The Junior Minister was so eager to greet her that he stumbled on the cobbles and almost fell into her arms, which xandre caught on camera and said they couldn't have done better if they had rehearsed it for hours.

But that was the last thing that did happen more or less according to plan, because as we were walking across the tarmac, a dark skinny man in a mac appeared from nowhere. Jervoise.

'What on earth are you doing here?'

'Liaising with the Flying Squad. Their orders are for us to detain the Minister here.'

'Why?'

'There's a security alert on, but they don't want it to look like a security alert, so if you wouldn't mind just standing around here and acting natural.'

'But it isn't natural to stand about on a freezing November morning.'

'If you wouldn't mind, sir, things are happening rather faster than they expected.'

'What things?'

But his answer, if any, was drowned by the roar of a large vehicle, a huge yellow digger the other side of the fence. At first I thought it was going to drive on round the perimeter but then to my amazement it turned and went straight for the fence, crashing through it at full speed. I could just see four men crowded into the cockpit before the digger rumbled on over the tarmac going smack into the double doors at the main entrance. There was another huge clanging crash and the giant digger disappeared from our view.

'I would never have believed it,' Jervoise said. 'Look there.'

'What?'

'That blue speedboat there, coming from the Isle of Dogs. That's the getaway bloke.'

We gazed at the wake of the speedboat curving across the water towards us. Behind it I noticed that the dredger had moved into a strange position sideways on in the middle of the river. Beyond us downstream the pleasure boat was also turning back into the middle of the river.

'Got him nicely bottled up.' Jervoise chuckled. 'If you wouldn't mind moving a little further this way, ladies and gents. If it gets nasty, you might be just in range.'

As the blue speedboat came into the pier, another launch appeared from nowhere and crowded in behind it.

'Christ,' said Jervoise, on his mobile now, 'they've taken a sledgehammer to it.'

'To what?'

'The Millennium Star, insured for 200 million according to the owners. Ah, now the boys are moving in. They've collared the first two by the digger. Now they're going into the vault. Jesus, a bloody great digger, who'd have believed it?'

Jervoise was jigging up and down with excitement as he pressed the mobile to his ear.

'Officer,' the Junior Minister said, 'would you mind telling us exactly what is going on here?'

'Sorry we couldn't brief you in advance, sir. We didn't want you doing anything that might give it away we were on to them. The heist of the century that's what it is, the heist of the century,' he said, chuckling with unashamed delight. 'They've got 'em, they've got 'em. What a peach.'

'They've foiled them, have they?' the Junior Minister said.

'They have indeed, sir, wrapped 'em up and tied the string, and they've cuffed the boatman too.'

'I'd like to go in and congratulate the officers responsible. Would that be possible, do you think?'

'Hang on, sir, I should imagine they would be most gratified but I'll just enquire. Yes, they say that would be in order. If you wouldn't mind following me, sir, we'll need to go in the back way.'

We followed Jervoise round the side between the slanting gantries and through a little door which led us into the main alley. Just opposite was the Head Zone where we were to make our spiel to the Junior Minister and Trull was to present him with the fibreglass model of the Brain Box. A bewildered knot of people from the office were standing on the translucent steps which led up to our exhibition space, but Jervoise led us on past them, through clumps of equally bewildered visitors, some of them clutching cappuccinos and mini-pizzas but frozen in mid-air as though they were victims of some new Pompeii. Round the next bend the air was full of blue smoke and we could see the back hoe of the digger thrust like the jaw of an enormous yellow dinosaur into the inner wall. The place was swarming with policemen and as Jervoise went over to speak to them, a detachment of uniforms, four of them perhaps, led past us a man in blue overalls cuffed on both wrists to an officer. He was cocky, fortyish, with a bright look in his eye. As they came past, he shouted, 'Twelve inches from payday we were, twelve inches from fucking payday.'

'As a matter of fact they were nowhere near. When the diamonds came back from Tokyo in September De Beers replaced them with fakes. But he had some cheek, that fellow. Winked at me when I cuffed him and said it was worth a try.'

'Well done indeed, Superintendent. Brilliant work. Fantastic.'

The Superintendent was jubilant and so was the Junior Minister. They stood together shaking hands in slow motion while xandre darted around snapping them from all angles.

Then the other three heisters came past, each with his clutch of arresting officers, and I couldn't resist a little spurt of fellow feeling. Some of us, too, had been twelve inches from payday or thought we had, though it didn't look like that now for us either. We probably looked more bedraggled than the heisters. People would remember them. Would they remember us?

We were turning to go when another little clutch of officers came towards us. This time they were walking alongside a stretcher carried by two ambulance men. There was a man on the stretcher covered by a blanket.

'Now this is an odd one,' the Superintendent said. 'We arrested him half an hour ago during the security sweep. An unrelated incident, we think. He was hiding in the scaffolding under your zone, sir. Carrying a revolver and a couple of grenades. One of the sniffer dogs got him. When we arrested him he started raving "I'll get the bastard" and then seems to have had some kind of seizure. We need to get him to hospital sharpish, but we had to wait till we'd sorted this little lot.'

The blanket was tucked in up to his chin and he had an oxygen mask clamped to his face, but even so we could see it was Joe.

'He would appear to have a grudge against one of you gentlemen. Would he be a shareholder? I understand you have had some financial difficulties.'

'No, not a shareholder, or in fact, yes,' Trull said, 'but he's an old colleague who's been having some health problems. We must get him to hospital.'

'Yes indeed, sir. But I think you'd better leave that to us as he's in police custody. He smells terrible, probably been living rough, I should think.'

I bent down to get a closer look at him. It was hard to disagree with the Superintendent. Joe looked rough all right. His mottled cheeks were covered with tawny-silver stubble and his tousled hair was full of dust, though that might have come from where he had been crouching under the stand. And there was a sickly smell coming off him. No doubt the smell would have been worse without the oxygen mask.

It was a dismal sight but – hard to say this without sounding callous – it was not exactly a shocking one. When you came to think about it, living rough was more or less what Joe had always done for a living. Even when he was dressed up in a £600 suit there had never been anything smooth about him. It was the roughness that was the making of him. That was what attracted all sorts of people you would never have expected – difficult women, sober investors, even me. This much I probably had an inkling of when I saw his freckled body caper round the dormitory forty years before. But what I was too young to know then – in fact, had only just come to realise – was that the roughness would be his undoing too. There would come a time when his rawness, his plunging on, his total lack of sensitivity unnerved people and made them want to be somewhere else as soon as possible.

When that moment came and Joe realised he was on his own again, his reaction was different from that of other people in the same situation, because it was more puzzlement than anger or despair, rather like the barking of a dog who cannot understand why he has been shut out of the house. Or at least that was how it had always been until now. He was always looking too hard for the next big thing to waste time on getting his own back.

So I saw that this must be the final act because the world had run out of adventures for him and there was nothing left but the icy nullity of revenge. That was the last shot in his locker and in his locker was where it was going to stay.

Just as well that his eyes were tight shut and he could not see Trull peering down at him with the cool appraising look of a consultant on his round.

'Oh, one of us must go with him. But I can't leave the Minister now he's come all this way. Christ, how awful.' Trull paused, looking around as though he was still grappling with the problem when I could see perfectly well what he had in mind.

'I'll go with Joe,' I said.

'Oh, will you, Gus? That's a load off my mind.' He gave me a look of anguished gratitude. Then he bent over the stretcher and patted Joe's head.

'We'll take the launch,' the Superintendent said, 'the chopper's tied up tracking the getaway van over the other side. He won't know yet we've nabbed them, but it won't take him long to guess.' He was having a good time. Trull was having a good time, so was the Junior Minister. Everyone was having a good time except Joe.

He was stertorous now, grinding and choking like a lorry struggling up a steep hill. A doctor had appeared at his side, a neat little man in an anorak with hair scraped across his skull. The doctor had pulled aside the blanket and unzipped the dark-blue fleece that Joe was wearing – not the sort of thing he usually wore these days, perhaps he thought it was the right thing for a hit-man. As the doctor bent over him, I caught a glimpse of Joe's bare chest, pale and freckled and innocent under the glaring lights. The doctor didn't take long to tell us that it looked like some sort of stroke, which I could have told him, and I chipped in to say that he had already had a couple. The quicker we get him to hospital the better, the doctor said, and I knew that too.

But it took us some time because the visitors who hadn't been evacuated had all crowded in to see what had happened and our little procession was becalmed between a Burgerbar and a McDonald's, and the smell of chips mingled in with the smell of the heisters' smoke grenade, which had drifted round from the vault. We began to move forward very slowly, trying to clear a path through the mob round Joe on his litter. They knew, I think, that there had been some sort of robbery attempt and must have assumed that Joe had been injured as a result, possibly in a heroic attempt to bring off a citizen's arrest. They gawped at him reverently, as a medieval throng might have gazed at some holy man whose ailments were a sign of divine blessing, perhaps amounting to stigmata.

We passed the Kentucky Fried Chicken stall, then stopped again opposite a baguette-and-coffee place decorated in the colours of the French tricolour. It was playing old French accordion music, a catchy, swirly tune with a melancholy fade. There was no vocal but just as we were moving on again the words came to me: '*voici la ronde de l'amour*'.

The round of love – what an awkward, meaningless phrase. It sounded better in a foreign language – *rondo* or *rondeau*. But even then, whoever thought love went *round*? It went up and down like a rocket, all whoosh and exploding stars on the way up, a silent sooty stick on the way down. Far from A falling in love with B who fell in love with C and so on until the circle was neatly completed, the whole process was brutally asymmetrical – B's life being utterly destroyed by the affair, C not falling in love at all, A going on to fall in love with D, E, F, G and H. If you wanted to bring geometry into it, the parabola of love would be nearer the mark. In plenty of cases, of course, the rocket never left the old milk bottle, me and Gracia for example, or Joe and Jade. But it never came round again, never.

And love was not the only thing that didn't come round again. Youth didn't, nor did middle age come to that, nor did most of the opportunities that you missed the first time round which you didn't learn until too late was the only time. It was poignant, really, the need to believe in eternal recurrence. That was another reason why we all had a soft spot for Joe, because he remained stubbornly convinced against all the evidence that if you missed this bus there would be another one along in no time.

It wasn't just cheap accordion music that ministered to this need. It was the same thing with classical music too. The first movement would set off with a grand sweep, inspiring, even jubilant, sometimes thunderous and fateful too. Then you had the second movement which might be soft and sad, or it could be lush and sweet and make you think of a meadow running down to a dappled stream, though you weren't supposed to think of that unless the programme told you you could, which would mean it was programme music and not the real thing, unless it was the Pastoral Symphony, which was all right. Anyway, one way or another in the end you came to the final movement and, as often as not, what did you hear? A sprightly country dance, or *rondeau*, or *rondo*, or 'round O' as the dictionary says that the backward English used to call it – anyway, music going round and round in a dancelike manner. I know that technically it doesn't have to be a dance. Technically I am sure you too are well aware a rondo is just a multi-sectional form, movement or composition based on the principle of multiple recurrence of a theme or section in the tonic key. All the same, it still sounds as if somewhere in there a dance is struggling to get out and be danced.

I know this rounding off is supposed to cheer us up, supply that sense of closure which real life so often fails to come up with, but it doesn't work for me. The thunder and the yearning of the earlier movements won't go out of my head. These are intimations that cannot be danced off. So far from leaving me adjusted and reconciled, the rondo only sharpens my thoughts of mortality. All the busy hopping, the glowing cheeks, the hearty cries only seem to bring closer the day when the eyes have shrivelled back into their sockets and the calves have gone stringy and the only thing that reminds you of castanets is the bones rattling. For me there's nothing upbeat about a rondo finale. It's more like a *danse macabre* and it doesn't sum up the human condition, or come even close, because the human condition isn't any kind of recurrence, eternal or otherwise. The human condition is just going on until it stops. Whether you think it's a bargain or not, it is an unrepeatable one.

The crowd was beginning to understand that we needed to get a move on, and the stretcher-bearers had room to break into a jogtrot and we passed out of reach of the accordion and there was a loudspeaker playing some old Motown numbers. The Superintendent held open a little door and we came out of the smoke into the chill air.